LUX

The Dark Between Series

RAE ELSE

Anchorite Publishing

ISBN 978 1 9169049 8 9

Cover design by Adriatica Creation

raeelse.co.uk

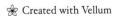 Created with Vellum

"And I think we could live forever
In each other's faces 'cause I'll always see my youth in you
And if we don't live forever
Maybe one day we'll trade places
Darling, you will bury me before I bury you
Before I bury you."

(Halsey, Ya'aburnee)

❧ I ❧

DREAM TO SELL

The shadowy figure was a blotch in the background. Jess drank in her finished drawing. Winged silhouettes of people and horses littered the foreground. Jess smudged the charcoal at the edges, trying to capture the dancing images that the faded had cast upon the cavern in the Silvan Mountains.

Other drawings lay on the bed around her. Mazes of wings and branches crisscrossed the paper, the eye drawn to the murky stain in all of them. Restlessness had driven Jess out of bed in the middle of the night, impelling her to pick up her art supplies. Materials obtained two weeks ago when they'd arrived here in the Seelie Court. Imber, the Seelie king, had bestowed an abundance of materials on Jess when she'd asked for paper and pencils. A treasure trove of art supplies was now hers—a collection she'd once only dreamed of owning.

Yet, Jess's jaded gaze slunk past the stash, drifting around the huge room. This bedroom was in one of the highest towers in the Sun Keep. The whole building was constructed from ignes-covered walls—the fire-eaters living in the rock gave it its name. The huge ceremonial rooms like the Sun Courtyard glowed day and night, but the private rooms like Jess's were paneled with rich wood and lit by candlelight instead. Each piece of furniture within was intricately carved, a chamber fit for royalty ... or divinity. King Imber *had* appointed this room to Jess and Rune: a chamber for Lady Silva and Lord Alba, the goddess and god who were the mirror image of each in power and love.

Once upon a time...

During their journey through the Silvan Mountains, Jess and Rune had learned that their destiny was no longer bound together. Jess still ached with the loss. They'd discovered that during the Great Divide, Silva had buried her seed magic in the twin shifters Romulus and Remus. Consequently, Jess, a descendant of both Romulus and Remus, was Silva reborn. Jess's blood had restored the feeling in Rune, enabling him to find his shadow self in the mists of Umbra and become the whole, living embodiment of Alba. Yet, with that accomplished, they'd learned how changed Jess's power was. By hiding her seed magic in the original twin shifters, Silva's power had altered. She'd become an Earthen goddess. The result being that Jess and Rune no longer fit together. Neither in magic or ... in love.

That first night here, they'd talked about everything that had happened. But the next day, Rune had granted her sole use of the room. She'd protested: she was a shifter and could easily be a nocturnal animal. Wasn't it fairer to take turns? Rune had explained that, with his godhood restored, sleep wasn't a necessity. Another of the *many* things that again separated them now.

But it wasn't the loss of their love that made the stillness of the night almost too heavy to bear. She fidgeted with the corner of the drawing, looking at the pages scattered like autumn leaves. Her gaze found the shadowy mark in each—the one that looked as if it were fading on the very page. She wrapped her arms around herself as the Sidhe's haunting stare filled her thoughts.

It had been two weeks since the Unseelie queen, Mara, had held both Jess and her shadow self, the Sidhe, captive. Two weeks since Jess had discovered the reason Queen Mara had long sought her: because the Sidhe had been dying. The blackouts that Jess had suffered from all her life had been her shadow self emerging and lashing out in fear. Each rage-fueled incident was the act of a dying being, fighting for survival. Something Queen Mara had known and calculated upon. The moment the Sidhe and Jess had conjoined again, Mara had tortured Jess and tried to tether her immortal soul—a goddess's sluagh.

A chill crept through her at the memory of the queen's voice: *"my magic merely requires pain, blood, and iron."* To tether Jess's soul, Mara would have tortured her to death. Fortunately, Rune had intervened in time. Mara had fled to the Ones Below—the Fomors, the ancient enemy who had caused Alba and Silva to fracture. Rune's restorative waters had healed Jess. She ran her hands down her bare arms, hating the reminder of torture she'd been subjected to. The scar tissue where the queen had shredded her arms was discernible to the touch and eye. Jess's nails bit into her arms as she imagined having Mara at her mercy instead. Her hands loosed. In Umbra, Jess would be powerless against Mara. After all, Jess's shadow self—the *Umbran* part of her—was dead. At the thought, the pain of her loss struck, raw and visceral.

Jess raked her fingers through her hair. The hollow in her chest grew as she thought of how misguided she'd been. When she'd come to Umbra, she'd been so *sure* she knew what she was doing. That she'd save the Sidhe and restore the goddess, Silva. She'd been chasing the sense of wholeness that she'd had when first conjoining with the Sidhe. The feeling that had convinced her that, if she only got to the Sidhe, all would be right. That she'd be *whole*. Instead, she'd almost gotten herself killed and her soul tethered.

Rune claimed he sensed great Earthen power in Jess. But she didn't know that for sure: she hadn't returned to Earth yet.

As soon as Jess and Rune had explained to King Imber and his closest court how they—the Umbran gods—had been fractured, they'd sealed Jess and Rune's need to stay in Umbra. It was Alba and Silva's absence from Umbra during the Fomor invasion that had diminished their power and left them all vulnerable. To prevent fear from blossoming in the Seelie Court, Jess had agreed to remain in the Shadowlands until all the Seelie had gathered and she and Rune addressed them. Until they explained Jess was no longer an *Umbran* goddess and her absence didn't weaken Umbra, she'd stay put. That gathering was *finally* due to happen tomorrow. King Imber had summoned all Seelie to the Aedis Cornu—the Temple Peak, for midday.

Trepidation swirled through Jess, but she wanted the truth to be out. She wanted to turn her attention to where her heart was: Earth. To her father who was Theo's prisoner. Theo was now High Mage of Enodia, having claimed the position by tethering para souls. Jess gritted her jaw, hating the thought of her father in the mage's hands. She'd gone against her feeling and nature by not going to confront Theo. But she'd allowed herself to be counseled by Rune, who believed a secure base in the Seelie Court with the Seelies' support had to be established if they were to combat the accumulating threats. Those threats marshaled through Jess's head. Mara had retreated to the kingdom of the Fomors but her forces would likely be bolstered by the enemy when she returned. And Theo and his coven were now even stronger, with their sluagh hordes strengthened by the para souls they'd tethered. At the thought of Theo's ruthlessness, another sting of worry for her dad swept through Jess. She tried to reassure herself. Theo wouldn't kill him. After all, he wanted something to hold over her. But it didn't mean that the night wasn't rife with what her father might be suffering at Theo's hand.

Pale light stole through the curtain.

How is it dawn already?

Jess scarpered off the bed. She'd agreed to meet Astra at Eventide. Pleased that she'd collapsed in yesterday's leathers after the late-night run, Jess ran her fingers through her hair and eyeballed herself in the mirror. A streak of charcoal was smudged on her chin. She licked her finger, rubbing it off. Her gaze snagged on the ornate dress reflected behind her that the Seelie maid had left for her. Part of King Imber's hospitality to Lady Silva entailed sending a fae maid to wait on her, as well as offering an array of dresses in materials as soft as silk.

But I'm no fairy princess.

Pulling on boots, Jess wrenched open the door, then shifted into her wolfish form. She bounded down the corridor. The golden hallways were decorated with fine rugs which slowed her down, her iron-sheathed claws in danger of catching in their weave. She savored the bare stone of the spiral staircase, bounding down them two by two.

In the lower gallery, the scent of amber filled her nose: most of the Rem Clan were staying in rooms on this floor. About half the Rem Clan had come to the Seelie Court. The clan was another reason Jess had wanted to go back to Earth. Her second, Dearbhla, had acted on her behalf, cautioning Jess about her presence on Earth—it would draw Theo's attention to the pack again. The last thing Jess wanted was to hinder the Rems from getting to the safety of Umbra. She had been eager to bring the pack as far away from Theo as she could. She worried that he'd use any influence he had over younger Rems to do the unspeakable—to slay their kin—for the promise of power and position that he could grant them as Enodian High Mage. Dearbhla had ensured that the Rem were apprised of Theo's threat, and at Jess's wish, had given the pack the choice to come through to Umbra or stay on Earth. Jess let the amber scent wash over her, grounding her.

Ever since her shadow self had passed on, she'd felt a great awareness of the Earthen magic in all shifters. She remembered that first night at Skiron's, how she'd sensed the Earthen energies in the house from a distance. It was one of the few ways she'd been able to start exploring her goddess power. For instance, if she were to reach out now, she'd be able to distinguish how many individual shifters were on this floor.

She knew, in part, this was because she had created them. In the deep past as Silva, she had crafted the twin shifters. And her seed magic that she'd buried in them had been kept within them, generation upon generation until it had come back to her in the form she now had. She was both mother of shifters and the amalgamation of all shifters who had come before her. And so, she was disappointed that so many of the Rem Clan had chosen to remain on Earth, regretting that only half had come through to Umbra. But like Dearbhla, those who were here were here by choice. Not because of any blood command to their Alpha. A blood bond that was a symptom of the Fomors' dark magic that had invaded both Umbra and Earth so long ago.

When Jess slipped outside, she proceeded around the walled keep. Pale sunlight spilled over its golden form. It was pretty in the dawning light, but unease beat through her as she looked up. Usually, it was called the Sun Keep, but she'd heard it referred to as *"Silvae Radices Aurea—Silva's golden roots."* So much of Silva—*her* —was embedded within the Seelie Court. So much that Jess remembered nothing about. That she'd *never* remember. Sometimes, the thought of these swathes of lost memory seemed like a great darkness, threatening to swallow what was left of her.

Hell, I can't even speak Umbran.

A fact she and Rune had explained to King Imber and his court through the changed nature of Jess's magic, now Earthen in essence. But by the end of today, everyone would know the true extent of just how changed she was. That she was, literally, a half-souled goddess. As worry climbed through her, the fundamental nature of her change consumed her. That first night had illuminated how different she was, when she and Rune had spoken. Her need for sleep and food indicative of her mortality. Of course, it wasn't as if *Jess* had ever thought of herself as anything other than mortal. The majority of her life had been spent thinking she was human. It was only in the last year that she'd come to terms with the fact that she was a shifter. But it was weird to think that before this lifetime, she'd been immortal.

Pummeling her worry into the ground, Jess made her way farther from the main walls of the Sun Keep, where mature trees and shrubs abounded. In the last couple of weeks, it had become a luscious jungle. Evermore blossoms flowering earlier—the greenery around the keep responding to the return of Umbra's gods.

To Umbra's god.

In legend, Silva was the one associated with seed magic, with the blossoming and fruiting of Umbra's vegetation. But it was Alba's vitality and power that Umbra's life was responding to. The trees and undergrowth didn't thrive on Earthen energy. Their substance was imbued with those ethereal shadows unique to Umbra. Ever since she'd come through to the Shadowlands, that substance had unnerved Jess. And she now felt the reason that was. These lands here contained only enough Earthen energy for her to transform into her wolfish form, but not enough for her to access and explore her powers as an Earthen goddess. The need to return to Earth twisted through her once more.

It was with relief that Jess stepped into a dust-covered court-yard, the greenery kept at bay for the sake of having a training ground. In the bare space, she finally felt as if she could breathe and the knot of tension in her loosened.

Astra was already doing warm-up exercises, a precursor to their dueling practice. They'd met for sparring practice for almost as long as they'd been staying at the Sun Keep. Other than Rune, Astra was the only one who knew Jess's shadow self had died. On the second day staying here, Astra had barged into Jess's room. Finding her wallowing, the fae demanded she spill her secrets. The rest of that day, Astra had stayed with her, making her feel better as they'd talked shit out together. There'd been jerky and wine involved, too.

Today, there was no such understanding on her friend's face

and not so much as a coffee offered. "Hurry up," Astra greeted her.

The only difference the truth had made was that Astra made Jess pour her feelings into training rather than eat her weight in jerky. Even when Jess had shared her uncertainties about her power in Umbra, the fae took that as more incentive to get to sharpening her teeth, claws, and scian. It was partly why they frequented the training area daily.

The Seelie around them were the *other* reason. Already multiple sets of fae were gathered about the courtyard, the clash of wooden weapons rending the space. Despite Astra having arrived with Alba and Silva, the Seelies' hospitality didn't extend to her. Astra had been on the receiving end of glares, snide comments, and meager portions at dinner. Of course, Jess had wanted to go all Lady Silva on them, but Astra had said that would be like getting your mom to fight your battles. Skiron had come up against as much pushback from Astra, too, who complained when he'd insisted on accompanying her everywhere. Instead, Astra had come up with her own solution: dueling dates. Admittedly, the fact that the Seelie hadn't escalated their mistreatment of her was largely due to these daily demonstrations that she wasn't a force to be taken lightly.

Amidst the other early risers, Astra's black wings contrasted starkly with the Seelies' white wings. Her petite frame contradicted the strength and agility she moved with. Astra's skin and hair had taken on the same hue as the dust as if she'd already been struck down and dirtied. But that hardly ever happened. More often than not, it was Jess who ended up on her ass.

Gods, I must really hate myself to agree to be her target practice.

Jess's thoughts softened knowing how much Astra herself had at stake here. She remembered the longing look which Astra gave to Skiron's house. The fondness that infused her tone when she'd spoken of sneaking off over the last year to be with him there. She saw her desire to be part of his world, to be able to build a home with the person she loved, rather than be stuck in the shitty world she'd been born into.

And gods do I get that.

Astra tossed Jess the hefty wooden cloidem. They'd progressed from fighting with scian to the larger swords. Jess had only just caught the blade when Astra lunged at her. The lightness and speed with which she moved were so graceful, the fae seemed to dance. Jess mastered the urge to tense up, loosening her shoulders with a breath as she blocked the fae's strike. With each charge and thrust, she did what Astra had told her to: pour her feelings into her strikes. Her frustration, heartache, grief, and anger were like a melting pot, fueling her motion.

With each beat of their wooden swords, everything Jess fought for seemed to sharpen. Adrenaline shot through her as she joined the dance with determination. They *would* show the courts, clans, and covens that the enmity that existed between each was unnatural, that it had been seeded by the Fomors' invasion.

They were weaving their way in a series of thrusts and blocks when the scent of evergreen distracted Jess. Her gaze swung away from Astra as if sweeping the area for a new opponent. Jess's eyes landed on a pair of shifters in their human forms. Matteo whirled a wooden fae spear against a female shifter. A dark braid whipped through the air as the female shifter blocked his attack. Piera. Jess's sister.

A lump rose in her throat as the presence of the two shifters threatened to steal her focus. Over the last two weeks, she hadn't seen much of them. Part of that was *her* fault. It wasn't as if she'd tried to tell Matteo the truth about her shadow self dying. Anticipation stole through her as she wondered what he'd make of her when he knew. But the memory of how he'd looked at her when she'd told everyone at Skiron's house that she was Silva tempered that feeling. That look had spoken volumes. That she was something *different*. Something he couldn't understand. Someone he couldn't be close to anymore. It was that look that had had her avoiding him as much as possible. She hardened herself, reminding herself that even with her shadow self gone, Matteo couldn't deal with who and what she was now.

Jess sidestepped Astra's blow, swinging her own blade toward the fae's open flank. Astra deflected the stroke effortlessly. Jess's frustration had her going in for another strike. Astra ducked as Jess's sword whipped past her head. Next moment, the fae shot forward, taking advantage of Jess's overreaching. She stumbled clumsily out of the way but righted herself just in time to meet Astra's next attack.

The aroma of fir and pine continued to needle its way into Jess's awareness. Things between her and Piera weren't any better. But this time it was Piera who avoided *her*. Jess had tried to approach her to explain that they would save their father, but she'd refused to speak to her. She yearned to explain that their father was a matter closest to her heart but that she must follow Rune's guidance. He was the sole Umbran god now. Anxiety threatened Jess as she wondered whether the truth would only make Piera hate her more.

Astra rushed her, landing a powerful blow on her flank which sent her sprawling into the dust. Jess's breath left her as pain blossomed down her back. With the wind knocked out of her, she blinked up at the pale sky.

Piera's barbed tone from the other side of the courtyard rang out. "You're right, this *is* making me feel better."

For a moment, Jess didn't have it in her to get up. She just lay there, feeling hollowed out. She had thought she'd known what she was doing. She'd been so sure that the path she was on was right. She'd thought she'd go to the Silvan Mountains and return with her strength magnified. With a goddess's strength. After all, that was who... what... she'd once been. A being invested with all the strength and power of the winds that swept through those peaks. But she wasn't that anymore.

And the hurt swelling through her chest wasn't because Piera thought her hard-hearted. A cruel goddess. It was because she *wasn't* that. In fact, she didn't much know *what* or *who* she was. But she feared that the family she'd always dreamed of having would be lost to her when Piera found that out.

2

WHEN YOU'RE NOT HERE

The river wended its way through the valley, a silvery ribbon beneath the moonlight, forty-foot shy of the outer walls of the Grian Turris—the Sun Keep. Rune's awareness of the water was as tangible as if the river caressed his skin. The current of Umbra's waters was as much a part of him as the flow of his own blood. A buttery light played on the river— the bright reflection of the Sun Keep.

In Rune's most distant memories, he saw it comprised alone of the simple circular court in which King Imber had received him and Jess. Rune's ancient memories worked something like the tide along the shoreline. Sometimes, its expanse was so clear that he walked its vivid path as if it had only happened yesterday. At other times, the seashore was submerged entirely. And *he* steered those tides because he *was* them.

In his day-to-day interactions, he allowed his distant memories to sink into Umbra's waters and shadows. It was easier that way. But at night, when he had the luxury of solitude and time, he sifted through them, exploring their depths. In fact, he'd found being within their tide as rejuvenating as resting. It was his way of resting instead of sleeping as a mortal would. In a way, the memories were very like the process of dreaming. He could guide a memory, but it was a deep subconscious part of him that conjured it.

The current took him to a recent memory: the day of their arrival. Two weeks ago when a hundred or so Seelie had gathered in the tiers surrounding Imber's throne. The lapping waters seemed like the awed whispers that had risen within the lofty chamber after Rune and Jess had shared their tale with the court.

Both the king and his subjects had been captivated. They'd gawped at Rune's shadow wings, watching them shift as if an invisible breeze played with them. Their wide-eyed looks and awed chatter had set the court alive, belief and hope stirring.

But it was the flap of other wings that had sanctified Rune and Jess's claim. Umbra's animals had breached the court. Within minutes, elen—golden-hued birds, ordinarily elusive creatures who kept to the thickest of forests—had flocked in the gleaming rafters. Meanwhile, fuathan, the Depth dogs had clustered in the courtyard, circling Rune and Jess. The animals of the Heights and Depths had blessed them. Happiness and faith had beat through Rune—he'd felt as if they were a potent oasis to which Umbra's wildlife was drawn. They *would* restore union to Umbra. They *would* purge the Shadowlands of the Fomors' dark magic. Belief had flooded the king and court too, the animals acknowledging the return of Umbra's gods.

But emptiness moved through Rune as he remembered what had happened then. King Imber had bequeathed Lord Alba and Lady Silva a chamber in the Sun Keep. When he and Jess had been left alone, she had joked about the animals—that he'd been like Snow White in the way they'd surrounded him. Rune had been struck by how she'd understood the significance of the animals but hadn't *felt* them in the same way he had. The sacredness and purity of having the animals bless their rule. Because, just as the fuathan had sensed the return of the gods when they'd been drawn to Cuill and the lingering Sidhe, the animals had been drawn to *Rune*. Not Jess.

For I am Umbra's only god.

Once again, Rune stood alone, picturing Jess in the candlelit bedchamber, alone too. The bower-like room had seemed to mock them with all they'd lost that first night. It wasn't merely that they would both have recently dreamed of sharing such a romantic space. It was that she wasn't the Silva who filled most of Rune's memories. An echo of what Jess had said in Norway skipped through him. "I hate the idea of you ... yearning for anyone but me." He remembered how Jess's look and admission had warmed him then. But now, everything they'd been to each other so recently felt pale in comparison to what they'd *once* been. And oh, how he did yearn for Silva.

Those shorelines that he'd kept submerged over the day rose like jagged rocks, tearing through him. A memory of Silva struck him—ebony skin, her midnight hair, her white gown trailing behind her. How many times had they strolled these banks together? It felt as if she would come to find him at any moment. For they were as constant as the moon holding the tide and the tide following the moon. The push and pull never changing. But that never-changing relationship *had* changed.

Rune remembered Jess's stray comment as she'd looked at the dress that King Imber had sent her. "I've worn enough white to last me a lifetime." She associated it with the Rem Clan. She didn't *know* that it was Silva's color, the white symbolizing how she reflected Alba. Jess's comment should have hurt Rune. But it hadn't. Because, in so many ways, Jess *wasn't* Rune's true love anymore.

Jess's associations with Alba were those of Earth's. Where Alba had been muddied with links to the drowned god, with Enodian legends of the god leaching Remus's coat when he'd brought him back from the dead. All true. But Alba, the white, had older associations. In his first form, Rune had fair skin and hair. Much more similar to the Rems. His coloring symbolized his most vital element—the frothing waves, the nutrients of the waters, bringing *new life* in his wake.

And it had always pleased Silva to wear Alba's colors. In turn, he had donned the ebony hue of her skin and hair. The soft black tunic he wore now was to honor her—the lady of the night sky. Long before she, too, had been bastardized by the Enodians and all their twisted portrayals of Lady Night.

The glimmer of the Sun Keep on his waters swallowed Rune's focus. He thought of when Silva had been called *"Swelsel— the roots of the mountain."* When her rock had merged with the seed magic, and she'd created the ignes rock. The very rock that the Sun Keep had been built from. It seemed as if *everything* was imbued with some memory of her that caused him to ache with grief.

The riptides of these memories felt like they were changing Rune. He was being reshaped by loss—by loneliness. Before they were fractured, he and Silva had had what Jess had spoken of only figuratively—lifetimes. Together. Their immortality and love— infinite. Now, the knowledge that he was the sole Umbran god seemed to slam into him as the waves of the Alban Sea now drummed upon Umbra's southern cliffs.

Rune wrenched himself from the ocean of memory. It was ironic that there was nowhere deeper than the corners of his mind, and yet he felt as if any one of these shallow eddies might drown him.

Alba's consciousness was vast. The tributaries that had flowed within the vamps upon Earth had returned to him, too. Rune had sensed it happen that first dawn after he'd claimed his shadow self. The tiny wisps of stray consciousness that had given those vamps their immortal blood had flowed back at Eventide. And with it, Rune had been complete. All the vamps on Earth had— like Sunny—become human again.

That first day, Sunny had been a comfort. Rune's ex-blood

brother may not retain any of Alba's consciousness, but he'd experienced it and knew something of its overwhelming abundance. They had talked much. But too soon, Sunny had gone back to Earth to spy for him and Jess.

By the Depths, I am *spending too much time alone if I actually miss Sunny.*

Clasping his hands behind him, Rune trod along the bank, grounding himself with reflections about tomorrow. At midday, the Seelie were due to gather on the Aedis Peak, to hear Alba and Silva. There had only been one hiccup earlier when King Imber had come to Rune, detailing the Triodian High Witch, Fern's displeasure—she was suspicious of Imber's recalling his troops from Earth at dawn. Imber had assured her that his soldiers would be back at dusk. It wouldn't be long before Fern's suspicion drove her to seek answers herself. Rune only cared that Fern kept Earth's paras' attention away from Umbra as long as possible. He wanted to attain the faith and backing of all Seelie before the politics of Earth's paras became involved.

Since the blood-sworn vamps, who had previously maintained the glamour upon Triodia's branches, had returned to humanity's ranks, the Seelie had been helping. Imber had deployed Seelie delegations to the Triodia institutes to glamour them invisible. The Seelie had also glamoured the ex-vamps previously in the Triodia's service to forget about the para world. Yet, because fae power only worked at Eventide, the units had to be there at dawn and dusk to maintain the glamour. It wasn't a long-term solution, not when all Seelie would soon be needed to defend their own lands. For Mara would return, likely with reinforcements from the kingdom of the Fomors.

The Enodians were, too, without glamour. Unlike the Triodians, they had no far-reaching alliance with the Unseelie. Some Enodians worked with Unseelie and vice versa, but it wasn't standard practice. The coven likely didn't have enough Unseelie allies to glamour all their strongholds invisible. Rune wondered how the

Enodians were managing the breakdown of their system. It was likely the reason that the invasions upon the Triodias had ceased.

Surely, Theo must suspect that the vamps becoming human had something to do with the successful restoration of Umbra's gods. Oh, how Rune would love to pummel that worthless mage with all the power of the Heights and Depths should he portal here. Not as much as Jess. Rune knew she was impatient to confront Theo, who held her father captive.

Yet, Rune knew that force couldn't be the means of truly defeating Theo and Queen Mara. Because the enemy responsible for bringing about their power, the Fomors, thrived off destruction. As evidenced even in this peaceful valley. Through the web of water, an undertone of iron lurked, brought from the forges that daily churned out iron weapons.

For too long, the Seelie had fought the Unseelie, barely managing to keep them at bay the last few centuries. But the Unseelie and their queen were a pale enemy in comparison to the Fomors, who were nourished by that very destruction. A flicker of the portal under the Iron Keep, through which the destructive energy from Umbra flowed into the Fomor kingdom, rippled through his head. He did not doubt that Mara would return with Fomor reinforcements, eager to feed off the nourishment of war. Rune didn't know how they were to defeat that enemy yet, but he would start with trusting in the gentler, nurturing ways of his people, in the same way they'd trusted in the signs and portents of the animals.

And it starts with the Storm-born.

He would show the Seelie that true power lay in restoring, not destroying. He would give his people another ally in the form of the Storm-born.

Rune's chest twinged as he knew what he had to do. The Aedis Peak this early in the year still bore much snow, and it was necessary to clear it to allow for the gathering of all the Seelie— over three thousand. So, he summoned that part of Silva's magic that now dwelled within him. Unlike the power he wielded so happily over the Depths, his power over the Heights felt... uncomfortable—an admission that Silva was gone.

But unclasping his hands, he relaxed his body, reaching out to the winds. He called down the Zephyr, the warm southern wind wafting up from the Alban Sea. Its current sang of blossoms, carrying seeds to scatter on the grass plains. Rune dissolved into its playful stream, encouraging its heat, relishing in sprinkling the kernels upon the lands beneath. He could feel the vigor of the storm flowing through his veins. This was the start of new life for his people.

Even if... it was an end for him.

3

A LOST CAUSE

Matteo landed on the Temple Peak on all four paws, feeling like a cat that had fallen off a ledge.

Without the nine lives. Seriously, no self-respecting shifter has any business falling through Heights portals.

His fur bristled down his back in discomfort. He'd thought traveling through the Depths portals when Dearbhla had brought him to Umbra was bad enough. But traveling through the Heights was worse. He still felt as if he were falling, even though he knew he was hundreds of feet farther up, on the Temple Peak of the Silvan Mountains. His body betrayed how unsettled he was, his claws refusing to let up their death grip on the rock.

Yet, knowing the next travelers would be coming through behind him, he forced himself to pad forwards. Being kicked in the backside was an indignity he could do without.

Around him, rested masses of wind-blasted rocks as smooth as pebbles rounded by the sea. Fae had claimed many of these as seats, while others stood along the mountain ridge as far as the eye could see. In the distance, he caught swathes of white fur, along with pale complexions and hair: shifters. He made his way towards the congregation of Rems, changing into his human form.

A fae nearby whispered, "Lady Silva carried away the snow in the early morning and wore down the rocks."

Matteo scowled as he pictured Jess—or didn't picture her as it were, a disembodied entity—and it felt as if the breeze playing across his skin was responsible for stealing her away from him. This conversation was a repeat of the sort that had swarmed around the Seelie Court for the last two weeks. *"Lady Silva this… Lady Silva that…"* The only thing more grating than being continually reminded about Jess's goddess status was the consistency with which her name was paired with Lord Alba's.

Matteo's expression eased as he saw Dearbhla amidst the other Rems. Although she sat with the clan, there was room on either side of her. He wasn't sure if it was her, well, difference from the rest of the pack—being half fae—or her position as second that disinclined the other Rems to socialize with her. To be honest, it could simply be her taciturn manner, but he had grown to like her company since they'd gotten to Umbra. After all, she had saved him and his Alpha from the Triodia. And by choice, Dearbhla continued to serve Jess steadfastly. Jess's second was generally quiet and kept herself to herself, but Matteo had spent plenty of dinners sitting in companionable silence with her and was comfortable with her aloof manner.

"I've never seen so many fae," Matteo commented as he sat down. The entirety of the ridge was occupied by Seelie. Matteo had portaled here from the Sun Keep. While a few hundred of these Seelie had likewise come from the Sun Keep, hundreds more had journeyed from farther afield.

"I'd say," Dearbhla answered. "There hasn't been a gathering like this since the fae wars."

Matteo's gaze roved the Seelie curiously. The most recent fae wars had occurred a generation ago. He remembered his mother talking about the lack of Seelie on Earth during her youth because they were defending their borders in the wars. Queen Mara's unrelenting attacks were the reason that King Imber had implemented the conscription of Seelie to be raised on Earth in the following generation. Skiron's generation. Looking around, it was clear that the shadow of war was never far: the standard blue-and-green hued leathers were what the majority wore. Yet the Seelies' coloring distinguished the various groups in the gathering. There were those like Skiron, the fae from the Seelie plains who bore triticum-colored hair, like the crop they grew. Their lavender eyes like the casia flowers, prolific in the fields, too. Then those that lived in settlements in these mountains, their skin the same gray-blue of the rock itself. Similar in kind to the dark-skinned seafaring fae. But they all shared the same white wings.

And Dearbhla wasn't wrong. War would usually be the only reason for such a gathering. Wasn't it the same with the clans and covens on Earth? Through mirror calls, Matteo had learned from his mother that the full Triodia Coven was gathered in its headquarters, along with the majority of Roms who had transferred their allegiance from Giovanni to the High Witch. An ugly part of Matteo had been exultant that the self-righteous witches and mages were holed up. But most of him feared for his clan, for the shifters, mages, and witches he'd worked and been friends with. He thought of his good friend, Gretta, and hoped she was safe. He'd been relieved to hear that his mom wasn't considering joining them. She was one of the few shifters who remained loyal to Giovanni. Having experienced enough prejudice from paras due to her love and marriage to Matteo's *human* father, she empathized with her Alpha's predicament. That was *one* good thing about the last couple of weeks for Matteo. He'd had time to catch up with his mom about everything that had happened over the last few months. And he was secure in the knowledge that his parents and brothers were as safe as they could be on Earth.

With all the vamps de-vamped and the Seelie stretched at trying to maintain all the glamours on the branches of the Triodia, things were precarious. Matteo's mom had informed him of multiple human reports of buildings just popping up out of nowhere. Of how the Seelie had to glamour civil servants into forgetting about these strange appearances. The veil between the human and para world was shaky, and with it, both the safety of humans and paras.

Matteo's stomach somersaulted. Today was the first step towards building a force to protect both Earth and Umbra. Ultimately, they needed to prove that the division that existed between each of the courts, covens, and clans, had come from outside. But bitterness wound through him as he contemplated whether some of them weren't too far gone for redemption. After what Theo and his followers had done—murdering and tethering their own parents' souls—Matteo couldn't help thinking that unity was a lost cause. How could the coven ever be whole again?

But the problems on Earth were, currently, on hold. Alba believed that the Storm-born would be instrumental in proving the existence of that true enemy to the Seelie, while giving them another ally too. A plan that hinged on Silva's winds restoring the Storm-born to their human-like forms. Yet, Matteo didn't picture the disembodied goddess the fae had been chattering about earlier. Instead, he pictured Jess lying in the dust as she had been this morning, convinced she'd been more winded by Piera's words than Astra's blow. Instantly, he'd wanted to go over and explain to her that Piera was angrier at Giovanni than her for keeping Jess a secret from her. Jess was simply an easy target for her anger, especially with Giovanni Theo's prisoner. It was far easier to blame Lady Silva, a goddess, who should be rushing off to Earth to save their father. As if such a course of action was no big deal. Of course, over the last couple of weeks, he'd tried to explain to Piera how much else hinged on Jess's actions.

Weeks.

It was hard to believe it was weeks ago rather than days that they'd sat at Skiron's house, listening to Jess and Rune concoct this plan they were about to embark on. But between ensuring that Piera didn't do anything rash at Eventide—like portal back with a Seelie unit to Earth—and with Jess so often being in talks with King Imber and Rune, he'd barely seen her. But it wasn't just her absence that had him feeling down in the dumps—it was the change in her since that first night she'd turned up. That blissful moment at Skiron's when she'd wanted him to hold her, had made him feel as if there might be a chance that she felt something of the rightness between them that he'd always felt.

But now, she seemed as if she wanted nothing more than to get away from him. Every time he ran into her, she always had an excuse ready: *"I'm about to go talk to Rune; I have to go see King Imber; I've got a report to hear from Dearbhla."* Jess seemed to have time for everyone but him.

It was the reason he'd found his way to the training courtyard this morning. After overhearing a conversation between a pair of Seelie that Lady Silva trained every morning with the Unseelie, he'd hoped to at least have some sparring time with her. But Jess hadn't stayed around long enough. Matteo *had* succeeded in upping his game with Piera though. Not that he'd won their match. He hardly ever did against Piera. Matteo was still rebuilding the muscle he'd lost while the Triodia's captive. But gods, he'd given Piera the best challenge she'd had of late, spurred on by the fact that Jess had left yet again without talking to him.

Matteo tried to fight the deflated feeling rising in him.

She's a goddess. She has the fate of two worlds to think about, as well as her father, and I'm disappointed she doesn't have any time for me?

"I'm glad those pompous peacocks didn't manage to get the king's ear," Dearbhla chimed in, pulling Matteo from his tortured musings.

He blinked, having zoned out completely, and unsure about what she was talking about.

"That Astra's flying," Dearbhla added, with a fierce look.

Matteo nodded. "Me too."

She was referring to the fact that some members of the Seelie Court thought it *"inappropriate"* for an Unseelie to be riding a

Storm-born. Of course, it was inappropriate for anyone to ride a Storm-born, given they weren't animals but shifters with humanoid forms. But in order for the Storm-born to be transformed, the two Storm-born leaders needed to be ridden—to be led—into Silva's transformative winds. Instead, the debate at court had waged around whether Astra should be allowed to ride alongside Skiron, despite that it was only she and Skiron who had any experience of riding the Storm-born leaders. Astra's treatment throughout her stay in the Seelie Court had been a daily reminder of how ingrained prejudice against their kin was here.

As Matteo mused, the portal that had remained open, showing the craggy outcrop overlooking the casian-colored fields, blurred as if a heat haze hung over it, and the next moment, King Imber floated through. With the arc of his white wings, he landed with the grace of a dove. Rune touched down next, his shadow wings unfurled similarly for balance. In contrast, Jess landed in a startled crouch with all four paws digging into the ground.

A fond smile quirked Matteo's lips.

Turns out you can't take the shifter out of the goddess.

Matteo glanced around at the Rem Clan he sat amidst, wondering if they also felt the swell of pride that Jess hadn't forsaken her shifter heritage. Surely, choosing to portal in her wolf form was a statement. Ownership of her shifter heritage. Or perhaps, just as his wolf had bristled beneath his skin as he prepared to portal, Jess's had, too. Warmth spread through him as the thought seemed to bring her closer to him.

King Imber led the way along the ridge, climbing up to the highest peak above the rest of the crowd. Jess shifted into her human form, walking beside Rune. The contrast between them was stark. Not just with the shadowy swirl of wings billowing behind Rune and the absence of Jess's. Rune was bedecked in a Seelie tunic of fine material, the ebony and gold like a night sky with fireworks. While Jess wore a simple pair of Seelie leathers. A fresh set from the dusty ones she'd worn this morning, but she looked more like a soldier than a goddess.

Seeing Rune and Jess standing together sent the usual sting through Matteo's chest. When he'd first heard how Rune had been able to feel again, through ingesting Jess's blood, he'd felt afresh the pain in acknowledging they belonged together. In the same way that Rune's mountain spring scent all over Jess that night at Skiron's had left no room to doubt they were together.

With the three figures upon the peak, King Imber addressed the crowd. "Thank you all for answering my call." He spoke in English to include the shifters in the audience.

The king's voice was audible to those nearby like Matteo, but as he glanced around at the crowd, he could see even those most distant listening attentively.

Matteo's gaze brushed the lines of Jess's figure. Was she projecting the king's voice on the breeze? She must be. Was it an exertion?

Lady Silva, Goddess of the Heights.

Matteo clenched his fists. Another tumult of unease spun through him. His palms grew clammy. Something in him didn't want to see her perform this magic as if witnessing it would be confirmation of how separate they were.

"My friends, I know you have all heard whispers and rumors about our Lord and Lady's restoration," the king continued. "Whatever remains unknown to you about how this has come to pass shall now be illuminated. But know that the restoration of our gods has been sanctified by the animals of the Heights and Depths and witnessed by king and court. I present to you, Lord Alba and Lady Silva."

Rune's voice rang clearly, projected in the same way as the king's had been. "My people, we come before you with our godhood restored. How we wish that we might, as in the days of old, be the answer to all your prayers. But the troubles ahead of us are not poor harvests, droughts, or floods. For they are not of *this* world.

"For centuries, our people have fought with their own— Unseelie against Seelie. We have believed that the enemy is one another. But it is not true. The enemy came from a different world. It invaded Umbra. It fractured our people. And Earth's. The enemy even fractured us. Umbra's gods. Our enemy is named the Fomors, the Ones Below. I will tell you how we discovered this truth.

"In the Silvan Mountains, within the Cornua, by herding the maelstrom and riding the race we have known as the pucca, we heard the true past from the Book Of Nature, uttered by the faded.

"They told us of how the Storm-born—a shapeshifter race who fled from the Fomors—sought aid in Umbra. We gods journeyed to Earth for a weapon against the Fomors; it was said that iron would defeat them.

"But before we gods could return to Umbra, the Fomors invaded from the Depths. I *am* the Depths—Umbra's waters— and the enemy fractured me. I became an inverted version of myself on Earth, not life-giving but life-taking. I became the first vampire. And the division that occurred in your gods, rippled on through your lands, severing the courts, covens, and clans in two."

Rune's regard swiveled to Jess. "It is only through Lady Silva that we have been granted this second chance. During the Fomors' invasion, as she also began to fracture she realized that only a creative act could counter the Fomors' destructive magic."

He gestured to the shifters. "Our honored guests here today are Silva's descendants. For it was she who created the original twin shifters and buried her seed magic in them, the ability to heal us gods lay within the clans, growing stronger each generation, until the love of a Rom and Rem came together, bearing Jess.

"A shifter born of both clans, a descendant of both Romulus and Remus, possessing the seed magic in her blood. In giving me her blood, feeling was restored to me. This led us to the Silvan Mountains, where I was able to face my shadow self, the fetch in the mountains, and become whole. Become Alba again."

Jess seemed to brace herself, her shoulders tensing then loosening. Her voice rang for the first time. "The moment has come for me to share something about my magic. I succeeded in burying my seed magic in the race I crafted, the shifters of Earth but... it changed me. My magic is no longer Umbran. It is Earthen."

For a second, sorrow tinged her voice. Her figure upon the summit looked suddenly bare as if her wings had been plucked.

Concern prickled through Matteo. He wished he was beside her so that he could tell her that it was her sacrifice—Silva's sacrifice—that had enabled Rune to have his shadow wings back, that had restored his power to what it was, that she was the key to the gods still existing at all.

But Jess's voice strengthened. "You all know the stories of my shadow self, the Sidhe."

It was instant. A tautness hung over the gathering as if the temperature had plummeted at the mention of the Sidhe.

Confusion rippled through Matteo, uncertain as to why Jess would choose to focus on a topic that would cause the fae discomfort. Surely to bring them together, she and Rune should be focusing on the positives.

Jess pushed on. "You know that the Sidhe has been connected to the faded for thousands of years. That she called for those who were about to die from the Between. There was a reason for that. With my becoming Earthen, my shadow self was no longer needed, and she began to fade. She was fading for centuries."

Tension as thick as fog hung in the air.

Fading for centuries...

"When I conjoined with her in the Shadowlands, we didn't merge. Instead... she died."

Matteo's heartbeat drummed in his chest as that word needled its way under his skin.

Died?

Jess's announcement continued though. "I need you all to know that I now belong to Earth, which suffers from the same division that Umbra does. Its covens and clans have been torn apart by the Fomor magic that polluted us all. Just as Mara harnessed that darkness, so has Theo of Enodia. The sluagh horde he wields has been magnified by the para souls he's tethered. I do not yet know what Earthen power I wield, but I promise you I will fight for the people I created *and* for you, to whom I once belonged. For both worlds."

Before shock could transform into chatter, Rune cut in. "As I am now Umbra's sole god, I have taken on Silva's power over the Heights, as well as the Depths. I will lead you in this battle against the enemy that fractured us, while Lady Silva will travel to Earth, to defend the other para races there. We may not be the gods of old, but we will stand together against our common enemy.

"For centuries we have given the Fomors what they wanted, our war with one another strengthening them. We must find a way to unite if we are to defeat them. I would have you witness today the power of restoration rather than destruction in the shape of the Storm-born. They who originally came to Umbra for help, were like us, fractured during the Great Divide. Their ability to transform into their human-like forms taken by the enemy and Umbra's winds emptied of the transformative power they needed. Now that I am whole again, so are the winds. I will restore the Storm-born. And we shall have another ally, with knowledge of the true enemy to stand beside us."

Rune's last word seemed to summon the winds. Once again, there was no leeway for talk. Streams of wind rushed above the peaks and … the Storm-born descended. Matteo made out the silhouettes of the mounted riders upon the backs of the lowest soaring Storm-born: Skiron and Astra on the herd leaders.

He had barely registered the approaching riders before his gaze turned back to the tallest peak. Rune stood alone upon its summit now. Matteo felt frozen as he traced the two figures who had retreated to stand below, where there must be some shelter from the winds. He watched Jess, strands of hair whirling around her face as the winds above strengthened.

Even amidst the booming gusts and wingbeats, it was the echo of Jess's voice that thudded through Matteo: "She was fading for centuries. She died..."

Part of Jess had died.

Matteo remembered the painful scream that had been torn from Jess when he'd first tried to get her to shift in the Cathedral. He bristled with frustration as the gathering storm winds and herd of flying shapeshifters above kept him captive where he sat. *All* he wanted to do was go to her. Now.

Why didn't she tell me?

Alarm ripped through him. He thought of the way she'd avoided him. He'd tried to put it down to her having too many goddess responsibilities—those of Silva. Goddess of the Heights. Mother of shifters. The Great Goddess. But her aloofness appeared in a different light now. And the things that he'd taken as her choice—to portal in her wolf's form, to address the assembly in English—appeared to him differently too.

He remembered that night at Skiron's when she'd entreated him to hold her. The memory of the vulnerability in her voice tore at him. *"Please, hold me."* That night Jess's shadow self had died. A dozen inklings bombarded Matteo all at once. Perhaps, Jess *couldn't* speak Umbran. Perhaps she was more at home in her wolf's form because that was the only part of her she had left. And perhaps, if she and Rune were no longer the mirror image of each other in power, they weren't in love either. Matteo quashed the heady, hopeful idea, ashamed of where his train of thought had taken him so quickly. Even if that *were* the case, it didn't matter right now. As his gaze locked onto Jess's stalwart stance, her attention on the Storm-born stampeding across the sky, he knew what did matter was getting Jess to talk. Because in all likelihood, being the stubborn and hot-headed shifter that she was, she'd pushed him away because she needed him now more than ever.

❦ 4 ❦

EVOLUTION

The maelstrom churned above the crowd on the Aedis Peak. Protected in the shadow of the summit, Jess watched as Skiron and Astra circled within its clutches, riding the Storm-born leaders. Astra's black wings were spread out above the Storm-born she rode; her ebony feathers arcing unapologetically like a massive *fuck-you* to the Seelie.

Jess smirked. Rune had been the one to sway the court to include Astra. In argument to the prejudiced courtier who had remarked that an Unseelie riding a Storm-born was inappropriate, Rune had retorted that perhaps his attending their transformation was inappropriate too. Over the last five hundred years, he had ridden tethered pucca plenty of times. Did his mistakes blacken him too much to be included in the Storm-borns' restoration?

At the time, guilt and shame had crashed through Jess. Her own crimes against the tethered Storm-born were much worse. She and her wolves had killed twenty tethered Storm-born when they'd entered Umbra. Something she hadn't shared with the Seelie Court; it seemed unlikely to help their cause. Said courtier had held his tongue after Rune's comment. Of course, the courtier hadn't known that excluding Lord Alba from this transformation would have been impossible—it was Alba who wielded the power over the Heights.

Something they all *know now.*

With eyes narrowed against the fierce winds, Jess squinted up at Rune. His determined figure was otherworldly, braced on the summit beneath the clamoring storm. His dark, loose hair remained still as if he were made from the stone of the mountain.

A prickle of anxiety stole through Jess. Umbra's flora and fauna had been powerful omens that had sanctified them as Alba and Silva to the Seelie Court. But Jess was aware after her truth that Rune *needed* to prove his power over the Heights, over the winds that had once been her domain. If the Seelie were to believe in them, to unite against the Fomors, then they had to have confidence in their god.

Please let it work.

Rune's conviction in his abilities was evident in the Seelie he'd stationed around the ridge intermittently. They held robes ready to clothe the Storm-born once they'd transformed—for the Storm-born had never yet possessed human form in Umbra and would be naked.

The first signature of Rune's power affecting the shapeshifters was evidenced as their downy, ebony bodies started to alter color. In the glare of the midday sun, their changing hue caught the light. Silvery glimmers cascaded over their shapes. Jess shielded her eyes against the glare, making sense of the change they'd undergone. Their equine bodies glinted with *scales*.

Jess's heart hurried. Was this because of Rune's Depths power? Was he struggling to harness the Heights? Struggling to unlock their human-like forms?

The swirling tornado of prancing horses above gleamed even brighter. Golden feathers like those of the elen birds—those that had appeared in the Seelie Court to bless their return as Umbra's gods—sprouted along the horses' frames. Jess found herself entranced. She remembered what the faded had said about Silva taking inspiration from them: a changeling race with both animal and human-like forms. Jess felt that pull of inspiration now as she watched their fluid frames begin to ... *change*. Her fingers itched for a pencil, to render the feeling that was building in her onto the blank page.

The vortex above seemed to be made of silver and gold, and the crowd gave an audible gasp as both Astra and Skiron spun out of it in a flurry of wings. The whirling Storm-born leaders must have been moving at a speed too great for the fae to remain mounted. The two fae hovered on the periphery of the churning maelstrom, but with a signal from Rune moved away from the tempest. Storm clouds amassed, their wisps and billows blotting out the sun so that the strange twister seemed closer now. Some of the fae sitting and standing along the higher peaks crouched down, wary of the gathering storm.

Jess smelled it before she heard the rumble. The scent of ozone. Memories of flickering thunderstorms rolling across Maine's national parks flickered through her head. A rumble of thunder growled across the Aedis Peak, and a fork of lightning almost immediately flooded the sky, piercing the maelstrom. The vortex ejected the first Storm-born. The shape-shifter's body was ashen as if made of the storm clouds still amassing above. As they descended, their shape became more comprehensible in the air: a head, shoulders, wide torso, wings, and limbs.

Jess's pulse stampeded. Rune had done it. Her eyes widened as she watched a winged man gliding down from the churning storm. The edges of his form still glimmered in silver and gold while the rest of him had settled to a gray.

Stunned silence engulfed the crowd of fae as the first Storm-born set foot upon the mountainside in human form, wings like shadows.

No, more like billowing clouds.

A fae nearby moved forwards, throwing a robe around the Storm-born.

Shortly, another form soared from the dark mass of clouds, the rumble of thunder and tracery of lightning every so often kept the crowd riveted and anticipating the release of the next shapeshifter. It wasn't long before a dozen Storm-born stood upon the Temple ridge, wrapped in Seelie robes, their own faces upturned to the storm and Rune, anticipating the release of their brethren.

Just like the rest of the crowd, Jess's gaze roved the trans-formed Storm-born. All of them possessed churning black wings, the color of the storm clouds above, their lines constantly moving and changing. Jess regarded their ever-shifting swirls with fascina-tion. Their skin tones varied from the gray of overcast skies to the pale blue of clear ones. As she stared at the wings of a female, the Storm-born's eyes met her own. Jess blinked in surprise as she took in the churning quality within them, too. As if something of the whirlpool above remained within them. They set off a memory in Jess—of the Cornua and the howl of the winds as they spilled through the passageways. Those winds that bore the voices of the faded.

The world seemed to tilt. Jess's throat went dry, and her heart battered against her ribcage. Memory stole through her, and she was back in the passageways of the Cornua when that sense of foreboding had taken hold of her. When she'd thought the many tunneled caverns with the voices of the faded were like the hives of the dead.

Alarm spiked through her, and suddenly she didn't want to be here. In the whirling commotion above, with everyone's eyes on Rune and the captivating spectacle, Jess realized that as a wolf she'd be able to slip down the back of the peak easily enough, and relatively unnoticed. With her heart racing, she shrank back into the shadows, inch by inch, and descended the ridge.

5

NATURAL THERAPY

The remnants of the storm stole around the lower reaches of the Aedis Peak. Cold crept through Jess's fur as she tried to tame her chaotic feelings. Her emotions felt as unsettled as the winds above.

And the whirlpool swirling within that Storm-born's gaze continued to whisper through Jess's memory.

Her wolf form did nothing to dampen these jumbled thoughts. Morphing into her human body, she took a seat on a rock. Taking a breath, she reassured herself that everything had happened as they'd wanted it to. Rune's position as Umbra's sole god had been aired—literally—in front of all Seelie, which left Jess free to set her sights on Earth.

She exhaled deeply, trying to steady herself. Another flash of the Storm-born's cloudy gaze shot through her. Unease stirred. The woman's eyes had seemed to possess the same quality as the maelstrom. Which made sense, Jess supposed. The Storm-born used the winds to transform. Why shouldn't their eyes contain something of that power? But why did it make her feel uncomfortable? Jess wondered whether it was because those winds had once belonged to her. Was this some kind of reaction to watching Rune use a power that had once been hers?

Is that what unsettled me?

The scent of evergreen cut off her train of thought. The nutty undertone engulfing her senses told her the Rom weaving down the crags was Matteo. She'd deliberately avoided looking at him as she'd addressed the crowd despite being tempted. He'd been so obvious amidst the pale-haired and pale-skinned Rem, like coal amidst snow. But her feelings had been chaotic enough without having to wonder *how* he'd react to her revelation. But now that he'd sought her out, half of her squirmed with unease, while the other half hummed with ... hope. Perhaps, he'd be *less* weirded out by her godhood now that he knew the Umbran part of her was gone. Yet, even as she thought it, guilt swam through her. She was *still* Silva. She'd had a shadow self. If Matteo couldn't cope with that then that was his problem. Not hers.

When his black wolf landed at the bottom, Matteo shed his fur, his tall, muscular body solidifying. Jess stood up. For a moment, she worried that she'd see that damned stiff expression he'd worn at Skiron's. But she was surprised to see the openness in his eyes as he gazed at her. "Why didn't you tell me?"

Jess shrugged but anger sparked through her. How could he expect her to tell him when he'd looked at her as though she were something incomprehensible? With bitterness, she replied, "I'm a goddess. I can hold things together myself."

"Don't be obtuse—you need to talk about this," he retorted.

Obtuse?

Nettled, Jess snapped, "I might have talked if you hadn't treated me like something alien."

Matteo frowned but with earnestness asked, "What do you mean?"

Now she felt obtuse. She really wished she hadn't said that. She'd avoided him *because* she didn't want to see that look on his face again. Now that she'd called him out on it, wouldn't he be forced to admit that he had struggled with the revelation about her godhood?

The fear of rejection made her bristle with anger, and she fisted her hands. She ground out, "At Skiron's—when I told everyone about being Silva—you looked so ... closed off. Like you wanted nothing to do with me." Jess avoided his gaze, unwilling to find confirmation of what she was afraid of stamped across his face.

"If I looked at you that night with distance, Jess, it was only because I was scared of losing you from my life."

His low, sincere tone had her heart thumping against her ribs. Her breath caught in her lungs almost painfully as she dared to look at him.

She was riveted by his brown eyes holding her. Full of the same steady reassurance that he'd *always* given her. That she'd thought she'd lost. Wasn't that why she'd had an excuse ready every time he'd tried to talk to her over the last couple of weeks? The risk of losing Matteo's affection after everything she'd lost already had been too much. So, she'd pushed him away.

"Don't you remember what I said when you first told me you were Silva—when you were here in the Silvan Mountains?" he asked.

Memory stung her and what he'd said on that mirror call came easily to her. "That you liked me when I was a Rem–"

"And that even part goddess you'd still be as difficult to talk to and bad-tempered. Bad-tempered, check. Difficult to talk to, check," he listed off her attributes on his fingers. "With how well I see the future, I think I must have mage blood," he commented with a wry tone.

A weak smile crossed her face but the lump rising in her throat and the prickle of moisture behind her eyes overwhelmed her. Desperate relief welled up and with it, tears started to fall. Before she knew it, her breath came in hurried sobs.

In a moment, Matteo's arms were around her. She couldn't

stop the sobs that racked her. Her stomach fluttered as she thought of how much Matteo had always been here for her. That he'd been her pillar of strength almost as soon as she'd entered the para world. That here he was again, flying to her side, to check that she was okay.

Fort Matteo.

"Shhh, I'm here," Matteo whispered, both his rolling tone and the way his hand stroked circles gently down her back, so comforting. Gradually, her tears subsided. And as her relief ebbed, she was left instead with an overwhelming awareness of Matteo— his strong arms around her, the feel of his sculpted chest beneath her cheek, the heady scent of his pine and nutty aroma.

Why was fate so cruel? Why was it that when he'd kissed her, she hadn't felt for him what she did now? Because she hadn't been able to, she reminded herself. Her shadow self had been a part of her then. Her Umbran self had pulled her inevitably towards Rune —towards Alba—with all the force of their immortal love. But now, her affection for Matteo that had such a firm foundation— built upon his unstinting loyalty and protectiveness towards her, burgeoned. The affection building within her wanted to spill over into something *more*...

There was so much more she could say. So much she wanted to. But self-consciousness prickled over her as she realized what a mess she was. She realized with mortification that she'd sniveled all over the front of Matteo's black shirt. It was *really* wet.

She pulled back, looking up at him, "I'm sorry."

"You've got nothing to apologize for." His steady, gentle tone had her both comforted and wanting to melt back into him. His hands still rested on her back. "Have you spoken at all about your shadow self passing?" he asked.

"To Rune, a little." She flushed, averting her eyes. Self-consciousness prickled over her as she mentioned Rune. A chaos of emotions tumbled through her as she thought about how awkward chatting about her shadow self passing had been with Rune. How obvious his own grief at losing Silva was. He had an ocean of memories about Silva to mourn. Whereas Jess had a void.

Matteo's hands fell away from her. More confusion whipped through Jess. Did he still think that she and Rune were together? They *were* Alba and Silva, after all. How did she even broach that subject? It *was* connected to the loss of her shadow self, she supposed.

Feeling flustered, she pushed that matter aside. It wasn't what Matteo had asked her anyway. "I talked a bit to Astra, too," she added.

"Someone who thinks the arena is a valid substitute to actually talking about grief," he said knowingly.

Jess's lips curled. He wasn't wrong. Other than beating out her grief in the ring, her therapy had consisted of nothing more than sketching the Sidhe's haunting form, hadn't it?

She was reminded that Matteo had been there from the first moment that her shadow self had reached out to her. He'd heard her painful screams in the Cathedral, too. And, as she had so many times in the past, it felt natural to use him as a sounding board to try to work out how she *did* feel.

"Do you remember what you said when you were trying to get me to shift in the pen?" she asked. "That I might get the blanks in my memory back when I shifted?"

Matteo colored. "Gods, Jess, I wish you wouldn't repeat what I said then. I was such an idiot. I thought I knew it all. And the way I treated you was appalling." He shook his head. "I hate myself for the way I opened old wounds for you."

Side-tracked, her thoughts spun back. Matteo *had* been immovable in his conviction that she was guilty, believing that she'd shifted and killed her foster sister, Caylee. He *had* incited one of her rage blackouts by needling her about all the times she'd lost control and lashed out at her foster siblings. Despite the heavy subject, lightness spread through her. For one thing, it reminded her of how much they'd been through together.

Jess's lips quirked as she thought of how she had first seen Matteo as proud and unbending. "You were an arrogant ass."

He looked surprised then huffed a laugh.

"But," she added, "only at first." She'd been so wrong to ever think him arrogant. "Just by listening to me, you showed more open-mindedness than any other rival clan member would have."

He frowned, shaking his head. "You're being far too kind."

Hardly.

Once again that burgeoning feeling made her overly aware of *all* of Matteo's merits. But before she could do more than be very much absorbed by his many physical merits, he steered the conversation back. "You're mourning your lost memories then?"

She *was* grappling with those blanks in her memory. Those from when she was growing up *and* her ancient memories. But she'd brought up the blanks from this lifetime, from the rage blackouts she'd suffered from because the overwhelming feeling about them was one of ... *guilt.*

With a squirming feeling, she admitted, "I never wanted them back, Matteo. And now that my shadow self's gone, even though I know she was dying for centuries, I feel like it's my fault. Like... I wished her away."

"Then you're just like the rest of us," Matteo said with firmness.

She frowned, confused.

"All of us wish away parts of ourselves. For instance, I would wish away the self-righteous, conceited, arrogant ass I was back in the penitentiary."

Once again, despite the heavy subject, he had her smiling again. Gratitude welled through her. How could she *ever* have been afraid that he saw her as alien when he had the most wonderful habit of making her feel the most normal she'd ever felt?

"Besides," he added, "you *knew* from the off something wasn't right. You told me that there was something wrong with your power, but I thought I knew better—"

Jess laughed.

It was Matteo's turn to frown in question.

"I think we're both really good at the self-blame," she commented.

"Perhaps," he conceded. "Shall we agree to be kinder to ourselves then? By *not* cutting ourselves off from friends and actually talking about things?"

"Deal," she said, a smile wended over her face. To be fair, she didn't think she *could* cut herself off again. She felt almost drunk on how good it was to finally talk to Matteo. Her expression felt like the goofy one she'd had in the Cathedral when they'd laughed together. His presence felt as comforting as Earth's forests. Like a balm for her soul.

Just then, the sound of footfalls above drew their attention. It was a Rem. At the foot of the ridge, the white wolf morphed into a male with blond hair and blue eyes. "Lady Silva, the Storm-born leaders are asking for you. Lord Alba has portaled them back to the Sun Keep. You're requested to meet them in the Sun Study."

Jess nodded. "Thank you."

As the Rem climbed back up, Matteo's gaze returned to her. "Talk more after your meeting?"

Jess bit her lip, his question reminding her of the *many* excuses she'd given him over the last couple of weeks.

"Why don't you come with me?" she suggested instead.

There was a beat as he looked at her. "Isn't this something best suited to Alba and Silva alone?"

The intensity in Matteo's gaze made Jess feel as if there were many more questions laced into the simple one he'd asked.

She held his stare. "I want you there. You make me feel more like myself than I have in ages."

"Then I'm there," he answered. His unwavering tone and expression had her heart somersaulting once more.

And, to avoid the danger that his steady brown eyes and handsome features seemed to pose, she threw out, "Race you to the top." Changing into her wolf, she tore up the mountainside, relishing in the head start that her abrupt challenge awarded her.

6

BOUNDLESS

I t was difficult not to stare at them. Rune schooled his features though, aware that he was in danger of being as distracted by their wings that moved like clouds riding the wind as most people were by his shadow wings. The Storm-born leaders were dressed in the loose-fitting robes the Seelie on the peaks had thrown upon them. They had crouched and knelt about the Aedis Peak, unsure at first how to stand on their legs in these forms. Soon, though, like newborn foals, they had walked and looked at each other with wonder. The open joy with which they'd hugged and kissed one another had had Rune's chest tightening.

Both leaders had gleaming gray-blue skin and ashy locks to the shoulders. As well as their wings, their irises had that wispy quality as if whorls of vapor or mist lay in their dark stare.

Rune had thought just as they'd had difficulty moving in this form, they'd be unable to communicate. But he'd been startled when the male leader had introduced himself to him in Umbran. His name was Tinthir, meaning highest sky, and the female, Samhradh, meaning summer. Umbran names, albeit archaic words, far older than the current dialect of the fae.

After all the Storm-born had successfully transformed into their humanoid forms, Rune had proposed to take them to the Sun Keep.

Samhradh's request had surprised Rune. "We would have discourse with Lady Silva, too." To Rune's chagrin, he hadn't realized Jess had disappeared. He'd been so involved with gathering the winds, with *being* the winds, those currents and eddies flocking around the Storm-born and furnishing them with their long-lost forms, that he hadn't noticed her absence. Guilt swept through him for his obliviousness. He'd sent a Rem to find her. Worry crept through him. Making that announcement to the Seelie Court had been no small thing. Her openly telling everyone that her shadow self had died. Was she mourning what she'd lost? He wondered how it must have been for Jess, witnessing him transform the Storm-born. Did it seem as if he'd stolen a piece of her?

As Rune waited for Jess's return, an air of anticipation hung over him and these two remarkable guests.

"These are olives, sundried tomatoes, and mozzarella—Earth's finest vegetarian fair," Sunny told the Storm-born in Umbran as he knelt by the antipasti platter on the glass table between them all. His light-hearted manner was at odds with Rune's tension. But even Rune couldn't help the flicker of a smile as he thought about how enamored with food Sunny had become since he'd returned to humanity's ranks. The few evenings that Rune had spent in his company the food and wine had flowed freely.

Sunny had been frequently on Earth over the last two weeks, looking in on the ex-vamps he used to know, who might be able to get into Castle Nox. To try to find out any news about Giovanni. So far, they'd all been unsuccessful. Theo was unanimously turning all ex-vamps away. Yet, as he watched Sunny spear more food with a cocktail stick, Rune thought it highly likely his trips to Earth were motivated by his stomach, too. Not that Rune blamed him. He'd noticed a surge in his own appetite.

Both Storm-born shook their heads, sitting on the sofa opposite, but spoke their thanks to Sunny, "Tapadh leat." Their cloudy gazes examined the Sun Study with obvious interest: its walls of books, the desk and chair, and the soft upholstered sofas they sat on before the lit hearth.

He noticed the Celtic nature of their pleasantry. It wasn't the first time that he'd wondered at the Celtic influence in Umbra's language. He remembered Cuill's long hunt to decipher truth from the roots of Umbra's language, and how the Celtic influence had been a mystery. After all, Silva and Alba had entered Earth during the Great Divide, so they brought the Latin influence into their language, but the older Celtic basis had been inexplicable.

But now, Rune realized with a start that these Celtic influences had come from the Storm-born. Parts of their language had been incorporated into Umbra.

As Rune thought about language, once more he wondered how the Storm-born had learned Umbran. Not wanting to offend them, he tried to ask delicately, "How do you come to speak such an old Umbran dialect?"

"We learned Umbran through the stories in the wind, from the faded, my Lord," Samhradh said.

"All of our knowledge of Umbra and of our own people's past comes from them, Lord Alba," Tinthir agreed.

Rune started. Of course. With no one to speak their language or talk of their stories or world, whatever beliefs they'd held had been lost to them. The look of wonderment that lit Samhradh's face, and the way both Storm-born leaders insisted on addressing him as "my Lord" took on new meaning. In a way, Umbra's language, its history, and even its gods had become the Storm-borns' own.

The way the Storm-born treated Rune was similar to the way King Imber and the Seelie Court did. King Imber had at Lord Alba's wish, gladly portaled back all the other Storm-born—there had been two hundred of them—and promised to oversee that they were given beds and food.

Rune didn't get a chance to question the Storm-born about the faded more as they were interrupted by the door opening.

Jess entered. And Matteo. For a moment, Rune's eyes took in the shifter as if he were an intruder, but he reminded himself Jess needed someone to confide in. Rune knew that he and Jess couldn't be one another's confidantes anymore. Not with how changed they were, not with how much grief and heartache muddied the water between them. But Jess needed friends. It was a good thing the stalwart shifter was beside her again.

With effort, Rune greeted them both equably, "Jess, Matteo, come meet our guests."

The Storm-born bowed to Jess as they had Rune, reverence for her godly status seeming to prevent them from being overly familiar. But he noticed as they had with Sunny, both Storm-born leaders greeted Matteo by kissing his cheeks. They seemed to be a naturally demonstrative culture.

With introductions made, Rune offered to translate for the leaders, reminding them that neither Jess nor Matteo spoke Umbran. That pang of awkwardness rippled through him as he highlighted the gaping hole in Jess's knowledge ... in her memory, which felt once again as if he were pouring salt into her wound, but Jess sat down on the sofa looking composed. Matteo took a seat beside her.

"When our ancestors first fled to Umbra, it was you, Silva, who restored our people just as Alba has this day. Thank you for all you have done for us," Samhradh said.

Jess blinked, clearly a little tongue-tied at being thanked for something she, personally, couldn't remember. But she was sincere as she said, "After seeing you transform, I totally understand why you were the inspiration for my own creations."

After translating her warm observation, Rune found himself studying Matteo. During the shifting process, Earth's shifters

were like mist and shadow, like something belonging to Umbra ...
and the Storm-born it turned out. But in their human forms, both
Matteo and Jess's strong features and statuesque physiques were
different from the willowy, softer-featured Storm-born.

"For us to be an inspiration to gods is another gift you've
bestowed on us," Samhradh said.

With these pretty exchanges of thanks given, the Storm-born
raised the topic of conversation they'd wanted to engage Lady
Silva in.

Tinthir's cloudy eyes brushed Jess. "We were telling Lord Alba
before you arrived that we learned Umbran from the faded. They
have furnished us with what we know of ourselves, of our
language and beliefs. But our connection to the faded and the
Between itself goes deeper than that."

Rune's regard sharpened as he translated Tinthir's ominous
opening. Everyone else's focus honed, too. Both Jess and Matteo
leaned forwards, while Sunny stopped eating.

"Your faded become part of the winds, which in turn become
part of us. The wind is what we draw our power from to shift. In
drawing from the maelstrom all these centuries, the faded have
changed us. They have given us our ability to travel through the
Between outside of Eventide. Our connection to the Between is
stronger than almost anyone else's. For nothing is as boundless as
the dead."

"Which is why the Unseelie tether you," Rune exclaimed, realizing how the Storm-born gave the Unseelie their ability to travel
in and out of the Between at any time.

Jess pressed. "What did Tinthir say, Rune?"

He realized he'd forgotten to translate and filled Jess and
Matteo in. His mind raced with this glimpse into the Storm-born
race and how they fit into the fabric of Umbra.

"Nothing is as boundless as the dead," Jess repeated. Her eyes
illumed with a strange light. "Stronger than almost anyone else?

You mean that I, too, have a unique connection to the Between, don't you?"

Tinthir and Samhradh shared a glance, and it was the female who answered. "With your shadow self cast into the Between, you already know that she was altered. So much that she sensed those who were about to die."

Rune stopped interpreting again, this time because he didn't like where this was going. He hesitated as he met Jess's expectant gaze. Was she never to get away from how much the enemy had changed her? A chill swept through him. He didn't want her to feel as if she would only ever be defined by loss. But it wasn't his place to keep this from her. She needed to know everything that could help her understand her new self. He translated Samhradh's words.

Jess's face darkened, but her tone was steady as she looked at the Storm-born. "I recognized the Between in your eyes. I felt a connection to that energy. You're saying that because my shadow self existed in the Between for centuries, I still retain some of that power?"

"Yes," Tinthir said. "Over your lifetime your shadow self connected with you. In doing so, she left you with some of the magic of the Between."

Jess contemplated this for a moment and murmured, "My blackouts." Her gaze moved to Matteo. "The blackouts left me with some of her power."

"Part of her *is* still with you," Matteo said, a warm smile on his face.

Rune felt anew the growing chasm between himself and Jess. And yet he was pleased to see Jess had clearly been talking through her loss.

Jess turned to Tinthir and asked, "Does that mean, like you, I'd be able to portal from Umbra to Earth outside of Eventide?"

Rune understood Jess's question. She had only ever portaled

on Earth. As her power was Earthen, perhaps she wouldn't be able to portal from the Shadowlands to Earth.

"Without doubt, Lady Silva," Tinthir replied. "Your connection to the Between would allow you to easily portal to Earth outside of Eventide."

Jess looked buoyed up by the prospect. Rune could see her focus turning to Earth, to Theo, and to her father.

Tinthir added, "In fact, the faded bring a message through us, my Lady. They advise you to do that: portal to Earth using the connection you have to the Between, to the faded, and to Earth's dead. And to use it when you confront your enemy in your world, too."

As Rune told Jess, he remembered how the Umbran dead had spoken with an animated awareness, acknowledging Rune and Jess's attempt to transform the Storm-born the first time. They weren't just voices of the past but had advised them about the present. They'd told Rune how to claim his shadow self in the fetch. They'd told them that only when his power was restored could Jess's shadow self be freed from Mara. But they hadn't said anything about how Jess's shadow self would die.

Realizing that the faded must have been aware of that fact but had held back, he voiced his concern. "The faded left out telling us what would happen to your shadow self, Jess. Do you think we ought to trust their advice?"

Jess looked solemn and took a moment to consider. "If it were based solely on their advice, perhaps not, but I feel this truth in my gut, too," she explained. Resolve settled over her face. "If I can portal outside of Eventide, then it will give me the element of surprise against Theo. What's the time?" she added, glancing at Matteo, who wore a watch.

"It's only three o'clock. We've still got three hours until dusk." He added staunchly, "I'm coming with you."

Gratitude and warmth softened Jess's face.

Rune felt a pang of regret. He couldn't aid Jess in this fight. He had to put Umbra first.

Sunny surprised Rune too as he chimed in. "I'll come, too."

Seriously, hasn't he stocked up enough on snacks?

Rune noticed he *had* single-handedly polished off the antipasti platter. Feeling the necessity to do something, Rune looked to Tinthir and Samhradh. "I would check on your people and see King Imber. Will you join me?"

He left Jess and the others preparing for an exit from Umbra in a couple of hours. Rune led the Storm-born leaders into the Sun Court, to the Sun Hall, where long tables were laid out with lots of fresh food. The entire hall buzzed with a celebratory atmosphere—flooded with the talk of hundreds of Seelie and Storm-born. Going past the tables, Rune noticed more than a few couples of Storm-born pairing off—some kissing openly where they sat, others with laughs and holding hands, going off to find quieter places to celebrate.

Rune supposed that locked in animal form all their lives, their eagerness to explore a whole new world of feeling within their human bodies must be great.

King Imber was quick to offer Rune his seat at the high table and sit the Storm-born leaders to his right as honored guests.

But after a brief update from Imber about the Triodian High Witch and the ex-vamps, Rune motioned for the king to stay put. "Thank you, but I need to see Lady Silva before she leaves for Earth."

Leaving the Storm-born leaders in Imber's capable hands, he turned to leave the hall. But not before his stomach gave a growl. He was just about to purloin a small quiche from the platter in the middle of the table when one of the Storm-born—a female with *fixed* wings, as well as *un*-smoky eyes, caught his attention.

As he stared at her, she waved. Like she knew him.

Bemused, he wandered towards her, a questioning expression on his face.

"Hi friend," she said.

As he looked further bemused, she chuckled. "Thank you for keeping your promise, to free my people. Also, sorry for leaving you stranded at the top of the mountain, but you look like you managed the descent fine yourself." She eyed his shadowy wings with a flicker of mirth.

Rune colored.

By the Depths.

This Storm-born had been the one he'd flown upon to the White Peak, where he'd confronted his fears in the fetch. As embarrassment twisted through him, his silence only lengthened as every possible apology sounded gods-cringingly awful.

How do you apologize for riding someone? Shit... See?

On top of that, Rune was desperately racking his brains to remember everything that he'd said in front of the Storm-born. That's when he remembered he'd started speaking to both Storm-born whenever it had been his turn to lead them up the mountains. He winced inwardly. Hadn't there been a particularly vocal afternoon on the journey up when he'd told the Storm-born all about his feelings concerning the blood oath that Jess had used against him? He'd dwelled on how betrayed and powerless he'd felt. It had been his way of trying to make reparation for all the wrong he'd done over the years by using them like animals.

Great idea, Rune.

"I'm Eilea by the way, my Lord." Another old-Umbran name, meaning *"Island to the West."* Rune thought of the western isle, which he, Sunny, and Cuill had traveled to. It was beautifully sheltered in the north, and he remembered watching some spectacular sunsets along its shore.

He felt completely tongue-tied in front of this woman who looked like she knew all his deepest secrets.

Because she does.

Oh gods, he almost blurted something about the sunsets being amazing on Eilea but, finally, managed instead to respond,

"Please, call me Rune." The idea of Eilea showing *any* subservience to him made his stomach roll.

"How is your companion who journeyed up the mountains with us?" he asked.

"Beinn is fine, too." She gestured to a similarly fixed-winged man at the table, out of place as well, amidst the fluid crowd of Storm-born whose churning wings made it look as if storm clouds were gathering for the feast, too.

Like a lightning bolt, it belatedly struck him that their fixed-ness was because they were tethered. Something that proceeded to make him feel even worse. He made a mental note to check with Sunny on the Unseelie contacts he'd borrowed the Storm-born through. Such as, how long did his agreement allow him to borrow them for? He recoiled at the idea of the two tethered Storm-born being recalled by their Unseelie masters.

Before he could make more awkward conversation, Rune excused himself. "I hope you enjoy the food and are suitably comfortable in the Sun Keep. If you need anything, please, don't hesitate to ask."

Eilea smiled. "Thanks, Rune."

And Rune retreated from the Sun Hall, feeling gods-damned un-godlike as he ruminated on how much he'd said in this Storm-born's presence, whose eyes seemed to dance with humor.

7

DINNER DUTY & DESTINY

Trying to find things to do to kill the hour before leaving for Earth, Jess joined Astra for dinner duty. It wasn't a coincidence that the one Unseelie in the court got allocated a *lot* of chores. Not that the Seelie kitchens were the worst place to be: the aroma of pastry, mixed with a sweet caramelly scent wafting through the space, was hardly unpleasant. Although Jess would have preferred a joint of roasting meat. On arrival in the kitchens, the Seelie were quick to greet her with bows and the head cook came forward,

"Is there anything we can get for you, Lady Silva?"

A fairer world. Equality. Some sign that there's the potential for unity.

Jess bit down the temptation to throw her dry comments at the kitchen staff. Clearly, her temper was too close to the surface for comfort's sake. Taking a deep breath, she forced a smile. "I'm just here to help my friend with dinner prep."

Whether it was the term "friend" for an Unseelie or the fact that Jess sullied herself by picking up a peeler, silence flooded the room. But Jess focused on peeling the annum—a woody root, a bit like cassava. They'd had them in stews while they'd been journeying up the Silvan Mountains.

Jess had already updated Astra on what the Storm-born leaders had said, having gone to her bedroom straight afterward. She'd related everything to Astra and Skiron. As soon as they'd heard about Jess's going to Earth at Eventide, they'd both declared they were coming, too. She'd also caught up with Dearbhla. Her second had wanted to join her on the rescue mission, but Dearbhla had agreed to stay behind to keep an eye on the Rem Clan. With a new shapeshifter race filling the keep and a celebratory atmosphere in full swing, her second had agreed to stick around to keep an eye on the clan.

Despite having already discussed their plans, Jess still found herself wanting to talk to Astra more. To have company in the lead up to portaling to Earth. As the minutes drew on, the strained silence of the kitchen, where none of the Seelie talked either, did nothing to ease Jess's nerves. Deciding to use some of her divine rights, she said, "Can we have the kitchen to ourselves, please?"

The half-dozen Seelie soon bowed before departing.

"Someone's prepping for returning to their Earthly kingdom," Astra joked.

Jess chuckled. It was miraculous—what with Tinthir's bombshell about Jess's strong connection to the Between and the dead —that she could still laugh with her friend.

But such is the awesome power of Astra Rainbow.

Jess shrugged. "Gotta prepare to be Lady Night, right?" she quipped, thinking of how in some ways the distortion of what the Enodians worshipped was what Silva—she—*had* become. If the faded, Storm-born, and her gut were correct about the power over the dead and the Between that she had. She remembered what Theo had told her in the penitentiary. That she was open to the sluagh. Open to the dead.

The anticipation of how that power over the Between on Earth might manifest sent a jolt of anxiety through her. Would Theo be able to sense her? Would Lorenzo's blood sluagh sniff her out? Would she have enough of this death energy to fight Theo? To destroy him and his followers? Tension of the unknown jostled through her.

Astra retorted, "If through being Lady Night, you can knock Theo on his ass, then embrace the dark side."

Jess's lips quirked.

"Ooo, do you think you'll be able to do that tree thing that the warden did in the penitentiary? What if you can turn a whole forest on Theo and his followers—set giant tree creatures stomping on all those puny witches and mages? Pew pew, pew pew." Astra's feet mimed squishing Enodians.

"What do trees have to do with the dead and the Between?" Jess asked.

Astra shrugged. "Rune said he sensed great Earthen energy in you, too. Your magic is Earthen, as well as this Lady Night energy."

Astra wasn't wrong, and nervousness wound through Jess as she wondered how these two aspects of herself would come together.

"Just don't discount Earthen magic, okay?" Astra said. "I totally want tree soldiers."

"Noted," Jess said with a smile. But her intuition told her that this link she still possessed to the dead and the Between would be the key to saving her father.

The Storm-borns' explanation and their message from the faded felt more like confirmation of something that she'd been on the cusp of realizing. It had explained the reason for that haunting, lingering sense she'd had the last two weeks. It explained the feeling she'd had on the Aedis Peak when the maelstrom had recalled to her the voices of the faded. And, mostly, it explained, on catching the eyes of that first Storm-born, why their gaze had conjured thoughts of the faded.

Because the faded were part of the Storm-born. In the same way that the faded and the dead were part of Jess. Her shadow self had been trapped in the Between and the faded had become part of her. And then, through Jess's blackouts—when her shadow self had emerged—the magic of the Between had become part of her too.

"Anyways, if I get to Theo first, that mage is mine," the fae added, bringing Jess back from her reflection. Astra really did look like she'd love nothing more than to skin him alive as she carved the annum viciously. In fact, Astra had been as desirous to take Theo out as Matteo was.

Jess's smile softened as she remembered how quickly and staunchly he'd declared he was coming with her. As soon as their plans had been decided, he'd agreed to fill Piera in. Jess had thought it better for Matteo to lay down the chain of command. She had the feeling that if she did it, Piera would be far more likely to defy her for the sake of it.

A grin spread over Astra's face. "Dork, you've totally got that I heart Geometry look again."

Jess blushed. Her heart galloped in a tell-tale way.

Do I?

She *had* been thinking about Matteo. *Again.*

Clearly, I've been spending waaaay too much time with Astra for her to read me so well.

Even with the worry about what she would soon face on Earth, the happiness she felt about having her friend back in her life still warmed her.

Sure, friend, because that's what this warm fuzzy feeling's about.

At the word *"friend"* memory sparked, her thoughts tumbling back to the gardens in Villa Silva. To Matteo's low voice, *"I hope you see me as your friend."* Yet his gaze had been filled with heat as he'd uttered those words. And the next moment, his lips had been on hers. Soft and forceful.

She flushed with self-consciousness as she admitted to herself now how much more she wanted from him than friendship, too.

Astra rightly interpreted Jess's blush and racing heartbeat. "What's stopping you then?" she pressed. "Is it the age gap?"

Jess frowned. "Matteo's only like twenty-two. There's four years between us."

The fae laughed. "Yeah, yeah. Sure, your human body's eighteen, but how many years has Silva been around for?"

She snorted but argued back, "That would be centuries between us then, but I can't remember that time."

Astra guffawed. "Sheesh, maybe it's a good thing you and Matteo haven't got it on yet—I mean, now you're so old you've got memory problems."

Jess buckled over, clutching her stomach as her friend's humor got the better of her.

Oh, gods.

It felt so good to laugh about how cosmically fucked her love life had become.

Jess dried the tears of laughter from her eyes, finally able to resume her peeling.

But Astra wasn't done. "Astra Rainbow, the hopeless romantic, here for one night only. Step up, step up, for all your Tassological needs," she joked, then tossed a long unbroken peel of annum down in front of Jess.

Jess stared at the peel in front of her.

Astra waved her fingers over the annum as if she were casting some sort of spell. "Do it. Do it. Do it."

Jess's thoughts raced back to the prison. To that moment when Lea had knocked the potato peel out of her hand and onto the floor, telling her that the peel would spell out the first letter of her true love's name. Her throat grew tight as she remembered the peel *had* spelled out "M". At the time, the para world and its magic had all been so new to her. She had barely believed that shifters existed, let alone that there was a type of Earthen magic —Tassology—that could predict your true love's name.

But now she knew better. And her gaze locked onto the

annum peel as if it were a coiled snake. Because yes, she had feelings for Matteo. She had *big* feelings for him. And suddenly the idea of casting that peel on the floor and getting anything but an "M" made her chest feel like it would implode. And even all the mucking around and laughter with Astra couldn't chase away the dread that churned in her gut. What if she'd waited too long to tell Matteo how she felt? What if he didn't feel what he had for her? What if they weren't destined to be together as they'd once been? And unable to face the fear swarming her, she turned away, barely hearing Astra calling her as she retreated from the kitchen.

༄

A SHORT TIME LATER, JESS STOOD ON THE RIVERBANK OF THE Sun Plains. It was an hour until Eventide, the strip of water wending through the valley still bright in the daylight. They had settled that Jess would attempt to open a portal to Earth, yet if she failed to access the Between, Astra or Skiron would open it in an hour. The two fae stood hand in hand behind her. Matteo and Piera, their ebony coats sleek in the light, stood behind. And Sunny brought up the final number.

Jess's gaze strayed back to her sister. She'd managed to get a stiff affirmative from Piera that she'd follow orders. That if Jess's power didn't work or wasn't enough against Theo and his followers, then she'd follow the chain of command to retreat.

As the seconds ticked by, anticipation hung heavy. They'd agreed upon La Alba as the exit point as it belonged to Jess. Technically, it was still under her control. If you overlooked the whole only half the clan had chosen to follow her. Portaling outside of Eventide would give them the precious few minutes for Jess to explore her powers. Then she had no doubt Theo would show up ... or at least be alerted to her presence when Lorenzo's blood sluagh came sniffing.

Jess's pale gaze wound to Astra. The lines of her friend's face

had stood as stiff as statues, poised to strike, began to relax, real-izing that Lorenzo couldn't see them.

The wolf padded towards the mansion.

Jess followed calmly, knowing that her boot wouldn't make any indentation in mud or emit noise. She and her friends were made of the ephemeral.

Of the past. Of the dead.

As Jess moved, even less substantial than a sluagh, she motioned for the others to follow. She watched as her friends froze in shock. Then, cautiously followed.

The lake was disturbed as an archway of fire lit its surface, and Theo stepped out of the waters. He'd never looked as abhorrent to Jess as he did when he moved from the lake. Like Queen Mara, he was something that had taken on the divisive power of the Fomors. Instead of seeing that energy as something that polluted him, he saw it as empowering.

Dressed in a long, black cashmere coat, his tanned skin and sandy hair stood out in the wintery light. With a hurried gait, he exited the lake, his green eyes glittering with distrust.

"You stupid dog. There's no one here!" Theo exclaimed.

Jess had no doubt that her camouflage ... *all* of their camou-flage would hold. But she saw the surprise stamped on the fae and Sunny's faces and in the shifters' pricked ears as Theo stalked right past the whole group.

Jess seethed the longer she looked at him. His lust for power and arrogance screamed from every aspect of him: his confident stride, his glimmering eyes snaking over his surroundings, and the cruel set of his lips.

A stab of despair cut through her. At first, she didn't under-stand where it had come from, but as she watched the amethyst glow of Lorenzo's blood sluagh flicker, she realized it came from her uncle's spirit.

His deep despair felt familiar. She'd felt it once before—in the Sidhe's painful need for peace. Lorenzo's stolen energy pulsed with the same need to be elsewhere, but Theo yanked on the tether like a leash, and the purply wolf petered out. Jess had never thought she'd feel sympathy for her hateful uncle ... but in this moment, she did.

With her new power and insight into the dead, looking at Theo now was like seeing him properly for the first time *ever*. And it wasn't pretty. The different hues of his sluagh horde surrounded him. Some she recognized from the descent into the human Netherworld—the black, gray, and white mists of human souls that formed the basis of his horde. But there were so many others now. She could see the magnitude of magic, burning in the blue, purple, and heliotrope glow of all the para souls. And at the heart of that swarm of stolen energy was Theo. An abyss. Like a black hole gaping in Earth's fabric. His soul contained the same festering magic as the Fomors because he'd embraced it whole-heartedly. He was a void stealing the light and warmth of all those around him.

In the swirling mass, Jess recognized that shifting soul, not quite of the human ones, but not belonging to the heliotrope of the paras either. She remembered seeing this energy during her descent to the Netherworld. Before Theo had tethered Lorenzo's blood sluagh or any other para souls.

Jess examined the being's energy. A human with magical abili-ties. Who had seen the future. The woman with the third eye, she'd been called by her community. Memories from the woman's soul shuddered through Jess: of a vineyard with fruits, flowers, and Theo's blood, tethering her soul to him forever.

The misery and yearning of this individual soul bled into Jess, choking her with anger. She wanted to free this soul from the detestable mage. To free all the souls bound to him. For a moment, the whisper of the murdered Rems, of their wandering souls seared through her, too, and the urge to tear into Theo as if she bore a hundred claws and fangs raged through her.

But Jess curbed the desire. Instead, she drank deeply of the

Earth's magic—the scent of dirt, of dampness, and decay. She used the blood and bones in the Earth to smear their very essences and mask themselves from Theo's notice as he stepped back into the portal, her own hidden person following.

I need to get to my dad.

Urgently, she gestured for the others to follow. Sneaking into Castle Nox and breaking her father out without Theo or any of the Enodians noticing would be the best possible scenario. With this death dust, Jess would be able to keep her friends out of harm's way *and* rescue her father.

And as they stepped through the Between this time, the whisper of trees seemed to sigh around them, carrying and camouflaging them.

8

DEAD OF NIGHT

The disgusting scent of decay clung to Theo as he exited the Depths pool in the catacombs. The smoke from the portal did something to combat the smell, and he breathed it into his lungs as if it were fresh air. He shrugged off his cashmere coat, sure the wool had absorbed that damp earthen reek pervading the grounds of La Alba as it followed him. Hurling the garment on the floor, he strode out of the fiery waters.

His sluagh crawled out through the castle, investigating the corridors and its grounds. His heart struck his chest as alarm grazed him. What if La Alba had been some sort of diversion? Sweat beaded across his brow as he tensed. He shouldn't have gone there. It was foolish curiosity to leave his most secure stronghold.

But Lorenzo was so sure he'd sensed Jess.

Theo's heart rate slowed as relief fluttered through him: all was quiet, only the energies of Enodians and sluagh evident throughout the castle and its grounds. As Theo took in the calm, the mantra that he'd uttered ever since the vamps had become human beat through his head.

My sluagh horde is immense.

My followers' hordes are additional protection.
Castle Nox is fortified with ancient sluagh.
Jess can't touch me here.

But the thought of the stories blossoming from the Shadow-lands, of thawing snows and gathering wildlife, countered his attempt to soothe himself.

Big whoop. Umbra's having an early spell of good weather. It doesn't mean anything.

But he felt deflated. For a moment, he'd thought he was about to get answers.

Theo mocked himself.

You'd think with how much Remi's on the brain, I cared about her.

But the truth was Jess had royally fucked Theo's entire world. He felt as if the whole damn castle were falling down around him.

Enodia's infrastructure *was* failing. There were no vamps to glamour their buildings invisible or allow for the tethering of souls from hospitals and care homes. And the ex-vamps didn't know what was going on any more than Theo did. Most of those that had been employed by Enodia had come begging for shelter and an explanation as to what had happened to them. Theo had threatened to set his and the rest of the coven's sluagh on them if they didn't fuck off. What use did he have for powerless vamps? He wasn't a charity.

Although, he'd soon need charity: he and his followers had been forced to reach out to the Unseelie they'd worked with over the last few years. And as Enodia's High Mage, he had granted and was granting an ever-growing number of favors to the Unseelie that they would want to collect before long. Yet, currently, the Unseelie were the only way that he could think of for maintaining the glamour upon Castle Nox and Enodia's other strongholds. Already the Unseelie who were maintaining those glamours had bargained for use of the strongholds whenever they desired them. At this rate, he would be gifting Enodia's fortresses to the Unseelie completely.

The fae had proved essential for turning away the curious humans who had come calling when Enodia's strongholds had suddenly appeared out of thin air. The first few humans had been killed outright by the more ancient sluagh tethered to the fortresses. Too quickly, the humans' law forces—the police and the military—had escalated the threat the humans' posed. Theo already had a war he wanted to end by conquering the final branch of the Triodia, the last thing he needed was another one against the human world. Once again, a cloying sense of uncertainty somersaulted through Theo. Part of the appeal of ruling as High Mage on Earth, had been the superiority that paras had over the fragile humans. But with the vamps' powers gone—such a vital part of the para world—that superiority was in danger of being overturned.

Frustration tumbled through Theo. What he really wanted to know was *where* Queen Mara was. If he could deal with the Unseelies' leader directly, maybe he'd be able to broker a more long-term alliance. The little he'd been able to get from the Unseelie working with him was that Queen Mara had left the Iron Keep. Her units patrolled the borders of her lands, but the fae he'd spoken to implied that there'd been no new orders for some time. What could have shaken the formidable Unseelie queen? And where was she if not the Iron Keep? All the things Theo didn't know felt like a yawning chasm opening beneath him.

Had Jess and Rune successfully restored the Umbran gods? Worst of all, he was *so* damn close to eradicating the Triodia Coven. His spies told him that the entire Triodia Coven had been confined to its headquarters for a week now. But even that was a source of irritation. If he were to attack the final branch, he'd leave Giovanni, his most valuable leverage against Jess, undefended here at Castle Nox. By the Night, he was as holed up as the Triodians were. Jess had turned him into someone he barely recognized. He wasn't exactly the staying-in type but, aside from checking out La Alba a moment ago, he hadn't left Castle Nox since the vamps had lost their powers.

For a moment, he considered reaching out to Bad Juju. If he had to stay in, he preferred company. But even that kind of pleasure was denied him; he was sick of all her fucking questions. Of all his followers' questions. Theo massaged his temples as their constant nagging pounded through his head. *What's happening? What are we going to do next? When are we going to attack the Triodia?*

Ironically, the source of information that had been most forthcoming was Jess's own clan: the Rems. Theo had captured a pair of Rems, intent on using soul warfare to betray information concerning their Alpha. But he hadn't needed to torture them; they'd talked willingly and freely, claiming that they had been given the choice to serve Jessica Remus or not. They'd opted out. They'd told him that she'd given them the choice to come to Umbra or stay on Earth too. That was the last word they'd had from their Alpha, delivered through Dearbhla, Jess's second.

Theo raked his fingers through his hair in frustration. Lorenzo's blood sluagh coalesced on the air, his ears drawn back, and he stalked across the catacombs.

"Sod off, you stupid mutt," Theo barked, snuffing out the shifter, sweeping him back into the ash of his sluagh horde as if he were putting out a cigarette butt. The shifter had too often been wandering off. Of his own accord. It had first happened that night that Jess claimed Lorenzo had invaded her dream. At the time, Theo had thought Jess mistaken and suffered a nightmare. But it seemed that had been the first of Lorenzo's breaking his leash. Could it be that Lorenzo was another thing that was going pearshaped thanks to Jess?

Theo wished he could beat the stupid mutt that had dragged him needlessly to Vicenza. A smile finally curled his lips as he thought of taking out his stress on another dog nearby. Fishing a hefty iron key from his jeans pocket, he proceeded through the main catacombs to a huge iron door at the back of the crypt.

Unlocking the door, his sluagh limned him in pale light. In the trickle of their glow, another body on the floor was apparent.

Giovanni Romulus, the Rom Alpha resembled a corpse. The skin that one could see beneath his unkempt beard, ashen. The angles of his face sharp and sunken. Only his chest rising and falling showed that he lived.

Theo's smile broadened as he realized he'd be able to sneak into the Alpha's dreams again. Lately, he'd found more delight in playing with Giovanni's fantasies. It soothed him to watch the Alpha's mind crack as he realized what he'd seen wasn't real.

Damping the light, so as not to wake the sleeper, Theo let his sluagh burrow into the slumbering Alpha, saturating the shifter's dreamscape.

The Alpha's mind was spinning like a merry-go-round—the tell-tale sign of how much Theo had been using this space as his playground. Spite filled Theo. For every inconvenience Jess had done to him, he would ensure he gave back a hundred times by fracturing her father's mind.

The person in the Alpha's dream was clear. A young woman, slightly older than Jess, but with similar coloring and features. Theo had seen the woman in the Alpha's thoughts and dreams often. Alessandra Remus. Jess's mother. Giovanni lay beside her. This dream was more of a tapestry of good memories stitched together.

Like he thinks he can knit himself a safety blanket.

But these stolen moments with the Rem girl who Giovanni prized so much were *exactly* what Theo enjoyed tainting and torturing him with best.

But beneath the wish to get his own back on Jess through her father, fear lurked. It seeped into the dreamscape before Theo could stop it.

"Jess is Silva, Gio," Alessandra whispered. Awe and happiness washed over her face.

Theo's dread beat through the landscape as the fearful thought that had haunted him of late dominated him:

I was so sure about using Jess for my own power grab. What if I could have squashed her like a fly before, and now she crushes me?

Giovanni smiled tenderly. "I know, my love."

But Theo's fury flooded the Alpha's fantasy, twisting Lessa's features and words with hate. "Your daughter's Silva, and yet, you're beneath her notice. Perhaps if you'd been there for her, for either of us, then she wouldn't have left you to rot."

The devastated expression, both on the dream Alpha's face and on the one in the dungeon, sent a jolt of satisfaction through Theo

Yet, like an avenging angel, the dream Alessandra suddenly chalked herself upon the air in the cell, crouching over Giovanni and looking as if she'd tear apart Theo limb by limb.

9

BURN FROM THE INSIDE OUT

I t was remarkable. Matteo still felt sure that if he rubbed his eyes, he'd wake up. Yet Lorenzo's blood sluagh tracked the area around them, his glow diminishing from where they'd all frozen in shock. The undeniable truth beat through him.

Jess's made us invisible.

Not that they appeared any different to Matteo's eye. His lupine gaze skimmed over the two fae and Sunny's figure, all looking tall from where he was hunkered on the bank in wolf form. But otherwise, they appeared unaltered. As he reflected on this novel form of magic, he realized that he... smelled it. There was a potent odor: moss, dirt, and damp. As if they were in an old forest in autumn when the leaves turned to mulch, and the mushrooms started sprouting. He felt it, too. There was something blissfully peaceful; he felt as if he could be in his favorite place in the whole world, Vesuvius National Park, wrapped in its wooded slopes and its mineral-rich soil beneath his claws.

But the miracle of what was unraveling was blotted out when Theo portaled out of the lake.

Everyone squared up, poised to strike. Their attention went to

Jess, ready to follow her order, but she merely held her hand up for them to wait.

Once more, amazement lapped at Matteo.

We're hidden from Theo.

The mage trod out of the lake, his eyes searching the land, but without seeing any of them. Matteo went rigid as the mage passed Jess, no more than an arm's length from her. Yellow and orange flame from the Depths portal crossed his skin like a tiger's stripes. Memories of this megalomaniac immobilizing tens of shifters all at once with his abominable waking nightmares flooded his thoughts. Apprehension needled through Matteo as Jess risked walking after the mage. But Matteo's sensitive ears discerned no footsteps; it was as if Jess didn't affect the world around her. She beckoned for them to follow, and he gingerly padded forwards, too. Beside him, Piera looked happier than she had in weeks, in an I'm-on-the-hunt kind of way. Her ears and tail pricked up, and her eyes pinned on the mage as if she dearly wanted to stalk him as closely as Jess. Despite their very different coloring, features, and physiques, the sisters' determination and alertness were the same. But Jess remained in human form as she shadowed Theo.

Astra, Skiron, and Sunny seemed to have gotten over the shock of their ghostliness and tentatively followed, too. Their gormless expressions and tip-toeing footsteps would have been funny if it wasn't for the presence of the mass-murdering mage. Piera alone had the gall to prowl just behind Jess. Matteo forced himself to pad quicker, intent on intercepting Piera should she do anything reckless and interrupt Jess's concentration.

Fascination prickled through Matteo as he watched Jess shadowing the mage. Tinthir had advised her to draw on her connection to Earth's dead, and Matteo wondered if Jess was drawing from the death that had occurred within these grounds so recently. It was only weeks ago that Dearbhla, alongside the Rem Clan, had buried those killed by Theo within these grounds. They should have been laid to rest in Cemetery Remus with their ancestors. But the time it would have taken to portal and bury them there would have put Dearbhla and the pack at too much risk. Instead, the Rem Clan had opted to bury them where they'd fallen.

Matteo imagined the fallen Rem roaming these gardens and its bordering wilds like Lorenzo's ghostly sluagh, longing to be at peace with the pack. Sticking close to Theo, Jess looked more ethereally beautiful than ever. Ethereal and yet determined in her path once more.

His chest tightened as he remembered the vulnerability she'd revealed to him on the Temple Peak. At first, he'd thought her avoidance of him had been because she was afraid of talking through her grief. But as she'd confessed how she'd misinterpreted his distant look at Skiron's and seen the way she'd barely dared to look at him, he'd seen how afraid she was ... of losing him. The barrage of thoughts that had whipped through him then had been deafening. If she was this upset about the possibility of losing him, did it mean that she had feelings for him? How he'd wanted to tell her that it was impossible for her to lose him because he loved her utterly. But he'd clamped his jaw shut. It had been best to omit the I-love-you part he told himself again. She was grieving for the piece of herself she'd lost. She didn't need him to complicate things.

Didn't I do that once before?

The memory of kissing Jess at Villa Silva threatened to chase away all his resolution, but he quelled the thought.

I will be there for her as the friend she deserves.

As Jess flanked Theo directly towards the still-open Depths portal, she gestured to them all. They all hurried towards her, stepping through the portal behind her.

They exited into a vast stone room, lit by torches, its vaulted ceilings flickering with shadow.

We're in Castle Nox.

Jess had snuck them, unseen, into Enodia's securest stronghold. At the back of the crypt, the mage unlocked a door. Jess followed. Could Theo have unwittingly brought them right to Giovanni? Hope beat through him as he peered into the small room, no bigger than the one he had been locked up in in the Triodia headquarters. His flews pulled back, but he swallowed the growl in his throat. Giovanni slept on the floor at the rear of the dungeon.

Matteo lengthened his gait, pressing his flank against Piera's in what he hoped was a reminder to stay back. He could feel the anger pouring off her in waves. But they had to wait. Wait for Jess's directive.

Tendrils of purple smoke wafted toward the sleeping Alpha.

Trepidation whipped through Matteo as Jess turned around, her eyes locking with Piera's. Her voice was a whisper, but Matteo heard it. "No matter what, get him out."

Matteo's heart quickened.

In the blink of an eye, Jess stood beside her father.

Theo backed away. "How did y-you...?" The mage's eyes slammed back to Matteo and the others.

He can see us.

"How dare you use my mother's memory!" Jess bit out.

Before Matteo could do more than wonder whether Jess's power could combat Theo's, the mage buckled over, a scream tearing from his throat—a scream that reverberated off the stone walls and echoed around the vaulted ceiling. An amethyst wall rose around Theo like a shield. He pulled himself up, eyes blazing with fury as he stared at Jess.

Footfalls sounded from behind them, farther back in the catacombs. More Enodians. No doubt Theo's followers with their own sluagh hordes, reinforced with para souls.

Astra, Skiron, and Sunny hurtled out of the door, going to confront the incoming Enodians.

Piera shot over to the back of the crypt, towards her father.

Matteo's gaze whipped to Jess as he followed. Her focus was locked on Theo's glowing shield, threads of its purple wound towards her as if she were plucking at the mage's protection, trying to get through to him.

Piera morphed into her human form. "Help me!" she said as Matteo shed his fur, too. Soon, Giovanni was slumped between them, barely conscious as they hauled him across the cell.

Matteo's focus shot back to Theo and Jess. Judging by the vein pulsing in the mage's forehead, whatever Jess was doing to him, he was going to make her suffer for it given the chance.

Clangs and shouts rang from the other room. He scanned the scene through the door. Two Enodians lay on the floor, but two others crossed blades with Skiron while Astra and Sunny were crouched on the floor. Matteo's pulse raced as he worried they'd been wounded, but as Sunny gritted his teeth, scowling up at the mages fighting Skiron, he realized the Enodians had incapacitated them with their sluagh hordes. If more Enodians arrived with more para sluagh, they wouldn't stand a chance of fighting their way to the portal. And they needed Jess to open the Depths again. Astra and Skiron's fae magic only worked at Eventide.

"Jess!" Matteo shouted. "We need to go."

He forced Piera, with Giovanni stooped between them, to halt. Panic beat through Matteo as he watched Jess. She seemed entirely lost in whatever she was doing to Theo. She hadn't so much as blinked as he'd called to her. Her face was strained as she teased evermore threads of violet away from the mage. Theo's knees buckled, and his expression twisted as he fought to keep that shield blazing between him and Jess. Was she so wrapped in hatred that she'd lost herself? Horror spiraled through him. Would she let the need for vengeance get the better of her?

Piera tried to move them on, but Matteo urged Jess again, "We need to go before the others are overwhelmed. Jess!"

Finally, Jess's gaze veered to him. Relief tore through Matteo as she came back to herself. Her pale face blanched as her attention went beyond Matteo to the sound of weapons striking off the stone walls.

Jess nodded, only turning to Theo to promise, "I swear I'll set every soul tethered to you free."

Theo's eyes burned with hatred, but he remained where he was, panting, his brow slicked with sweat, and tremors racking his body.

Understanding pierced Matteo. She hadn't been trying to tear through Theo's shields to get to him; she'd been freeing the souls within his sluagh horde. The tide of relief that rushed through Matteo as he heard Jess's quick steps following them through the catacombs was immense.

Skiron had managed to cut down another of the Enodians and Sunny was back on his feet, helping the fae fight the remaining witch. The Depths portal ahead of them prickled with that whisper of magic that had brought them from Umbra to Earth. Matteo anticipated the feather-soft touch of those comforting waters, their gentle promise of safety.

He heard Jess step over to Astra, hauling her up from where she crouched on the floor, still besieged by the Enodian's sluagh. The scent of dirt and dampness filled the air as Jess's magic swept aside the sluagh from her friend.

"Go," Jess ordered as she pushed Astra over beside Matteo. The fae's face was ashen and her wings drooped.

But the next moment, the portal petered shut, and Jess cried out.

In an instant, Matteo darted around, ushering Astra to take Giovanni's weight.

Theo was upright, stalking across the catacombs toward them. Towards Jess. The mage crushed something in his fingers, his green eyes glimmering as they ran over Jess on her knees.

The fiery torchlight washed over something pale in Theo's fingers.

Jess's hair. Theo has a lock of her hair.

The wash of Theo's heliotrope sluagh volleyed towards Jess.

Jess buckled and would have been on the floor had Matteo not caught her. She writhed, her back arching as her face twisted in agony as the sluagh washed over her and ... into her.

A heartrending cry flew from Jess's mouth. "Matteo!"

Matteo's heart punched at his ribcage as if it would burst from his chest at the anguish as she shouted *his* name. Laying Jess down, Matteo's wolf tore through his skin instead, his savage claws and teeth arcing toward the mage. He had to get the lock of Jess's hair out of Theo's clutches.

Tendrils of amethyst pierced Matteo, their blinding force ripping into his innermost landscape. A flash of Jess as the remote goddess he feared her becoming, standing by Lord Alba, blistered his insides; she rose into the Heights, and he knew she was leaving him behind forever. But he tore through the fear because it wasn't as bad as what was happening right now: Theo cutting into Jess with her worst fears. Failing her again was his real worst fear. And he wouldn't. Not when she was, literally, screaming his name for help.

Matteo caught the glimmer of surprise in Theo's eyes just before his teeth sank into the mage's arm.

As they tussled on the floor, Theo unsheathed his scian.

But Matteo felt the return of powerful magic. Like the call of the woods, it emanated nearby with great strength. He heard the whisper of the Depths portal open again, and the scent of dirt bathed the catacombs. Jess must have recovered.

Theo's stunned pallor said so. The mage scrambled back, clutching the lock of hair, but yelled out in surprise as the pale strands suddenly burst into flame.

Matteo darted away from him. But it wasn't Jess who stood at the Depths portal. It was a witch Matteo didn't know. A witch whose brown eyes were still on the burning lock of hair at Theo's feet.

"Erika," Sunny exclaimed. The other Enodian had now been cut down and lay at his feet.

"Sunny," the witch said, a flicker of a smile on her face. "I sensed you needed a hand."

Shifting into his human form, Matteo rushed forward. Jess was still on the floor. His pulse catapulted up a notch as he realized she was out cold. He scooped her up into his arms. Piera was already going through the portal the witch had opened, supporting Giovanni with Astra's help.

Matteo was completely of the same opinion. *Whoever* this witch was, Sunny knew her, and she'd just saved their hides. She was definitely a welcome traveling companion.

Skiron hurried into the portal next. Sunny took his sweet time as he stared at the witch as if there wasn't a dangerous mage still loose in these catacombs. Erika gestured towards the portal, and Matteo didn't need to be told twice. Plunging through, he clutched Jess fiercely as if the Between might take her from him.

10

DE-VAMPED VS. UN-VAMPED

Jess couldn't see the light. Darkness pierced her. The iron-tinged were holding her frozen in place. Their icy touch seared right to the bone. No, Queen Mara's *scian* was causing that blinding pain, carving the flesh off her bones. The bitter sting in Jess's soul bled into the agony flooding her body from the blade.

"Where are we?" Matteo asked.

Jess stilled, mind-blowing relief coursing through her. The rumble of his voice resonated through her head, and she realized she was pressed against his chest. He carried her. His voice had always had a musical quality to it, but it really was music to her ears. The happiest, most beautiful, poignant music she'd ever heard.

"Risør in Norway," Sunny answered.

For a moment, Jess realized she couldn't remember how they'd gotten away from Theo and Castle Nox, but she continued to feign unconsciousness as she didn't... *couldn't* withdraw from Matteo's warmth. From his *aliveness*.

The violent images that Theo had knocked her out with guttered across her mind again. At first, she'd been in the circle of iron-tinged sluagh while Mara shredded her flesh from her arms—the queen intent on torturing her to death and tethering her goddess's soul. Throughout that waking nightmare, the high-pitched pain of Jess's shadow self, yearning to move on, had been her greatest torment. Until... a black wolf had leaped at Queen Mara.

Panic slammed into Jess as she remembered the iron-tinged sluagh and Mara transferring their attention to the wolf. Anguish had consumed her as she, still suspended by the iron-tinged, hadn't been able to move ... Hadn't been able to do anything as the wolf ... as *Matteo* howled ... as Mara cut into his body and ... gut-wrenching silence had fallen.

Jess breathed in the scent of evergreen and the whole world shrank to the beat of Matteo's heart resonating through her head and washing through her body.

"And why'd you bring us here?" Astra asked, her tone suspicious. Jess didn't need to see the fae to know her russet eyes were sweeping the area, her hand poised on the hilt of her cloidem.

"I needed somewhere safe to talk to Silva," an unknown voice answered. A woman's.

"This was where Erika and I first met," Sunny explained.

Jess couldn't help it. Her eyes snapped open. "Erika?" she said.

A witch stood slightly apart from the rest of them. Her brown eyes met Jess's. The witch who had been a vampire. Who Sunny had believed had been killed by the Triodia Coven when she'd become one of the scourge hundreds of years ago.

Jess remembered the hope Sunny had recently voiced about Erika. After the faded had explained that there were other worlds, that the Fomors had come from outside of Umbra and Earth, Sunny had suggested that Erika—who had mastered all three branches of magic like a witch of Earth's original coven—might have managed to travel to a different world after becoming a vamp.

Sunny was right.

Jess's gaze raked the witch. She didn't have the pallor or gaunt-ness of a vamp. She'd become human, just like Sunny and the other vamps. The witch's amber skin was heavily tattooed, the one patterning her temple and feathering down her neck domi-nating. And most beguiling of all, Jess sensed that death dust that she had used to cloak them all at La Alba emanating from the witch. She realized Erika was shielding them all with the same energy. Jess stared at the witch; her eyes bright with questions.

Piera's impatient voice interrupted, "Can we make introduc-tions once we find shelter?"

Jess stirred in Matteo's arms, her eyes darting to where Giovanni was slumped between Piera and Skiron. Guilt whipped through her. Instead of rescuing her dad, she'd gotten distracted by Theo's sluagh horde. Her gaze tracked her dad's hanging head, his chin resting on his chest, and his weight very much held by Piera and Skiron. He hadn't regained consciousness.

Matteo's grip tightened on Jess as she tried to move. "Theo knocked you out. You need to rest, too, Jess."

She didn't try to move again. Instead, she laid her head against his shoulder, only transferring some of her weight by draping her arm around his neck, enjoying having an excuse for this closeness. Enjoying giving in to his demand, a demand that her whole body echoed, not out of tiredness, but with the need to feel him.

"I have a house on this street," Sunny interjected.

Jess narrowed her eyes on the back of Sunny's head, wondering how the witch had known about Sunny's house. Had he already met Erika since she'd returned to Earth? Sunny *had* been portaling back from Umbra frequently these past two weeks. On the pretext of checking on vamps and spying on Theo to try to get news of Giovanni. But Sunny had never been particularly honest about his actions. Wouldn't it be just like him to have omitted the fact that he'd met up with his long-lost lover while on Earth?

Jess's gaze veered to Erika who walked beside him but lagged back a little. Her brown eyes were, again, pinned on Jess. A prickle of awkwardness stole through her as she averted her eyes from the witch. Erika had said that she needed to talk to Silva. Restlessness stirred through her as she wondered what the witch wanted.

They came to a row of darkened houses. A few lampposts lit the quiet road. It was still dark, but against the bright white snow, the facades of the houses were clear. Soon, Sunny showed them into a large house set on the roadside. Soft lighting spilled over them as he led them down an airy hallway, the ceiling soaring high above.

"There's a bedroom at the end of the hall for Giovanni," Sunny said, directing Skiron and Piera with the Rom Alpha.

Matteo went to follow, with Jess still in his arms, but Erika interrupted, "I need to talk to you now, Silva."

Jess frowned, her gaze unwilling to leave the hunched figure of her father as Piera and Skiron steered him down the hall.

"I'll make sure he's all right," Matteo said.

Warmth spread through Jess at the thought of how much Matteo cared about her dad and sister. "Thanks."

Taking her into the living room, Matteo deposited Jess on the sofa before leaving them. Meanwhile, Astra slumped down beside her. She looked pale. Jess remembered the other Enodian in the catacombs who had set his sluagh horde upon her. Feeling both shaken and grateful that they'd all made it out, Jess inched over, impulsively wrapping her arms around Astra. She expected the fae to push her away and accuse her of being mushy, but Astra cleaved to her. Jess wondered what her friend had seen in the fears the Enodian had projected. She swallowed the lump in her throat as her own nightmarish fears threatened to swarm her again.

When Jess's attention went back to their companions, she found Sunny had turned on an electric burner, while Erika sat on the other end of the L-shaped sofa where she and Astra rested. In the glow of lamp and firelight, her amber face looked tired. Dark circles rested under her eyes.

Jess noticed how Sunny made to step towards the sofa but stopped short. He couldn't stop staring at Erika and seemed stuck in the No Man's land between the heater and sofa. His overawed expression and uncharacteristic silence made Jess change her mind about her earlier supposition that he'd met Erika the last two weeks.

No, he totally looks like he's seen a ghost.

Because he sort of had, Jess reminded herself. Sunny said he'd seen Erika's death in the Silvan Mountains, in the fetch. But *clearly* Erika hadn't died. Jess eyed the woman, her gaze straying to the tattoo patterning her temple and feathering down her neck, both beautiful and fierce looking.

Gods, this must be so weird for Sunny.

The love of his life had just come back from the dead after hundreds of years. Taking pity on him, and in an attempt to unfreeze him, Jess asked, "Can we have some water, Sunny?"

Jerking from his daydream, he nodded. "Of course." He crossed over to the kitchen, retrieved a pitcher from the fridge, and brought glasses to the coffee table, handing them out before taking a seat in the corner of the sofa.

"Why choose to portal to Risør? Did you know Sunny had a house here?" Jess asked, scrutinizing the witch.

Erika's lips twitched. "Am I under interrogation? Didn't I just save *you* from the Enodian Coven?"

Jess nodded. "Exactly. I want to know why."

A noted smile crossed the witch's face now. But she answered calmly, "When I became human again, I suspected the restoration of Umbra's gods must have caused it and began my journey back to Umbra to seek them. But I sensed something I didn't expect— your death energy. It isn't something Silva was renowned for in legend as far as I know, but it was strong, so I tracked it until I world walked to Earth this evening." Her gaze strayed to Sunny, and she added, bitingly, "And as for here, I suppose I banked on Sunny still having some fond memories of this area enough to keep a place."

Sunny's pallor looked positively vampiric now. What Sunny had told Jess in the Silvan Mountains skittered through her head: *"Despite my failure in bringing about a solution to healing the divide, I was still driven in my quest to restore Silva. I was still ... torn. Sometimes, it seemed as if only Erika and I mattered then the pull of the quest would get me hunting Umbra for months."*

Okay, clearly these two still have some unfinished business.

Frustration prickled through Jess as worry about her dad gnawed at her. She wanted to be with him, not a third wheel to this awkward reunion between two ex-lovers. But the fact that Erika had been tracking *her* energy didn't allow Jess to give Sunny time to muster his courage. No matter how merciless the witch's answers were for Sunny, Jess needed to find out why she was here. And judging by Erika's demeanor and answers so far, something told Jess her return wasn't simply on account of her and Sunny's long-lost love. "Why are you interested in my energy?"

"Understanding how the magic of Umbra's gods was restored might help other worlds that have been divided by the Fomors."

Of course. Erika had spent centuries in other worlds. They'd already heard from the faded how the Storm-born fled the Fomors, who had invaded their world. It followed that there were more worlds that the enemy had invaded, too.

Jess's inquisitive gaze prickled over the witch again. Erika *was* using the death dust to cloak them all right now; the same power Jess had used earlier tonight. Was this something else she'd learned how to do in other worlds?

"You're veiling us with the same energy I have," Jess said. "How?" She scrutinized the self-contained witch, seeking to understand her motivations.

Sunny interrupted, "Erika never tethered souls. She learned the art of attracting the dead without tethering them. Like the original witches of the single coven before the Great Divide, Erika's long been able to use them as a magic source."

Jess almost rolled her eyes.

Way to focus on the wrong *thing Sunny.*

He'd told Jess that he'd once thought his feelings for Erika were infatuation and admiration for her magic. Likely it was one of the sources of tension between the two lovers. Therefore, immediately concentrating on your lost love's *magic* probably wasn't what Erika wanted to hear.

Jess's thoughts also took her back to months ago when she and Rune had been in Norway together. When Rune had first told her about Sunny's history and mentioned this witch and the Enodian mage whose magic he'd fostered. *"By raising them together in the arts of each other's magic. Sunny taught them to understand the three strands of magic that the coven in the beginning practiced, and from which their name stems from "tri— three", and "odia—paths.""*

"Understanding the three paths allowed you to find your way into different worlds then?" Jess said.

Erika nodded. "Before I became a vamp, I discovered that the raw material of the Between was souls—and the way to open portals into other worlds."

Jess thought of the feather-soft touch of Umbra's faded as she had called upon the Shadowland's dead to portal to Earth. She recalled, too, how it was the network of branches and roots, and that festering undertone of the dead on Earth, that had released her here. And it would be that that she'd use to portal through the Between back to Umbra.

On the surface level, it was the Heights and Depths that were used to portal Between Umbra and Earth. But just as the Storm-born contained the faded within them, and that whisper of death dust roiled through Jess, the dead were the deepest magic of the Between.

"But how come world walking is possible between Earth and Umbra without understanding that?" Astra piped up.

In her gut, Jess knew it had been her and Rune's ancient selves that had caused that connection and answered, "Because of my shadow self and Rune's fracturing on Earth. They were thrown back into Umbra, while Alba's corporeal self was left on Earth, along with my seed magic sown into the twin shifters. In so many ways, Umbra and Earth bled into each other."

Astra blinked at her, then settled for muttering, "Dork."

The witch looked between Jess and Astra, before segueing back to what she'd been saying, "So, yes, when I became a vamp, I didn't know if I'd still have my witch's magic, but I did. And so, I took the plunge and world walked."

The quiet that settled felt loaded. Jess knew that Sunny hadn't wanted Erika to become a vamp. Knew that that was a decision Erika had taken anyway by getting a vamp sworn to the Triodia to make her into one. And Sunny hadn't known about Erika's discovery of other worlds. Hadn't known she'd world walked. Instead, he'd thought that she'd been killed by her coven.

The witch added, "Besides which, I've found other ways in other worlds to magnify that power." She drew out a piece of what looked like crystal from her pocket; it was limned in an orange glow. "Speaking of which." Her eyes roved over Jess. "Are you well enough to take over the veiling, Silva?"

"I actually prefer Jess," she replied, but Jess nodded her agreement. She felt for the death dust that she'd summoned so easily in La Alba. Despite the modern interior of the house, she felt the layers of earth beneath her answering her call and drew it up as easily as roots would water in rain-drenched soil.

As Jess felt the whisper of her death dust settling over all of them, she nodded again to the witch.

Erika leaned forwards, the light from the crystal diminishing until it went out completely. So, the crystal had been the means of magnifying Erika's power to keep them veiled. The relief in not having to use that magic was visible in the way she slumped back on the sofa.

Jess's gaze wound to the door, wondering where Matteo was. Had her dad woken up yet? Maybe now that she'd veiled them again, she could go...

Erika interrupted Jess's train of thought though. "So, Jess, will you share with me how your and Alba's restoration came about?" The witch's gaze glimmered with undisguised interest.

Jess knew that Matteo would come get her if her dad's condition worsened. Quashing her restlessness, she decided to share what she knew as quickly as she could. If such knowledge could help other worlds, it was right to share it. "Firstly, it came about through my heritage," she said. "I'm born of both shifter clans."

"The divided's blood," Erika said.

Jess nodded. She knew from Sunny that when Erika had been on Earth hundreds of years ago, Sunny had interpreted the Eventide prophecy as the Triodians had: the sacrifice of the divided's blood to the Between would unify the courts, covens, and clans, and restore Alba and Silva. He'd admitted to Jess that he'd plotted a union between Erika and an Enodian mage, Inis, believing that the sacrifice of their child would fulfill the prophecy.

Questions buzzed around Jess's head at Erika's interjection. Had the witch known Sunny's intention? Jess couldn't help but think that here was another woman who knew what it was like to love an Alban heir, who both loved and longed to kill a part of you. Sunny had said she and he had been together for a decade. How had Erika managed it?

Jess quelled her own curiosity and continued her explanation. "When I entered the para world last year, it set off a series of events. Perhaps none more important than me giving Rune, an Alban heir, my blood.

"Rune?" Erika said, confusion creasing her brow. "I thought that..." Her gaze wavered to Sunny.

There was a sincerity in her expression that made her look much younger. Her mistaken supposition hit Jess. Erika thought that *Sunny* had become Alba. That Jess and *he* were together.

Sunny's voice sounded hoarse. "Rune, another vamp made after you left Earth, is the one whose feeling was restored by Jess's blood. He now holds Alba's entire consciousness."

Erika's eyes widened with shock.

The air was charged with unspoken words. Surely, Sunny would tell Erika what he'd told them all in the Silvan Mountains? That he believed Erika's blood hundreds of years ago *had* restored his feeling. That he *had* loved her. That seeing his greatest fear in the fetch—her death—showed that.

Jess had the urge to pull Astra off the couch and slink out the room, but just as she moved, Erika released a laugh and suddenly got much chattier.

"Anyone want some cran?" The witch withdrew a bag from the fur-lined pocket of her jerkin. Both her jerkin and trousers were pale and made of a soft-looking material like suede. The odor of fish flooded the room as she untied the bag.

Astra wrinkled her nose. "What's cran?"

"Dried shrimp," Erika said, popping a piece in her mouth.

Jess, ordinarily a connoisseur of dried meat products, didn't want it near her, let alone in her mouth. The expression on Astra's face suggested she wasn't enamored either.

"It's small and high in protein. I couldn't carry much, but this kept me going while world walking the last two weeks," Erika elaborated.

At the sight of Erika pulling out her own refreshments, Sunny took a break from awkwardly staring at her long enough to fill bowls of chips and bring a bottle of wine from the kitchen.

Or maybe he's just trying to escape the cran.

Both Erika and Astra readily accepted a glass of wine when Sunny returned. Jess eyed Astra a little concernedly as she noticed her drinking quickly.

"Jess," Erika said, "why is your energy so Earthen then, and how have you come to wield energy from the dead? As far as legend has it, isn't Silva the goddess of the Heights?"

Jess fought back an eyeroll. Maybe she should record herself. That way she wouldn't need to keep explaining how their restoration had come about. "When Alba was fractured," Jess explained, "he became the first vampire, leached of life, while I had time to bury my seed magic in the two shifter twins I created before I fractured. Our shadow selves—the Umbran inner parts of us—were thrown back into the Shadowlands for millennia. Rune's was the fetch that appeared in the mists on the White Peak, while mine was the Sidhe. She was trapped in the Depths, cut off from the rest of my magic on Earth, so she faded and was dying for centuries. When I joined with her recently, she passed on." Her voice thickened on the last two words. Even though she'd talked about it more frequently of late, not to mention in front of a crowd of thousands, the words still hurt.

"Which is how you came to have this connection to the dead and the Between," Erika surmised, understanding in her eyes as they flicked over her.

Jess nodded.

"Huh," Erika said, her expression thoughtful. "I don't know what I was expecting when I set out to find out how Umbra's gods had come back from the brink of destruction." She took a gulp of wine. The witch was doing a good job at keeping pace with Astra. "But I can safely say it's not the clear-cut picture I expected."

Jess huffed a laugh, realizing for one thing the witch had clearly thought that it was Sunny, her ex-lover, who had become Alba, and was still likely reeling from the discovery that he wasn't attached to Silva in any way. Jess felt as if she could *definitely* relate to the witch's rollercoaster of a journey. Especially with how she was feeling about her own current love life.

But Jess merely commented, "You're telling me." Her gaze wound to Astra, tempted to remind her it wasn't juice she was drinking.

But Erika asked, "Pray, how did an Enodian mage come to have a lock of your hair?"

Jess felt like the biggest idiot ever at the question. A flush stained her cheeks. Thoughts of how different things had been when she'd first met Theo flipped through her head. No, not really, she mused. He'd just concealed his intent well. And Jess had been desperate to find a way out. No matter the cost. To think that despite all her new godlike powers, that mistake could have cost her her life and those of all her friends. Jess admitted, "I gave it to him."

To her surprise, Erika didn't look judgemental, only thoughtful. "I burned it before we portaled out. I once gifted a similar token to an Enodian mage. I truly believed that I could overcome the divide between our people. But I learned that that breach between our covens wasn't something I could undo myself, which is why I went looking for answers elsewhere."

Jess reckoned Erika wouldn't have made light of her foolishness quite as readily if she'd still been under the mistake of thinking Sunny was Alba. And thus, Sunny and Jess an item.

Erika drew out a flask from another pocket. Uncapping the flask, she said, "I think tonight calls for something stronger." She offered it to Sunny first.

"What is it?" he asked.

"Ligue, harvested from Kemdo's underwater forests. It's... potent. One sip's enough," Erika told him.

"Is that where you were?" Sunny asked, accepting the flask.

"Kemdo was the world I was in when I stopped being a vamp," she replied.

From the meaning in Sunny's tone and eyes, he hadn't just been asking where she'd been recently. But he took a sip and grimaced, his eyes watering slightly as he passed it to Erika, who offered it over the coffee table to Jess.

She shook her head. "No thanks, what with maintaining the death dust veil," she explained, feeling very much like the designated driver, and that somehow the discussion that had started was swiftly descending into some sort of party.

Astra had no such qualms. Grinning, she took a sip. "By the Depths, that's delicious."

Erika leaned forward. "One—"

But Astra had already taken another gulp. The fae passed the flask back to the now sheepishly smiling witch.

"And I call it un-vamped," Astra shared. She relaxed into the sofa, her wings shifting around her, too, draping over Jess. A musky sweetness wafted from Astra, and Jess examined her friend's now dilated pupils.

Oh hells, this is so gonna be like a bacae berry night.

Finally, a heavy step had Jess turning around and meeting Matteo's stare. "How is he?" she asked quickly.

"Still asleep. Piera's staying with him. Thought I'd check on what... He trailed off and grimaced. "Is that shrimp?"

The warmth of the room had brought out the odor of the cran to a pungent degree.

"Good nose, my friend." Erika laughed. "It's cran, want some?"

"It's from a world called Kemdo," Astra added, "where Erika was when she was un-vamped."

"De-vamped," Matteo countered, the corner of his mouth curling, telling Jess he'd overheard Astra's earlier comment.

"Uh-uh, too much like de-fanged," Astra retorted.

"Well, they were, and then some," he said.

Astra snorted. "Fair play."

Despite all that had happened tonight, Jess's mood felt buoyed up as she listened to her friends bantering.

The witch whose gaze was taking in Matteo with interest, then Astra, arcing to Sunny, shrugged. "It's not every night you're back in your home world for the first time in five hundred years." Then, like Astra had, she took *another* gulp of ligue. "Two rival fae, two rival shifters, and a pair of ex-vamps. I think we're much farther along the road to that mythical unification than we ever got, Sunny."

Her gaze dilated, too, the same languor affecting her limbs as Astra.

Sunny frowned, looking like he very much wanted to say more, but seemed to realize that any meaningful conversation with Erika tonight was off the table.

Astra piped up. "Where's Ski?"

"He's outside on guard," Matteo answered.

"Awww, Ski. He's too *good*. I'm gonna go kiss him and tell him I'm glad he's not gone."

A pang struck Jess's chest, knowing all too well what sort of waking nightmare Astra had been subjected to tonight in the catacombs, too, with that deceptively simple word, *"gone."* No wonder the wine and ligue had gone down a treat. Jess knew her friend wasn't the best at dealing with her emotions. Instead, Astra had tried to use the alcohol to numb whatever she'd experienced. But the ligue had pushed her inhibitions out the window, and with wine glass in hand, Astra wandered out the room to find Skiron. Jess felt a rush of happiness for her. Even if it was on account of the ligue, she was going to tell the person she loved most in the world how special he was to her. And as that warmth filled her, instinctively, Jess's gaze strayed to Matteo in turn. Unable to resist her own desire to look at her favorite person in the whole world, her gaze clasped his tall, muscular form, reassuring herself that he was there, he was alive and close to her. His brown eyes met hers with both protectiveness and gentleness. That combination of strength and softness that was so beguiling. So Matteo. The feeling of what she wanted from him, everything, all of him, flooded her gaze, and it was all she could do to remain silent and not make an idiot of herself by telling him in front of an audience everything she felt.

Thank the gods I didn't have any ligue.

RIGHT THROUGH ME

Rune sat in the window seat, perusing the same page he had for the last few minutes, still without taking anything in. *A History Of The Faded* lay open in his lap. This was King Imber's Sun Study; the reason there were so many tomes that he would never have known existed a few months ago. He wondered if he'd ever get over how foolish it had been to overlook the Seelies' gentler wisdom for answers. If he'd only listened to the voices in nature, in the animals, and elements, Alba might have been restored so much sooner.

Whenever Rune wanted some inside time, he took refuge in this room. He found its book-lined walls especially comforting tonight as he'd tried to fathom more about this link to the faded that the Storm-born leaders had spoken of. The link to the Umbran dead that Jess had successfully used to portal her and her companions to Earth.

And then what?

Restlessness about the danger Jess and the others might be facing pushed him up out of his seat. He abandoned the book upon the other two he'd been skimming for the last few hours: *Stories of The Faded* and *Tales of The Drowned*.

At least Eventide wasn't far off. Perhaps a half hour and he'd be able to send a Seelie through to La Alba ... if Jess hadn't returned by then. She could portal back outside of Eventide.

So, why hasn't she yet?

Over the last few hours, Rune had considered asking one of the Storm-born leaders to portal through to Earth. But he worried about sending them into potential danger. Besides, there was no knowing whereabouts Jess and the others would be.

A knock issued on the door, bringing a swell of anticipation. Could this be news? "Come in."

Eilea entered the room. "I had a feeling you'd be up." She was dressed in Seelie leathers, carrying a tray of food.

Rune closed his mouth, realizing he'd been gaping. He'd expected King Imber or Dearbhla perhaps, anxious for news of Jess. But this was the second time the Storm-born had unexpectedly appeared carrying a tray of food. Last night, she'd sought him out after their awkward meeting in the Sun Hall, bringing him a quiche and salad. He'd been in a talk with King Imber so hadn't been able to speak to her properly, but Eilea had interjected that as she'd gotten in the way of his dinner, she'd brought it to him.

"Thank you," Rune said, venturing to the desk where she laid the plate. "But you don't need to wait on me, you know?"

The Storm-born shrugged. "I just can't get enough of carrying things for you, you know?"

He colored, his thoughts fluttering back embarrassingly to those moments in the Silvan Mountains when she—*this pretty, young woman*—had been his steed.

"I'm just messing with you," she joked. "You're way too easy to wind up."

Rune's mouth was in danger of falling open again, so he opted to take a seat at the desk instead, the scent of the sweet warm pastries on the plate already tantalizing his tastebuds.

Eilea went over to the window seat and sat down, looking out at the view. In the glow of the ignes rock, the closest trees, shrub-beries, and flowers would be visible.

As he took a bite of the flaky pastry, he realized it was Eilea's flippant manner that was throwing him.

You're seriously complaining about someone treating you like a normal person?

Ignoring his derisive internal commentary, Rune couldn't help contrasting Eilea's relaxed manner with almost everyone else's deference. If the king or any other Seelie had visited him, they would have been cordial, but it was unlikely they'd have checked the reverence with which they regarded him. Even the Storm-born leaders in their conversation last night had treated him in a way befitting a god. Eilea seemed completely unfazed by his power and status, and he didn't really know what to do with that.

Her teasing comment still had him embarrassed. But he chided himself. It had been a joke. She really didn't seem to bear him any ill will. Surely, she wouldn't choose to stay in his company if she'd been serious? Uncertainty rippled through him as he wondered why she had sought him out again.

His gaze brushed her willowy figure; her slender limbs were swallowed by the Seelie leathers she wore. Her skin tone was a brighter blue than the Storm-born leaders' bluish-gray. Her features, too, were delicate, almost lost behind the thick, black hair she wore to the shoulder. It was shorter, though, than the other Storm-born; a difference likely accounted for by how the Unseelie who had teth-ered her had shorn her horse's mane. All of Queen Mara's pucca were groomed to look uniform when ridden as part of the unit.

Eilea turned around, her fixed dark eyes catching Rune's as she caught him studying her.

Endeavoring to find something to say, he asked, "Why does your Umbran differ from the other Storm-born?" What he really wanted to know was why she was so different in her manner to the Storm-born leaders and the rest of her people, who bowed and greeted him with his godly title. But once again, Rune took refuge in analyzing one aspect—her language—which was noticeably more modern, like Astra or Skiron's way of speaking.

A shadow crossed her face. "I learned the modern dialect from listening to the Unseelie and his kin, who tethered me."

By the Depths. Of course. I just thought that her haircut must be because of them, so why not her language?

He seemed to have a habit of putting his foot in his mouth every time he spoke to her. "I'm sorry—"

"Why? You didn't tether me."

Her blunt comment brought a flash of Queen Mara carving her scian into Jess's arms. Rune's stomach quailed at the thought that Eilea had been through a similar sort of pain. Marked. He knew, theoretically, that the Unseelie similarly marked the Stormborn with iron: the pain, iron token, and their mingled blood bringing about the abhorrent magic that bound their soul to the fae's. Consequently, they were at the behest of their master's call. Of course, that hadn't prevented Eilea or Beinn, the only tethered pucca who had been part of the wild Storm-born herd, from transforming into their human forms when Rune had unlocked them with the Umbran winds.

Like a fool, he realized he hadn't told her that he'd spoken to Sunny who had procured both Eilea and Beinn through his Unseelie allies. Likely Eilea was worried that the Unseelie would soon call them back.

Rune broached the subject, "I spoke to Sunny, my friend, who..." he trailed off wondering how to word it without giving offense again.

"Purchased the use of me and Beinn," Eilea provided.

He nodded, fighting back the grimace. "Sunny assured me that the two Unseelie through whom he obtained you will keep to their bargain—they didn't specify a timeframe for your return. And they aren't the sort who would recall you so they can join

Mara's army, but more of the mercenary types who will sell their services to the highest bidder."

A dark look came over Eilea's face. "I know, Sunny paid them well."

Once again, Rune was reminded that she must have been present when Sunny had bartered for her, albeit in animal form.

She added, "Thank you though, for asking on our behalf."

He shook his head, feeling weary. "The least I could do." Silence threatened as he wondered—if she already knew the lay of the land concerning the Unseelie who had tethered her and Beinn —why was she still here? What more could she want to discuss with him?

He couldn't assuage the guilt roiling through him. His igno-rance over the centuries had done great damage to Eilea's people. A people Alba was supposed to have protected, too. "I may not have tethered your people, but I was so deaf to the intricacies of magic right in front of me, in the Storm-born and in Umbra's elements."

"The magic in the Storm-born and in Umbra's elements speak to emotion," Eilea argued. "The Fomors robbed you of your ability to feel. Just like they robbed my people of our ability to transform. So, you can't blame yourself. Besides, as soon as you were a feeling being again, you treated us Storm-born with respect." She added with a glimmer of mirth, "Such as talking to us on the way up the mountain."

"It was to assuage my guilty conscience that I started speaking to you and Beinn. I won't allow you to give me credit where it's undue."

"Won't allow my Lord?" she teased. But she added, "The fact that you felt so much guilt makes you a good person, Rune."

That shut him up. He blinked at her. He felt suddenly bare beneath her dark gaze. As if she could see through to his deepest, most private thoughts.

That's because you did *use her as a sounding board for your deepest thoughts, you fool. She just referred to it again.*

Rune racked his brain to remember what he'd said in front of her and the male Storm-born. Then, the realization struck him that the Storm-born had been *there* when he and Jess broke up, too. Yes, in horse form. But they'd been very much present.

With his mortified look, Eilea seemed to catch his train of thought. "Look, can we just agree that whatever you said in front of me and my friend, Beinn, is forgotten?"

"Agreed," he conceded readily. Scrabbling for something else to say, he asked, "How is Beinn doing?"

A grin crossed her face. "Very good, I think. Last night, I left him at the feast with a Storm-born, Uisge, who he used to date before he was tethered."

A flicker of the couples Rune had seen kissing in the Sun Hall filled his thoughts. Grasping at what to say, he almost said that he hoped Eilea had enjoyed the feast, too, but silenced himself, realizing that could be misconstrued as asking whether she had enjoyed herself in a *similar* way to Beinn. And that, *certainly*, was none of his business.

Eilea seemed oblivious to Rune's discomfort and picked up one of the books beside her. "Stories of the Faded. I know quite a few of those."

Feeling as if she'd tossed him a lifeline, he ventured over to her.

Finally, back to the safety of books.

Wasn't she the perfect person to talk to about what he'd been searching these books for? He'd sought to try to understand more about Jess's connection to the faded, the dead, and the Between. He sat down on the window seat, beside Eilea, taking the book—well, more of a sheaf of papers—from her. Besides, he realized as he sat there staring at the open sheaves, that what he'd been searching for couldn't be read about; it had to be *felt*. Just as Eilea had expressed it so succinctly about the intricacies of magic that belonged to the Storm-born and Umbra's elements.

"What does that part of your magic feel like?" Rune asked quietly. "This Between magic? That's part of Silva now?"

Seriousness settled over her slight features for a moment. "It's been so long since I truly felt it myself, it's hard to describe. Since I was tethered seven years ago, that part of me, the part of me that belongs to the maelstrom, that contains the faded, and links me to the Between is in part with the Unseelie that tethered me."

Seven years. Abhorrence for the fae who had bound her seared through him. Rune knew that Unseelie hunting parties had, for centuries, traveled into the Silvan Mountains to hunt and tether the wild pucca. The desire to rid Umbra of the detestable magic that had allowed this crime to happen had never seemed so important now that he was speaking to the real, talking, feeling woman who had been used as a beast of burden and weapon by the Unseelie. Doubt churned through Rune at the thought of how much darkness the Unseelie had tainted themselves with. He wondered as he had on so many occasions, how the courts could ever be united. How could there be any coming back from tethering another soul?

"But I suppose when I travel through the Between," Eilea continued, "and use the power of the faded, it feels feather soft. Like the blanket of a thousand wings pulling and guiding me through."

A lightness spread through him. She hadn't described anything dark or strange in having this connection to the Between. And relief settled over him that Jess's changed power shouldn't be something she would struggle with.

Just then, Rune's stomach decided to growl.

Eilea smirked. "You know, you eat like a horse?"

He chuckled. "I don't even need to eat, it's just enjoyable."

Her lips curled. "I promise to keep the heights of your hedonism under wraps."

Rune's stomach fluttered strangely now. With nervousness and ... anticipation. Despite Eilea's innocent, jokey comment, he pictured a *different* type of hedonism as his gaze dipped to her plum-colored lips. Confusion tumbled through him. He and Jess *weren't* together anymore, but he still mourned what they'd lost so recently, as well as for the memory he had of Silva. But his body didn't seem to care about that. Instead, his blood pounded. His mouth grew dry.

Just then a knock sounded on the door. A Seelie steward entered. "My Lord, Lady Silva and the others have returned with Alpha Romulus. They've just portaled through onto the top of the Sun Keep."

Rune's heart quickened. Jess was back. And with her father. What had happened with Theo?

Eilea prompted, "Go see them."

For a moment, Rune's gaze swept Eilea. Had she noticed his distraction? Had she noticed that sudden urge that had come over him? But Rune abandoned examining his discomfiture, and with a nod of agreement, started to the door.

Eilea's voice drew him back, "Wouldn't the window be quicker?"

Another flicker of uneasiness, this time concerning his power over the Heights, affected him. That usual stab of contemplating his power over the winds. That it meant Silva was gone.

But Eilea was right. Especially if any of them were hurt and needed his healing ability. Opening the shutters, Rune dissolved into the winds. The cold ebb of night air was refreshing, and he felt his thoughts sharpen.

At the top of the Sun Keep, he solidified and took in the group of travelers, gladdened by the sight of Jess looking unharmed. She was distracted though, seeing to her father along-side Piera. Matteo and a Seelie eased the Rom Alpha onto a kind of stretcher that the Seelie steward must have brought for them.

Rune hurried over to examine Giovanni. Drawing upon the

nourishing part of his power, he examined the currents in the Alpha. "He's not injured, just exhausted, in both mind and spirit. He's on the cusp of waking," he assured them. The Alpha's face was sallow and gaunt, a testament to how much Theo had tortured his mind.

The Seelie steward and Matteo soon lifted the Alpha and moved to the door.

"Take him to my room," Piera directed, following them.

Rune had time to take in the others now.

There was an unfamiliar dark-haired, amber-skinned woman amidst them, dressed in a pale tunic and trousers. Sunny seemed to almost be carrying her. She had her arm draped around his neck for support. Was she injured?

Alarm beat through him as he took in Astra's similar state: Skiron was supporting her, too.

"What happened? Are they hurt?" Rune asked quickly. If they went down to the river, he could heal them with his waters.

Jess shook her head, opening her mouth to explain.

But Astra interrupted. "So, Jess made us invisible, we followed Theo, but he attacked Jess, and this un-vamped Triodian witch showed up and saved us, and gave me the best sea water I've ever had."

Rune's eyebrows shot up. "Is she—?"

"Drunk as a skunk," Skiron said with a sigh. He walked to the door, lifting the fae, who despite her petite size seemed quite a handful as she wriggled in his arms. She kept stroking his face and saying the same thing over and over: she was glad he wasn't gone. "Later, guys," he called back.

Rune's gaze went to the witch, who seemed in a very similar state. As in she was finding it difficult to stand, not that she was stroking Sunny. Rune had absorbed Astra's description, though, and felt there was only one person who could answer to it.

Sunny affirmed it in the quiet dawn. "This is Erika."

So, Sunny had been right. The witch *had* world walked.

"Is this why you've been returning to Earth so frequently?" Rune asked, his temper fraying. Wasn't it just like Sunny to omit information that could prove valuable?

"Rune–" Jess interjected.

"No, actually," Sunny answered. Bitterness tinged his voice. "Erika only arrived back on Earth today. As it is, she came back for you, Lord Alba and Lady Silva. She believes that understanding your restoration might help heal other worlds divided by the Fomors. Something we can talk about *tomorrow* when she's in a fit state to do so." With that, he stormed past Rune and into the keep, as much as he could with a drunken witch in tow.

Surprise beat through Rune. He hadn't considered the magnitude of destruction that the Fomors had waged. Of course, he knew that they were responsible for the division wrought on Umbra and Earth's paras, as well as the Stormborns' world, but to think of the scale they may be dealing with was mind-blowing. The enormity of the enemy they were dealing with loomed even larger and more terrible in Rune's thoughts.

Suddenly, left alone on the rooftop of the Sun Keep, he looked at Jess, trying to gauge her dazed expression. "Do you trust this witch?"

"Not around Ligue and Astra."

He frowned.

"The very potent seawater Astra was talking about."

He shook his head, fighting back the urge to smile. "But can we trust Erika? If she came from another world, who's to say that she didn't come from the Fomors? Or isn't an ally of Mara's?" He looked towards the door of the keep. "Perhaps I should station a guard on her room."

"She *did* save us from Theo," Jess answered. Her expression darkened. "I got distracted by him, and it could've ended really badly if it hadn't been for Erika. As it was, Astra, Sunny, and I were attacked by Theo and other Enodians' hordes."

Rune examined the tension in her taut expression and shoulders. "Are you all right?"

Jess nodded. "Only my pride's hurt. My stupidity came back to bite me in the ass." At his questioning stare, she explained, "Theo used the lock of hair I gave him to attack me with his sluagh. Otherwise, he'd never have been able to affect me."

"Gods," Rune exclaimed. It felt like another lifetime—Jess and Theo exchanging locks of hair to communicate in the penitentiary and at Castle Nox.

"Erika managed to burn the lock of my hair," Jess added, "before getting us out of there. So, yes, I trust her," she concluded with a thoughtful air.

"The Enodian's attack was why Astra got carried away with the Ligue tonight. And Erika, I think, let loose for similar reasons —as calm and collected as she seemed at first, seeing Sunny was emotionally charged." She paused before adding, "Something complicated by the fact that Erika thought Sunny was Alba, and that me and him were together."

Rune blinked. He felt a pang of sympathy for his ex-blood brother. "It seems to be something of a package deal, doesn't it? Being an Alban heir and having a complicated love life." A wry smile crossed his face.

Jess blinked in surprise, then laughed. They stood in companionable silence for a moment, looking out from between the buttresses of the keep at the grass plains, more and more becoming visible as the last of night ebbed away.

Rune wanted to understand fully what had happened on Earth with regard to Jess's powers. "Astra said you made them invisible?"

"Yeah," she answered. "I used the connection to Earth's dead to shield us. I'm calling it death dust," she added, casting a conspiratorial look at him. "And at Castle Nox, I managed to untether hundreds of souls from Theo. I think if I had access to enough Earthen energy, I could untether thousands at a time."

Rune's chest swelled as he looked at the resolve forming on

Jess's face. Even tired, with dark circles under her eyes, Jess had the determination and confidence that he'd missed the last couple of weeks.

He commented, "You found yourself on Earth like I knew you would."

"I did," Jess said. A glimmer of softness filled her gaze. "Through and through an Earthling."

The memory of him uttering those words to Jess in the Cornua, after they'd realized how altered Jess's magic was, how separated they were, swept through him. But that brittleness that had been there then, was absent now. The past couldn't weigh that phrase down anymore. Instead, it seemed to flourish with all the things that Jess had found on Earth, and with the promise of her powers complimenting Rune's. To defend their worlds. Together.

"If you untethered the sluagh, do you think you could untether the Storm-born from the Unseelie?" he asked. His heart picked up a notch. If Jess could do that, their duty to the Storm-born could be fulfilled. They'd be able to free their allies from the slavery they'd been subjected to in the Shadowlands.

"I don't see why not," Jess said. She looked towards the keep door before she added, "Listen, you said my dad would be awake soon. Can I go check on him and then talk to you about plans in a bit?"

He realized she probably hadn't had a moment with her father since rescuing him. Due to having to escape Theo and Erika's sudden appearance.

"Go see him," Rune said with a smile. "I'll be in the Sun Study."

"You're the best, Rune." She gave him a quick hug before departing.

On top of the Sun Keep, Rune reflected on his and Jess's interaction. For the first time in weeks, it hadn't felt stilted or burdened with the past. He found himself examining the budding feeling in his chest with wonder: a sense of something unfurling. He mused on what Jess's mastery of her Earthen and Between power might mean for the war at large. Perhaps Erika's return would bring them yet more knowledge of the enemy, too. A strange feeling caught Rune up: anticipation and restlessness made his body tingle. And he watched Eventide caress his lands with awe. Its gentle touch like the faintest of whispers, hinting of new beginnings.

12

ROOTS & BOUGHS

Jess hesitated when she reached Piera's door. Her heartbeat began to dash. By the Heights, it wasn't just Matteo she didn't know how to look at or what to say to. There was her sister, too. There hadn't been time yet, what with Erika's insistence to talk, having to concentrate on portaling everyone back to Umbra while maintaining the death dust veiling over them all, and then clueing Rune in on what had happened on Earth, to even think about what she was going to say to Piera.

Would she blame her yet again for getting distracted by Theo's sluagh horde? Jess had gambled with all their lives and jeopardized their father's rescue. While she stood there, the door swung open, framing Matteo, a questioning expression on his handsome face.

Gods, he totally heard my heart trying to knock down the door, didn't he?

"I didn't know whether to knock," Jess mumbled, trying to get her skipping heart under control. She walked past, trying to stifle her awareness of Matteo's pine and nutty scent. But the memory of being enveloped in it as he'd carried her in Risør made her feel as if the room were closing in around her. It was only the sight of

Giovanni's now reduced form laid up in bed that finally allowed her to rein in her feelings.

Piera sat on the right side of Giovanni's bed. Jess hesitated at the foot of the bed, guilt swelling once more that she'd almost failed her dad. Her gaze brushed the sunken cheeks and dark circles of Giovanni's face. He looked haggard. And everything he'd been through was because of *her*.

"Come sit," Piera said.

Jess started, meeting Piera's eyes. Their chestnut hue seemed warmer than it ever had.

Tentatively, Jess took a seat on Giovanni's other side.

"What did you see Theo plant in his head?" Piera asked.

Jess's mouth had grown dry at the mention of Theo, thinking Piera was going to ask about the fears he'd planted in *her* head. But her thoughts swung back to Giovanni's nightmare. Jess kept her eyes on her father's worn face.

"My mother," Jess answered, voice thick. "She was accusing him of not caring about her. Or me. She told him that that was why I hadn't come to save him."

"You did. Save him," Piera said slowly. "You didn't understand your power and you went in there anyway. Thank you."

A lump rose in Jess's throat, and all she could do was nod and keep her eyes on her dad. But something lightened in her chest. Piera wasn't blaming her for the mistakes she'd made. A tentative feeling of connection with the girl beside her that hadn't been there before settled over Jess. And their shared vigil over the man in the bed was its own form of communication.

Matteo had taken a seat in the armchair in the corner of the room, and they all sat in comfortable silence for some time.

After a while, Matteo asked, "Can I get either of you anything?"

Giovanni's gruff voice sounded, "Prosciutto, salami, and nduja."

Piera gasped and Jess's gaze blurred as she took in her father's eyes fluttering open and his lips curving. She felt as if her heart had both slowed and was doing double time; to see his face animated with life and his voice infused with humor left her reeling.

Matteo was soon up, standing behind Piera, grinning down at his Alpha. "The Seelie don't have much in way of meat, but I'll see what I can do."

"You break a wolf out of prison and drag him to the realm of the veggies? Haven't I suffered enough?"

At the word *suffered* tears spilled down Jess's cheeks.

He did suffer. All because of me.

An image of Theo limned in that awful darkness, the trickle of light from all those stolen souls the only warmth illuminating his hideous, hungry expression as he'd moved towards Giovanni flickered through her head.

How many times did Theo torture him like that? All because of me.

Piera chuckled and squeezed her dad's arm. "Sunny might have something." She whipped around to Matteo. "He's got a stash of food from Earth."

"I'm on it." Matteo's step was quick, and he was gone in a flash.

Giovanni's brown eyes swept Piera, and his hand was soon in hers. "It's so good to see you, darling." He glanced at Jess. His face crumpled in concern. His other hand reached for her. "Sweetheart, I'm all right."

But Jess shook her head, her hands retreating to her lap. It was too much. That he should be concerned for *her* when everything that had happened to him was her fault. "It's all my fault..." she choked out the words. "What Theo did..." They came in bursts between tears. "He twisted mom's face. Her words..." she trailed off, her sobbing not letting her voice how much she condemned herself—for not going to Earth sooner, for ever getting close enough to Theo for the mage to target her loved ones.

"You saw her," Giovanni said, sounding as if all the breath left him. After a moment, he ordered, "Look at me." His tone reminded her of the prickle of command that she'd once felt from him as he'd ordered her to stay in the penitentiary when he'd tried to persuade her from portaling away. Before she knew who he was to her.

But he wasn't using a blood command over her now. That wasn't what had her looking up. She wanted to look at her dad's face in the same way she'd been mesmerized by the vision of her mom. Something deep in her bones longed for a connection with him. Even though she didn't deserve it.

"I'm glad you saw her too, Jess," he said. "It's felt like an eternity since I saw her, since I heard her voice. I felt as if I'd forgotten her but then she was there with me. With us." His own brown eyes brimmed with tears. But they weren't sorrowful. "Theo didn't mean for it to be, but to see her again was a gift. One I'm glad you got to share in."

Instead of reliving the bitterness in Alessandra's voice, Jess pictured her stubborn mouth, her quick eye, and the fierce spirit that she possessed in a way Jess had never known before. Never been able to know. Until now. A tentative smile spread across her face.

"But nothing brings me joy like having you *both* here," Giovanni said quietly. He looked at Piera. "I hope you know that you've always been a joy to me and your mother." Then he reached for Jess's hand and, this time, she let him hold it. "But having you come into my life, Jess, it's like having a piece of Lessa come back to me." He looked between his daughters. "You are both as vital to me as the call of the woods. You are my roots and boughs, my past and future."

He beamed at them, and his happiness was infectious. Both Jess and Piera laughed as they hugged him. Well, Jess laughed/cried, but they were happy tears. And when Piera and Jess took each other in, the dark-haired girl shrugged, a softer look than Jess had ever thought her capable of coming over her face. "I always liked the idea of having a sibling to boss around."

A strange flutter shot through Jess's chest. A dozen things seemed to zip through her head at once. The gazillion times that different foster siblings had foisted the term sis on her. An image of Caylee scampering up into the oak in the back garden and hollering, "*I'm the king of the castle.*"

And there was the lump in her throat again.

Oh, shit, am I really going to cry again?

Jess wanted to explain to Piera that she wasn't ordinarily a crybaby, but the thickness in her throat made her incapable of anything coherent.

"Speaking of which, go see where Matteo got to with dad's order."

Jess gladly went to the door, able to turn her back on them and dash the tears from her eyes. She knew Piera had been all too aware that she was about to blubber and sent her packing. Whether it was because she wasn't good with tears or knew that Jess didn't want to cry for the second time in front of them, Jess was grateful.

More contained, she smiled back at them. "One meat platter coming up." She would bribe, demand, or steal Sunny's stash for her father. The weight of everything settled on her as she wandered down the hallway. That sense of belonging as Giovanni had taken her hand and pulled her in for a hug overwhelming her.

And Piera.

My sister.

She hadn't thought it possible for her to extend an olive branch, let alone suggest that they might be able to develop a relationship as sisters.

Thinking about Giovanni's take on what Theo had done to him as a gift because it had brought Lessa back to him made Jess reflect on her own experiences at the mage's hands. Even in the golden light of the Sun Keep, warmed by the daylight, Jess felt the chill of that vision. The burn of Mara's blade, the iron-tinged immobilizing her, and the awful certainty seeping through her that when she died, she'd still be there. One of the sluagh's number and bound to the queen. She hadn't believed there *could* be a deeper fear than that.

But the memory of Matteo's black wolf arcing into that circle and the queen burying her blade in his flesh instead had flooded her with mind-blowing, gut-wrenching agony. Because ... she *loved* him.

Jess remembered her paralyzed body in the vision, racked with terror. The overwhelming sense that had flooded her system was that she couldn't *do* anything. She was powerless to act.

But you're not now.

Jess wanted to quell her stupid internal voice. It *wasn't* talking about her power. It was talking about how she could *do* something about what she felt for Matteo. She could *tell* him.

But even as panic started to swarm her, she knew she had to. Because Jess understood exactly what her dad had meant about her mom's appearance in his head being a gift. Because the opposite had been true for Jess concerning her nightmare. She'd never felt as happy as when she'd regained consciousness and been overwhelmed by Matteo's presence, waking to love for him crashing through her every fiber.

13

WAITING GAME

Matteo felt dazed. Sitting in the Sun courtyard on the front tier, he stared at the golden corridor where Piera's room was located. He'd come across Sunny quickly and garnered a selection of cold meats. But the packet felt weighty in his hands as he contemplated going back to fulfill his Alpha's request.

Not that he didn't want to gratify his Alpha. If anyone deserved comfort food, it was him. And gods knew how happy he'd been to see Giovanni's face animated with good humor again despite all he'd suffered. That he'd returned to the land of the living little worse for wear was more than he could have hoped for.

But that was part of it, wasn't it? Since the moment at Castle Nox when Jess had cried his name, he'd begun to hope again. To hope for a lot. To hope for ... *everything*.

Matteo remembered when Theo had inflicted soul magic on him in the penitentiary. His deepest fear at the time had been the thought of Jess breaking out to confront Lorenzo herself. In the waking nightmare, he'd watched the monstrous Alpha approach her. Matteo remembered the cruel smile across Lorenzo's face. Then the way he'd transformed into his wolf, his claws and teeth speeding toward Jess. It had seemed to carve itself on his heart because he'd known, even then, how deeply he cared for Jess.

The need for her seared through him as the echo of her crying out *his* name in the catacombs rang through his head. What had she seen in her deepest, darkest nightmare? The echo of her heart-rending cry, although terrible for its pain, contrarily made him hope. To hope like never before.

He remembered the way Jess had clung to him as he'd carried her into Sunny's house. As if she'd been burrowing into the safety of the undergrowth, her breathing deepening as if there was nowhere she'd rather be than in his arms. How hard it had been not to react to the feel of her soft fingers around his neck or the awareness of her full, curvaceous body in his arms. He'd tensed when her resiny scent threatened to chase away all rational thought. He'd felt the prickle of his wolf so close beneath his skin, the desire that licked through him raw and wild. He'd wanted nothing more than to carry her into a room, bolt the door, and talk about what had happened at Castle Nox.

Okay, perhaps, not talk.

He imagined, as he had in Risør, running his hands down Jess's face, his fingers lifting her defiant chin, and his lips claiming hers. Imagined how their bodies would soon tell the other what they were too damn wilful to tell each other in words.

But Jess had needed to rest after being attacked by Theo's sluagh horde. Then there'd been the witch, insisting on talking to her. There had also been Giovanni's welfare to think of, too. And then Jess had had to maintain the death dust veiling and portal them all back to Umbra. And now Giovanni had woken up and Jess was likely dealing with even more.

Are we never going to get a break?

His nostrils flared and he looked up, drinking Jess in. She

came towards him. The Seelie leathers she wore were marred with the scent of dust from the catacomb floor. Again, the echo of her crying out for him pounded through his memory. But her slightly red eyes and harrowed expression soon claimed him.

"What's wrong?" he asked.

"Nothing." She sat down beside him, the abstracted expression still on her face. "They sent me to find you," she explained, her eyes turning to him.

Here he was sitting idle when his Alpha and friend who had been tortured for weeks had asked for a snack. Gods, could he look any more selfish?

"Got it," he answered, flourishing the packet needlessly. "I'll get it to him." He made to get up.

Jess gestured for him to remain sitting. "Wait a moment."

His brown eyes grazed her face; it was paler than usual. "Are you all right?"

She hesitated then said, "Piera ... told me she's always wanted a younger sibling."

Warmth spread through Matteo. He smiled. "She's a hard nut to crack, a bit like someone else I know, but underneath, she's a big softy."

Jess's answering smile tugged at his heart. But his own smile fell away. Because, despite being happy that she'd found the family she'd longed for, that she'd deserved her whole life, he wasn't, technically, part of it. Sure, earlier he'd wanted to stay with his Alpha and Piera, to stay with his friends, but mostly he'd wanted to stay with Jess. He'd wanted to bask in the sight of seeing her happy. He'd wanted to stay because he desired to be part of the reason for that happiness. No. He needed to be the main reason for her happiness.

Gods, Jess, it's killing me to love you.

"Earth to Matteo," Jess said, a frown flitting over her face. "What's wrong?"

He rubbed his forehead. "Tired. I need to get some shuteye." He eased himself up from the polished tier.

"Will you come running with me?" She blurted in a rush.

He frowned. He'd just said he was *tired* and she was asking him to run?

"After you sleep," she explained. "Maybe this evening. We could ... portal back to Earth. Go somewhere..." Her voice thickened. "Just us." Her eyes seared into him, searching, and ... a beautiful blush spread over her cheeks.

She wanted to go running with him.

Alone.

She was looking at him again as she had in Risør. When the uncharacteristically gentle words that Astra had expressed about Ski looked like something Jess had related to. Wholeheartedly. And her eyes had turned to Matteo.

Jess's expression tautened and he realized he still hadn't said anything in reply. Yet, despite wishing for nothing more than alone time with Jess, reservations flocked at her suggestion.

"Don't you need to talk to Erika when she wakes?"

A breath left her. Of relief? "It's already noon. I think after she's slept, she and Sunny will need to talk first. As long as we're back for dawn then..." Her unspoken words and the hopeful look in her eye had Matteo's heart pounding.

But the witch hadn't been his utmost concern. "What if Theo senses you again?"

Jess shook her head. "He won't. I've cloaked us twice before. It'll be easy to do it again. And he doesn't have my lock of hair anymore."

His mouth went dry, and anticipation threatened to make him tongue-tied. Exerting himself, he said, "I know just the place. How about a run in Vesuvius National Park? Shall we say dusk at the river?"

Jess's face lit up with an unusually shy smile, and the light in her eyes was as beautiful as the dawn's, soft and searching. "See you at Eventide." Bewitched by the promise in her voice, he barely registered that she was holding out her hand.

Oh, Giovanni's food.

She took the packet from him, her smile growing, then wandered back the way she'd come...

And Matteo finally remembered to breathe.

14

WORDS RUN FREE

Jess spent the rest of the afternoon in the Sun Keep with Rune, sharing exactly what had happened on Earth. The room was scattered with books—the pleasant aroma of parchment, leather, and wood smoke from the roaring fire filling the space. She was touched to find that Rune had been reading up on the Between and the faded, eager to find anything that might help her master the new element of her power when she returned.

Yet, after hearing about everything that had happened on Earth, he soon tidied away the books, declaring that she clearly had no need of studying. Jess found herself reveling in explaining the naturalness with which she'd portaled through the Between, in relaying how she'd used the death dust to veil herself and the others, and, lastly, the triumph of liberating all those hundreds of souls from Theo's sluagh horde.

A few hours later, Jess and Rune had the bare bones of a plan. One that—if all the pieces came together successfully—would enable them *both* to draw upon the full extent of their powers in Umbra against Mara's Unseelie forces and her Fomor allies. Rune agreed with Jess that Erika might prove a useful ally in the fight ahead. But with the witch still resting, they put a pin in any more plotting for the day.

Making plans had provided Jess with a useful outlet, but with their strategizing put aside, she soon became a bundle of nervous energy. Unable to keep still, she got up from where she'd been sitting opposite Rune and started to pace.

She'd been putting off explaining the *full* version of what she'd seen in the waking nightmare Theo had struck her with. But she knew she had to tell Rune that she was portaling to Earth this evening. And, more importantly, she wanted to tell him why. She wanted to be open with him. Apprehension thrummed through her. Gods, the last thing she wanted was to hurt him.

Jess looked out the window, then paced to the other one, her churning thoughts preventing her from really seeing the view.

Despite their earlier joking about Alba's complicated love life, it wasn't without awkwardness that Jess contemplated sharing her feelings with him. She knew they couldn't be what they had been to one another. But would he be all right if she moved on? She knew it was quick. On the surface of it, two weeks seemed *insanely* quick. But Jess knew now, she'd always been torn. Torn between her feelings for Rune and Matteo. Her Umbran self had pulled her towards Rune, while the Earthen part of her had desired Matteo. And she couldn't hold back from confessing her feelings to Matteo any longer. She needed to tell him.

Tonight.

"Are you going to tell me why you're wearing a groove in my study floor?" Rune asked.

She stilled at the window, her gaze settling on him.

"Just watching you is exhausting," he added. "Quite a feat, given I don't sleep these days." With his legs sprawled out in front of the fire, his shadow wings spilling out in slow movements down the back of the sofa, he did look languid.

"There's more to the waking nightmare I had at Nox," Jess began. "In it, I wasn't alone when Mara tortured me. Matteo was there." Her gaze fastened onto Rune, wondering how much she had to say for him to understand exactly what that meant.

"Have you told him?" he asked, instantly catching her drift. Yet, his tone was calm and steady.

She released the breath she hadn't realized she'd been holding. "Not yet. I'm going to talk to him this evening. We're going to portal to Earth."

With earnestness, Rune said, "I'm glad you're reaching for the happiness you deserve, Jess."

"That's very magnanimous of you," she said, her tone light-hearted but her gaze tracing the lines of his face, searching for any tension.

"Noble Lord Alba at your service," he retorted, amusement creating the only lines around the corners of his mouth and eyes.

His face seemed so familiar and yet so different these days. So full of wonderful memories and yet absent of the feeling it had once evoked. Instead, the dynamic between them was easy. Intimate yet comfortable. The weightiness of loss had faded. But her thoughts took her back to what she'd seen that first night here in the Sun Keep. She'd glimpsed Rune's raw edges. Seen how cut up he was about her shadow self passing. And how could he not be? An eternity alone beckoned before him.

"Will you be all right by yourself?" she asked softly. Her breath caught in her throat again, knowing that Rune knew she didn't just mean because she loved Matteo. There was so much in those words, *"by yourself."* Guilt swelled through her. She'd alluded to the eternity stretching out before Rune, but she needed to know how he felt.

Seriousness bathed his face and he huffed out a sigh; more in contemplation she realized as he looked ahead of himself unsee-ingly for a moment. "I actually think I will be … Somehow. I have faith that you and I will save our worlds. And… I'm looking forward to seeing what comes from that. I'm looking forward to rebuilding the Shadowlands and seeing it become all I want it to be."

Her chest was full: of love and pride. She imagined the whole lifetime before her, too, in which she got to witness Rune reviving the fae lands with peace and prosperity. Along with all the possibilities that a similarly peaceful period on Earth might bring for the para world. And with the glimmer of hope suffusing his words and expression, it seemed as if he would find fulfillment and a new beginning in the prospect. Jess's gaze swam with tenderness, and for the third bloody time today, she seemed far too close to crying.

"Now, shouldn't you get cleaned up if you're portaling out of here with that oversized shifter?" Rune asked, his gaze running down her dusty leathers, which she still hadn't changed since getting back from Castle Nox.

"Hey," she remonstrated at his *"oversized"* remark. "What happened to noble Alba?"

Rune shrugged, reaching for one of the books he'd tidied away on the table. "Alba the Honest is one of my epithets, too, I believe," he said. "So I've got to say it like it is, and that shifter's a goliath."

Jess sighed, but as well as realizing she *did* need to get washed, the shocking realization that she had nothing decent to wear, soon gripped her. Leaving Rune in peace, she hurried off to the hot springs on the ground floor. Afterward, she fretted again over having nothing but fae clothes. She really wanted something other than combat leathers tonight.

I mean, nothing says romance like battle gear.

She had the dresses King Imber had gifted her, but they weren't exactly very *her*.

Inspiration finally struck—Piera might have something that fitted her.

What are sisters for, right?

When she showed up at Piera's room, her sister asked her

what the occasion was, but Jess only told her that besides leathers, she didn't have anything other than the dresses that King Imber kept presenting her with. Piera was a little smaller in size than her, but she gave her a pair of ripped jeans, a pale vest top, and a leather jacket that she reckoned should fit her.

When Jess got back to her room, with only enough time to change, she thanked her lucky stars that she managed to squeeze into everything. Her backup plan had been to go and raid Astra's wardrobe. But if Astra Rainbow had gotten wind of where she was going, she'd have grinned as if watching her own personal romantic movie. She'd thought that Astra might visit her this afternoon, but she'd likely been sleeping off the massive hangover, courtesy of the ligue.

Before she knew it, dusk was falling. Exchanging flesh for fur, she barrelled down the staircase and out of the keep. Making her way down towards the river, her gaze clasped the tall, broad figure at the river's edge in the distance. Matteo stood, waiting in the shadow of the keep. In a black T-shirt and jeans, he was clad more casually than the usual shirt and trousers he tended to wear.

Pre-occupation with how *she* looked whirled through Jess's thoughts. She reminded herself, she'd at least made an effort by not turning up in combat leathers. As she reached him, all the weird twisting feeling in her stomach allowed her to do was gesture to the water like an idiot.

But clearly, Matteo got the gist, morphing into his black wolf. Reaching out to the faded, Jess opened the portal, its whisper rippling through her. She stepped through in her human form, with Matteo's wolf beside her.

On the other side, she breathed in the scent of moss, leaves, and bark. The descending dusk on the land seemed as soft as the whisper of silk against skin. Anticipation stirred through her. Most of the trees on the hillside were still bare of leaves, but the hint of spring was just detectable in the earliest scent of shoots on the boughs.

Jess didn't forget to pull up the death dust from the earth and veil her and Matteo. It answered her call with ease. She did *not* want any visitors tonight.

This night is mine.

Her gaze brushed Matteo whose ebony fur dissolved as his tall, black-clad figure filled the space instead.

Our night. Hopefully.

The tapping of a woodpecker startled Jess. She pulled up the collar of the leather jacket, her nerves making her fidget. Her breaths were shallow, her pulse pattering with agitation.

Matteo's calm voice sounded. "We're about two miles from Ottaviano. You can just make out the sequoia and yew trees in the distance"—he pointed over the dipping hills—"that's the park's headquarters."

Jess moved closer to him, following his eye line. She could feel the distant vibration of magic coming from the yew trees. The hum of their power washed over her, grounding her as much as Matteo's steady tone.

"The building's beautiful but this is the closest Depths pool," he said. "This whole section of ancient forest is glamoured. Although, we can't be sure given the current state of things of course."

Jess shrugged. "I've veiled us. We should be fine even if there are people around."

Matteo's gaze brushed her. A gleam of admiration swam in his eye, making her pulse quicken.

The squeak of bats punctured the air, and Jess smiled up as she discerned them flying through the avenues of old trees around them.

"Greater Horseshoe Bats and Geoffroy's Bat," Matteo explained.

She moistened her lips, aware of how closely Matteo was watching her take in their surroundings.

She looked ahead at the dirt path snaking through the trees, gradually sloping upwards.

How many national parks in Maine had she explored? They'd always given her such comfort: the echo of Silva's magic buried in her thrumming through every woods she'd ever set foot in. Jess could feel the same gladness infusing Matteo's voice as he detailed the environment he knew so well. She wondered how often he came here.

"Is this your favorite place to run?"

"It is," he affirmed. "Ever since my mom first brought me here as a pup when I was eight."

Jess smiled, imagining a young Matteo scampering through these woods, liking the canopy and every tree that her eye lit upon even more. How right it felt to be standing here with him. She remembered how she'd experienced this feeling with him before, sitting in the gardens of Villa Silva. When they'd been basking in the beauty of the night together.

And here, with the sky clad in branches and the tree trunks like pillars, she felt as if they'd found another temple to worship in. To worship the trees, the night, and that inner wildness that called to them both. A religion Jess had always subscribed to. Even before she'd known she was the goddess who had started said religion, she thought dryly. And here she was with Matteo, who she knew was as eager to take part in the call already summoning them.

Eagerness to explore the place enveloped her. The ripple of expectation was mirrored in Matteo's open stance. She knew the demand of the woods—the way it called to him to shed his skin— was as deep as her own. To let that wildness tear through you and become one with the forest.

With a dare in her eye, she said, "So, are we running or what?"

One dark and one light silhouette marked the air, and then they were streaking through the woods. And yet their shapes were for their eyes alone. The death dust that Jess had cloaked them with meant that not even the other wildlife within the woods saw or heard them passing.

They took hairpin turns, crisscrossing past stone pines, chestnuts, maples, and oaks. The swathes of trees seemed to reach out to stroke them as they careered past. When Jess started to lag behind, Matteo only increased his gait, challenging her to push herself. Jess answered, forcing herself on, telling herself to outstrip him. When Matteo's pace shrank, she reciprocated in turn, and he was pulled on by her refusal to stop.

It wasn't until both of their tongues were lolling and they were desperately panting that they skidded down a deep verge to a flowing stream. Lapping up the cool water, they drank their fill. When Jess's lupine eyes looked up, she was mesmerized by the sight of Matteo's brown stare holding hers from across the stream. Her gaze traced the silver beads of moisture around his muzzle, glittering in the dim light, and even in wolf form, she imagined how much she'd like to lick the spray from his muzzle.

Then Matteo's furred outline blurred, and his human form sat on the bank. Butterflies fluttered in Jess's stomach as she followed suit.

He eased off his sneakers and socks. Rolling his jeans up, he dunked his feet in the water. It was exactly what she felt like doing and, with relish, she lost herself in the cool water and air on her clammy skin.

"The locals call this the Valley of Hell. The Romans believed this whole area had entrances to the underworld." Matteo's gaze brushed the mostly bareish trees.

She looked at him in surprise. "Um, that's kinda dark."

"Somma is part of Vesuvius—the volcano that buried the ancient city of Pompeii. The Romans believed the tremors and gases released all those centuries ago were the gods of the underworld. When it did erupt, it killed thousands in Pompeii. It's still active today."

Jess swallowed, thinking of how she'd felt that energy in the soil, beneath the roots of the trees and hillside. All that death had been why her summoning the death dust had been so easy. And why maintaining the veil upon them felt as easy as breathing at the moment.

"You felt it," Matteo said, "when you used your power to veil us."

Was that why he'd brought her here in particular? So that she had easy access to the death energy? Then she remembered he'd said this was his favorite place.

Jess nodded, her eyes weary. "And with all that, *this* is your favorite forest?"

"Yes, it's my favorite," he affirmed. "Stone pine woods, chestnuts, Italian alders and maples, holm oaks, and black locusts." He gestured to the forest sweeping the hillside, inhaling deeply as if trying to breathe in as much of its perfume as possible. The movement strained the fabric of his T-shirt, and Jess's gaze dipped over his contoured muscles before forcing her gaze back to his face. "All this diversity, along with the insect and animal life, all this beauty only exists because of the rich soils, reinvigorated by death."

Jess's pale eyes held Matteo's burnished stare. His words weren't just about the landscape; they were about her. He was alluding to her power through the land, his earnest expression and hallowed tone implying that just as this place was beautiful...

So am I...

As Matteo's gaze returned to the lines and folds of the land, Jess broached, "But aren't people here afraid to live in the shadow of a volcano?" But she wasn't talking about *them*. Her analogy, like his veiled comparisons, was her asking about him. Did he fear her?

"I think it *attracts* them," he uttered, the emphasis sending a tingle down her spine as his gaze lingered on her. "Living so closely to death reminds them to live their fullest lives, to seize what they want." Now, his brown eyes pierced her with a challenge. Would she seize what she wanted? Did she have the courage to live to the fullest? To make this moment count? She could feel her blood pounding through her as he dared her to take what she wanted. Just as he'd dared her to push herself as they ran. But this was the hardest kind of bravery, revealing what she *felt*. In a way, just as her gut reflex had always been, these last few weeks she'd *still* been running. From her feelings. But she had to brave the unknown if she truly wanted to live.

It's time to tell him everything. To lay myself bare.

Jess began quietly, "When Theo attacked me at Nox, at first, I saw Queen Mara and her iron-tinged encircling me. She was torturing me, trying to tether me. That's what happened with my shadow self. Mara had always known that part of me was dying. And when she captured me and I conjoined a second time with the Sidhe, Mara cut me ... meaning to kill me and tether my goddess soul."

Matteo gritted his jaw, looking appalled. His brown gaze hardened with rage, and she could see he was torn between wanting to let his wolf out or to comfort her.

Jess forced herself to go on. "But then, in the waking nightmare at Nox, I wasn't alone in the circle. You were there, and Mara turned her attention to you..." A lump rose in her throat and Matteo leaned forwards. She ground out, "I watched you die. And ... it broke me.

"That's when I knew for sure, with my whole being, that I had to tell you how I felt. How I *feel*. Almost as soon as we met, I cared about you, but when I went to Umbra that feeling deepened."

Jess thought about how even journeying up the Silvan Mountains, just thinking about Matteo a month ago had brought the first upswell of desire. Then when she'd finally seen him in the mirror pool—when Dearbhla had rescued him and her dad—she'd experienced another thrum of longing.

"And when my shadow self passed on, it was like the waning

connection to my ancient life was gone, and everything was clearer. I felt different. I felt more in touch with my foundations. With my Earthen power. And that energy in others. *Especially* in you.

She shook her head. "I'm explaining this badly. It's not about power. Ever since you backed me in prison, ever since you were there night after night at Villa Silva, I needed you." Jess clenched her fists. She wouldn't dilute her words. "Theo's vision forced me to admit my deepest fear. Losing you. I hate him, but he made me see what I've been too stubborn to see for ages. I love you."

Matteo was watching her with an alertness that reminded her of the way she felt when she crouched in the grasses, listening for the tiniest of sounds. Ready to bolt ... or strike.

"And you and Rune?" Matteo said. "Silva and Alba?"

She shook her head. "We don't feel what we did before. The connection that existed between us belonged to the past. We'll always love each other in a way, but our connection was to bring about the restoration of Umbra's god. And now that that's happened, our connection, our feelings for one another have gone. That part of me that was ancient—my shadow self—has passed on ... And I'm ... just me."

Jess's temples pounded with nerves. And fear. That sense that baring herself in this way would only lead to being left alone ate at her. But she wouldn't let her insecurities devour her. She rushed on, the words breaking free from her, pushing her recklessly on, afraid of what would happen when she stopped, when silence fell. "I know I've been pushing you away recently, but it's only because I'm afraid of losing you. Afraid that what you felt—"

Matteo moved, splashing through the stream. He knelt before her. Inches away. He had that hungry look of desire that she hadn't seen since they'd been together at Villa Silva. Her heart pounded. This close, his pine and cedar scent flooded her awareness. It was intoxicating.

She took in the change in the length of his hair. He still hadn't cut it since he'd broken out of the Triodia. He'd regained most of the weight he'd lost in captivity, his handsome features more like those she'd called proud. Heady expectation pulsed through her as her gaze brushed his strong jawline, tracing the chin dimple that Astra had egged her on about in prison. *"No one's immune to a chin dimple."* And as she drank him in, she realized how devastating his rugged beauty was.

"Felt?" he whispered. "My foolish heart has *never* given you up, Jess. I tried to be the friend you needed me to be—and I always will be—but I've never stopped loving the beautiful girl I fell for in the Cathedral."

With the joyful charge her heart went into, she was sure it was in danger of exploding.

The affection he held her with, as boundless as the horizon, took her breath away. The blue light of night falling softened his face, and the memory of being this close in the gardens of Villa Silva came to her again. But only the light was the same. What she'd felt back then for Matteo was a shadow of what she felt now. Then, she'd been attracted to him; now, she *loved* him. Completely. She wasn't torn. There was only him. The magnitude of the realization left her frozen. Heart-pounding, dry-mouthed expectation engulfed her. Only her eyes seemed to work, tracing Matteo's long lashes, then his lips. She remembered their feel, forceful yet soft.

Matteo's hand grasped hers, bringing her to her senses and tugging her closer to him. He ran his thumb over hers, tenderly, lovingly, and just that little movement sent tingles through her. And the way he looked at her with reverence, not because she was a goddess but because he *loved* her, undid her.

The bounds of uncertainty that had held Jess broke, and the pads of her fingers stroked his jaw, brushing the edge of his lips in anticipation of tasting them. But Matteo shot forwards, claiming her lips first. It wasn't the gentle kiss Jess had expected. It was a kiss that spoke of hunger. Of wanting. His tongue invaded, tangling with hers, and setting her alight. His hand cradled the back of her head, before caressing her neck. Her greedy fingers stole into his silken hair, caressing and tugging. A low rumble escaped his throat, and the sound sent a delicious shiver through her.

The violent need to be closer to him ripped through her, and she melted into the powerful wall of his body. Pleasure beat through her as her nipples pebbled against his chest. Her mouth so satisfied with exploring Matteo's lips now longed to explore *other* parts of him.

They were still kneeling. She wanted to be closer. Her hands swept up his chest, seeking to guide him back.

"Not here," Matteo rasped out as he drew back, his hands stilling her.

Jess pouted. "I'm having you in these woods, Matteo."

He chuckled. "There's my beautiful savage." His gaze held so much that she felt as if she'd combust. He pulled her up from the bank. "There's a warmer spot I want to take you."

Jess reluctantly allowed it, despite thinking that the only warmth she needed was a Matteo-shaped blanket. She kept her hand laced with his as he led her farther up the slope.

A few minutes later, they stood outside a gaping black cave. At her less than enamored expression, Matteo laughed again, the belly-deep laugh making heat pool in her. She wanted to make him laugh like that all the time.

He gestured for her to wait, then disappeared into the darkness. A moment later, the warm glow of firelight lit the bare rock walls. When Matteo drew her into the cave, the sight of an oil lamp nestled in the nook of a wall, bathing a nest of brown fur blankets and pillows, met her.

"How?" Jess asked, blinking at the simple but enchanting sight.

Matteo shrugged. "I stashed some stuff here years ago. I come here whenever I feel like getting away from it all."

Jess drank in the simple cave walls and soft fur bedding, feeling as if she were standing in a palace. "It's beautiful."

"It is now," he said, his eyes grazing her and setting her skin aflame once more.

He came closer, resting his hands on her hips.

Fire licked through her.

She had been so afraid of the unknown, of putting herself out there. But she hadn't been prepared for how right this felt, for how being this close to Matteo felt like being home. Every touch made her feel more grounded, safer ... cherished.

Memories of how close she'd been to realizing this in the past tripped through her head. The way he'd been there for her in the penitentiary had kindled the first flourish of this. Then when she'd been on the run, the way Matteo had tried to find her, to keep her safe, and guide her to the Rom Clan—*his clan*—had sparked a deeper feeling in her. Part of her couldn't help regretting that her feelings for him now hadn't happened then. She knew she hadn't been able to love him. Her shadow self had pulled her towards Rune as it had been meant. But still, a bittersweetness filled her.

Matteo tilted her chin up. "What is it?"

There *was* an undertone of sadness to her happiness. She shared her thoughts. "You've always had my back. Always tried to protect me. To fight for me. I'm sorry it's taken this long to appreciate that and recognize how I feel about you. Everything I felt for you was there from the beginning, but it was so obscured, it was almost lost."

Matteo smiled. "All of it's been leading here. There's nothing to regret, dearest."

Her eyes glistened as the endearment tugged at her heart and reminded her of their journey toward this moment. The word evoked what her father had said to her at Villa Silva. That his pack would protect all he held dear. Matteo had used the same phrase when he'd broken it to her that Theo had captured

Giovanni: *"I'm sorry that I failed to protect all you hold dear."* That had been the moment Jess had first felt *this* overwhelming sense of completeness, standing with Matteo, she'd told him, *"I hold you just as dear, Matteo."*

It's what her lips told him now as she kissed him fervidly. There was nothing else. No one else as dear.

His lips journeyed down the column of her neck, his tongue on her skin making her gasp. Matteo's hands traveled the curve of her breast, down to her hips. Heat flared along her skin, everywhere his hands stroked, a feverish trail of need bloomed.

Her hands swept over his statuesque body—his shoulders, his arms, his back—glorying in the feel of the masterpiece beneath them. Wanting more of him. All of him.

Gods, the exploration of his firm yet gentle hands and kisses was maddening. She wanted—no, needed—every inch of his rock-hard body against her.

Now.

She pressed herself to him as she'd dreamed of doing for so long; the feel of his length through his jeans against her stomach sent her wild. Heat bloomed below her navel. She quivered with heady arousal. Something akin to a growl sounded from Matteo, and her core turned molten.

But through the intoxicating feeling, the shimmer of Jess's death dust over them... *wavered.*

"Mmm, Matteo," she whispered, her voice hoarse.

As he came up from where he'd been kissing her neck, she reluctantly said, "I don't think I can keep our veiling and..." She blushed, unsure of how to finish that sentence.

Feel so much? Orgasm?

Even just with his hands on her hips, his mouth on her neck, and the feel of his length against her, she'd been in danger of feeling too much. Her concentration *had* faltered. Yet, part of her still wanted to keep going, damn the risk.

His eyes dark with desire cleared a little, and he smiled. "We can take our time." But his hands, still on her back and waist were like the heat of the midday sun, firing through the Earth and heating all of her, and something she didn't want to relinquish.

The hard warmth against her lower stomach seemed to demand her attention, too. The idea that her hands might still be able to continue their journey of discovery had them wandering up to trace circles along his sides. Undressing him with her eyes, she suggested, "We could still do *stuff*... I mean, I could do stuff for you."

"That's not a fair bargain," he retorted, his gaze traveling over her body with tantalizing heat. "Until you can reciprocate fairly, you're not getting a piece of this," he added sassily, gesturing to himself with a flourish.

Despite the very uncool gesture that made her grin, her hungry eyes told him how much she wanted a piece of that.

More than a piece ... I want to devour him.

Disappointment fluttered through her as he withdrew. "What are we gonna do then?"

Stooping down by the nest of blankets, he pulled something from under a pillow. "I've got it. Scopa?" He held out a pack of cards.

"Never played."

"Then you haven't lived, my friend."

She settled herself cross-legged on the fur blanket, unable to stop thinking about where those hands should be as she watched him dealing out the cards with deft movements. When she suggested doing forfeits—strip-poker style—Matteo's stare intensified, and he looked like he might waver. But, he managed to get them back on the straight and narrow by bringing out her competitive side in a different way. He suggested they play for truths. With a bit of beginner's luck, Jess claimed the first one. For a moment, she considered asking about previous girlfriends, or about his first kiss, but dismissed the idea. If she couldn't be kissing him, she didn't want to think about others doing so.

"What's your favorite movie?"

"Finding Nemo," Matteo answered swiftly.

Jess chuckled. "That's a kid's film."

"It's also the best film ever, about the lengths you'll go to for friends."

Warmth spread through her chest as she thought of how perfect he was. Of course his favorite movie would be about friendship. She thought about how he'd always been there for her almost as soon as they'd met. Offering understanding and help and asking for nothing in return. She thought of what he'd said to her earlier. *"I tried to be the friend you needed me to be—and I always will be..."* She felt so lucky that she got to call him that. Friend. To think that she'd once thought that she didn't need one of those. That she'd set so little value in the word. Now, she had a group of friends and family that she would do *anything* for. But, still, now that they'd finally shared their true feelings with one another, her heart sang at the thought that she got to call him something infinitely dearer than friend.

With their physical closeness curtailed, they soon sought to bare themselves as much as possible with their truths. As Matteo claimed a forfeit from Jess, he asked gently, "You tricked me into taking you to the Cathedral that last time in the penitentiary—to steal the bit of yew that got you out?"

It was barely a question. He already knew the answer. Jess nodded. "Yes." But there was so much more to that choice that she wanted to explain. That she'd only done it because she was desperate to find a way out, that she'd felt justified in using his feelings for her against him because of the barbs he'd thrown at her to incite the rage blackout, but all those words felt hollow now. Excuses. Given how much she regretted not slowing down to take stock of what she felt for Matteo, all her reasoning seemed so flawed.

The memory of the way he'd looked at her that last time in

the Cathedral came to her: his earnest expression and voice like a gift that she'd been oblivious to.

So instead, she admitted, "I don't deserve you, Matteo."

"Don't deserve me?" he exclaimed. "If it hadn't been for you, I'd never have woken up to the truth of the para world. To its inequality. To its corruption. To my own insufferable presumption that I was better than those on the other side. Without you, I might have been blind my whole life."

She'd never questioned how much Matteo had done for her since he'd entered her life. But to hear that he saw her as someone who had helped him, too, had her heart swelling once again.

When Jess claimed a victory, she asked equally tentative, "What did you promise the vamps in Venice in return for them giving you Dearbhla's name?"

His expression clouded. "I let them feed on the stretch I patrolled in Naples. It's the most shameful thing I've ever done. I watched the vamp feed as much as I could. And, of course, I would have intervened if he'd lost control."

Her heart both ached for what that had cost his conscience and soared with love that he'd been willing to cross a line he never would have but for her. Jess settled then that she'd spend the rest of her days making sure Matteo knew he was loved.

I might even let him win the occasional round of Scopa.

Later, Jess reciprocated by teaching Matteo Rummy. With victory hers, and the low light of the oil lamp kissing his strong features, she asked, "Aside from Villa Silva, when was the first time you wanted to kiss me?"

"When you crashed into the Triodia reading room," he answered swiftly. "It felt like something from one of my dreams—you just appearing like that, in that skimpy black dress, your hair loose, your cheeks aflame." Matteo's gaze roved down her body. "Same question."

Jess smiled playfully. "That's not how this works. There are rules, you know?"

"When has that ever bothered you? You like to break rules," he retorted, looking very much like he wanted to break the rules as his gaze lingered on her lips again.

"On the mirror call," Jess answered, "when I was in the Silvan Mountains. You had panzerotti in the corner of your mouth and … I wanted to lick it off you."

His Adam's apple bobbed. "Panzerotti are the best." His voice was thick.

Jess gave him another of her deepest truths for free. "That was the first time I wanted to kiss you, but I knew much earlier that you were important to me. Almost as soon as I met you, you made me feel safe. The safest I've ever felt. It's why I nicknamed you what I did in the penitentiary." She pictured Fort Kent with its oak tree with ribbons in the breeze. "My foster sister, Caylee, had all these forts—the oak in the garden and the living room cardboard castle, another book one in her bedroom—all called Fort Caylee, of course." A bittersweet smile crossed her face. "When you opened up to me about your shifter-human heritage, when you took your time to listen to me, I knew I'd found my fort: my *Fort Matteo*."

There were no more card games or forfeits. Only more kisses and caresses. Kept to the edge of what was too much. And the night quickly passed with so many more truths freely given.

15

FORTRESS

Darkness was thinning. Daybreak near. Perhaps another half hour. Matteo sighed, not wanting to leave. He always had a hard time leaving Vesuvius National Park, exchanging the wilds for the trappings and responsibilities of real life. But leaving this fertile countryside wasn't going to be half as much a wrench as untangling himself from the heavenly body beside him. Jess's arm lay across his chest, her leg over his, and she ran her fingers through his hair, playing with the ends that were beginning to curl.

I really need a haircut.

He hadn't had a chance since getting out of the Triodia to sort it. He idly wondered whether the Seelie Court had barbers. Until Jess's fingers brushed his scalp again, sending a frisson of desire through him. Matteo's chest tightened as he thought about the confessions they'd shared. They had been as blissful as what he imagined making love to her would be. And oh gods, he'd imagined it. It was impossible not to with her curves and softness pressed against him all night. Only a saint could have lain, enfolded by these limbs, and not let their thoughts go down that road.

His favorite of her truths, perhaps, had been the gift of her nickname for him: *"Fort Matteo."* It's what he'd always wanted—to be the one who she'd run to, the place where she belonged, to have what she deserved. A true home. His arm tightened around her.

Oh gods, I didn't know happiness like this existed.

"Do we have to go back?" Jess whispered, sharing his reluctance to move. But there was obvious trepidation in the seriousness of her tone.

"How about we just get Erika's top ten destinations and go world-hopping for a bit?" he quipped.

She huffed a laugh, but he felt the tension sweep through her shoulders as she began to worry. How he wished they *could* slip away into the Between. He'd gladly disappear anywhere with her. If he was reluctant to leave, she must be so much more so. Returning to Umbra for her meant returning to the weight of Lady Silva's responsibilities. The fates of two worlds resting on her shoulders, alongside Rune. As well as sharing all their heartfelt confessions with one another, Jess had told Matteo about the plan she'd already devised with Rune. She must be contemplating everything that needed to happen to prepare for the looming battle, as well as sharing these plans with their friends later today.

"*Silva*-lining," Matteo said. "You won't need to camouflage us in Umbra. And I promise to distract you from your divine duties."

His heart skipped a beat as she raised herself. Was she going to say that they couldn't in Umbra ... that they needed to keep things from Rune? But she looked down at him with a salacious smile on her face. "I see what you did there, and that's a definite *Silva*-lining."

It made his heart sing to hear her joke about her godhood after all the apprehension she'd suffered about it.

But it was Matteo's turn to be beset by apprehension now that he'd thought about the personal complications surrounding their new relationship. "What about Rune ... Should we... Do we tell him about us?"

"Scared of the big bad god?" Jess ribbed.

"Oh, I could take him," Matteo said, turning onto his side to meet Jess's playful gaze. "You know if he fought fair and not as a storm or flood or whatever," he caveated. In truth, he didn't fancy being on the receiving end of a god's wrathful jealousy and would definitely prefer to know the lay of the land. He added honestly, "If I were Rune and I found out I'd lost you, I don't think I could be held accountable for my actions."

A tender smile crossed her face, and she assuaged his doubts. "Rune knows about my feelings for you. He kinda granted his blessing, told me I deserved to be happy the last time we spoke. But," she added with a frown, "we should probably try to lay low in the Seelie Court. Probably not the best timing with a looming war for the fae to find out that Lady Silva is shacking up with someone else."

He ran a hand down her bare arm, loving the fact that she no longer shuddered as she had when he'd first touched the scars Mara had made. He'd kissed away her self-consciousness of them until she only shivered with pleasure as his tongue had teased the sensitive skin of her midarm and forearm, coming close to the bounds of what was *too much*.

His hand journeyed down her back, savoring the intimacy between them that he'd fantasized about so many times. "Shacking up? Is that what we're doing? You know I don't actually live here, right?" he joked.

"Whether it's a cave or castle," Jess answered earnestly, "I'd live anywhere with you."

His heart felt full to bursting as he stared down into her beautiful, clear gaze. Her tender words sparked a million thoughts at once. He imagined introducing Jess to his mom and dad. They'd love her as soon as they saw how competitively she took a round of Scopa; he imagined whiling away the hot summer nights out for drinks in bacari with his brothers and their girlfriends. He imagined taking her to try street food in his district, her hungry lips on his afterward, tasting better than any of the delicacies on offer. Imagined choosing an apartment in Naples together. Scrap that, they'd both prefer the countryside—a crumbling down villa that needed work but that they could make their own.

But he didn't tell her any of these things. Because if he told her everything he dreamed of doing with her, there was no way he was leaving this cave. Because at the top of that list of dreams was making love to her. And flickering death dust or not, he was in danger of telling her to get better at multitasking.

But he didn't intend their first time together to be marred by an audience of Theo and his sluagh horde. So instead, Matteo declared, "And that's why we need to go back to Umbra. It's what we're fighting for—to keep our worlds from fracturing anymore." He added with a smile, "Besides, we're important proof that there's a way back from the invading dark—a Rom and Rem living together without fighting, have you ever heard of anything so indecent?"

Jess latched onto his last word, biting her lip. "Totally inde-cent," she said with a wicked gleam in her eye. And, soon, Matteo was fighting her off, practically dragging her out of the cave, with murmurings of "savage" beneath his breath, and in between attacks of kisses and laughter.

16

RESTLESS WAVES

In the evening, Rune knocked on Ski and Astra's door. Ski opened the door.

"How's Astra doing?" Rune asked,

"Not yet emerged from her cocoon," Ski replied. He opened the door fully, and Rune took in the outline of Astra's horizontal figure on the bed, enveloped in blankets, as well as her own black feathery wings.

Astra's wings eased back, and she grumbled, "Ligue is a fearsome opponent. I hope you never face it, Rune."

Rune laughed and called in, "Feel better soon."

As he took his leave, he knew he should go check on Sunny, too. Guilt rippled through him as he thought of how quickly he'd jumped down his throat earlier, supposing Sunny had been going back to Earth to secretly meet with Erika these last couple of weeks. While in reality, the witch hadn't come here for Sunny, but rather for the sake of other worlds. Worlds to which she'd vanished, leaving Sunny to believe that she was dead. Something he'd believed for over five hundred years.

Coming around the corner to where Sunny's room was located, Rune's steps were curtailed by the sight of his ex-blood brother propped up against the wall, his legs sprawled out across the hallway.

So, things with the witch are going well.

Rune wondered if he should disappear—literally—and pretend not to have spotted Sunny sitting outside his own room. But the weary, overwhelmed expression that was on Sunny's face made the decision for him. Wordlessly, Rune came over and eased himself down next to him.

"I'm sorry I assumed you went behind my back," Rune opened with.

Sunny sighed. "It's not like I haven't been a conniving git in the past—there are precedents."

A wry smile crossed Rune's face. Such as scheming to sacrifice Jess to the Between. In the first few days here at the Sun Keep, Sunny had owned up to him and Jess that he'd been the one to tell Fern Trever about Jess's Rom heritage. That he was responsible for the Triodian High Witch capturing Jess and almost success-fully killing her. Jess had claimed the right to thrash Sunny in the training arena. She'd called in Astra as backup, too, and he'd soon, deservedly, been beaten.

It was strange to feel the absence of anger that would have been there at the thought of Sunny's underhandedness, only weeks ago. But now Rune knew, at the heart of all the Alban heirs —him, Sunny, Cuill, and all the heirs before them—the Fomors' magic had lingered on. Consequently, their interpretation of the Eventide prophecy had been colored by the enemy's destruc-tiveness.

Rune shared his reflection. "In many ways, the Fomors' magic continued to divide us—their destruction coloring our outlook and in turn keeping us broken."

Sunny chuckled. "Is this Alba absolving me of all wrongdoing then?"

Sunny's laugh did nothing to dispel the shared wrong they'd done in their centuries existence. Something Rune knew his ex-blood brother felt as much as he did, despite the nonchalant façade that had long been his armor.

Rune didn't know if it would ever be possible to forgive himself for all the cumulative wrong he and the other Alban heirs had caused while Alba was fractured. But ... he recalled Eilea's words of wisdom. *"The Fomors robbed you of your ability to feel. Just like they robbed my people of our ability to transform. So, you can't blame yourself..."*

Rune locked his gaze with Sunny's. "Our enemy robbed us—Alba—of our ability to feel. So, yes, I'm telling you to stop turning your anger inwards. Direct it towards the enemy where it belongs."

Sunny's green eyes blinked in surprise.

No doubt, since Erika's return, much of his regrets centered on how he'd spent centuries trying to bring a Triodian and Enodian together to produce the divided's blood to fulfill the Eventide prophecy.

Rune wondered how things had stood between Erika and Sunny before she made that move to become a vamp and leave Earth.

"Did she explain why she left?" Rune broached.

Sunny was silent so long that it seemed he wouldn't answer. But, finally, his voice hoarse, he said, "On Earth, Erika spent her whole life trying to win my love. I fostered her and Inis's magic. Which in itself is fucked up enough for her to leave this world. But no, despite our wretched beginnings, it wasn't that. My own words caused her to leave me. I told her I couldn't love her as a vamp. I told her if she became the half-dead thing I was, the affection that existed between us, would die. It's hardly surprising she chose to walk into a world without me in it."

"You weren't a being capable of true feeling," Rune reiterated.

"And yet some part of me *was*," Sunny said. "I saw the vision in the fetch of her coven killing her. My deepest fear was of her dying. Something that shows I truly cared for her."

"Did you tell her about the vision of her death in the fetch?"

Sunny's golden brows drew together. "No."

Rune suppressed a smile. "I'd tell her."

Sunny swept his hand over his face in exasperation but nodded. Then, in a far more habitual way, he deflected attention from him, turning his perceptive stare on Rune. "And how is Alba himself doing?"

Rune hadn't really caught up with him much over the last week and a half. Gods, how did he sum up everything that had changed of late?

For a moment, his thoughts went back to his earlier conversation with Jess. Today, their long talk had felt relaxed: a natural kind of intimacy flowing between them. Even her admission about what she felt for Matteo had left no bitterness. With her half-hopeful, half-*terrified* expression, Rune had wanted to tell her that he was certain the shifter was nose over tail in love with her, but he had seen Jess's doubts in her fidgety body language and known that only the shifter confessing his own feelings to her could assuage them. Instead, Rune had told her with sincerity that he was glad she was reaching for the happiness she deserved. And in that moment that she'd asked him whether he'd be all right by himself, he had, for the first time felt as if he would be. Feelings of anticipation and confusion whipped through him as he reflected on that. What had changed?

But, by the Heights, he wasn't ready for a heart-to-heart about his emotional state with Sunny. Instead, he focused on what he and Jess had strategized today.

"Jess will be going to the Triodia tomorrow—not just to call upon the support of the shifters and the Triodians against Mara and the Fomors, but to claim the Earthen power in the Cathedral."

"She's going to portal the ancient grove to Umbra," Sunny said, instantly deducing what he meant.

"Yes, giving her access to her Earthen energy here," Rune said. "She untethered hundreds of sluagh from Theo."

"She could aid you in destroying the iron-tinged that Mara and the Unseelie wield," Sunny reflected.

Rune nodded. "On the topic of untethering, I might need you to call your Unseelie contacts to Umbra or meet them somewhere on Earth under the guise of "giving back" the Storm-born tomorrow, too. Jess wants to see if she can untether the Storm-born successfully from the Unseelie who bound them."

The little white lie came out smoothly. *Jess* hadn't suggested it, but wasn't it important to see if she could untether the Storm-born? There were many Storm-born within the ranks of Mara's army. If Jess could free them all, then they were another weapon that Mara and her forces would lose. Rune told himself that's why he was interested in doing so. He was thinking about the strength of their forces. And he was thinking about the duty he had to his allies.

That's all.

"Of course," Sunny agreed. "We'll discuss it tomorrow when Jess is around."

Anticipation for tomorrow stirred through Rune. For a moment, he thought Sunny would ask where Jess was. Yet Sunny's gaze traipsed once more to the door of his chamber, clearly preoccupied with the hard truths ahead of him.

Rune wished his ex-blood brother good luck, then wandered outside into the dark. The glow of the ignes never allowed the keep and its surrounding gardens to be claimed by the night completely, an ever-glowing light amidst the darkness. Drinking in its golden walls, for once Rune's mind didn't drift to the past. Instead, only the simple pleasure of the present washed over him. The glimmering light stroking the trees, shrubs, and blossoms of Umbra's bountiful lands—a beautiful sight that he took the time to admire.

Yet, something within him called for movement. Like the

breathlessness of the night that spoke of storms brewing, a quiet-
ness whispered through him. But what it meant he didn't know.
Farther afield, he felt the high pressure above the Alban Sea on
Umbra's eastern shore. He could coax out that pressure system
and bring down those winds until he drove the waves into peaks
that mirrored the Heights.

But Rune stayed in his human form, not wanting to exist in
the abstraction of the winds or waves tonight. His steps wended
down the bank towards the river, keeping closer to home. The
charged feeling grew as he walked. He told himself it was his
preoccupation about what information Erika could provide about
the Fomors tomorrow. He told himself it was eagerness about
presenting his and Jess's plans to their friends.

But as he drew out onto the plains by the river, his steps led
him to the Storm-born camp. Expressing their preference to
Imber to be out in the open rather than beneath walls and ceilings, the king had soon furnished them with tents and facilities
for fires. It was remarkable to see that in the space of only two
days, not only had they set up tents and campfires, but many had
thrown themselves into learning from the Seelie. Cookery and
music were the dominant activities. Savory and sweet fragrances
wafted through the night; pots and pans were settled over fires
while the Storm-born and Seelie mingled, talking and laughing.

An array of instruments sounded from the area. Skilled fingers
plucked the chords on luids and lips whistled through phiobs.
Here and there, tentative movements tried to mimic the music.
Rune walked through the night, witnessing the camaraderie
springing up between Seelie and Storm-born of all ages.

For a moment, he thought of far-flung places that his
centuries' existence on Earth had taken him. When he and Sunny
had sought out distant Triodian and Enodian branches, looking
for signs of the seed magic on Earth. He remembered paras in the
Amazon Forest who had lived in a similar style, out in the open
thanks to the exotic climes. But then his more ancient memories

sparked, and he remembered such a scene as this with the Storm-born when they'd first entered. Yet, those Storm-born had had the luxury of having possessed their human form as well as their animal ones *all* their lives. And their own music and cookery had been as skilled and vibrant as the Seelies' now. But even with the dissonant chords and hollow half-formed notes, Rune felt a massive sense of deja-vu, listening and watching the two races connect.

"Penny for your thoughts?" a voice asked from beside him in English. Eilea had come up next to him stealthily like one of Umbra's shadows. But as Rune started, his eyes drank in her very real warm and vibrant figure. She wore a dark green Seelie dress, its fit drawing the eye to her slim figure.

He wished for a moment that he hadn't been thinking about the past. That he didn't have to tell her that he'd sunk into those waters that were him, but that, inevitably, was so alien to the way that everyone else experienced the world. To the way *Eilea* experienced the world.

But Rune answered honestly, "I was thinking of how I remember this from before. Before the Fomors invaded when your people first came through to Umbra. This could be that time in so many ways."

"What else do you remember about the Storm-born from then?" Eilea asked, her voice peaking with inquisitiveness.

Rune's black gaze veered away from the campfires and people to look at her. Eilea's expression like her tone was only infused with interest.

What did you expect?

Before Rune's internal commentary could tell him that she would judge him, he said, "I remember that your people were master storytellers. They would use their shape-shifting skills to act out their stories while others narrated.

"I remember the jumbled phrases through which we learned one another's language. That your people, like you, always had a natural flair for language. We learned each other's tongues through exchanging common words, broken phrases that became more with time."

Four Storm-born nearby were currently dancing to some of the Seelie music, their crouched forms with their cloudy wings sparked another memory in Rune of the Storm-born talking and acting out where their power came from. "I remember before the Fomors, your people said that the creative force at the heart of your world was called Anu. Your word for the storms that gave you your shape-shifting power. That when the enemy came, it was Anu that they'd becalmed."

Self-consciousness prickled over him as he worried that he'd let the magnitude of time's tide moving through him be too apparent. How could someone not be disturbed by you uncovering great swathes of memory as if they were only yesterday's?

But Eilea's face lit up. "Anu," she breathed with awe. "You have to write this down. You have to teach us to write these stories down, too. Everything that happened BF."

He frowned. "BF?"

"Before Fomors," she answered with a quirk of her lips.

An easy smile immediately spread over Rune's face. The distant shores that he'd walked alone of late didn't feel so isolated. He realized that the vault of knowledge that was his wasn't just his alone. He could bring back a world of memory to a race that had been robbed of theirs. Rune knew what it was like to lose your past. When he'd been turned into a vamp and Alba's consciousness thrust upon him, without the depths of Umbra to sink into, he'd felt robbed of his human life. Robbed of the memory of home, of the memory of his mother and sister. But through Jess's blood and love he'd felt again, and experienced what happiness lay in those remembrances. The past could be restorative. It needn't be something that detracted from the present. And it could enrich the future.

Eilea's request reminded him fondly of his blood brother,

Cuill, who had taught him to read and write. Her unfettered joy
was a breath of fresh air. She made everything seem more possible. Doable.

BF. Before Fomors.

Reducing the damage of what the enemy had done to those
two simple letters was a feat of genius—the abbreviation seeming
to reduce the enemy themselves.

He gazed at her with open admiration. "I'm not going
anywhere. I'll tell you everything and teach you and your people
to write these stories. Until you're sick of the sound of my voice."

"I think the only reason I'd get sick of your voice is if I
wanted your lips to do other things," she quipped.

The suggestion had heat prickling over his skin. But at the
same moment, confusion somersaulted through him. So, she *had*
noticed the way her lips had ensnared his attention last night.
This time it was the challenging look in her dark eyes that had his
heart pounding against his chest.

Eilea laughed. "Does my frankness make you uncomfortable,
Rune?"

His thoughts spun.

Yes. No.

But as she stood in front of him, with that teasing light in her
eye, he admitted to himself that that was *exactly* what this restlessness and anticipation was about.

Her.

It hit him like a ton of bricks, that he was feeling attracted to
this quick-thinking, outspoken Storm-born.

In a hoarse voice, he acknowledged, "You make me feel
uncomfortable in the best possible way." The intermingling of
nervousness and desire moved up his spine as he watched a
pleased smile spread across her face.

Wasn't this part of what had made it possible to tell Jess
honestly that the concept of eternity stretching out before him
wasn't as frightening as it had been? This feeling had come out of

nowhere. But there was an undeniable spark between him and Eilea. And ... he was looking forward to exploring it.

It was why, too, he'd asked both Jess and Sunny about untethering the Storm-born from the Unseelie. He hadn't been thinking strategically about his forces. Nor had he been thinking about his duty to his allies. He'd thought of how much he wanted to liberate this wonderful vibrant being from whatever bastard had tethered her. The god within Rune rumbled with wrath at the thought and vowed that tomorrow, Eilea and her friend Beinn would be freed from their slavers.

The longer Rune stood in front of her, the more he felt how much he'd wanted to see her again. That he'd actually missed her since only *this morning*. He liked the way that she kept him on his toes, unsure whether the next thing out of her mouth would be a wisecrack or a blunt observation.

It wasn't an accident that only minutes ago, he'd found himself quoting Eilea's words to Sunny. She was an insightful, stimulating woman, who he was looking forward to getting to know. The temptation to get caught up in the encouraging glimmer in her eye and let his lips dip down to taste hers was strong. But Rune settled on earning that kiss.

Rune uttered, "Your people had a saying: 'A-màireach, bidh speuran ùr-bhreith ann gus do thogail suas a-staigh.'"

"Tomorrow, there will be newborn skies that lift you up inside," she translated, her dark gaze growing thoughtful.

"I feel the promise of all those skies when I look at you," he told her. "Though in Umbra, the night sky has its own magic. Will you dance with me, alongside your brothers and sisters?"

The music nearby was dominated by the voices of the Storm-born: the raw chant of the males in the group was like the deepest of winds reverberating through the caverns, while the higher voices of the females were like the gallivanting gales across the jagged peaks. It touched something within Rune. Like it was the song he'd been needing to hear ever since he'd joined with his shadow self. Thrumming through the music was the song of the Heights, the other part of him that he'd barely scratched the surface of.

Eilea took his hand, switching to the same ancient Umbran, something of the archaic Celtic influence coming out as she said, "To new-born nights, Rune."

He watched the gleam of her eye and felt as if he were breathing in hope. After everything she'd been through, there was such liveliness in her voice, and it matched the thrumming pulse singing through his own body. The one that *wanted* to dance to the music and taste the bacae wine that was going around.

When they joined the dancing, Eilea's first steps were uncoordinated and tentative, but as Rune guided her, the Storm-born's steps grew surer. Initially, the crowd watched in surprise as Lord Alba joined them. The gathering gave them a wide berth, staring and whispering. But with time, the other Storm-born and Seelie returned to their own celebrations. And Rune felt the magic of Umbra's night bloom: in the music, in the dancing, but most of all, in Eilea's vivacious company.

❧ 17 ❧

A DEAL WITH THE DEVIL

Theo trod through the dim corridor, his steps tentative, unsure of where he was or why he was there. His faltering steps infuriated him, the sense of caution ... of *fear* teeming along his skin like sweat.

"Your specter blooms in the night, I wish I could hold you tight." The voice wrapped around him like a summer's evening.

Von.

The musician he'd met in Italy, in the villa where he'd tethered Donna's—the woman with the third eye—soul. Theo's heart drummed against his ribcage as he realized that's where he was. The Tuscan villa.

"Like smoke whispering through me, you're there then gone..." Von's ethereal song seemed to suffuse the murk with color. He followed her voice with surer steps, his pulse pounding for a different reason—her tone was as full of want as her lyrics.

Want for me.

Rounding the doorway, Theo's gaze struck Von—raven-haired and eyed, her pale face swam in the gloom, her parted lips an invitation. She wore the same high-collared lace blouse and tulle skirt she had when they'd fucked. As if she'd never left.

As if she's been waiting for me.

Within seconds, Theo crossed the threshold, his mouth devouring hers, his kisses heavy with the same want that had filled her words. His hand fisted those raven locks, his other ripping the tulle skirt.

So damned kissable and rippable.

But something crackled, distracting Theo from Von's voluptuous lips. His eyes darted around, shock hammering through him as cracks wound down the walls and across the ceiling. The place was falling down. Theo tried to pull Von towards the door, but she wouldn't budge from the bed: a dead weight in his arms.

Theo wanted to run; new urgency filled him as pieces of rubble rained down around them.

"Von!" he screamed, the terror in his tone grating on him to such a degree that he pulled at her with more violence. His wrenching of her arms should have broken them, but she didn't budge an inch. There was no softness or animation about her now. He watched with horror as cracks ran over her as if she were part of the crumbling structure. Yet, her mouth unsealed and sang, "These walls stand tall, but they will fall unless you name them the home they are."

And with that, Von's form crumbled, dissolving into dust and enveloping Theo. His heart seemed to bulldoze through his chest and right into the remaining walls as they caved in around him.

Theo thrashed awake, his sheets strangling him. His heart pounded through his temples, his skin slick with sweat. He gasped for air, his mouth tasting like chalk. This was the second time he'd tried to sleep since Jess had escaped Nox with her father. Both times, Von had appeared in the unsettled landscape of his dreams.

Jess has fucking done this to me when she untethered those souls from me. Like Donna.

The woman with the third eye had been ripped from Theo. Along with *hundreds* of other souls from his horde. The magnitude of that devastating loss filled him. He and Jess couldn't have been fighting in the catacombs for more than a few minutes. But in that time she'd severed hundreds of his sluagh from him. Loss swept through him. Heat prickled along his skin as if he were feverish.

Once more his thoughts stagnated. On Donna. She'd been the first soul with para abilities that he'd tethered. Now, she was just *gone*. He felt her absence like a gaping hole in his own being. He still didn't understand how Jess had ripped his sluagh from his own soul. But that's what she'd done. Theo ran his hands through his hair, unsticking the strands plastered to his forehead.

She's fucking ravaged my soul.

As his breathing and heart rate quickened, Theo's thoughts wandered to the Tuscan villa he'd just occupied in his nightmare. To the room where he'd seen Von. He remembered lying in bed with her a whole afternoon, talking about Donna, about what else the band knew concerning the spirit haunting the villa. He remembered that quivering feeling across his skin as he'd sensed Donna's presence on the periphery as surely as he'd felt Von's fingertips and lips upon his skin.

That must be why he was dreaming about Von—in his subconscious, she was *linked* to Donna. Yet, something in him, something irrational, made the singer foremost in his thoughts. The wish to see her consumed him.

Perhaps... I could portal to Italy. Perhaps it would be good to take my mind off Jess.

A smile wound over his face as he imagined charming Von all over again. She'd had her memories of him wiped by the para unit who had caught Theo before putting him in the Triodia Penitentiary. His heart cramped as he remembered when he'd been captured by the para unit and Von's memory of him erased. He'd wished there might be some lingering memory of him left in her mind. And the dream, with those lyrics about him in her music, was that again: a wish for her to remember him. After all, he knew exactly what attracted her, the otherworldly, the strange and unusual.

In other words, me.

Just as he was contemplating gallivanting off to Italy, a knock sounded on Theo's door. "High Mage, there's a mirror call for you," a muffled voice called from the other side. One of his followers.

Ferocity ripped through him. He'd *told* them he didn't want to be disturbed. "Unless it's Jess—"

"It's Queen Mara," the mage responded swiftly.

Shock hit him. The Unseelie Queen. Mara had disappeared while Jess was in Umbra. Adrenaline erupted through him. Theo remembered the glimpse into Jess's fears that he'd gotten: Queen Mara torturing and trying to tether Jess's soul. Her *goddess's* soul. *Silva's* soul.

A smile spread over Theo's face. So, Mara sought information on Jess. No doubt, the queen had heard of Giovanni's escape from Castle Nox. There were enough Unseelie employed by him to maintain the glamour over the castle that word had reached the queen. Of course, if Mara wanted something from him, he was gonna make damn sure that he got what he wanted in return.

He slung a silk robe on before striding out the bedroom. The mage who had brought the message hurried after him.

"Does the queen call from Umbra?" Theo demanded.

"No. An Unseelie arrived in the night and gave us a white orb to open the mirror pool. Looks like some sort of coral, I think," the mage answered. So that confirmed that Mara wasn't in Umbra at all. If she'd been calling from the Shadowlands, the usual hebena token of the Unseelie's native tree would have been used. The orb had been white. Coral, the mage said. Theo imagined Mara taking up refuge in some remote corner of Earth. Calling from a mirror pool with coral. He'd give orders to his followers to cross-reference areas of coral, along with any clues he gleaned from the mirror call he was about to join. That's if Mara didn't divulge where she was herself. If she needed sanctuary on Earth, the scales were definitely tipping in Theo's favor.

The mage accompanying Theo ran ahead to the door of the Xibalba Suite, opening it for Theo who strode in. Before the previous High Mage's death, the suite had housed Nox's biggest library. Now, it had a small collection of tomes Theo had carefully condensed into his own personal collection. It was one of the few major changes to Nox that Theo had made since his succession to High Mage. The whole room looked as if it was part of a cave system, its mystical pools reflecting the now sparser collection of books throughout. Xibalba had been designed to symbolize the power one could wield by mastering the Night and Netherworld.

But he knew that was only a half-truth now. It took *all* three branches of magic to truly have power. He'd used Tassology—the Earthen branch of magic—to discover who his and the other Enodian youths' parents were. By doing so, he and his followers had been able to kill and tether their parents' souls. The para souls they now wielded. The greatest form of magic any Enodian had possessed before.

Theo had been in the procedure of integrating that missing branch of magic into the room's design. The yew trees Enodia had claimed from the Triodia institutes they'd conquered had been portaled and were now rooted throughout Nox's outer grounds. In triumph of his knowing that it took *all* three branches of magic to truly rule on high, he intended to have all of the woodwork redone in this room, carved from the yews of Silva's groves. Unfortunately, the matter of redecorating had been put on hold by Jess's reappearance.

Still, his gaze did skim over the burnished woodwork in the room, imagining the satisfaction he'd feel when wood from Silva's Cathedral adorned his room. When Jess's most ancient and potent wood was cut up and used to symbolize his victory over the three branches of magic ... and, most importantly, over *her*.

A beat of alarm struck him as he thought of that strange witch who had portaled through the Depths into the catacombs to rescue Jess. Another who seemed to have mastered all three branches of magic.

But as Theo approached the dais in which the sunken mirror pool rested, he schooled his features, readying to search for signs as to where the queen might be in the clues of her skin color, which was ivory. Fae had the most wonderfully helpful tendency to blend with their surroundings. But the bone-white rock behind her, and—was that a distant waterfall in the background?—did nothing to clue Theo in on where she might be.

"You left Umbra," Theo said.

"A temporary removal while I gather troops," Mara said.

"Troops to fight Silva and Alba?"

Mara's lips curled minutely. "I thought you'd call them by the names you already know them."

Theo's heart skipped nervously. She suspected him entirely ignorant as to what events had taken place in Umbra. But at least through Jess's break into Castle Nox and through glimpsing that vision of her fear—that memory of Mara trying to tether her—he knew that Jess *was* Silva restored.

"Even displaced and altered gods are still *gods*. Besides, I saw Jess recently, she is *god-like* but... not invulnerable."

Theo watched the queen still. That got her attention. He'd been right about her wanting information concerning Jess.

The queen shifted where she sat, her armor-like dress caught the silvery light of her surroundings. "I've removed to my allies, the Fomors' world, whose forces I shall use to help me attack Rune and Jess—Alba and Silva," she allowed, her expression serious. "I want to know what power it was that Jess had that enabled her to escape from Castle Nox with her father recently?"

The Fomors' *world. Another world.*

Theo's thoughts pitched. The scale of unknown magic that stretched before him was astounding. To think he'd once wanted to avoid dealing with Umbran magic. Possibility beckoned and a trill of excitement sang through him; a giddy feeling that reminded him of the joy of contemplating a tethering ground soon to come into existence.

Besides, such a thing as avoiding Umbran magic was impossible with Jess and Rune's threat darkening his rule over Earth. He'd decided that he would be involved with Umbran magic. In fact, one of the prices he intended to name in his bargaining with Mara relied on iron-tinged magic.

Consequently, Theo said, "I will tell you everything that I witnessed and sensed of Jess's power if—when your war with Umbra's gods is over—I have dominion over Earth."

"Naturally." She looked pleased, as though she didn't expect him to ask for more.

As if.

Theo glanced at the nearest case of books on display. With the mirror pool open and Mara's iron-tinged able to come through, there was little doubt that they'd investigated which books his library consisted of. So, he added, "As your iron-tinged have, no doubt, mentioned, like my predecessor, I have an invested interest in possessing the immortality that you've managed to obtain." Theo *had* taken over Jorah's research of delving into the matter of Mara's immortality. The High Mage's notes and references to his reading materials had been copious. Most of Theo's collection gathered within this room belonged to that topic.

But Theo had more urgency than Jorah had to discover the secret to Mara's immortality: his followers. No Enodian wanted to procreate now that doing so would put their life on the line. They'd all agreed that there would be no more witchlings and magelings swelling the ranks of Enodia. But lately, Theo had caught wind of this causing unrest within the coven. He'd heard pesky questions murmured: *What is the plan for Enodia's future? Are we to be the last of our coven? How will we endure?* Theo had silently raged at the Enodians for asking such questions. At most, they were in their fucking *twenties*. Immortality hardly seemed pressing now. Right? But after reading more on the subject, Theo had set himself the challenge of solving the answer of long life.

A task that his reading, paired with that vision of Jess's shadow self disappearing into Umbra's shadows, he'd finally solved. Umbra's landscape was saturated with its own shadows, as were its gods, all of it was *enriched* by shadows. By making the iron-tinged sluagh on Umbran soil, Mara had tapped into the Shadowland's magic. The iron-tinged enriched the queen in the same way Umbra's shadows did its lands. So, if like Mara, he tethered souls on Umbran ground and spent enough time there to be nurtured by its shadows, he, too, could be immortal.

Theo laid down his conditions. "I want an area of land granted to me in Umbra, where I can create my own iron-tinged and spend enough of my time there to be eternally sustained by the Shadowlands."

The queen's jaw tightened almost imperceptibly. "Your discovery of your own brand of divisive magic, High Mage, was impressive. I admit to listening about and following your journey from afar with interest. The fact that you have discovered the requirements to my own divisive magic is, perhaps, even more so. You are far shrewder than your predecessor."

"I need to be," Theo said honestly, "if I'm to survive the new order I've created by doing away with the natural order of procreation in my coven. The favor I would have you grant me I intend to share with only a select group."

Mara's lips curved. A smooth segue back to his demands, the expression said.

Theo continued, "I will choose only an inner sanctum to share immortality with me. It would be something the rest of the coven strove towards. If I had a piece of land granted in Umbra, perhaps from the soon-to-be conquered Seelie lands, then I could spend and practice the magic necessary to prolong my life and any of the followers I chose fit."

The queen's expression and voice were serious. "What you ask is no small thing. Land—the right to practice iron-tinged magic that is my creation. What will you give me other than knowledge about what magic Silva wielded to escape you?"

"I and my followers will fight alongside the Unseelie and the Fomors," Theo stated.

Mara's dark eyes studied him as if searching to understand his motivations.

"I would thus earn through battle the land I would have and annihilate the Triodia Coven, who will, no doubt," he added with mockery, "stand by the Great Goddess's side."

"You would fight against Enodia's own gods, Lady Night and Lord Netherworld?" Queen Mara countered.

Theo frowned, totally perplexed by the reference to Enodia's gods.

Mara laughed. "Clearly, you are not wholly informed of the Umbran gods' history." She looked too pleased about Theo's ignorance. He wondered if this was going to be an obstacle to their working together. The queen continued, a shrewd look coming over her face. "It was the Fomors' magic fracturing Alba and Silva that turned them into Lord Netherworld and Lady Night."

Theo blinked. "My coven's been worshipping a form of Silva and Alba?"

"In a way, yes," Mara said, her eyes delighting in his shock.

But it was Theo's turn to smile, "As High Mage, I believe it's time then for an overhaul of Enodia's deities."

Queen Mara soon agreed to his terms. So, he told the queen of how Jess had portaled into Castle Nox invisibly. He could see Mara's burnished eyes trying to disguise the lust swimming in them: for Jess's soul. He omitted the vision of seeing Mara trying to tether Jess's immortal soul. So, too, that in that vision he'd sensed Jess's loss, that he somehow knew that despite the power she possessed over the dead, that her shadow self was gone. Why tell Mara that when he could see that that was *exactly* what she still hoped to tether? The queen must have left Umbra before witnessing Jess's shadow self die.

Whereas half a soul, or whatever remnant of power that lay in Jess's, was exactly what Theo wanted. And by agreeing to be on Umbra's battlefield, he intended to get it. After all, half a soul or whatever was left in Jess was *plenty* soul to patch up the holes she'd ripped in his.

Nor did Theo say anything of the witch—an adept in the three branches of magic, who had portaled Jess and the others out. Who had come through the Depths portal, free of fire and tethered souls. Theo hoped that said unknown witch would be another distraction on the battlefield for Mara. One that Theo wanted to avoid. He remembered the acute power with which the witch had targeted the lock of Jess's hair in his hand. Gone before he could so much as blink. And the power with which she portaled through the Depths pool but without any sign of teth-ered souls. Yes, he needed to steer clear of her.

As Theo's plans came together, he mourned the loss of Jess's lock of hair. That token that had so easily subdued her. But she had another Achilles' heel. The way her nightmare had altered as Mara's iron-tinged had pressed in on her, to include the black wolf leaping through the circle, told him all he had to do. When he captured the shifter, Matteo, he'd once more hold Jess like putty in his hand.

18

THE MARROW OF WORLDS

Back in her room, Jess had only returned from the hot springs located on the ground floor of the Sun Keep when a knock sounded at the door. Still in a half state of dressing, Jess peeked around the door. Dearbhla stood there.

"There's a message from Lord Alba," her second explained. "The witch is awake, and Alba's asked for you to meet them in the Sun Study."

Jess thanked her lucky stars that she and Matteo *had* portaled back with the dawn.

"Thanks, Dearbhla." Jess hurried to towel dry her hair before shoving on a fresh set of Seelie leathers and her boots. She did a quick recon to get Matteo. She wanted him to hear whatever information the witch might share, too. But when she knocked softly on the door and he opened it—dressed only in a pair of jeans—thoughts of what she was *actually* here to do flew.

The width of his chest and shoulders was ... well, fort-like ... Her gaze brushed over the sculpted muscles of his defined pecs and abs...

And this is Matteo building *muscle!*

Jess's thoughts assembled into helpful musings on how they could build muscle *together*.

She would likely have succumbed to tackling him into the room if the click of a door snapping open hadn't sounded. Meeting Matteo's dark stare, it was gratifying to see that there was a lingering heat in his eyes that said his thoughts had gone to similar places.

Astra's voice sounded. "Oh, hey, Dork, you're back!"

Jess rolled her eyes. Crap ... if Astra knew she'd been away last night, had she guessed–

The cheesy smile on her friend's face confirmed Jess's unfinished thought. The fae unabashedly took in Matteo in all his topless glory. "Good night, Geometry?"

Matteo let out a belly laugh while Jess blushed crimson, especially as she'd just been drooling over Matteo's triangle body. Gods, she'd told him about Astra's nickname for him and both the potato and annum peel story last night, too. They'd laughed over Jess's refusal to trust in Tassology readings, when, in a way, they came from her; from Earthen power, from the Great Goddess, from Silva.

"I knew it," Astra squealed, clapping her hands together as she drank in Matteo's knowing laugh and Jess's beet-red face.

Skiron loped down the hallway, sighing. "Sorry guys, I've never met someone so unromantic who's so into *other people's* love lives." He tugged a now arguing Astra down the hall.

"Some people just need a helping hand..." Astra's voice trailed away.

Matteo leaned down towards Jess, his voice low. "Have I ever told you how utterly stunning you are when you blush?"

Breathless, Jess shook her head, aware of her pounding blood, no doubt staining her cheeks more. But the gods-damned devastatingly carnal expression on his face made her skin tingle as if he were already touching her. But half a meter still rested between them: they'd agreed not to touch each other in public, something she thoroughly regretted now. She bit her lip, aware that if Astra had come upon them, another fae could at any moment. "Remind me why we didn't come straight back to your room?"

At the river when she'd suggested she follow him back, Matteo had said he needed far longer than a morning to make love to her.

"Because I'm the biggest idiot of all time," he replied, the musical lilt to his voice making her melt.

Jess smiled but forced herself to remember why she'd come. "Erika's awake. We're all meeting to discuss plans."

"I'll throw something on."

She pouted. "If it were a private audience with Lady Silva, this would be fine."

"Good to know, *my* lady." Jess's heart pounded with the emphasis he put on *my*; she had no qualms about being addressed as such.

It took every ounce of self-control to stay outside the bedroom.

Why is there always a world to save?

Giving up on her wallowing, Jess morphed into her wolf form. Once Matteo had joined her, they both padded along the golden hallways until reaching the Sun Study.

Changing into their human forms, Jess exchanged a reassuring look with him before traipsing into the study. There were three sofas around the circular room arranged around the hearth where a fire burned. Skiron and Astra naturally shared one; Rune and a Storm-born occupied another. At first glance, Jess thought it was one of the Storm-born leaders but realized this female's wings were unmoving. They were black like Astra's. But her wings weren't the black downy *feathers* of a fae. They were more like Rune's shadow ones. Only fixed. Like a black cloud hovered behind her. Otherwise, her svelte figure and delicate features were very like the other Storm-born Jess had encountered.

Jess took in Erika, sitting on the other couch *alone*, while

Sunny had opted to stand by the mantlepiece, where he leaned. Looking as if he wanted to be anywhere but here.

Jess supposed five hundred years apart was quite a gulf to repair. Twenty-four hours was hardly going to be enough to unpack everything the two had to discuss. Despite there being a seat by the witch, Jess felt unwilling to give up sitting beside Matteo. So, she clasped his hand and pulled him over onto the rug in front of the fire.

"We dogs can't resist the warmest spot," she joked.

Astra laughed.

Feeling a little self-conscious, even though she and Rune had talked openly about it, her gaze was a little wary as it traveled to him.

But there was nothing but warmth on Rune's face. And instead of focusing on the fact that Matteo and Jess held hands, he drew their attention to the Storm-born. "This is Eilea. Eilea was one of the Storm-born we journeyed up the Silvan mountains with."

Jess's eyes bugged out. She stared at the Storm-born's *fixed* cloudy wings. This was one of the tethered Storm-born, who was still yoked to an Unseelie. This woman was one of the beings they'd used as a *pack horse*.

Eilea read Jess's shame in her shocked expression. The Storm-born shrugged. "I told Rune the past's water under the bridge. We're here to discuss what's to come."

A flurry of questions occupied Jess. Rune had mentioned the Storm-born who had been tethered by Unseelie the last time they'd spoken. He'd proposed that she untether them from the Unseelie who had bound them. She'd thought he'd been talking about the tethered Storm-born in general. After all, there must be hundreds in Queen Mara's units. But now, Jess wondered if the topic of conversation had been motivated by more than strategy. Was his motivation something more personal—what with this tethered Storm-born present? And Eilea *had* called him *Rune*. So far, even the Storm-born leaders had been as reverent as the Seelie in the way they spoke to both Rune and Jess. Always referring to them as Alba and Silva or my lord and lady.

But Jess quashed her curiosity. Eilea's reminder that they were here to look ahead was exactly what she needed.

Jess pinned her gaze on the witch. Erika still had that slightly sallow look to her face, but she looked better rested than she had in Risør. She'd clearly bathed, the scent of Seelie blossom and fruits on her skin evident to Jess's shifter nose. Erika's hair was plaited in a thick braid on one side, leaving the tattoo that patterned her temple and feathered down her neck on the other side even more visible. But the witch hadn't taken advantage of a change of clothes that her fae hosts would have offered. Erika looked as unlikely to wear a dress as Jess, but Seelie leathers would have suited her. Instead, she still wore the felt-like tunic and furs. Jess suspected they were tougher than they looked. She'd already gauged the witch wasn't the type to leave herself vulnerable. Perhaps she trusted this material more than fae leathers. Or did her clothes hold more meaning than pure function?

"Will you share everything you know about the Fomors with us?" Jess asked the witch.

Erika nodded. "The Fomors need those they target to share a deep affinity to their environment. Indeed, it is also true of world walking in general. The worlds I have been able to enter are those that recognize my magic. The affinity to Earth, and to the Night and Netherworld." Her eyes flicked to Rune and Eilea, then to the fae. "Or to the Heights and Depths if you would rather express it that way. In all worlds that we can enter, there must be at least one of these elements present."

"Water makes up most of the Fomors' kingdom," Rune said. "It's how they breached Umbra, and I felt the enemy's waters more recently when I closed the gouged entrance to their world beneath the Iron Keep."

Jess blinked at him, feeling as if it had been an age since they'd been by that polluted pool to the enemy's world. Had it really only been a space of weeks?

Erika nodded her agreement. "Theirs is a world of murky pools, of terrifying abysses and torrents that seek to consume all that comes their way. Across worlds, they have many names: world-breakers, devourers, the gathering dark.

"It is their waters themselves that are nourished by the division they forge in the lands they invade. Each conquered world sends a stream of nourishment back to the waters Below."

Jess remembered the way that Mara had cast some of her iron-tinged sluagh into the pool. A chill crawled down her spine as the pale, jelly-like skin that she'd seen on the other side of the portal swam in her memory: the black ink of the iron-tinged sluagh visible through the thing's transparent body.

"I saw Queen Mara feeding some of her iron-tinged to the waters beneath the Iron Keep, to creatures with transparent bodies," Jess said.

"Yes," Erika said, "you witnessed the waters spawning and nourishing new creatures, who will one day march in the Fomor army. When darkness is sown into a world, discord and a desire for dominion spread through that race. In turn, the hundreds of lives that are taken—whether in the form of destruction in general or through the individual spirits of the dead, like Mara's iron-tinged that she sacrifices—all of that energy spawns new Fomor foot-soldiers within those waters, who in appearance are said to be an amalgamation of all they conquer."

Rune summarized, "Umbra's faded said every divisive act we have ever taken against each other continues to nourish the Fomors."

Erika nodded.

Eilea interjected. "What of the way the Fomors invaded the Storm-borns' world? We are a race who worshipped the storms—Anu. That's where our transformative power came from." Her gaze brushed Rune. "But the Fomors tethered us in our animal forms. Why?"

"The Fomors do take physical resources from worlds they invade, too," Erika agreed. "Which is the way other worlds speak of them doing to the Storm-born. Invading through the waters, they used their power over the storm rains to becalm your world and take away your ability to transform. Then their foot soldiers captured and enslaved your race in their animal forms and were used as beasts of burden in their world."

"How many worlds have you been to?" Matteo asked, intrigued.

"Five, not including Earth and Umbra. Two of those worlds had been conquered by the Fomors. The other three have not."

"What's happened to the other worlds they've invaded?" Eilea asked.

"The same division that the Fomors have sown in our worlds is rife in them. In Gorta, there are two tribes—one with an affinity to land and one with water. In Gorta, they say the stones themselves are hungry. When a Gortan comes across a Draci, they allow their lands to feast upon their muscle and strength. Many Draci are wraithlike creatures, wandering the luscious plains of Gorta."

"That's horrific," Skiron exclaimed, his brow drawn.

Jess looked at the revulsion on his face and felt as if she understood his reaction. To a Seelie, there was nothing more magical than the flora and fauna of their world. She felt as a shifter a similar feeling about Earth. Its forests and open spaces like the national parks she'd always loved. Like the sanctuary she and Matteo had enjoyed recently. And here were the Fomors tarnishing that beauty by making the land something deadly. Something that actually *consumed* one of its races.

"What about the Draci?" Astra asked, leaning forwards, asking about the Gortan's rival tribe. In fact, all their attention honed, morbid curiosity making them hang on Erika's every word.

"The Draci drag Gortans into waterways, washing away their memories. They distill those memories and sell them. It's a ravenous world. I didn't stay long."

No kidding.

"Tell them about the whole worlds." Sunny's voice sounded behind Jess for the first time. So, Erika had shared something of this with him first. Unease wound through her as Jess considered that sharing hadn't seemed to fix the obvious tension between them. In fact, Sunny's tone had a definite bite to it.

Erika said, "I've been to Gorio, inhabited by a people who do not sleep: the Grigori—those who are awake. They have golden wings, similar to the fae. They are a people who love the sky and the high places of their world. They have outlawed travel to worlds affected by the Fomors. In Vrasi, inhabited by the Iyan warriors, they outlaw travel to conquered worlds, too."

Nervousness beat through Jess as she digested this. She hadn't considered that other worlds might outlaw travel to other realms. She wondered how the witch was received in such places. Had she shared with other races where her home world was? Certainly not in Gorio or Vrasi she supposed, if travel to conquered worlds was outlawed.

Erika continued, "But what I've never come across in all my travels was a race that had *come back* from the division the Fomors wrought."

"But our races haven't come back from the division wrought," Rune said. "The Unseelie and Seelie are very much still at war."

"As are the covens and clans," Jess added.

"But Alba and Silva *have* returned," Erika said. "The first glimmerings of a unified world, of unified *worlds*, is evident right here." She glanced around at the group. "A descendant of a Rom and Rem." Her gaze brushed over Jess then strayed to Matteo and his clasped hand in Jess's. "A Rom and Rem together; an Unseelie and Seelie together. A Storm-born re-furnished with her long-lost form. And ex-vamps returned to humanity's ranks."

Jess felt for the second time through Erika's spoken words what a wonderful thing their group was. Through their age-old love, Jess and Rune *had* returned. Albeit changed. But they still sat together, united in their regard and desire to save their worlds and people. Alongside an ancient ally—a Storm-born—they'd managed to bring back from the brink of destruction for the second time. What seemed like a simple gathering of friends was so much more. There was her heritage, a wonderment in itself. The result of a Rom and Rem overcoming their enmity and falling in love. A powerful thing that echoed in her and Matteo's newfound love. And then the Unseelie and Seelie who loved each other, no matter how *"unromantic"* Astra claimed to be. Jess had witnessed the longing and regard that she'd had when speaking about Skiron, his family, and home, and how thrown she'd been by the idea of losing Ski when it was planted in her head by the Enodian.

Erika addressed them all again. "I think that's all the information I can assist you regarding the Fomors. If there's anything else you'd like to ask me, be my guest, but I'm going to head off later today."

Jess startled. "You're not staying?"

"No. I came back to find out how you and Alba were restored. I think it's important that I have that information but it's time I got back home."

Everyone stared at the witch. Except for Sunny. Jess noticed that he'd gone utterly still. So this was the reason for his sharp tone earlier. He'd told Erika to tell them about the whole worlds she'd visited. One of which she called *home*. Where she was returning rather than staying to help them.

Jess's heart fell. It wasn't just information she'd hoped to get from Erika. She'd hoped the crystal the witch carried, which magnified her power, might strengthen the other Triodians power, too.

"Don't you want to help the coven you were raised as part of?" Jess asked.

"This isn't my world anymore," Erika answered without hesitation. "There are other worlds that I have spent many more centuries in than the few short decades I did here."

Sunny stepped away from the fire, walking away from the circle of sofas and moving to the far window.

Evidently, Sunny's confession about what he'd seen in the fetch hadn't been enough to repair what was broken between him and Erika. Jess felt a pang of sympathy. She knew Sunny was hardly the most deserving guy. In fact, recently she'd enjoyed beating the crap out of him when she'd discovered that he was the informant who had enabled Fern to capture her. But even with the war looming over them, she couldn't help wishing everyone could be as happy as she was. With Matteo's hand still in hers, an undertone of warmth hummed through her. And right now that warmth even extended to Sunny.

"But I hoped that crystal that magnifies your powers might help the Triodia Coven at large," Jess pressed, holding Erika's brown gaze.

"The witch with the magic crystal, eh?" Erika commented dryly.

Astra giggled.

"It's called thokkal—sky-melted iron—from Thokcha," Erika clarified.

"Another world you've been to?" Rune interjected.

The witch shook her head. "I've never been there, but I have a Thokkian friend, Micha Xi, who gave me the sky-melted iron. Thokkians believe the iron was sent to them by the gods. They are a mighty race of warriors who seem like gods in the strength of the magic they wield. But I can't stay and teach you to wield it. As I mentioned earlier, my home world outlaws travel to conquered worlds. I can't risk staying here too long."

"It's Kemdo, isn't it?" Astra said. "It's that delicious cran," she suggested to the witch, "you just can't get enough of it."

Ski bit back a laugh. "Don't play coy, you just want her to provide you with a lifetime supply of ligue."

Astra groaned and shut her eyes. "Too soon, Ski."

Jess knew the fae were trying to diffuse the tension, but disappointment thrummed through her.

She exchanged a glance with Rune. Erika's leaving was a blow, but it *didn't* change their plan. Rune nodded, telling her to share with the others what their plans were to protect their worlds.

"Well," Jess announced, "I'm going to visit Triodia's headquarters before Eventide today to call the Triodians, Roms, and the rest of the Rems to Umbra to stand against the enemy. I'm going to portal all of the ancient groves belonging to the Cathedral into Seelie lands. With access to such potent Earthen energy, I'll be able to use my death dust to untether Mara's iron-tinged from her and the Unseelie, like I did with the few hundred sluagh I did from Theo—"

"Wait. What?" Erika interrupted. "Sunny, you didn't tell me Jess untethered *hundreds* of sluagh." The witch's penetrating stare flew back to Jess, "How long did that take you?"

Sunny whipped around at the window, his frown indicating his confusion, but alertness settled over him as he watched Erika again.

Jess shrugged. "Not more than five minutes, I'd say, and I didn't have that much Earthen energy to draw from. With my ancient woods in Umbra, I could likely untether many more in that time." She forced herself to sound surer than she felt.

If something about untethering many sluagh quickly had impressed Erika and gotten her interested in fighting alongside them, then she'd talk up her skills, even if she hadn't had a chance to test them much yet.

Erika watched her with startling intensity for a moment, then fixed Rune with her stare. "Perhaps, there is *more* we can do. With your powers, Alba, keeping the enemy occupied in Umbra, Jess could go to the root of the problem."

Both Jess and Rune stared in bemusement.

Realizing they didn't have a clue what she meant, Erika explained, "That water that I spoke of in the world of the Fomors is mostly comprised of souls. Of divisive magic. Think of what your magic, Jess—that can untether the divided souls from those who have dominated them—might do if taken down to the Ones Below. If the energy of all that soul magic was moved on from those pollutant waters, the Fomors would fall, and with them draw out all the divisive energy they'd sown into conquered worlds."

Matteo's hand tensed in Jess's as he realized what the witch was proposing: Jess to infiltrate the enemy's territory. Her thumb stroked Matteo's. A habit she'd picked up from him. Throughout the night, he'd had a cute way of running his thumb over hers as if holding hands wasn't enough.

Jess swallowed the lump in her throat. "You want me to go into the enemy's kingdom and push on all the souls in the Below?"

The witch nodded.

Alarm tore through her. The memory of Erika's description of the Below filled Jess's imaginings. And her own memory of seeing that jelly-like creature through the pool beneath the Iron Keep, feeding on the iron-tinged sluagh, sent ripples of panic through her.

Maybe I hyped up my skills a tad.

"And while you infiltrate the Below, I could magnify my power over the death dust with the Thokkal iron," Erika said. "I can also teach your Triodians—certainly those with a strong connection to the dead—to wield that energy against the enemy ranks, giving you yet more troops who could fight the iron-tinged." Her tone had taken on fervor.

Jess blinked at the intensity that had come over the witch. Why was she all for fighting the enemy now?

But Rune interjected forcefully, "This isn't what Jess and I planned. We will fight the invading army together. I will harness the storms and riverways and break the enemy's ranks. While Jess releases the iron-tinged, as well as untethering the Storm-born within the Unseelie ranks." Rune's black eyes bore into Jess with confidence.

Erika retorted. "And you'll likely expel the enemy's armies from your worlds, but for how long? Do you think they'll stop in trying to reclaim your worlds? The Fomors are a poison, infecting and growing ever stronger the farther they spread."

Jess held the witch's idea in mind, looking it over from different angles, and, theoretically, thinking through exactly what she meant by moving on this poison from their worlds and others. "By untethering and pushing on all divisive magic, you mean that all those who have tethered iron-tinged, sluagh, or Storm-born—any Enodians or Unseelie that have tethered another soul–"

"Would die," Erika finished.

Shocked silence flooded the room. Unease prickled over Jess's skin. It seemed one thing to plot and plan to meet their enemy on the battlefield. But what the witch proposed was more like Enodian soul warfare. And the magnitude of it struck Jess. All Enodians, all Unseelie, and other peoples in other worlds who had tainted their souls by tethering another would *die*. Jess's stomach roiled.

A great cleansing.

"Those who have tethered another's soul are beyond redemption," Astra said evenly.

Jess's gaze flicked to her friend. Astra's rigid look told her that she was suppressing the emotion that was buried deep, deep down. Because the fae's parents—yes, those who she barely knew —were part of that group she condemned.

Eilea's steady voice seconded the fae's, "I agree. There's no coming back from stealing a part of another."

Jess didn't know how long the Storm-born in their midst had

been tethered to the Unseelie she was bound to. But her look and unyielding voice embodied what they all knew: some acts were unforgivable.

That question that Jess and Rune had spoken about while battle planning, and that she had discussed with Matteo when recounting those plans, drummed through her head. If they succeeded in defeating the enemy forces, what would they do with the survivors? With this plan, there would be none. And there shouldn't be. Couldn't be. The quiet seemed to grate at Jess, and she had the sense that they were each considering this notion.

With the dangerous plan Erika was suggesting, Jess needed to understand the witch's motivation entirely. She knew this wasn't going to be easy for the witch or Sunny, given their history. She was uncertain of what truths they'd shared, but Jess forced herself to ask for Erika's full story,

"If you're not fighting for our worlds' survival, which world are you fighting for? Which is it that you love?"

The witch's brown eyes widened slightly, and her fingers strayed to the feather on her neck. Jess banked that whatever world she'd gotten that tattoo in and those furs she hadn't changed out of was the same world.

"Vrasi," Erika said quietly. "The first whole world I came to after leaving Earth. I met Phyrra there, an Iyan warrior who fixed something in me I thought was broken forever. I learned in Vrasi, too, of how Earth had been divided by the Fomors' invasion. That I came from what Vrasi saw as a dying world. Phyrra used to say that I would find a way to save Earth." Her lips twitched. "Towards the end of her life, she got blunter and told me I needed to go back to my world, even if I couldn't save it. That my framing of world walking as adventure and exploration wasn't the truth, that deep down, I knew I'd always be running away from my past if I didn't return to my home world." She took a deep breath. "It's her memory I honor by returning. It's for the sake of

Vrasi that I wanted to know what could heal a conquered world. It's for the Iyans I'll stay and fight. Because if the enemy ever targeted Vrasi, I know I'd never forgive myself for passing up this opportunity to stop them."

Silence flooded the room as everyone contemplated her words.

It was Astra who broke it. "And I suppose these Fomors won't bat an eye at Jess if she goes swanning into their kingdom?"

"That's more than we can hope for," Erika said. "We'd need to wait until the enemy invades Umbra to give you the best chance of penetrating deep enough into the Fomors' lands. But I think if we trust in a suitable disguise for you all, you'll go unnoticed for longer." As Astra frowned, the witch added, "There are Unseelie units who have gone with their queen to the kingdom Below, an Unseelie leading a *prisoner* wouldn't look out of place."

"A prisoner?" Matteo probed, the edge in his voice telling Jess he didn't like this idea one bit.

"Remember, I mentioned there was another world I'd been to that had been fractured by the Fomors. It's a place called Yin. The Suang are nature spirits that gift favors to its people. The guise of a *wolf* isn't uncommon amongst the Suang of the forests."

"Why do I feel like the Suang don't get a happy ending any more than the Gortans do?" Ski interjected.

"Their rivals, the Yingan, hunt them, skinning them of their coats and thereby obtaining the favors they would bestow," Erika said. "A bound white wolf—a Suang—led by an Unseelie through the kingdom of the Fomors would not look out of place. Especially," she added, her gaze straying to Eilea, "if said Unseelie were riding a *tethered* pucca."

Eilea's fixed gaze regarded the witch before veering to Jess. "If my presence can help, I'll come with you, Jess."

"Thanks," Jess said. Yet, she *was* surprised that the Storm-born would put herself in harm's way so readily to help a group of people she knew so little about. But as she felt the tension emanating from Matteo beside her, she couldn't help noticing Rune's taut body language, and the fact that his black stare was very much centered on Eilea now. Something had happened between the pair of them, Jess was sure of it. At least, if it hadn't yet, she was sure Rune *wanted* it to. Despite the mounting tension with battle plans becoming more complicated, once again happiness stirred through her.

Holy Crap, I'm getting as bad as Astra Rainbow.

Astra called Jess's attention to her. "Count me in then. I'm your wing woman too."

Ski chuckled. "Yeah, literally."

Jess grinned at the pair. Only Astra Rainbow could be unfazed by the prospect of infiltrating an enemy kingdom.

But Rune's forceful tone dominated the room again. "This is absurd. Jess, in the deep past this is how the enemy was able to weaken us—because we left our world. We should remain in Umbra and fight the Fomors and Mara together as planned."

Behind the anger in Rune's voice and black stare, Jess detected the desperate imploring note.

"Rune and I need to discuss some things in private before we come to a decision on this," Jess said. "How about you guys all go get some breakfast and we meet back here in a couple of hours?"

Rune relaxed visibly.

Erika frowned but with a nod agreed. Astra and Ski were quick to vacate their sofa. She suggested to him, "We could get a round in in the arena before eating?"

"I'm going to go see your dad and Piera," Matteo said, claiming Jess's attention, "tell them about portaling to the Triodia this afternoon."

She smiled. "Thanks. Can you ask Dearbhla if she'll come too? I want her to reach out to the other Rem."

He nodded. His dark eyes told her he had a hundred other things to say but that they'd speak about them soon.

In this way, Jess and Rune found the room quickly vacated, and the two of them were left alone.

Jess felt a weird mix of relief that she and Rune could chat about everything, but the suddenly emptied room made her feel the loss of their friends.

Rune frowned. "I don't like this plan, Jess. It puts an unfair amount on your shoulders."

Jess shook her head. "You heard Erika. We'll only be able to infiltrate the Fomors' kingdom once it's emptied of its armies. There'll be plenty to do here too."

"But should we really be trusting Erika? We know so little about her. And what if her information about the Fomor kingdom is wrong? Does she even know enough to allow you, Astra, and Eilea to penetrate it safely?" Rune asked.

Under the barrage of questions, Jess found it hard to know which to answer first.

"If we proceed with this plan," Jess said, "Erika will have to go through everything step by step. She'll have to lay out what we can expect entering the Fomor kingdom. She spoke of needing to penetrate to its heart. We'll find out why. We'll talk about what dangers we have to avoid. A prickle of apprehension shot down Jess's spine as once more that jelly-like creature—Fomor spawn Erika had said—swam through her thoughts.

Rune looked bereft as he said, "But that's just it, it won't be *we*, it'll be *you*."

There was so much feeling written in his black eyes. In his taut expression. Her heart felt bruised as she considered how much he'd lost. Saw how it was the fear of losing more to the enemy that had him pushing back against this plan. Wasn't that why he'd thrown out that comment about them sticking together in Umbra? After all, Rune knew as well as she did that her power wasn't tied to Umbra anymore.

But she forced herself to speak the truth, "The very fact that I can leave Umbra, that my power's tied to Earth and to the

Between now, is an advantage, Rune. What if this is what we need? What if I can push on all that divisive energy into Oblivion?"

Rune sighed. But he didn't argue. The seriousness that bathed his face showed he was contemplating this new angle.

"And as for trusting Erika. The way she spoke about Vrasi is how I feel about Earth and you—"

"Feel about Umbra," Rune finished, a resigned look on his face.

What Jess now felt for Earth was staggering. She knew she belonged there with her whole being. To be honest, she already missed it, and it had only been a morning since she'd left. She'd always want the best for Umbra: for those she loved here, Rune and Astra, but it wasn't the place where she felt most complete, where she and the person she loved most belonged. And despite it being a tall order for today's agenda, part of her buzzed at the thought of going to the Triodia, to her most ancient woods, to rally the Earthens to her.

She felt her magic itching beneath her skin at the prospect of standing in the Cathedral again. Where her magic was strongest. She wondered what power she'd be able to channel with such a potent source.

She thought of what she'd got Sunny to agree to when she'd beat him in the arena a few weeks ago. That he'd come with her and help explain Alba and the vamps' history. He would be the voice of Silva as it were. Despite all he'd done in the past, Jess felt a pang of sympathy for how cut up he'd looked in here earlier.

"Besides, if we go down this route, it means Sunny's got a chance to fix whatever he's messed up," Jess suggested slyly.

Rune's eyebrows shot up. "Seriously, the fact that this plan might help Sunny's love life get back on track is meant to make up for the amassing mortal peril?"

Jess shrugged but grinned. "What can I say, I'm feeling sappy."

Rune's lips twitched. "You do seem less fidgety."

Jess laughed. She couldn't help drawing attention to the obvious developments in Rune's love life. "So, you *totally* have a type."

At Rune's confused expression, Jess tried to do Astra's waggly eyebrow thing despite knowing she sucked at it. "Shapeshifters, eh?"

Color crept over Rune's face. But the mixture of nerves and hope was clear in his expression. "Eilea's been here for me far more than I deserve."

"We gods sure have a poor view of ourselves, don't we? Don't you think we both need to work on our self-image?" she joked.

"You're right—a few golden idols about Umbra wouldn't look amiss, would they?" he quipped.

Jess chuckled as she saw the effects of Eilea working their charm on Rune's spirits already. And, as impossible as it had once seemed, they actually whittled away far too much of the morning making bad jokes about their separate love lives, only managing to rein it in when the others returned.

19

THE HEALING GLADE

Fern Trever stood on the outskirts of the blackened grove of the Cathedral. Here the tree-lined corridor near the library had only received superficial damage. Enough of the Great Goddess's magic pulsed in the trunks and boughs of yews to portal anywhere on Earth. Yet, Earthen energy alone wouldn't get Fern to Umbra. Portaling to Umbra required the Depths or Heights.

Not long ago, the High Witch wouldn't have deviated from the protocol for portaling to Umbra, proceeding to the Heights of Eurosky Tower with a Seelie. But she didn't have time for protocol. Nor the inclination to worry about upsetting the delicate sensibilities of other Triodians. She knew when she poured the wine, already nestled in the nook of roots nearby, that some standing guard around the courtyard would look upon her with judgment. But the spirits drawn by the offering, and mingled with her Earthen magic, would give enough potency to open a portal to Umbra. By using the spirits to guide her through the Between, she could get to Umbra under her own steam. And most importantly, *without* King Imber's knowledge.

Because Imber's hiding things.

Imber had given her enough Seelie troops to veil the Triodia's institutes from humans and to glamour the infuriating ex-vamps. But his information had been paltry of late. He'd affirmed that he'd heard the same rumor from Unseelie that had reached Fern: the queen had *gone* somewhere. But Imber claimed not to know where. Or why.

Bullshit.

There were too many whispers about happenings in Umbra. The latest Fern had heard by stationing her own Triodians to eavesdrop on the Seelie glamouring the various institutes was the rumor about transformation; the Seelie had spoken of the pucca being transformed by Umbra's winds into *human-like* forms. Talk that now caused unrest through the ranks of Triodians and Roms. What if they decided to uproot and go to Umbra themselves in search of a solution to the Enodian threat? Fern couldn't afford to lose *one* soldier. Yet, even with every Triodian and Rom soldier here, she knew that if the Enodians were to attack, they had little chance of survival.

The open-aired glade in the middle of the cathedral was as black and ravaged as the night Theodore of Enodia had burned it down. A constant reminder of what was waiting to happen to all of them—the last of the Triodia—if she didn't find answers. Soon.

The fading day couldn't disappear quickly enough. But as Fern continued to wish the day away, a tingling of magic pervaded the center of the main courtyard. The blackest section. The dead section. There wasn't enough Earthen energy for it to be an Earthen portal.

Fear pounded through Fern.

It can only be...

A prickle of more potent death energy tingled over her skin.

This is it.

The Enodians were portaling into headquarters. The Triodian guards, the hundred who had been stationed, interspersed with the hundred Roms in wolf form, felt it, too. Howls punctured the air, the Roms sounding the alarm to all the other Triodians and Roms within the building.

So, this is our final stand.

Sweat prickled along Fern's brow, its cold touch sliding down her back. Dread threatened to run rampant. She waited for the sulfurous stench to descend, for the soulfire of the Enodians' sluagh hordes to permeate the pale afternoon. Vehemence and horror twisted through the High Witch as she anticipated the ghastly glow of tethered para souls.

Instead, two black wolves morphed into the courtyard. Only the whites of their eyes and teeth contrasted with the ravaged black ground.

Roms.

Between the two, a human form manifested. Pale hair, complexion, and eyes, but clothed in black.

Jessica Remus.

Then *white* wolves portaled in next. Lots of them.

Fern glared at Jessica. She hadn't expected the end to come in the guise of this brazen girl. But, perhaps, she shouldn't have been surprised: Jessica *had* concealed Theodore of Enodia's evil. Through her concealment, the girl had allowed him to usurp the role of High Mage of Enodia and would be the downfall of Earth's paras. The Roms around the Triodians held their wolfish forms, their flattened ears and crouched bodies telling how they felt cornered in their den. More Roms were gathering in the corridors, answering the howled summons. Triodians flocked into the courtyard, most with their scians already in hand.

Then a fae form morphed from out of the portal: King Imber. As well as the Seelie King, a tall, golden-haired human who looked familiar joined the gathering in the blackened glade. A flash of recognition shot through the High Witch. The golden-haired human was the vampire—or ex-vampire—Greine, who had shared the true story about Jessica's divided heritage. Betrayal pierced Fern as her eyes hardened on Imber. The Seelie king *had* lied to her. He'd said he knew nothing about the reason the vamps had returned to humanity's ranks. And here he was in the company of this mysteriously ancient ex-vamp as well as Jessica Remus, who had used *spirits* to portal into Triodia's headquarters.

At Jessica's command, the wolves around her all morphed into their human forms. Fern recognized Matteo and Piera Romulus who Jessica stood between, as well as Dearbhla Remus. Were their human forms supposed to make their portaling into Triodia's headquarters less aggressive? The feral glint in their eyes couldn't hide the beast beneath their skin.

King Imber's steely voice jolted Fern. "By the Heights and Depths, tell your people to stand down. *My* people currently protect your institutes and sacred forest, Fern, wouldn't you say attacking me and my friends is inadvisable?"

Begrudgingly, Fern gestured to the hundreds of assembling troops lining the courtyard and surrounding hallways to be at ease.

Imber's clear voice carried around the destroyed glade. "The time is right for you to know the reason for the vampires' return to humanity and the reason their memory cannot be permanently erased."

Jessica Remus stepped forwards. "My blood *was* that which could heal the divide."

Anger shot through Fern: Jessica Remus had waltzed in here to tell them what they already knew? Jessica *was* the one who could have healed the divide, could have saved the covens, clans, and courts, but hadn't. Most infuriatingly, the girl's words captured Fern's troops' attention. The High Witch felt it like a change in air temperature as though a storm gathered.

The dangerousness of this girl, of her affecting Fern's troops, forced the High Witch to find her voice. "You admit that you could have healed the Between, could have unified the covens, clans, and courts, but, instead, joined with Theodore of Enodia?

You are, indirectly, responsible for bringing the Triodia and Roms to the brink of extinction."

Jessica looked completely unaffected by the accusation, her voice sounding calm. "The divide prophesied to be healed with my blood was never the Between. It referred to the fractured Umbran *gods*. The gods who shattered when they first portaled to Earth. One of whom, Alba, became the first vampire."

The first vampire was a god? What nonsense is this girl speaking?

The golden-haired ex-vamp stepped forwards and said, "You knew, Fern, that the oldest vampires had *something* different about them from the majority. The Triodia had teams of mages and witches studying those captured from nests to try to understand what made them different."

There *had* been Triodian units whose job it had been to analyze the blood of the vamps captured from destroyed nests. Teams of witches and mages had endeavored to understand the calmness that the older scourge seemed to develop with age.

Fern's gaze flicked to Greine, remembering the wonder and terror she'd felt as he'd spoken to her about the Eventide prophecy. His awareness of the Triodia's history, of their most secret documents about the prophecy, had seemed to imply that he'd been around *since* the Great Divide. Over two hundred millennia ago, when the first Enodians were said to have conjured the Night and Netherworld and cleaved the coven, clans, and courts in two.

The High Witch's palms grew clammy, shock and ... a dawning tide of understanding ringing through her, making her re-examine the past. When the first Enodians were said to have conjured the Night and Netherworld, the dark god and goddess ... What if they had never conjured them? What if the fae gods had portaled to Earth like Jessica said and fractured?

Fern's brown eyes hardened on Greine. "If you are the first vampire, Alba, why did *you* want to sacrifice Jessica to the

Between then? And why did you say that the Triodia's goals had aligned in the past with vampires?"

"Before, when I was a vampire, *part* of Alba's consciousness was in me," Greine said. "I was motivated by the god's need to restore Silva. But the thing about being Alba, about having his consciousness after the Great Divide, was that he was fractured. He didn't *know* what had happened during the Great Divide. *That* we only ascertained recently, when Rune—another Alban heir—was made feeling by Jess's blood and reunited with his shadow self in Umbra."

King Imber piped up. "Umbra—the Shadowlands—is known for the shadows that imbue all of its life with magic. It is its core essence, just as on Earth, Earthen energy is yours. Most of you will have heard rumors of the tales of the fetch in my lands: the mists that pilgrims say show their deepest truths. The Fetch was Alba's shadow self, thrown into the Heights during the Great Divide."

The words landed like blows on Fern. The scourge had been imbued with unnaturally long life, not because they were a *blight* on the para world, but because they had been fragments of a *god's* consciousness. Those vampires that the Triodia had bound by blood oaths to them. These were the beings who kept coming back to the Triodia. The Seelies' glamour that wiped away their memory of the para world, coming undone every Eventide.

Greine spoke again. "I, too, misinterpreted the Eventide prophecy. All the vampires did. I did awful things in pursuit of fulfilling the prophecy. My machinations affected generations and ruined countless lives."

Fern's stomach squirmed as she thought of Triodia's reformation and rehabilitation bill. She thought of her predecessors. Of how many High Witches and Mages had been determined to reform Enodians all to bring about progeny born from an Enodian and Triodian. Only a few babies had been born from such unions over the centuries. But that handful had all been

THE HEALING GLADE 185

innocent blood. Innocent blood spilled to the Between. By the Triodia.

Fern felt the ramifications of this revelation running through her like tremors. The High Witch's gaze swung to Jessica Remus again: the girl whose blood had healed Rune. Whose blood had healed *Alba*. Memories of that night she'd tried to sacrifice this girl to the Between surged through her. She remembered that feeling of connection to Jessica. Fern had sensed so much Earthen magic flowing from the girl. She'd been so sure it was a sign from the Great Goddess that Jessica was the divided, the necessary sacrifice. But now as her eyes roved the girl, she wondered whether she had sensed the goddess's magic in Jessica because...

"Does that mean you are—"

"Silva," Jessica finished. The statement was as clear as her crystal eyes.

Fern's legs shook beneath Jessica's pure gaze.

I cut open Silva...

Fern clenched her fists, her knuckles turning white as she shook her head against the memory.

"Before my power was shattered during the Great Divide," Jessica continued, "I created the two original wolf shifters. But even those new creations, the sentinels of my power, were affected by the darkness that splintered all races: *gods*, clans, covens, and courts. It wasn't until one shifter of each clan came together that I could be reborn."

Fern shuddered as she realized that the very thing that had brought about a suitable vessel for Silva's return—the pairing of a Rom and Rem—was something she'd recently publicly condemned. The High Witch felt the swathe of black wolves surrounding the courtyard with a new prickle of awareness.

"And just like Rune—Alba—my counterpart," Jessica continued, "it wasn't until I reclaimed my shadow self in the Depths— more commonly known as the Sidhe by the fae—that I was fully restored."

So, this was the riddle to the death energy Fern sensed around Jessica. The way Jessica's—*Silva's*—power worked. It was how she'd used the power of the dead to portal in here. Like a Triodian witch or mage of old, the Great Goddess rang with both the light and the dark. With both life and death.

Jessica looked around at the Roms within the ranks of the Triodians. "And when I buried my seed magic within Romulus and Remus, my magic altered. My essence became Earthen. Today, I return to you, every part of me the Earthen goddess you have worshipped for centuries."

"You have come to defend your sacred grove from the Enodians," Fern exclaimed with hope.

"No." Jessica's lips quirked before she added, "I have come to ask for *your* help, High Witch. To come to Umbra. I ask for the help of *all* the paras of Earth. The same threat that fractured us Umbran gods, and all the para races of the Shadowlands and Earth, threatens us again.

"For the same dark magic that Queen Mara has encouraged in her court and that the Enodians wield, that originates from the ancient enemy that caused the Great Divide, threatens again. Queen Mara has returned to the world of our ancient enemy, the Ones Below—the Fomors—and this very moment swells her forces with theirs, readying to do harm to our worlds."

Fern's ire grew as she listened to Jessica. King Imber had concealed the fact that Queen Mara was becoming a greater threat. And now these... *Umbrans* deigned to come to her and her forces demanding help?

Rankled, the High Witch said, "If you, and Alba, and the fae," she added, looking at Imber, "are responsible for *causing* the Great Divide by portaling here, isn't it your responsibility to fix it, not ours?" Rage crept over her as she once more thought of how her gut had always told her that the fae *were* invaders. And they had invaded Earth. They had been the ones to cause Earth's coven to fracture.

Imber came forwards. "*We* have a responsibility to unite, Fern. We, in positions of leadership, have allowed this cycle of destruction to go on and on, pitting brethren against brethren. For too long, we have fought the enemy on our own soil, without truly exploring the way that each of our races was similarly affected by the Great Divide. The true enemy that fractured our courts, covens, and clans is about to rise anew. We need to unite if we are to defeat it or all of Umbra and Earth will be plunged into a second greater darkness than before."

Fern's gaze grew flintier as she contemplated Imber's words. Wasn't it *fitting* that his people would fight when it was *his* lands that needed protecting? Where had he been as the different Triodia branches had fallen one by one to Enodia until all they'd been left with was the Cathedral in which they stood?

"The Fomors feed off of destructive acts," Jessica said. "We need *all* of you to come together just as we have." She looked around at those gathered nearest her, and Fern took them in properly. Two fae, an Unseelie and Seelie, stood with hands clasped. Dearbhla and Matteo, one dark-haired, the other pale: a Rem and a Rom, another contrasting pair. Then the dark-haired, female Rom who stood beside Jessica, pale-haired and eyed, presented another striking sight.

The female Rom, Piera Romulus, Alpha Giovanni's daughter, spoke for the first time. "My sister, Lady Silva, will not demand your allegiance. Although she is both the mother of all shifters and the descendant of both clans, she will not command you. She will not taint herself with the divisive magic that the Fomors planted into our races when they invaded. Where the blood command and oaths stem from. She is giving you all the same choice she gave her own clan, to choose whether to fight with us and protect our world and loved ones."

Another jolt went through Fern as she ruminated on the blood bonds—the very blood oaths that they'd used over the blood-sworn scourge to keep them bound to the Triodia. The blood oath that she'd gotten the Roms surrounding her to swear to her, transferring their allegiance from their blood traitor of an Alpha. Jessica and her group of allies were sullying all that had kept order within the ranks of the Triodia.

Feeling the acute regard of the surrounding shifters and Triodian troops, Fern clutched at straws as she demanded of Jessica, "And what of our sacred grove? What of *your* glade, the most ancient heart of your power, already ruined by the Enodians? Are we to abandon it to them? Let them capture the last of our ancient yews, pulsing with *your* magic, so they can root them in the sluagh-infested soil of their strongholds?"

"How about we take them with us?" Jessica suggested, an enigmatic smile on her face.

And with that, Jessica's magic pulsed. The Enodian scent of smoke ingrained in the burnt trunks and roots faded. The blackened Earth beneath their feet lightened, moss and lichen mottling the dirt and clambering up the roots of the trees now *healing*. The charcoal trunks seemed to breathe in the earthen energy flooding the glade, new bark forming. And where branches had been broken, they started to stretch out, reforming, until the open sky of the oculus was once more rafted with fresh growth.

The trees around Fern as she turned in awed contemplation seemed to sigh with contentment. And the High Witch's bright green dress whipped around her as she turned, trying to drink in as much as she could as the transformation occurred; the tree branches reaching and the roots sinking, above and below, declaring what her pride hadn't allowed before: their maker, their mother, their goddess, stood amongst them.

As the coven and shifters took in the sight of the new cathedral, housing the Great Goddess beneath its rafters, silence rang, the sound of hundreds of believers standing in awed contemplation.

I believe...

The Roms in the courtyard had their paws outstretched, their heads laid to the dirt; meanwhile, the witches and mages around the space went to their knees, their eyes lowered in reverence. The holy walls of the trees had never seemed so rich in fragrance or the prayer rug of moss so soft.

And the High Witch dropped to her knees, prostrating herself upon the moss alongside the rest of her coven.

20

CRYSTALS & COMMUNION

J ess sat by one of the Depths pools in the forest, bordering onto the Herba Terra. The Unseelie were barely patrolling their borders at the moment, having withdrawn their patrols to nearer the Iron Keep. In Queen Mara's absence, Erika had suggested that Jess spend some time in Unseelie territory to simulate an environment similar to the Fomor kingdom as much as possible. The deep portals throughout the dense Unseelie forests were the closest thing around to the watery chasms of the Ones Below. Paired with that, the Unseelie, some with iron-tinged sluagh tethered to them, gave Jess the chance to feel and commune with the sluaghs' divisive energy. That which the Below teemed with.

It had been four days since she'd healed the Cathedral of Silva and portaled it back to the Seelie Court. The ancient woods were now rooted along the riverbanks near the Sun Keep. Healing the trees in the Triodia's headquarters had been as easy as breathing for Jess. The magic within the Cathedral had reached out to her, recognizing her as part of it. The power running through her was the same as that that sang through the trees. So, she'd driven her magic through the destroyed roots, trunks, and boughs until they'd blossomed with new life.

Jess had added to the grove a few days ago, too. Veiling herself with her death dust, she had snuck into the grounds of Castle Nox again and portaled the stolen yew trees into Umbra. She still wished that she could have seen the look on Theo's face when he discovered the woods he'd stolen from the Triodia institutes gone. But Jess had fought the temptation to hang around Nox and confront Theo. She'd needed to get back here and begin her own preparation for the mammoth task ahead: penetrating the Fomor kingdom.

She'd spent the majority of the last four days exploring the Unseelie lands, drawn to areas that rang with divisive magic. She couldn't afford to raise the alarm by untethering the iron-tinged and Storm-born tethered to the Unseelie armies. But other discordant energy abounded through Mara's lands—wandering souls—Storm-born and human who lingered where they'd died. Centuries of warfare meant that the lands weren't exactly empty of the dead. Of course, there'd been no fae souls amongst those wandering. Any fallen fae had passed into the winds and waters of Umbra and become the faded.

Now, as twilight fell on the fourth day, Jess felt a sense of peace that thanks to her practicing, a few more souls had managed to move on into the Between. A prickle of anticipation stole through her as she observed the falling light. At Eventide, spirits were naturally drawn to the Between. She remembered all those months ago when she'd first been staying at Castle Nox, how she'd wondered at the sluagh being drawn to open portals. Now, she knew it was the Between calling to them. Their yearning souls longed to dissolve into it and travel into Oblivion.

Jess had gotten into the habit of opening a portal at Eventide, to focus on the dead in the Between. Over the last few days, she'd reached out so deeply into the Between that she'd felt the weave and weft of Earthen magic. On one side she'd had the sense of the feather-soft faded and on the other the whisper of branches.

The deeper she reached, the surer she felt about her task of moving on so many souls in the Below. But just as she was about to reach out to the pool before her, she felt the prickle of magic pouring from the waters.

Someone was portaling through.

Instantly, Jess yanked a veiling over herself with her death dust.

At the sight of dark braided hair and the tattooed temple, Jess's quickening heart slowed.

"I needed a break from the Triodians," Erika explained as she emerged from the portal.

Erika had kept to her agreement and was training Fern and a handful of the Triodian coven to magnify their power with the Thokkal iron. She'd allowed the Seelie metalsmiths to melt down the iron and forge rings for the witches and mages.

Jess's thoughts stagnated on Fern. For all the Triodian order that Fern had supposedly upheld, the High Witch had cultivated an abundant following of lingering spirits, similar to Erika's. Fern said that her ancestors from Mexico had always respected Dia de los Muertos—the Day of the Dead. She'd spoken of her practice of carrying sweet cakes and wine to coax the dead to her when she wanted to strengthen her Earthen magic. Jess hadn't hidden her disdain that Fern would practice such magic in secret while preaching that only *Earthen* magic should be practiced in the Triodia at large.

Yeah, Jess didn't envy Erika's task of working alongside Fern. But they needed all the troops they could get. Through Sunny's Unseelie contacts—those who he'd borrowed the tethered Storm-born from—he'd heard that it was rumored the Enodians would be joining Mara's armies when they invaded Umbra. Anger seared through Jess. In a way, she wished she could be here on the battle-field and shred the souls from Theo's. Yet, she smothered her frustration down. If she succeeded on her mission in the Fomor kingdom, Theo's, and all the other Enodian and Unseelies' divisive magic would be purged from Umbra and Earth.

Erika drew out a ribbon from her fur-lined pocket, tying it on the nearest hebena tree. Jess had a flash of an oak tree with ribbons fluttering in the breeze:

Fort Caylee.

Spending so much time around the Between and dead did have its drawbacks. Jess pushed away the melancholy sting of grief. "What are you doing?"

"A practice they have in Yin. The people dress the trees in the forests with ribbons, clothes, and food, asking the Suang for their heart's desire."

The Suang were the nature beings that Erika had spoken of—the disguise that Jess would be using when she went into the Fomors' kingdom. She'd be posing as a Suang who had been captured, a gift being escorted by an Unseelie from Queen Mara.

Most of the discussion Jess had had with Erika about infiltrating the enemy's kingdom had centered on logistics. Such as that Jess should stay in her wolf form as much as possible because the Suang commonly had darker complexions and hair than Jess in their human guise. The white dress that Jess now wore was part of her disguise, too. If she did need to transform into her human form in the Below, she'd at least be dressed in the style that the Suang commonly wore. It was day two of wearing one of the gods awful Seelie dresses, and it felt weird.

Jess watched in bemusement. "If I'm going to be in wolf form in the Below, how is understanding Suang rituals important?"

Erika didn't answer but continued to tie the ribbons upon each branch. Jess wondered at the care with which she fastened the tokens. She found herself almost believing that a Suang would step out from between the trunks of hebena trees to bestow a wish upon the witch.

Then, a scent pervaded the air: spicy, a bit like cloves, and a sweetness like cinnamon, which was when Jess realized the mate-rials Erika hung were infused with something.

A flutter of energy that marked dusk—Eventide—brushed Jess's skin. That feather-soft whisper that rang from the Depths, from Umbra's faded, made Jess's whole being tingle. The sensa-tion lapped against her, back and forth. Now that she could access her goddess's power over the Between, Umbra's magic didn't feel so strange against her. Not now that she knew that through the faded she could harness her death energy.

"I remembered that I had a few spices from some of the worlds I've been to," Erika turned around and explained. "I infused the ribbons with them. Hopefully, when you open the portal, the scent might bring some of the souls from those worlds."

The sight of the fluttering ribbons filled her with anticipation. So far, she'd only been able to practice moving on stray human and Storm-born souls into the Between.

Her heart climbed into her throat. Its pulse was all she could feel for a moment as her blood pounded through her temples. With a deep breath, Jess opened the portal.

At first, the breeze alone fluttered through the ribbons, but then, something else disturbed them.

Souls. One ... Two ... Ten...

They tore through the branches, slashing at the ribbons. They weren't human or Storm-born. But Jess wasn't afraid; these *were* souls and felt similar to the iron-tinged or the sluagh tethered to Theo. They ached with sorrow, not malice. Barely looking at Erika nearby, Jess reached out to them.

She quashed the worry worming its way through her at the idea of contact with these shades. They continued to rip out of the Between. There were dozens and dozens of them twisting through the material hanging from the trees now. And they kept coming. A constant stream of these souls poured out of the portal. As they whipped around the ribbons, Jess got the sense that they were caught in the strips.

She had an overwhelming feeling that something about them had been horribly *bound*. As she reached out with her essence to one, she got a flash of pain and deafening silence. She felt the way the being wanted to wail. To shout. To roar. But *couldn't*. Jess sensed the same blinding need that she had in the Sidhe. And in those souls tethered to Theo. To be free. To be unencumbered. For their surroundings to be boundless.

She reached out with her energy, and it was as if she roared into the Depths. She felt and witnessed the souls that had arrived with the evening sink back into the Between. And with her thunderous power, they dissolved, rushing on into Oblivion.

As Jess's magic fell away, she stood firmly beside the beribboned hebena tree, the sight of the still scraps making her glad. Calmness and a wonderful sense of happiness flooded her.

Erika's stunned gaze snagged hers. "I'm sorry. I didn't expect those souls. I only infused the ribbons with spices from Yin, Gorta, and Kemdo."

"Who were they?" Jess asked, curious about the souls she'd just set free. She was eager to deflect attention from herself, too, as a prickling sense of discomfort came over her at the witch's amazement.

"Souls from Eor, I think," Erika said, sounding a little breathless. "I've never been there, but the Eorosh use language to hold people to their oaths and promises. A twisted race, where nothing is frivolous about the tongue. Many have taken to living in silence. Some even cut their children's tongues out to avoid the treatment they would suffer from those who abuse the power of words too freely given. There are too many who delight in tricking others into swearing oaths that enslave them."

Jess felt the uncomfortable echo of their pain, the snarled feeling of their souls. Of being bound to another's will. And the oppressive sense of silence in others. So much anger had swarmed through them with no outlet. They'd longed to roar. Then the thunderous manifestation of Jess's power had given them the sound they'd craved.

Jess didn't ask whether it was a world where the Fomors had sown that division, or if it was a division that was innate to the Eorosh's own race. It didn't matter. It was divisive magic like this that the suffering souls existing in the Fomors' primordial pool oozed with; the long-suffering energy that Jess *would* likewise push on towards peace.

A dazed look still rested on the witch's face. "I've had centuries to master my power over the Between and still I can't do what you did."

"You can with the Thokkal iron," Jess said, thinking of what the witch had promised to do on the battlefield when Mara and the Fomors invaded: untether the iron-tinged and the Storm-born, alongside the Triodians she was helping train with the Thokkal iron.

The witch nodded. "True, but Thokkians say that iron came from their gods." Her gaze brushed Jess with significance. "But then you are an iteration of a goddess. You have *had* whole lifetimes to accumulate this power."

The witch's marvelling threatened to dampen the natural calm that Jess had achieved.

Not wanting to examine things too closely, Jess thought she'd call it a day. "I should go portal to Astra, Sunny, and the Storm-born."

Like Jess training in Unseelie land, Astra and Eilea were nearby, practicing their riding and flying within its borders. The idea being that if they did come across any Unseelie patrols, their disguise and manner of riding should allow them to pass without question. And if they managed to pass as an Unseelie and tethered Storm-born in Unseelie lands, then they should pass in the Fomor kingdom.

And Jess was able to sense Astra and Eilea. The more she'd

focused on detecting the souls in the vicinity, the more aware she'd become of individual energy signatures. She prepped to portal to them.

But Erika interrupted, "Sunny and Beinn are with them?"

Sunny and the other tethered Storm-born, Beinn, had decided to join Astra and Eilea today. The borders were barely being patrolled, and Sunny had decided there was minimal risk of them being spotted. He'd helped give Astra advice on correct riding etiquette as he'd been around the Unseelie for centuries. Having far more experience than the one-year Astra had in Unseelie lands.

"Yeah," Jess answered.

"The reckless fool," Erika muttered. The witch fidgeted with the Thokkal ring on her finger. Was she worried about the group drawing unwanted Unseelie attention and risking their disguise? Or was this concern for Sunny?

Yesterday, Erika had seemed unperturbed when Sunny had been sent back to Earth by Rune: to meet the Unseelie that he'd borrowed the Storm-born from. Sunny had successfully captured both Eilea and Beinn's Unseelie masters. The Unseelie were now prisoners in the Sun Keep. With Eilea being such an essential part of the plan to infiltrate the Fomors kingdom, they couldn't risk the rogue Unseelie summoning Eilea back at an inopportune moment. Surely, Sunny had been at risk on Earth, too, dealing with the rogue Unseelie?

Then again, yesterday when Sunny had agreed to go back to Earth, there'd been lots of them present: Rune, Jess, and the Storm-born. With only Jess present now, Erika didn't look half as composed as she ran her hand over the Thokkal iron on her finger. Was she trying to sense Sunny now—to check he was okay?

"Why did you leave Sunny behind when you world walked?" Jess blurted out.

She couldn't help her curiosity. After all, she knew what it was like to fall for an Alban heir. To love someone dangerous to you.

Before Rune had sworn the blood bond to Jess, part of him had wanted her dead. To sacrifice her to the Between. Similarly, when Sunny had met Erika, he'd endeavoured to bring about a relationship between her and the Enodian mage, Inis. In the hope that their union would produce the divided's blood. Hardly a romantic beginning, but, somehow, Erika had fallen for Sunny.

The witch's hand fell from the iron ring and her gaze met Jess's. "When I discovered there were other places besides Earth and Umbra, I hoped to convince Sunny to come. I knew he'd never relinquish his search for Silva, but I thought he'd agree that other realms might have answers.

"I never saw him, or vamps in general, the way he and the Triodia did. As something cursed. Yes, they subsisted on blood, but as long as one managed to control that craving without killing, what they had was a world of opportunity. What Sunny had seen—five hundred years on Earth—was a blessing, not a curse. So, when I discovered other realms, I naturally wanted to seize the opportunity of unlimited time to explore other worlds. But when I broke the latter part to Sunny, he wouldn't allow me to become a vamp. Eventually, he vowed that if I did the little love that was between us would die." A wry smile curved her lips. "There had never been much love on his side anyway. You know how it is—Alba is incapable of love except for the perpetual hunt for the seed magic and Silva. So, I became a vamp, and world walked alone."

"But didn't the fact that Sunny saw a vision of you dying in the fetch after you disappeared help a little?"

"The fetch?" Erika asked confusedly.

Oh Sunny, you really never can tell the truth, can you?

Realizing she couldn't backtrack now, Jess explained, "Sunny told me that after you vanished he went to Umbra to look for you. In the mists, he saw a vision of you being killed by your coven after they discovered that you'd become one of the scourge. Having recently learned that the fetch was Alba's shadow self, he reckons that it was *you* and *your blood* in his system that caused him to see it. He reckons he might even have managed to restore Alba that day, to merge with his shadow self in the mist, if he hadn't run from his deepest fear."

Judging by the abstraction on Erika's face, this was *all* news to her. Jess had the urge to shake Sunny the next time she saw him and demand what was the worst that could happen by telling the whole truth to Erika himself?

At the thought, Jess offered to portal a now thoroughly discombobulated witch along with her. Maybe she and Sunny could talk things out. But Erika shook her head, merely muttering something about seeing them back at the Sun Keep.

21

OPERATION SHADOW SILVA

"Where's Matteo?" Giovanni asked as Jess snuck into his room. Well, Piera's room. Their dad had taken occupation of it. Piera had moved into the one next door.

"Nice to see you too, Dad."

He chuckled. "Sorry, love. I just wanted to pick his brain on my latest idea."

Giovanni had paper and pencil in his lap. He was doing what he could from bed, thinking over battle formations and the like. Still mentally exhausted, Giovanni slept a lot, and unless Mara and the Fomors held off their invasion for weeks yet, it was unlikely he'd be fit for battle.

Dearbhla had been gracious and worked through plans with Giovanni for the shifters. Gratitude towards her second swam through Jess, for her unwavering loyalty, knowing that whatever latest plans were in front of him would have come from her second. Dearbhla had also managed to get the Rem to Triodia's headquarters. Where Jess had managed to onboard the rest of the clan. Thanks to Jess's second, they had the full force of shifters in Umbra now.

But Jess smiled knowingly at her dad as she slumped into the armchair beside his bed. *Really* his exclamation about where Matteo was, was likely him prying into how things were going between them. Last time she and Matteo had been back in the Sun Keep together, they'd visited Giovanni and told him the news that they were an item. Not that Jess and Matteo had been able to keep it under wraps. Even in her dad's company, she'd been unable to stop hugging Matteo or keep the massive grin from her face.

Giovanni seemed a lot more in favor of her latest boyfriend than her last. Although, her dad had had to admit his error in tarnishing Rune with the same brush as all the other vamps. In fact, he'd had to take back his words about vamps not being able to be trusted when he'd learned that Rune was Lord Alba. Not to mention the fact that Lord Alba had frequently visited Giovanni to check on his recovery. Rune had tried his healing powers on him. But the tiredness of mind and soul that Theo had left him with, would only be cured by natural rest. And so, the Rom Alpha had reluctantly adhered to bed rest. He'd taken more readily to the snacks that always seemed to be present. The plate on the bedside table was piled with ham and salami.

The click of the door sounded and Piera joined them. "I thought I heard you," she said, looking at Jess. "How was training today?" She flopped onto the bottom of their dad's bed, her chestnut stare piercing.

"All good. Erika had a few things from other worlds, so I got to push on souls from different realms."

"I'd love to have seen that," Piera said, leaning forwards to pinch a piece of ham from Giovanni's plate. Curiosity prickled over her delicate features and Jess knew from the past few days she was about to start quizzing her about the ins and outs of her new powers. Piera had been fascinated since she'd begun to explore her powers over the Between. But unlike Erika, who had referred to Jess's godhood and made her feel self-conscious about it, Piera had a knack of asking questions, without making her feel uncomfortable. In fact, often her sister's questions had led Jess to some helpful realizations. For instance, it was Piera's curiosity about Jess's sensing magic that had had her honing her skill to pinpoint individual energy signatures from a distance, such as Astra's. Something that might well prove useful in the Below.

"I'll see if Erika's got any more tokens from different worlds and you can come watch tomorrow if you like," Jess suggested, swiping a piece of ham from Giovanni's plate, too.

Their dad interrupted, "What I still don't understand is why Rune can't go instead—he's a *full* god."

Jess held back a sigh. She explained to Giovanni for what seemed like the millionth time, "Rune's absence would weaken Umbra. It's how Umbra and we gods fractured in the beginning. Whereas because my power is linked to Earth and the Between, my absence won't affect anything."

Giovanni frowned. "Yes, but once again you're putting yourself at risk. I don't like it, Jess. Neither does Matteo."

Jess's lips quirked. "I'd be pissed off if he did."

Piera laughed. "What's with the white by the way? Is this you keeping the peace with the clans? Black one day, white the next. Have you ever thought of just going grey and being done with it?"

Jess snorted. "Part of my uniform for infiltrating the Below. Apparently, female Suang wear white dresses."

"As do maidens for sacrifice," Giovanni griped, unwilling to leave off voicing his dislike of what Jess had signed up for. Now probably wasn't the time to mention that she hoped she wouldn't have to transform into her human form in the Below. Her outfit being the least of her worries with her pale complexion and hair in danger of giving her away.

Piera drew the battle plan away from her dad, examining the sketch and numbers. "Did you get Matteo's opinion?"

"Not yet," Giovanni said, his eyebrows drawing together as he once more fell into contemplating the plans before him.

Oh, he really does want Matteo's opinion. Perhaps I am too naturally suspicious.

"Why don't you go get him, Jess?" Piera said. Her voice was innocent, but Jess caught the gleam in her eye and the knowing smile about her mouth. So, Matteo had mentioned to her how little they'd seen of each other lately. Since the night they'd portaled the Triodia and shifters back to Umbra, there'd barely had any time alone. A few stolen kisses before inevitably being interrupted was all they'd managed.

Trying to keep her voice sedate, she agreed, "Sure. I'll be back soon."

Piera fought back a smile, rearranging her expression as Giovanni drew her attention to the diagram in front of him.

In the hall, Jess morphed into her wolf's form. Her ears twitching, eager to pick up on any sign of someone ahead. She didn't plan on wasting her sister's help and getting cornered by someone en route. Lately, it had felt as if everyone wanted to speak to her. Astra and Eilea often wanted to go through the plans for infiltrating the Below. Astra had needed Jess lately, too, to talk through her feelings. Something Jess certainly didn't begrudge her. She may have spoken in a stoic way about the Unseelie being irredeemable. But after a few glasses of bacae, she'd voiced to Jess her guilt about how their plan meant that she was, basically, killing her parents. It had taken time to convince her that she wasn't a bad person, and a few more berries to allow her to tolerate the sappiness of Jess assuring her that she, Ski, and all her friends here *were* her real family.

But tonight, luck was on her side, and as Matteo's door came into view, no one waylaid her. Morphing into her human form, she gently rapped on the door. Jess's heart charged in her chest as the door swung open. As soon as Matteo appeared in the doorway, Jess pushed her way in, shutting the door as quickly as she could.

With a sly smile, her gaze stole over Matteo. Barefooted, and dressed in a black T-shirt and jeans, he looked delectably laid-back, as though he'd been lounging in bed.

Where I'm about to get you back to.

Her hands roved up Matteo's chest, relishing that they were alone. She pressed herself against him, enjoying the evergreen of his aroma, feeling herself relax in an instant. His arms came around her, and she let out a contented sigh.

"You all right?"

"I am now," she replied, looking up at him with a smile. "I've been fantasizing about this all day."

He stroked her cheek, but his expression remained serious. "How did practice go?"

"Let's not kill the mood with death dust stuff," she whispered, pressing her lips to his. All they ever seemed to do with the few moments they snatched together was give status reports on magic and troop positionings. A flicker of the page her dad had been studying came to her. But, instead, she chose to recall Piera's teasing tone as she'd told her to *"go get him"*.

But instead of his lips answering her in the way she wanted, he drew back, a searching look on his face. "You know, you don't need to go to the Fomor kingdom. We'll find another way to defeat them."

She frowned. Apparently, her dad *hadn't* been kidding when he said Matteo wasn't happy about the plan either. As she took in Matteo's furrowed brow, she realized how worried he was. And it was hardly surprising. They'd barely had the chance to talk properly about things since concocting this plan that Jess would infiltrate the Below and will the stolen energy of souls onwards.

His brown eyes gleamed with concern. She took his hand and pulled him over to the bed, tugging him down beside her.

"I promise I wouldn't be doing this unless I thought I could," Jess said earnestly, holding his gaze. His hand was still in hers, and his thumb began to stroke her own, both arousing and comforting. "I pushed hundreds of souls onward today."

"I don't doubt it..."

Jess remembered the longing pulsing through those souls that had swept through her, tugging at her heart, making her *need* to release them earlier. "Besides, if there's a chance I can free all those souls from the Ones Below and give them the peace they deserve, I *want* to."

"And you're amazing for that," he said, affection swimming in his eyes. "It's just, it always seems as if you're running off to somewhere I can't follow. I wish ... I could be there with you."

He knew it was a stealth mission. That they couldn't afford another *captive* with them in the Fomor lands. As it was, an Unseelie going *away* from the battle in Umbra, leading a captive Suang, could definitely look suspicious. But as she took in Matteo's worried expression, it occurred to her that there might be a way of communicating with him while they were apart. Perhaps even in separate worlds. Because Jess's energy *could* traverse the Between itself. She thought of the bridge she'd formed over the last few Eventides—between Umbra and Earth. She should be able to reach out from the Fomor kingdom to Umbra in the same way. She should be able to speak to Matteo. Soul to soul. After all, just as she'd worked on sensing Astra to keep track of her in Unseelie territory, she'd traced the nuances of Matteo's soul enough to know it as well as her own.

"Maybe you *can* be with me ... in a way. Let me try something. Close your eyes."

He gave her a questioning look but followed her instruction.

With her death dust, she reached out, melding with the hues of Matteo's energy signature. *Fort Matteo?*

He started, his eyes flying open. "That felt very Enodian, Jess."

She rolled her eyes. "Don't be such a Triodian. Communicating through souls isn't dark magic. It's what you do with it that makes it so. Close your eyes again and reach out to me. Form the words in your mind and with me connected to you, I should hear you too."

He looked unconvinced but closed his eyes again. His features relaxed and heat pooled in her as she remembered his peaceful expression as they'd laid entwined together, breathing in each other's kisses and truths. His lips distracted her. She turned away from him. Not trusting herself to stay focused, she closed her eyes too.

Jess...? The musical lilt of his voice flowed through her head. *I don't know what to say. This feels very like I'm talking to myself—*

I'm here.

It's weird, isn't it?

No weirder than death dust.

Show off. His melodious tone permeated her. His usual scent, cedar, pine, and that undertone of nuttiness, wafted through her. As well as that, his voice made her feel warm like sunshine pouring through a forest canopy, heating her skin.

"So, I should be able to reach through the Between," Jess said aloud. Matteo opened his eyes, too. "Even from the Fomors' kingdom. Whenever I can, I'll reach out to you. I get that I'll be sneaking into the Below and you'll be fighting but—"

"You'll reach out to me," he answered. His gaze wandered over her with that look of devotion that instantly kindled that fire beneath her skin.

Curiosity flared through her as she wondered what her own voice evoked in this disembodied form of communication. Agitation stole in though: what if her scent was of smoke, of darkness ... and death? But if there was *anyone* she could ask who she didn't mind being vulnerable in front of, it was Matteo. She'd already bared herself completely by asking whether he could love her. And he *did*. She already had his love.

In a moment of clarity, Jess realized that she'd spent most of her life believing that people only ever interacted with you for what they could get. It's what her childhood had taught her. Being shunted from home to home, caregiver to caregiver, and that the only way to protect herself was by building walls around her that no one could climb. If they were high enough, then she'd never get hurt. But with a moment of breath-taking stability, she knew she never needed to build those walls again. Not with Matteo. It wasn't a transactional relationship. She had his love, unconditionally. So instead of feeling vulnerable, she reached out and wordlessly asked, *What does my voice smell like?*

Matteo laughed. *Before this conversation, I would have been totally stumped by that question, but I get what you mean. Your voice smells like resin, like sap from a tree. Warm and ambery. The same as your skin.* He moistened his lips, capturing Jess's gaze.

She knew exactly what he meant. Matteo's evergreen scent pervading her head was precisely the scent she'd tasted when kissing him. *You taste like summer in the forest,* she told him.

Jess had now entirely forgotten the purpose of this communication, feeling only what a turn-on it was to have his lilting voice in her head. She craved more and asked, *So, if my voice was a season?*

Christmas. He smiled. *Not a season per se, but you're spicy and sweet...*

Does that make me your Christmas present? Her pulse picked up a notch, her mind already imagining his forceful lips and ... teeth on her skin.

Matteo drank her in, and Jess felt very much like his gaze was *unwrapping* her. Everything that they'd buried for the last few weeks—no, *months*—surfaced in the way their eyes held each other. And the next moment, they collided. Hands, lips, tongues. Any restraint broke. There was no more reaching out through their souls. Only their bodies would do for this communication. Their mouths moved fiercely and abrasively, bruising their lips. The violent need Jess had felt in the cave slammed into her and she relished that—this time—their touch had no limits.

She climbed on top of Matteo, her dress pooling around her thighs and waist.

Okay, I might be able to get onboard with dresses.

But it was still too much material. Matteo clawed at it. Jess raised her arms as he tore it from her, her bralette following swiftly. With her breasts freed, he kissed and suckled them until his teeth grazed them, eliciting a gasp from her.

A spicy smile painted Matteo's face.

She savored the much rougher taste of his kisses. "Who's the savage now?" she murmured against his lips.

The heat flaring in his eyes was the only answer before his mouth consumed hers again, promising nothing but savagery. She scrabbled to liberate him of his shirt, melting into his bare chest as his skin against her pebbled nipples drove her wilder. Her heart raced violently as he brought her closer to him. His hands tracking the line of her hips, her waist, and up her back. All the while, their mouths devoured one another, sucking and savoring.

When Jess came up for air, she moved her assault to Matteo's ear, eliciting a pleasurable hiss from him. Nibbling a trail down his neck, her fingernails grazed his scalp until he groaned. Heat pooled between her legs, the feral sound, making her ache for *more*. Matteo's hips thrust and his hard length pressed against the barrier of his trousers. A moan escaped her, her attention pinned on the delicious pressure of his arousal. Her hands found their way to the buttons of his jeans, freeing him of both his trousers and boxers.

Carnal delight lit her face as she drank in the sight of him.

Gods, he is *a goliath.*

She reached out, wrapping her fingers around his length, fisting him in her hand. The grunted breaths that he let out as she stroked him sent heat coiling through her. His shoulders heaved and his eyelids flickered shut as she continued to massage him. His parted lips demanded another incursion from hers, and she kissed him again, her tongue enjoying the taste of him as much as her hand savored his silky hardness.

Jess inhaled the jagged soundtrack of Matteo's breath, reveling in giving him the pleasure she'd longed to in the cave. She watched him shiver, captivated by his rugged beauty, and loving watching him lose control beneath her touch. But his strong hands took hold of her waist, and he flipped her onto her back. The delicious weight of his body pinned her down into the mattress. His intense stare locked onto hers, the heat and demand in it sending a thrill through her.

Matteo tugged her knickers off. His fingers found her entrance, stroking the slick, warmth between her legs. Gasping, Jess arced into his touch. Her moans came in a steady stream as his fingers invaded her. Her eyelids fluttered shut, the world now consisting of nothing but the feel of Matteo's deft touch, drawing her ever closer to the edge of release. As pleasure rippled through her, she ached for all of him.

"Matteo..." she ground out. "I need you."

The tip of him was suddenly against Jess's entrance. She whimpered as he slid into her. A low growl escaped him as he inched into her. She arced up, wanting more of him. She couldn't get enough, even as his delicious width stretched her.

With slow thrusts he filled her until that edge came closer. She felt herself quiver. Rising. Falling. Both. Then, shattered. Suddenly she felt as boundless as she did in the Between. Until the fullness, of Matteo, came back. But he started to pull away. She wrapped her legs around his hips, pressing him into her.

"I need to get some protection, dearest," he murmured.

"I've been taking a Seelie tonic," she explained, refusing to let him go.

In answer, Matteo slammed into her, making her see stars again. Any restraint evaporated, and he buried himself inside of her with ever quickening thrusts until... his expression tautened, and he groaned out his release. Her nails dug into his shoulders as the feel of his warmth spilling through her sent more eddies of pleasure rippling through her. Wave after wave of his climax filled her and she tightened around him in another heady rush of release.

Spent, Matteo collapsed on top of her. Jess ran a hand through his hair.

For a while, they lay together, the shared wildness of their breath and hearts, and their fused bodies feeling almost as good as the pleasure they'd shaped together.

Then, Matteo rolled onto his side, his brown gaze brushing her. "That was…"

"How every day's going to be," she finished with a grin.

He laughed. "Every day?"

Her lips quirked. "Don't think you've got it in you?"

Instantly, Matteo was above her, looking very much like he was already *up* to the challenge.

But then, a rush of whispers stirred around Jess; she recognized them instantly: the voices of the faded. Although they were distant, their calls shuddered across the Shadowlands. The network of energy she'd watched the last few days teemed with disturbance, too, vibrating with darker magic that suddenly crashed into the fae lands, sending a tremor through her body.

Jess blinked her eyes open and drank in Matteo now watching her with concern.

"They've entered Umbra," she said.

Matteo's expression tightened. He didn't ask how she knew, only, "Where?"

Jess shook her head, sitting up. "I'm not sure, but I feel the spirits being drawn to the gate they've cut into the Unseelie lands."

Just then, the sound of horns resounded: the Seelie were summoning everyone to war. Their din blared out, echoing across the plains. Their shriek like a manifestation of the tension palpitating through Jess.

Matteo's features sharpened with purpose. He got off the bed. Offering her a hand, he tugged her up to her feet. He stooped to pick up his boxers, pulling them on. Likewise, Jess retrieved her scattered underwear. Her hands shook as she picked up her bralette.

Matteo tugged her against him. "How about we just put A-Do-Not-Disturb sign on the door?"

The tension hanging in the air lightened a little, and Jess's lips twitched, grateful for the loosening in her chest. She splayed her fingers across his chest, letting the feel of his heartbeat beneath the smooth muscles of his chest soothe her. "We're totally getting one of those when I get back."

"I'll hold you to that," he said, the firmness of his grip and gaze fortifying her. "Every day," he added, his heated stare and his curling lips, making her knees go weak.

A tender smile skirted her lips, and she kissed him softly. She *would* come back. And they *would* bask in each other's company for days on end.

Once dressed, they hurried from the room. Transforming into their lupine forms, they tore down the spiral staircase, right into the Sun Court. Quickly, they morphed into their human guises.

Rune sat on King Imber's throne. Not because he was governing the multiple streams of Seelie running off to the armaments and up to the top of the Sun Keep, but because he was in pain. Jess noticed the tell-tale signs: his knuckles white with tension as he grasped the stone armrests of the throne. His expression was carefully neutral, too much so. Rune felt the gate in Umbra like a wound in his own body. He must be itching to attack.

"Where have they entered?" Jess asked.

"They've gouged an entrance in one of the Depths pools, next to Herba Terra." Rune answered. "They didn't even use the safety of the Iron Keep where the old gate was."

"So much the worse for them," Eilea said, standing beside him, her hand resting on his forearm. Her lips curled as she added. "The riverways and storm winds have much better access to the Unseelie grass plains than to the Iron Keep."

The Storm-born was right. The might of Rune's power over the Depths and Heights would be able to wreak havoc on the enemy ranks out in the open far more than if the enemy had entered the Shadowlands beneath Mara's keep.

But as she saw Rune's onyx stare settle softly on Eilea, her heart squeezed. Rune had made Jess promise that she'd do everything she could to keep the Storm-born safe on the mission they were about to embark on. Only yesterday, Rune had shared how torn he was about having the Unseelie who had tethered Eilea captive in the Sun Keep. He'd confessed how tempted he'd been to end his life. But Eilea was adamant that she remain tethered so as to help in this mission. Beneath the quiet, brooding anger on Rune's face, Jess knew the fragile hope that was growing: for Umbra's unity, for a future here, for one day, and perhaps not too far away, love.

Astra and Skiron skidded to a stop as they landed gracefully from the open roof of the Sun Court.

"Ready for Operation Shadow Silva, ladies?" Astra asked.

The tension skyrocketed. Those of Operation Shadow Silva were the only ones who would be flying over the Seelie lands tonight. The others would be portaling through the Heights from the Sun Keep, out into Unseelie land where they would draw the enemy into battle and away from the gate. By the time Eilea flew Jess and Astra into those lands, they hoped that the gate would be clear of the enemy portaling out.

Sunny and Erika were the last to push through the streams of fae, shifters, and Storm-born already making their way up to the Heights of the Sun Keep to portal. Erika's earlier braided hair was wild and loose, and as Jess's gaze roved to Sunny, she took in the serious case of bed hair afflicting him.

So, we weren't the only ones.

Jess exchanged a look with Astra Rainbow, whose toothy smile said the pair's appearance hadn't escaped her notice. Jess had a moment of being pleased that she'd blurted things out to Erika about Sunny's feelings earlier. And the happy look that Sunny shot Jess had her inwardly doing a victory dance.

Erika brought Jess back down to Earth. "Remember, don't risk your human form unless you have to."

Jess nodded, trying to master her nerves as the thought of where she was about to go and what she was about to try to do threatened to smother her. Thankfully, there was Matteo, and as his arms gathered her up, she felt her whole world reduce to that one perfect point where she was safe, where she'd always been running to, and where she'd damn well make it back to.

22

SEA OF ALLIES

Matteo plunged off the top of the Sun Keep, closing his eyes against the winds clawing past. His stomach somersaulted as he dropped toward the ground. But he knew he'd portaled successfully when the horns calling the allied forces suddenly died. The Heights spat him out, unsympathetically, into Unseelie territory.

He scrambled out onto a craggy hillside, alongside hundreds of other shifters. The wolves, fae, and Storm-born traveled through the Heights portals that their various units had been allocated to. Depths portals were only being used by the witches and mages to portal through the groves of trees by the riverbank. With the enemy being most attuned to water, it had seemed best to minimize portaling through the Depths.

Matteo was almost pleased of the dizzy feeling as he got his bearings, following the stream of shifters. The uncomfortable disorientation numbed the ache in his heart. But... not for long. The memory of Jess in his arms just before she'd left tore at him. When he'd seen the rising chaos in her eyes at the task looming, he'd crushed her to him. But now that embrace didn't feel enough —not to hold *him* together. He didn't know how he was supposed to survive what he'd just done: let her leave. He should be with her.

I should always *be with her.*

Beneath the night, the ranks of sure-footed wolves around Matteo swarmed down the crags above the Herba Terra. His assessing gaze took in the intermingled lines of black and white wolves around him. Like the original shifter twins, Romulus and Remus, they ran united. The magnitude of this moment flooded him, and, once more, he wished that Jess was beside him to witness this magic. Matteo gathered himself, remembering that it was *their* march that would draw the enemy away from the gate that was her entry point. It was the shifter unit, alongside the other para units, that would allow Jess, Astra, and Eilea to infiltrate the enemy camp.

The enemy who had sundered the clans, covens, and courts all those thousands of years ago. The enormity of the moment echoed in the swift beat of the shifters' paws that seemed to shake the earth with a demand for freedom.

Matteo was one of the first wolves to enter out onto the flat lands of the Herba Terra. The Grasslands. These plains felt even more alien than the Sun Plains. The lusciousness of the Seelies' parklands was enriched by Alba's restoration, a renewal that hadn't reached here. Instead, the deep thickets of dark hebena trees gave the area an unnerving quality. As if all that divisive magic that Jess had been studying in these lands the last few days had gathered in these forests. Matteo had never thought that trees could creep him out.

But there it is. These ones are totally creepy.

There was a pack of fifteen hundred wolves gathering in the grasses. They stilled, waiting for the next unit to assemble from out of the nearby Depths portal. Earthen magic thrummed near as the Triodian witches and mages burst from the lake. The Triodians were slower joining the wolves on the plain, but their rallying was accompanied by spectacular groans and creaks, and Matteo knew that the Silvan groves had been portaled in.

Sure enough, as Matteo's wolfish gaze whipped out across the plains, he drank in the sight of a moving forest, lurching forward as the mages and witches assembled. Matteo remembered the beings created from root and soil that Warden Whitmore had cast in the penitentiary, but these were much mightier specimens. These were the great yew trees of Silva's Cathedral and the ones Enodia had stolen, now marching alongside the Triodians, their roots scuttling over the plains like feet.

As the Triodians surged forward along with the forest, Matteo and the other shifters set off with them, padding on slowly. The huge, ancient boughs and branches grumbled and sighed above the shifters, moving to embrace all of Earth's paras until a huge, moving shield of woodland protected them. As the Triodians and shifters crossed the plains, the first shot of an arrow whizzed through the night. The moving forest protested, the trees' boughs whipping through the air to take the iron arrows for the wolves and Triodians beneath them.

Matteo smelled the ancient Earthen magic that Jess used flood the air. Erika, Fern, and a few others within the Triodia Coven, adept at communing with the dead, were using the spirits to help them against the Unseelie fae. The aerial units were starting to rain down attacks using their iron-tinged sluagh. Matteo's shifter nose took in the scent of cold iron stealing through the night. Anxiety tightened his muscles, every moment anticipating that cruel touch of cold on his fur, that if he were unlucky, might remove him from the fight before it had even begun. He focused on every sound eroding the night, willing himself to be alert enough, fast enough, to dodge the coiling shadows of iron-tinged invading the moving forest like poisonous gas.

Beneath the shifting, rustling forest, shouts and screams, growls and whines pierced the air, the Unseelies' iron-tinged striking plenty of their targets. With the rising cries, both human and animal, echoing through the forest, the sanctity of the woods felt tainted; a place of magic transformed into nightmare.

Through the darkness, Matteo's wolfish eyes caught the first sight of the true enemy. Their formations glowed like moonlight; their pearly, luminescent skin and the sheen of their armor and weapons catching the starlight.

The Triodians were to take Mara's aerial units, while Imber's Seelie and the Storm-born were to combat her pucca units. Everyone had agreed that it was vital to get the tethered Storm-born away from the enemy ranks before Rune targeted them with Umbra's Depths and Heights. So, Rune planned to first transform the tethered Storm-born with his winds, as well as meet Queen Mara in battle.

That left the Fomor foot soldiers to the shifters. They needed to battle their ranks until Rune could summon the waters and winds to purge them. To purge these lands with the elements, just as Jess was about to do in the Below with the soul energy she wielded.

As the lines of Fomors marching closer loomed towards the great army of wolves, Matteo, in step with Piera, Dearbhla, and hundreds of other wolves, swarmed forwards, disturbing the strange, droning insects and releasing a spicy aroma as their claws tore up the grasses. Their howls cut through the Shadowlands as they broke out from the coverage of the moving canopy.

As Matteo rushed toward the enemy line, the agglomeration of foot soldiers that formed the army dominated his senses. What Erika had said about them being formed from a mixture of those they'd conquered was clear in their diversity. Every soldier bore different features and forms. Some had wings while others had horns; some looked more human, others more animal. But where the individual forms should have been interesting for their uniqueness, there was that deep-seated knowledge beating through Matteo that none of these attributes *belonged* to the individual. Instead, as his wolf eyes drank in the sight, it was as if each Fomor was dressed in trophies butchered from innocents: the horns, hoofs, wings, and tails they wore as if they'd bedecked themselves from fresh corpses. And that's what their white, translucent skin reminded Matteo of most—the bones of those they'd slaughtered. He sensed it, knew it, something deep in his own bones warning him that these very beings were born from the bodies, blood, and souls of those they butchered. An army of the dead, even more grotesque than what Matteo had witnessed from the Enodians or the Unseelie.

These are the Devourers. World-breakers. The Gathering Dark.

Matteo charged, pushing himself faster as he heard the beat of his brother and sisters' paws beside him take up the song of the kill. He felt a rush of savage pride for what he was, for what his pack was: beasts who didn't shy away from the frightful flesh that stole toward them.

We are shifters. The descendants of Romulus and Remus. We will claim the skins of those who rent our clan.

Matteo aimed for a huge Fomor, who tried to hide his translucent skin behind a chest plate of armor and the fur cloak adorning his hulking frame. With the fur, the Fomor's horns seemed like even more of a mockery. Matteo's claws slashed at the exposed flesh of his enemy's neck and relished the sound of his choke as he hit the dirt.

Erika had said that the Fomor were beings born from water, and Matteo felt it in the cold, blue blood coating his paws. He felt as if the liquid were something festering and longed for a cleansing pool. Instead, his eyes sharpened, homing in on the exposed area of white on the flank of the next Fomor. Matteo's jaws needled into the creature's jelly-like skin, its blood and entrails spilling out onto the grass.

As Matteo's black wolf darted into the enemy ranks, his claws and teeth searching for the next weak point, the sound of a whine or howl escaping from the line of shifters around him spurred him on, urging him to fight for his brothers and sisters. For the pack's survival. But, most of all, the thought of a fair wolf stalking lands where this filth originated from forced him ever on. The deeper he fought into their masses, the more it seemed as if their lines were never-ending. And the white flesh he kept tearing into seemed to belong to the underbelly of one gargantuan beast. One that even a thousand pairs of teeth and claws had no chance of bringing down.

23

FOREIGN SOIL

Maintaining the veiling Jess cast over herself, Astra, and Eilea through Seelie land was effortless. She drew her power from the faded and she and her companions bled seamlessly into the night. Astra held the reins loosely in her hands; she wouldn't need them until she posed as a proper Unseelie once in the Fomor kingdom. Jess was seated behind her, her arms wrapped tightly around her friend's waist.

Ahead, the first sign of the enemy ranks—a kind of diamond-like glimmer on the horizon—came into view.

Jess's heartbeat quickened and her breath caught in her throat as a dozen wonderings flocked through her head.

How many Fomors are there? Have the others portaled through the Heights yet? Have the shifters marched against the Fomors already? Is Matteo okay?

For a moment, Jess's death dust ebbed and the veiling flickered.

Cursing, she drew it back over them. Calming her hammering heart—they weren't yet near the portal—she told herself to focus. Jess was in human form, as it was easier to channel her death dust in this body. But that meant she and

Astra—an Unseelie and *a Rem*—flying into the enemy ranks wouldn't go unnoticed. Jess's veiling *must* hold. She mustn't get distracted.

Jess directed Eilea, "Fly to the right of the white. I sense the gate lies that side of the plain."

How tempting it was to look left to where the Fomors gathered. A low rumble sounded like the roll of distant thunder, but she realized it was footfalls. They were marching. Jess concentrated on the muted whisper beneath that, the faded, focusing on keeping her and her companions safe. The last thing they needed was to be spotted by Mara's aerial units. Speaking of which, the airborne Unseelie gathered in bands above the white mass, their black wings and dark iron contrasting starkly with their allies below.

It became increasingly clear where the gate to the Fomor kingdom lay as Eilea carried them deep enough into the forests, bordering the grass plains. They had a birds-eye view of the streams of the enemy, still marching and flying out the portal in droves. Without instruction, Eilea drew them a little farther away from the droves of airborne Unseelie flying, perhaps, a hundred feet away, towards the Herba Terra.

A few more of Eilea's strong wingbeats took them within line of sight to the gate. Still, the enemy proceeded to pour out of it. Eilea slowed her pace, circling above a stretch of dense hebena forest. Guilt tumbled through Jess as she wondered how long the Storm-born could go with the two of them seated on her back like this. And that was without all the flying that lay on the other side of the gate.

Jess's gaze wound over the ever-increasing force that showed no sign of stopping. She dug her nails into her thighs as her concentration wavered. The whisper in the tops of the trees beneath them wafted through Jess's awareness, and she let the soothing energy of the faded lap over her and her friends. All else disappeared while Eilea continued in her holding pattern.

Astra's voice broke through Jess's trance. "Looks like that's the last of them. Let's go." The Storm-born arced down.

As they drew towards the gate, tension spiked through Jess. But she drew the death dust over them, willing it to conceal them from the enemy's sight. Everything seemed to slow as Eilea touched down on the ground, a mere ten feet from the portal. Jess concentrated on her breathing and on the whisper that lapped over them all. On the veiling that screened them from the very real eyes of the enemy nearby. Two Unseelie mounted on Storm-born stood on either side of the gate like sentinels.

Jess's heart cramped for Astra. She must feel just as tense if not more than Jess did, sneaking past her own people. But her friend's loose grip on the reins and steady breathing didn't falter. As Eilea's hoofs took silent, masked steps ever closer to the gate, Jess's eyes raked the tiny details of the Unseelies' uniform and armor and the tack of their steeds. Everything that Astra and Eilea were furnished with was the same, right down to the iron on the trim of the saddle and footholds of the stirrups. They looked the part. They moved the part. They were authentic.

I mean, Astra is *an Unseelie, and Eilea* is *a tethered pucca.*

The surrealness of the moment spilled through Jess's thoughts. As her nerves mounted, her musings went down ever weirder rabbit holes. To think that when she and Astra had first met, she'd spent a large amount of time picturing her friend on a winged horse. And here she was. Here they both were.

Despite her anxiety, Jess's death dust blanketed them as they plunged through...

The first thing Jess was aware of was the humidity of the air. Mist curled around them. As it dispersed, three moons came into view. Eilea was flying again, the shudder of her wings pulling them upwards. Jess drank in the sight of the moons that she'd seen through the mirror pool in the cavern beneath the Iron Keep—two half-moons and a crescent one.

"It's show time White Wolf and Storm Horse," Astra said.

In spite of everything, the code names that Astra had given them as part of Operation Shadow Silva, buoyed Jess up. "Roger that, Winged Warrior." As Jess recited the script that Astra had impressed upon her, she realized her friend had spent *way* too much time talking to them the last few days as if they were part of a Special Ops team.

Eilea nickered in appreciation. She took them higher, the vapor continued to disperse, giving them the first sight of huge strips of water below. In the moonlight, the surface of the Below glittered almost prettily. The curling mist, too, gave the watery lands a softness. But then the first shudder of movement broke the surface, curved, pale jelly-like flesh breaking the illusion of any wholesomeness. The fleeting glimpse was enough to make Jess's skin crawl. Something Eilea seemed to agree with as she nickered, her wingbeats increasing and taking them higher still.

The memory of the pheist wrapping itself around her leg and dragging Jess downwards flickered through her head. A swell of gratitude swept through her for Eilea's beautiful cloudy wings that allowed them to climb safely above the dark waters. Something that continued to beat through Jess, as every so often, one of these half-formed Fomor creatures breached the water below. Otherwise, the smooth waterways stretched out, on and on.

Until... the light altered. A ribbon of bright light issued ahead, and hope beat through Jess. Could it be sunrise? The two times she'd seen into the Fomors' world, the moons had been evident. What was the bet that this miserable place was a sunless world? But what was that light then?

As they flew on, Jess took in the scattered, warming glow below the surface and realized it was another doorway slashed into another world; it must be sunrise or sunset there. As they progressed, they witnessed more patches of light illuming the depths in different glows. Jess felt as if each cut was like a growth or cyst upon the world that it opened into.

As the patches of light multiplied, so did the movement in the water. Jess's shifter senses roved below, and she could feel the thrash of movement. Down, down the jelly-like creatures herded the energy that gathered like shoals of fish as if for safety, but the ravenous half-formed Fomors drove the shoal up. Here and there, the mottling of light broke the surface: souls. But the Fomor spawn were right behind, snapping and absorbing the souls. Jess's stomach lurched as she watched the fledgling Fomors consume these offerings. Jess dulled her hearing, pleased she wasn't in wolf form, or too much of their feeding frenzy would be audible to her.

But her heart quickened with nerves. As part of the plan, Jess needed to go down into those waters. Well, her soul did. She crushed her worry down.

One step at a time.

Finally, as Eilea's strong wings brought them on, the scape beneath them altered gradually: the water-ridden land gave way to swampy areas, and the first sign of plants and trees came into view.

This was their cue to alter their journeying style. The sight of the marshlands meant they would have to now continue on foot. According to what Erika had learned of the Fomor kingdom through her travels in other worlds, flying from this point on was prohibited. Jess took in the distant shapes of towers on the skyline, too, now.

The spires of three jagged towers were clearly discernible. Erika had said that she'd heard tell in other worlds that the Fomors' spires were said to be built in the deepest part of the Below. Much more of their construction existed below the waters than what was visible above. A submerged city lay at the center of the Below. It was within these depths that Jess would find the majority of the divisive energy; it was there that they had to aim for so she could move enough of these trapped souls on. Their cover story entailed them going to the same place. In Vrasi Erika had heard tell that the Fomor lords inhabited these towers.

Eilea brought them down, whinnying as her forelegs squelched into the mulch.

Astra chuckled. "At least you're about to be rid of some weight."

"Hey," Jess griped, more to try to distract her from the rising tension than from any real offense.

The fae shrugged. "Doggy-style from here on in, White Wolf."

She took the fae's order, sliding off Eilea's back and into the marsh ground, before changing into her wolf.

Jess felt very much like a misunderstood pooch as Astra attached an iron collar to her, the leather leash tight in her hand.

Prisoner. Remember.

Jess sniffed the strange purple and blue greenery around them, distrusting the mimicry of life. She thought of the way the Triodia's wards in the penitentiary had prevented access to any magic, resulting in a barren environment. But *this* was even worse: nature here felt *wrong*. Broken ... dead. There were some familiar specimens along the marshland path, too, which Jess recognized with a lurch: the black hebena trees and the dark green-black leaves of nyxcornua, reminding her that even Umbra's flora had been stolen by the Fomors.

Jess's heart beat nervously as she considered the next part of their plan and all that hinged on it. Soon, Astra would be questioned as to why she was here. Erika had said it would be impossible to get close to the towers—close enough for Jess to reach the deep divisive magic she needed to move on—without reporting to guards who patrolled the area.

In fact, that was the next sign they looked for. According to Erika's instructions, once they came upon some guards, they'd have penetrated deep enough. Astra put tension on the reins of Eilea's halter—not because she needed steering, but because this was the fae and Storm-born getting into disguise, acting like an Unseelie and pucca. Eilea's head and neck were jerked back into an uncomfortably upright position. Jess saw it in Astra's sudden ramrod posture, too.

The fae tugged Jess onwards. The marshland got even drier as if feet passed this way often, and it felt as if they must soon meet someone. Anticipation blanketed them all. Each of Eilea's footfalls and Jess's own sounded too loud. Jess's heart began to hammer in her furry chest, and she had to fight her instincts that were telling her to lurch into the undergrowth and trees for *some* cover at least. Her wolf ears swiveled, uncomfortably alert for the faintest sound.

As they came around the bend of some tall silvery trees, a pair of Fomors tracked their way toward them. One walked with great loping steps, the other jerkier. It wasn't a lie as Astra half-dragged Jess onwards; a creepy, crawling feeling came over her as her wolfish eyes grazed the pair. One Fomor had spiky barbs over the back of his skull and going down his spine. The other had leathery wings and a lizard-like tail, his nose more reptilian, too. They both wore pale gray leathers and boots and carried swords on weapon belts. The lizard one held a spear.

"State your business," the lizard barked in Umbran at Astra.

"I bring a re-conquering present from Queen Mara for the Fomor lords." Astra tugged on Jess's leash, and she growled, the sound drawing the Fomors' attention solely to her.

Jess's stomach lurched at the feel of their eyes on her. Their gazes were pale, milky almost, blending with their white skin so it almost felt as if they were eyeless. Like the sinuous creatures they'd flown over in the lake, these foot soldiers would have spawned from there. How many souls had they consumed before they'd been able to crawl from the lake? Their different features seemed like a testament to all they'd stolen: an ugly patchwork of stitched-together things. The one with barbs over its skin had slits in his neck—gills—and its second pair of eyelids created a murky coating over them as if it hadn't long emerged from the water.

"What is it?" the one with gills asked.

"Queen Mara captured her—a Suang for the lords to skin," Astra replied smoothly.

"Her, eh?" The lizard's forked tongue poked through its lips, and Jess had the disgusting sense it was tasting the air for her scent.

"I've never seen one," the one with gills said.

"Me neither," the lizard replied.

Jess breathed an internal sigh of relief. But too soon because the next word out of the lizard's mouth was, "Transform."

Jess snapped, baring her teeth at the lizard.

"Order it to transform," the lizard barked at Astra.

"Shift, Suang," the fae ordered, yanking the leash so that Jess was strangled, but she refused, making a display of rebellion as she snarled, even though Astra's leash made it hard to breathe.

But the Fomors weren't done. The lizard one aimed a kick at Jess, making her curl in upon herself. Unable to fight it, a whine escaped her.

As if from afar, Jess heard Astra's feigned indifference. "My queen ordered she be unspoiled for the lords."

Through watery eyes, Jess took in the lizard's grinning white face, his nostrils flaring as if he could smell her fear and pain. Maybe he could. The Fomors fed on destruction. His enjoyment made it clear that his abuse might long continue and make her unfit for the task she was here to do.

Taking a gamble, Jess shifted into her human form. Neither of these Fomors had seen a Suang. But that didn't mean they didn't know they were ordinarily dark-haired and dark-skinned. She crouched down on the ground, her jaw tight as if she'd spring at the Fomors and try to tear them apart even in this form if they came close.

"Reckon the lords will enjoy her flesh in more ways than just skinning," the lizard said to the other Fomor as he eyed Jess's face and figure, a lewd expression on his face.

The other snickered.

Jess's Umbran was poor. But it *was* getting better. She caught the gist. She had thought that the Fomors were all spawned in the festering waters around them. But the shock of hearing that some conquered peoples were brought here for the Fomor lords' pleasure made her blood boil.

The look of shock and revulsion etching itself across Jess's face made the pair guffaw again.

"Filthy Yingan!" Jess shouted.

They ogled Jess and she wondered if shifting had been a bad idea. Had she chosen her insult wisely enough? She'd spoken in Umbran. Should she have? The Yingan were those who hunted the Suang in their home world. Who skinned the Suang to seize the blessings they would otherwise grant to the people of Yin. Jess found herself envisaging the hebena tree that Erika had draped with ribbons: the ritual from Yin. In her thoughts, it fused with the memory of the be-ribboned oak of Fort Caylee. As she glared at the Fomors, all the anger and loss for herself and the worlds that had been ripped apart swam in her gaze.

Finally, the lizard waved Astra on. As the fae jerked her leash, Jess stumbled on, a mixture of anger and shock tumbling through her.

24

ALBA THE WHITE

As Rune flew through the Heights portal from the Sun Keep, with Imber and the Seelie at his back, the fury of Umbra's elements swelled through him. The Great Alban Ocean roaring at the coastlines looked out of Rune, drinking in the hundreds of Unseelie pucca riders on the Herba Terra as though contemplating a fleet it wanted to devour. The Storm winds, churning through the Heights of Umbra, seemed to drool over the Unseelie aerial units, too. They heaved above the Triodians' marching forest, contemplating the Unseelie like berries to be plucked and dispersed.

But Rune soothed the frothing waves and grazing winds. "Not yet. But soon," he whispered to them.

He couldn't let his anger get the better of him. He needed to transform the tethered Storm-born using the winds first.

Yet, the temptation to unleash the full force of his wrath prickled over Rune's skin like a flush of heat. But he pummelled his rage into his wings, thrashing the air and bringing him ever closer to the enemy.

Towards the throng of hundreds... No, thousands. The most prominent of which was the thousands of white foot soldiers glimmering on the plains ahead. The mass of Fomor units was great. The number of the enemy had been a complete unknown, with Erika only able to detail what had been rumored in other worlds about their invasions. It was said that the Fomors invading party usually consisted of thousands. But they didn't know if that number was in the few thousands, which the conjoined forces of shifters, Triodians, and Seelie could equal, or tens of thousands. The vastness of white choking the plains was a sobering sight, and Rune realized that the Fomor unit alone looked like it was ten thousand strong.

Rune's dark eyes stole over the frontlines of those formations and realized they were on the move. Their assorted shapes blurred with speed, and he spied the chaotic forms of his allies, the shifters, breaking the ranks of those first lines. His blood surged, and once more, Umbra's waters writhed: the northern sea slammed up into the river mouths, longing to wash away the foul enemy as quickly as possible. But he fought the pull of those waters again and flexing his fully stretched shadow wings, his muscles relaxed, and the foaming riverways subsided. Rune *would* aid the shifters in combatting the Fomor force once he'd dealt with his current target.

Steadier, he focused on that target. Rune homed in on the discordant energy of the pucca riders. Over a thousand strong. And, amid her riders, Queen Mara rode, enshrined in a protective circle of hundreds of iron-tinged, too.

The Unseelie pucca riders started to move. Breaking into a charge across the Grasslands, they soon took to the skies, their steeds bearing the fae up. The queen and her pucca units ascended, their sights set on Rune, Imber, and the approaching airborne Seelie.

Rune heard the rush of wingbeats accelerating as his other allies joined him from the higher reaches—some shaped like horses, others shaped like the feline mountain cu, even their double rows of teeth painting the air. Other Storm-born changed into snaking pheist, their huge, churning forms undulating through the sky as if through the Depths. Rune's heart swelled, feeling as if they were honoring his dual elements in the fearsome display they shaped as they charged.

And, finally, as Rune hurtled towards the frontline of Unseelie pucca riders, he uttered to his clawing winds, "Now."

His gusts coiled around the Unseelie, dismounting the first front row as if spears had been thrown up before the line. Then, Rune's winds embraced the Storm-born, their animal forms shimmering in golden and silver light, before the first Storm-born from the enemy ranks were released to their human forms. The lines of Storm-born traveling with Rune were quick to pick up their brothers and sisters, carrying them back into the safety of the herd. Meanwhile, Imber and the Seelie targeted the dismounted riders, and the first war cries and clash of iron echoed through the skies.

Again and again, Rune's attention went to the ranks of tethered Storm-born, reaching out with his gusts like welcoming hands while the same currents ripped the Unseelie riders off their steeds. Every time his winds tore at the Unseelie, he felt like a ship in a squall, rounding up into the wind, his anger threatening to claim him. But the Storm-borns' need for his restorative winds guided him back into the calm.

Besides, thoughts of Eilea reminded him of what he owed to this race. He'd made a promise to her that he'd free all her people, that he'd furnish them with the past that had been stolen from them, and with the ability to record it. Rune wished that she was here to fly with her brothers and sisters, to see more of them freed from their animal forms. But with each stroke of his wings and rush of his squalls, he reminded himself that he was closer to honoring the promise he'd made her.

The thought of Jess's assurance buoyed him up. She'd come upon him yesterday, just as he'd received word that Eilea and Beinn's Unseelie masters were imprisoned in the Sun Keep. The same anger that blistered his insides now had threatened to get the better of him then. How easy it would have been to take a blade to those Unseelie and steal their lives. Just as they'd stolen Eilea and Beinn's freedom. But Jess had reminded him that that was Eilea's decision to make. Just as it was hers to remain tethered to help infiltrate the Fomor kingdom.

Admiration beat through Rune for the fierce and quick-witted Storm-born. For the lengths she'd go to for her people and for Umbra. He felt the newborn skies that he'd whispered about to her growing within him.

A high-pitched whistle grated through Rune, throwing him and his winds out of rhythm. The mounted Unseelie charging forth in front of him bore down on him, cloidem in hand. He drew his own, the rush of the winds beneath his wings making the fae no match for him, but he gave his enemy a quick death, piercing his heart cleanly.

Rune's attention charged to the Storm-born who were turning back into their animal forms. Against their will. Multiple horses flew back toward their masters who had *whistled* for them. A flash of Eilea once more pierced Rune, all that vivacity and intelligence that had been tempered and bound.

And ... he let rip. The rider and those others who had *dared* to whistle for their steeds as they reclaimed them weren't just wrenched from their mounts—the gusts encircled their limbs, ripping them from their bodies.

The impact was immediate and silenced any more whistles. The Storm-born who were still mounted by the Unseelie now tossed and bucked, many of them successfully dismounting their riders themselves. Their reward of Rune's transformative winds awaited them, and like falling stars more Storm-born fell from the night sky. Here and there, Rune's wind clawed off the last of the Unseelie pucca riders, feeling a swell of success as the last of the freed Storm-born were illumed in silver and gold and brought into the safety of the herd.

Now, the Seelie rushed upon their dismounted brethren, the ring of metal and shouts roiling through the air struck like the clamor of thunder. Satisfaction blasted through Rune as, with the last of the Storm-born released from their animal forms, his way was clear. Clear to approach the enemy that the coiling anger in him craved.

Like the eye of a storm, Mara hovered in relative calm, her blade drawn but unused; instead, her black tendrils pierced any Seelie who dared approach her. Rune's temperate winds managed to catch the latest Seelie who Mara's inky-black coil had just knocked out. His gusts brought the Seelie safely down to the plain as he approached the Iron Queen.

Mara wore the same iron-scalloped dress. How she could fly in that he didn't know, perhaps her iron-tinged bore her up, as well as fighting her battles for her. Rune thought she'd never seemed more like something from the fetid Below, the cloud of cold iron staining the air around her like a devilfish's ink.

The closer Rune flew, the more obvious Mara's smug expression was. He recognized that ugly light glutting her gaze. She believed she had the advantage. Rune searched the skies around them, alertness prickling over him as he drank in the Seelie and Storm-born fighting the Unseelie and iron-tinged.

But it was from the ground that Rune felt the disturbance. A distortion ricocheted through the fabric of Umbra. Death energy flooded the Shadowlands—and Rune. Earthen, Heights, and Depths magic poured in, and a dazzling heliotrope glow exploded from beneath the moving yew forest of the Triodians.

The Enodians have portaled in.

So, Mara believed that Enodia's involvement was unknown to them, and enough to tip the scales in their favor. But thanks to Sunny's Unseelie informants, they'd known to expect the other coven. Besides, Erika and the Triodians with the Thokkal iron could magnify their Earthen and death energy and should be able to keep the Enodians at bay until Rune could help.

With relish, Rune flew closer to the Iron Queen. He summoned Umbra's shadows as he had in the cavern beneath the Iron Keep, the last time he'd confronted the queen. But then he'd had little time to fight Mara. She'd swiftly fled to the Below. Now the natural shades of the Shadowlands congregated around Mara's twisted darkness. They seethed with the same grim satisfaction that heaved through Rune.

He locked eyes with the queen, issuing the vow he'd uttered beneath the Iron Keep anew, "Umbra deserves its vengeance, Mara."

At the words, the shadows surged forth, piercing the iron-tinged sluagh around the queen. Rune's black stare burned with divine wrath and the darkness around Mara started to pale. Ashen cloud swam around her. Her coiling tendrils tried to shoot forwards, to attack Umbra's shades, but each time the blackness lightened.

Fury pulsed through Rune as he thought of how Mara had known what had happened to Umbra's gods—and yet chosen the Fomors over the land she had been birthed in. He thought of the way she had allowed him and the other Alban heirs entry into Umbra. Of the wrongs she'd had him commit—bringing human babes to the Shadowlands to make iron-tinged from. Of her desire to stay apprised of whether they came close to fulfilling the Eventide prophecy. The twisted version of the prophecy that would have had Jess conjoining with her dying shadow self, only to be tethered by Mara.

The queen's gaze darted around, an incredulous look bathing her face. Only now did she seem to realize that she was fighting a *god*. Fear flooded her burnished stare. She jerked upwards as if she meant to flee, but... Rune wasn't finished. Umbra's winds slammed into her from above. She shrieked as she crashed into the invisible ceiling. Umbra's shades crawled around her, leaching the darkness until ash started to rain down.

She thrashed her wings like a caged bird. Her eyes darted

around, frantic for a means of escape, but Rune's merciless winds held her. All the while the inky gloom around her disintegrated until even the iron of her scalloped dress started to dissolve. Rune watched as each of the tokens that had tethered an iron-tinged to her fell away like teeth crumbling from a mouth.

Mara screamed, and there was nothing queenly in the sound. Fear clawed from her throat. A fear that was all too mortal. As each token fell away, Mara's burnished eyes drained of color and her almond skin turned wan. The last scalloped piece of Mara's armor shattered, and the unnatural vigor that had animated her for three centuries dispersed back into the shadows, from where she'd stolen it.

With wilted wings the Iron Queen plummeted, spiraling down until her lifeless body thudded upon the Grasslands.

25

ON THE EDGE

After they'd moved for a few minutes away from the Fomor guards, Jess and her companions took the first opportunity to slink into the dark undergrowth and trees aligning the path. Jess's breaths were shallow as pain bloomed in her stomach and ribs every time she tried to inhale. With their disguise still of paramount importance, Astra stayed seated on the Storm-born's back even as Eilea's legs sunk into the marshland, each step an exertion as they picked their way off the track. Although the ground was more unstable, at least the plants grew thicker: they needed camouflage, a place to lie low for Jess to channel her magic. They pushed through vines and thorns that bit into Jess's fur and Eilea's coat, drawing scratches and blood from them.

Jess's head jerked back the way they'd come, taking in the obscured spires. A shiver crawled down her spine at the idea that they contained the Fomor lords who were responsible for decimating so many worlds. But, mostly, the thought of the unseen roots of their structures, beneath the waters filled her thoughts. Where her soul needed to go next.

From her position down low in the undergrowth, she reck-

her eyes. *Fort Matteo? This is White Wolf. We're safe in the center. About to dive deep. Over.*

The seconds that ticked by felt like an eternity. But as the beautiful scent of fresh pine permeated her, she heard, *Hear you loud and clear, White Wolf.*

Her heart leaped, and she couldn't resist. *Love you.*

Love you too.

Roger that, Fort Matteo. Out.

The high she felt at having heard him. Having heard he was all right. That he was *alive...*

With effort, she pushed thoughts of Matteo away. She could only help him and all those she loved by doing what she'd come here to do.

As she blinked her eyes open, Astra still hadn't shut her mouth. "You spoke to him?" Her whispered words made her awe sound even funnier.

Jess suppressed a smile, trying to seem casual. "Yeah, I reached through the Between. He's fine."

Astra's russet eyes bugged out.

Jess took a steadying breath. "I'll reach out to you when I can too. I'll only be able to hear you when I connect to you, but I'll do it whenever I can."

"Yeah, yeah, I know the drill," Astra said casually.

She and Jess had practiced holding their disembodied conversations recently as part of the planning process. It was when Astra had given them code names and insisted that they spoke as if they had Walkie-talkies.

Jess was surprised it had taken her so long to think of the possibility of reaching Matteo in the same way. But then again, it was only days ago that she'd managed to reach through to Earth from Umbra.

Despite Astra's supposed nonchalance, she asked. "Is there anything you want us to do while you're gone?"

"I don't think so," Jess answered. In terms of what to expect,

she didn't really know. All she knew was that her soul had to penetrate to the deepest point of the Below and move on the divisive
magic. In turn that should set off the flow, so that the rest of the
dark magic here would move on through the Between.

Simple.

Jess fought against a shudder as a flash of the white sinuous
spawn breaking the water's surface threatened.

"What about you?" Jess asked. "You going to be okay here?"

The fae's lips twitched. "If we're disturbed, my cover story is
you broke your leash, ran off, and rolled in something icky."

Jess's chest tightened, her stomach knotting with worry and...
love. She didn't want to imagine such a scenario, part of her didn't
want to leave her friends in this awful place at all. But at least
Astra had her next plan at the ready.

The rising tide of anxiety cloyed at Jess. The magnitude of
what she was about to try threatened to overwhelm her. The scale
of this place... But she remembered how many souls she'd already
pushed on into the Between, how she'd formed a bridge from
Umbra to Earth, and reached out to Matteo as easily as she might
have made a phone call on Earth.

Jess steadied her breath. She realized it was probably best she
lie down—

less likely to be seen and probably safer for her body, given
that her soul was about to leave. She wriggled back, her back
settling into the earth and her shoulder blades relaxing, as much
as she could in the dirt. A smile curled her lips.

*Who am I kidding? This was my natural environment or would be if
the mud wasn't empty—soulless—of Earthen energy.*

Whispering, she shared her thoughts with Astra who hunched
over her, "My natural environment."

Astra tried to smile, but it was strained. Her voice was taut,
"Good luck."

Jess closed her eyes. The prickle of awareness that had washed
over her each time she reached out to the dark magic throughout

the Unseelie Court emanated through the undergrowth. She let her consciousness travel on towards the waterline, and then, with a shiver of revulsion, plunged in. The shock of its touch was immediate. Like being immersed in ice water, her soul cried out at the repellent feel of it. It was as if she'd been submerged in polluted waters, as if a brownish, oily slick coated and suffocated her.

Disorientation swam through Jess. She felt as if she were walking but knew that her consciousness journeyed into the dark waters. She fought back the urge to retreat, every part of her wanting to shrink away as the sense of vertigo threatened to catch her up. The sensation was similar to when she traveled through a Depths portal. Which way was up, which down?

Jess felt her body, distantly, reacting to her soul's fear. Her heart beat wildly and her palms grew clammy.

Mastering her alarm, her shallow breaths deepened, her awareness arced out, and the diseased wasteland opened up around her. Jess distinguished farther out and deeper down in the water. Fomor spawn. The way their energy arced and snaked made her envisage their sinuous bodies moving through the Below all too clearly—dangerous, deep-water dwelling creatures. Creatures who *feasted* on whatever came their way. Bodies and bones, for sure, but also *souls*. A prickle of terror darted through her, feeling as if the strength of her spirit—half a goddess's soul—made her a mouth-watering feast.

But the divisive magic in these waters, even in the beasts circling deeper, wasn't the strongest one she sensed. Deeper still, there was a hint of pulsing rot that she intuited from its strength was where she needed to aim for. The place where she needed to attack and push the most potent discordant energy onward.

She had the sense that eyes crawled over her. Her being felt as luminous in the dark waters as much as her silver hair and pale complexion had. She thought of the way she'd camouflaged her body with mud in the undergrowth where she currently lay. She knew she needed to go deeper, to get to the most concentrated Fomor magic at the center of these waters.

How do I camouflage my soul?

The answer came to her as her sweeping awareness cottoned onto the first glimmer of light.

Other souls.

She remembered sensing them coming to the surface, chased by Fomors, together in the safety of shoal-like groups. As she got nearer the light of the beings, she realized it was a stream from one of the gouged gateways to another world. And reaching out to them, the essence of this one tore at her with a sense of familiarity: these souls seemed to howl, a wildness ripping through them that she shared, making her ache for Earth and the call of its woods.

Jess realized these spirits were the souls of Suang. She felt as if she could taste their sorrow for their woods and home world like salt in the water. She called out to them with the same note of pure yearning that she'd wished for the Sidhe: to be at peace, to give her what she'd wanted for centuries, promising that she'd move them on, too. Then, they were traveling around her, like a pack of ghostly wolves they joined her descent.

As Jess descended, she drew other essences to her, their textures and colors as varying as the different worlds they came from; most of which she had no knowledge of or shared language to understand the memories that some of these beings gave to her as their consciousnesses brushed against her own. Yet, they spoke with the universal language of emotion. The same yearning, longing, and pain made them kindred spirits, and Jess's pack grew.

As she descended, Jess reached back up to Astra, identifying her energy before mingling with it. *Winged Warrior?*

Despite protocol and all the scripts Astra had insisted on, she responded, *Fuck. That's so trippy.*

Jess felt sure her body back on the surface must be grinning. *I'm descending. I'll reach out again when I can. Out.*

Roger that, White Wolf.

Around Jess, the dissonant magic deepened, and she identified its force in the tall shafts rising from the deep. The towers. Erika had said most of their structures were submerged. The jarring note of their rot grew stronger the farther she dived, stemming from their bases.

Wriggling creatures suddenly shot out from around Jess, going for the souls around her as she and those in the center dove on. Her soul thrummed with fear, and although her body wasn't here, she had the sense of her blood pounding in her temples, of sweat crawling down her spine. Whatever strand that connected her consciousness to her body tautened with shrill panic as she raced to get away from the predators around her.

Jess had a distant sense of someone holding something over her mouth.

I'm panting ... Loudly.

Jess forced herself to calm down. For her friends. To keep them safe where they were hidden with her body. She hastened on, calling those around her with that promise of pushing them on.

Soon.

Jess wanted to reach out to Astra again to reassure her that she was okay but didn't dare let her attention wander now. Amidst the glimmering essences surrounding her, Jess felt the undertone of the discordant deep energy. Very near. She'd almost reached the deepest part.

The feel of the iron-tinged was strong here. There were the essences of centuries' worth of human souls—tortured, killed, and bound, only to end up here—decomposing in these waters. Their cold touch was no different to how they'd felt holding her frozen in Mara's circle in the Iron Keep, but Jess fought the icy fear, remembering that they weren't the dark weapons they'd become, but human souls. They didn't deserve this.

Amidst the spirits Jess had no name for, she once more intuited the identity of some from Erika's stories about the worlds she'd visited. Her being seemed to curl in upon itself as she recognized the souls of the Gortans and Draci in the slick waters. Their coagulated souls seemed to sandwich the rotten roots of the towers to the waterbed. She felt the ghosts of the husk-like Gortans consumed by their own land and the Draci washed hollow of memory by their waterways. Their world must have been conquered by the Fomors long ago, as the remnants of their decaying souls were some of the greatest in number, and those that the Fomor underwater kingdom seemed to be raised upon.

Their congealing souls in the waters were frightening and sickening. A flash of Jess's body came to her as her distress stretched the strand between her soul and body, and she knew Astra had turned her onto her side, the dry heaving afflicting her body gradually subsiding.

This was where the deepest infestation was. Jess knew it. She had to open the Between. She had to give all these suffering beings a place to move on to. So, despite every touch being like glass against her being, she opened the harsh waters around her. Acting as a gateway to the Between, she felt the souls streaming past, their torrent rushing on.

Jess started to pull at the energy beneath the towers' bases, too. Like roots in the earth, she yanked at it. Already dead and disintegrating, these roots had no stability, so as she yanked and wrestled them, they came away, dissolving and dissipating into the Between.

Then, the divisive energy of the Below started to flow onward, too. Sensing the rushing energy whip past her, Jess felt as if the waters around her were emptying. But it was the discordant energy within them that was dispersing into the Between.

Shock pulsed through her.

I've done it. The souls, they're moving on...

But from out of the wastewater, sinuous energy struck out. Jess darted around, but the pack that had been with her had passed on into the Between. Alone, numerous Fomor spawn attacked. Sharp pain broke through her...

Jess felt her breath cut through her lungs as if she couldn't get enough air. The faint touch of someone's hand on her brow did nothing to stop the sting radiating through her whole being. She yelled. Distantly, she felt someone's hand clamp over her mouth.

But movement whirled nearby. More of the souls from the waters around were streaming towards Jess. Most shot by her, rushing on into the Between. But some congregated around her and struck the Fomor spawn. They were *defending* her.

Amidst the beings guarding her, Jess recognized the Eorosh—that race who lived in fear of the spoken word. She detected the Eorosh's taut silence and strangled rage. As they grazed the beast that had attacked her, she caught snippets of images—of stumps in mouths ... words suffocated beneath silence and pain—but they had access to the energy of the Between, and a boom hammered through them, ricocheting through the Below.

The twisting bodies of the juvenile Fomors reared and shrieked. Their essences fired with pain as those souls they had feasted on, still unabsorbed—literally—burst out of them. The flow that Jess had set off, gained momentum. It was as if the Between called to all the energy around her. Like tributaries, they recognized it as the main body through which they were destined to flow.

Jess identified the enormous hulks of dying energy dropping through the waters around her: the heavy masses of Fomor spawn spiraling down like great whale carcasses. A rumble resounded around Jess and panic surged through her. Disorientation threatened and she flailed within the rushing movement. She thought it was another Fomor beast but realized as the roar flowed past her and into the Between, it was the Eorosh who had intervened between her and the Fomor spawn; they'd been defending their exit and now moved on with the rest of the souls that Jess had freed.

As the danger in the waters waned, the Eorosh's essences flickered out, and the wash of free-flowing souls echoed on into the Between like the soothing tones of a stream. Her whole being breathed a sigh of immense relief. And gratitude. She tried to send out her thankfulness to the Eorosh moving onwards.

I did it. The divided souls are moving on.

Jess detected, too, those Fomor juveniles in the water who hadn't been split apart by the unabsorbed energy in their bellies, now shrieking in pain, too. As the discordant energy around them drained from the Below, their life forces started to ebb as well.

The Fomor spawn are all dying.

On the periphery, she was just aware of Astra.

A beat of excitement hummed through her as she caught Astra's muted voice, "The towers are falling."

But Astra was muffled more than she had been. Jess hurried to rise. If the towers were falling, she needed to get back.

She tried to reach out, to surge up, but that's when she was aware... her surroundings had *altered*. No longer was she in the dark waters of the Fomor kingdom. The water she was in was too clean, too pure, too... fucking colorful. The startling array of colors flowing by was spectacular. As if it were dawn or dusk and the sun's rays were painting the surface of the ocean with a thousand different hues.

Dawning comprehension somersaulted through Jess. It must have been when the Eorosh had whipped past her, in the whirl of movement when she'd gotten disoriented, she'd drifted farther in. She could feel her soul keeping the Between open through which the destructive energy continued to drain away from the Fomor kingdom, but... she was on the *other* side of that doorway. The weight and tide of all the flowing energy was too great ... and had pushed her farther on.

Again and again, she tried to push back against the torrent rushing past her.

Alarm hammered through her.

She was beyond...

She was in the Between...

Deep in the Between...

Panic swirled through her.

A distant memory echoed through her head. *"...don't step into its flow or Oblivion will wash your soul away."* Theo's warning. From when his sluagh had guided her into the human Netherworld. She'd reminded him at the time that he'd said para souls didn't stay in the Netherworld. *"Nor do they, but if you get caught in its current, it will take you to wherever we para souls go after this life."*

And she knew that's where she was going. Through the Between. She was on the edge of Oblivion. So close to flowing on.

She wanted to scream. But felt, suddenly, like the Eorosh. Bound in silence. Unable to break through to where she had a voice and the ability to truly move. She was muffled. Frayed. Diminished. The flow of souls moving past her was a barrier against getting back. A flow that was only getting stronger the more the energy from the Below poured out.

That weird sense of feeling thin, feeling muted came over her again. She thought of how the Fomor spawn had struck her. Their bite had been when this feeling started ... when this weakening had started. Dread tore at her. The spawn had sapped her soul of energy.

Jess started as she felt something across her face. A slap. But it was *so* far away. Then pain. A nick across her arm. "Jess? Wake up." She felt Astra's touch on her skin distantly and realized it was only when the fae touched her that she heard her.

Fuck.

Jess realized that her friend could stab her and she still wouldn't wake up.

She felt Astra shaking her, her fingers brushing against her neck as she shook her shoulders. "It's not nap time. Come on. Walkies. You love walkies." Beneath the fae's joke, she could hear her brittle tone so close to breaking.

Jess tried to reach Astra, to send her energy upwards and connect, but again that sense of thinness, of weakness came over her. Despite knowing that she didn't feel Astra's energy, Jess tried. *Astra? Astra?*

Jess's panic climbed. Both the fae's attempt at waking her had failed, and her own attempt to reach Astra had, too.

As terror dominated her, in a last-ditch attempt to communicate, Jess thought of how she'd reached through the Between to Matteo earlier. Longing pulsed through her. She knew his energy signature better than anyone's. Maybe, even weakened, that connection would be enough for her to reach him. And maybe through him, she could get help from Erika.

Sure, easy to get witchy advice on a battlefield.

But Jess was scared shitless enough not to stop for fear of distracting him. Or for the little likelihood that Matteo would be able to reach Erika amidst the chaos of battle. Besides, if the Fomor energy was dying and moving on, perhaps the Fomors in Umbra were already falling.

Steadying herself and admitting she *needed* help, Jess reached out.

Matteo?

Matteo?

Please.

For a moment, she thought she detected pine accents. But the energy that struck her *wasn't* Matteo's. Gnashing fangs and arcing claws leaped towards her: Lorenzo's amethyst blood sluagh sprang at her and then ... past her...

Jess watched in shock as his color became mottled by a thousand different others, the waters of Oblivion as beautiful as the Northern Lights of Earth. But there were more souls following in Lorenzo's wake. Another was familiar to Jess. The color of lichen muddied the waters around her, and she recognized the previous Enodian High Mage, Jorah, being pulled on by Oblivion's tide. As the heliotrope glow of para sluagh continued to pour past Jess, warning flared afresh through her. This was Theo's sluagh horde. The divisive magic of the Fomors was flowing from Umbra, into the Between, and on into Oblivion.

And the sheer force of its convergence threatened to wash Jess's soul away forever.

❧ 26 ❧

OTHERWORLD

When Theo and his Enodians portaled into the walking forest on the plains of Umbra, it was as if they'd set off a bomb. The spectacular bursts of their sluagh hordes flooded the trees, targeting the Earthen mages and witches without mercy. He'd ordered his coven to decimate the Triodia. To make them history. To put them in the ground once and for all. And the Enodians were doing a spectacular job, the shrieks and huge detonations making it seem as if minefields littered the Grasslands.

Before leaving Nox, he'd shared with his coven the knowledge that Queen Mara had already granted him the means of immortality and that when they returned from Umbra, he would be choosing those who won him the most glory, the privilege of practicing such magic with him.

Nothing like the promise of more power to get an Enodian's blood pumping.

That, and he thought like him, his followers were simply overjoyed to be out in the world once more. Albeit in the Shadowlands. The coven's way of entering Umbra tonight had been novel, too. Some of Mara's iron-tinged had allowed them to portal in outside of Eventide. Another benefit from the Iron Queen that had impressed Theo's followers.

Through the alliance brokered with Mara, he was allowed to create his own iron-tinged. A right he fully intended to exercise tonight by capturing and claiming Jess's soul.

He'd only shared with his coven that he had a side mission—one that entailed him surreptitiously getting away from where his coven fought the Triodians. He deliberately hadn't used his para sluagh horde when he'd entered and as he fought his way through the covens. Like a wide-eyed fledgling who had forgotten how to use his greatest magic in the chaos of battle, he carved his way out of the fighting with just his scian. His sluagh acted as extra eyes only. He'd taken the precaution of looking low-key—donning a simple black sweater and jeans, and tying his sandy hair up in a knot. He wasn't Enodia's High Mage erupting out of the portal and fighting his way through in a blaze of glory. Instead, his bloodied hands and clothes were more like something that belonged to the ranks of the shifters and Fomors, whose very ranks he fought to get to.

He plunged his scian into the chest of a Triodian mage, pushing him off his blade and savoring the dull thud of his body in the grass.

Back to the Earth where you belong.

Yet, as he fought, his confidence in how his coven had been doing in their battle against the Triodians wavered. Theo's gaze darted around, taking in the lay of the land. He sensed and then watched as he took momentary cover behind a tree, a Triodian dispelling the amethyst shield around an Enodian.

Theo's throat tightened as he noted the similarity of the scene to the magic that Jess had used against him. His heart punched the wall of his chest as he watched the Enodian's sluagh horde be picked apart, threat by threat.

The Triodians are wielding Jess's magic. They're untethering our sluagh hordes. How?

As he skulked on, continuing to cut his way through with his blade, he noted the Triodians combatting the iron-tinged that the airborne units of Unseelie fae unleashed down upon them, too. Lots of the witches and mages shielded themselves from the iron-tinged, while others actually scattered the iron-tinged. No doubt, this development had much to do with the witch who had wielded the three branches of magic in the catacombs. Theo had spied her shortly after entering Umbra, quickly dodging out of sight. He wondered, too, with the death energy the coven wielded against the airborne Unseelie, whether Jess was within their number somewhere. But, if so, that was another reason to give these units a wide berth; he needed to capture Matteo before he came up against her again.

Speaking of which...

He hurried forth, dodging the tree root that suddenly lifted up. He spun out of harm's way as his sluagh, sensing the witch behind the tree's trunk, warned him of the flying scian she'd thrown at him. His temper flared and he dashed towards her, slitting open her belly. His sluagh—still his eyes and ears, even if he didn't use them to detonate the area—kept him safe as he navigated the moving wood of yews. The same trees he was sure Jess was responsible for stealing from Nox's grounds. As another one almost tripped him up, he swore that those that didn't grace the woodwork of his study would be firewood before long.

As Theo came out of the canopy of the forest, he risked a tiny glow of purple to shield him from any iron arrows or Triodian magic that might slow his progress. His attention went to the bruised skies. The night was that washed-out hue, telling that the magic of Lady Night was soon to recede.

The thought of Lady Night jarred Theo. What Mara had told him of how the goddess Silva *was* Lady Night had tarnished the dark beauty that Theo had venerated. That Enodia had unwittingly worshipped a form of the Umbran goddess for thousands of years, sickened him. And he swore again that when the Umbran

OTHERWORLD 253

gods were once more torn apart, he'd construct a whole new hier-
archy of idols for his coven to worship.

Storm clouds and an inky mist of iron-tinged were responsible
for prolonging the dark: Rune and Mara hovered in the thick of
the mingling gloom. More people Theo was desirous of giving a
wide berth.

Luckily, they're hard to miss.

Finally, he was on the periphery of the units he wanted to be.
The wolves were fighting the Fomor foot-soldiers, their luminescent flesh looking more like bone, their armor doing little to
protect their soft skin that, judging by the blood and gore on the
grass, had been easily punctured by the shifters' teeth and claws.
Here and there the torn body of a shifter laid still, but the piles of
fleshy Fomor corpses were more.

The sheer volume of the Fomor army stretching out ahead of
Theo momentarily gave him pause for thought. His nose crinkled
in disgust as one of those *things*, a Fomor, his brother-in-arms,
passed close by. The Fomor lunged at a shifter, spearing the white
wolf with one of its serrated claws. The thing had barbs down the
back of its head and spine, sticking out from its leathers. The
Fomor was efficient, Theo would give him that but *damn* was it
ugly. Not that he gave a rat's ass about who he was working with.
If it got him his prize, then screw who his allies were.

Theo sent his sluagh out, slinking throughout the fighting
army of Fomors and shifters. His horde pierced the black wolves
it came across, wafting through them, probing and prizing open
their souls. Annoyed at the ever-reaching field of Fomors battling
shifters, Theo wondered how long this was going to take, when—

A flicker of silvery hair and crystal eyes shot through the mind
of one of the wolves Theo's sluagh had slunk through.

Bingo.

Theo tore past the fighting pairs, lurching towards his target,
just as a Fomor with a long snout and fangs bit into the black
wolf's shoulder.

Oh brother.

Theo rushed the Fomor from the other side, sinking his blade into the thing's lower gut before twisting it deep into its kidney.

Does it even have kidneys?

Meanwhile, the black wolf who had been mauled, now catching its breath, lurched to its feet, blinking at its unlikely savior. Choosing not to examine the Fomor's anatomy too closely, Theo launched himself—figuratively speaking—at his prize: his sluagh horde lanced through Matteo's wolf. Remembering how the shifter had broken through dozens of his sluagh when he'd last tortured him, Theo wasn't gentle and pierced the wolf with the force of a hundred souls.

Matteo was pinned down, and Theo took the opportunity to put the scian to his throat. The wolf's shoulder was a bloody mess from where the Fomor had clawed him. But it was a shallow wound. The shifter would heal, even in human form.

As Theo removed his sluagh from the wolf, the pain cleared from Matteo's eyes. "Change, shifter."

A growl threatened from the wolf.

Theo pushed the blade against his neck. "Shift," he commanded.

This time, the wolf's body shimmered on the air until Matteo, caked in sweat and blood, his huge chest rising and falling with exertion, ate up the space.

"On your stomach," Theo ordered. "Hands behind you."

Matteo looked murderous but complied.

Good boy.

The mage knelt on the shifter's back, careful to send his sluagh shooting through Matteo once more as he bound his wrists with the leather ties he'd brought.

A flash of Jess in a bone-white landscape with deep lakes and writhing undulating creatures transmitted from Matteo's fearful thoughts to Theo.

What the fuck?

Theo withdrew his sluagh momentarily. His gaze flew around, the battle still wild around him. He needed to remove them from the thick of it. Indiscriminate, he cleaved a path, his amethyst sluagh sending out explosions as they fired through shifters and Fomors alike.

Fuck 'em all.

Irritation shot through Theo. He'd been worried about the Iron Queen beating him to Jess. But now, his thoughts skittered on the danger Jess was in if she'd portaled into the enemy world. He was damn well going to tether her soul *today*. He would seek her out. He'd go to the Fomors' world if he had to. He'd hold the scian to her lover's neck until she delivered herself willingly into his hands. An exchange. Pure and simple. He could sense the gouged gate not far from here. The sense of its foreign magic leaked into Umbra.

Theo picked his way carefully from the fray, kicking his captive ahead of him. They had gotten to the outskirts of the battle.

"Let's go find Jess, shall we?" he taunted Matteo.

But before the shifter could do anything but whip around to face him, his expression rebellious, the changing color of the sky caught Theo's attention. He drank in the graying light around Rune and Mara where they hovered and fought.

Is that dawn changing the color of Mara's iron-tinged?

But Theo blinked in stunned shock as the queen's sluagh billowing around her like black clouds turned from ashen to white. He stared, dread blossoming through him as the Iron Queen plummeted, her body tumbling like a rag doll through the sky.

Disbelief battered Theo.

The look on his face must have been transparent because Matteo laughed. "He's a god, you asshole, you seriously underestimated him ... and Jess."

Theo's mind scrambled in panic. He'd seen that Jess was in the

Fomor kingdom. Before, he'd been so eager to capture the prize that Mara had been after—Jess's soul—that he'd only thought of following her there to obtain it. But now, as the knowledge and shock that the fearsome Unseelie queen was dead shook him, he wondered *why* Jess had gone to the Fomor world.

But once more Theo didn't have a chance to latch onto his train of thought as a rumble like thunder resounded through the Shadowlands. His gaze darted up to search for Rune...

No, fucking Alba.

Theo thought to find the sky cracking open with forked lightning—the weapons of a god. But his heart skittered as he drank in instead, the turmoil of frothing waves, their formations swallowing the ranks of the Fomors farther back on the Grasslands.

Lord Alba. The Drowned God. Lord Netherworld.

A chaotic whorl of thoughts slammed through him as terror struck Theo. Rune was decimating the Fomor ranks with the waves of Umbra themselves. He could control the immensity that was Umbra's waters. Once the thought of dealing with Mara's magic had seemed too immense to Theo, and now Rune ... Lord Alba had fucking slain her.

The magnitude of it all squeezed the breath out of Theo's lungs. He needed to leave. Needed to get away. To the moving forest and find some iron-tinged to portal him back to Earth.

Now.

But, in that moment that he'd decided to run, something barrelled into him. He slammed down on the Grasslands, his back and head resounding with the impact. Only then did he blink his eyes open and realize Matteo was on him. Even with his hands bound, the shifter had used his massive bulk to send him sprawling.

"You're not going anywhere, you little weasel," Matteo growled.

Theo had the urge to laugh for a moment as the shifter clearly couldn't do much with his hands tied behind his back. But then

Matteo's forehead smashed into his own, and blinding pain rang out behind his skull.

Fuck. I'm going to kill this dog before I leave.

Yet again though, before Theo could regain control of his thoughts and master the splitting pain ringing through his head, something else caught his attention. His sluagh horde crackled. More specifically, Lorenzo's blood sluagh bloomed beside Matteo. The glowing white wolf sniffed and pawed at the shifter on top of Theo. And that's when something else tugged at Theo. An ambery scent wafted from the shifter.

Jess's perfume.

He stared up in bemusement at the shifter.

Then, a wave of dizziness hit Theo, intensifying the blinding pain behind his eyes. Theo squeezed his eyes shut. Panic bled through him as he detected his sluagh dispersing into that amber scent. The sensation reminded him of the way that Jess had picked at his sluagh in the catacombs at Castle Nox.

But she's not here. How is she doing this?

Theo writhed against the ground, his body racked by the assault against his soul. "Jess," the name fell from his lips. And at this point, he didn't know whether it was a question, a plea, or just a statement. Her whole being seemed to dominate his own. Her ambery scent was in his lungs, in his mind, on his tongue, coating all of him.

Then, memories assaulted him...

At first, Jorah's dominated. *He was in a jungle. Jorah surveyed prone bodies strewn out in the undergrowth like felled trees, lacerations and bruises across their skin. Satisfaction bristled through him—so many thousands of souls to reap.*

Theo's body tensed, and his head thumped against the ground. Agony tore through his mind. Not from the impact, but from the lacerations ripping through his own soul. Something dug into his being like pieces of flying shrapnel. He couldn't breathe. His back arched. His body spasmed.

Then a new image dominated: *A huge, white wolf loomed over a screaming baby that lay on the floor in a disarray of blankets. The wolf's muzzle dripped globules of fresh blood onto the white bundle. The natural sweet odor of young flesh flooded his nose. What could be easier than sinking his fangs in? The moment drew out, the cries of the baby piercing him and yet grinding him to a halt.*

Theo knew this memory, too. Lorenzo's. The same one he'd used to tether him. To drive home the fact that it was his mercy that had stopped Lorenzo from killing Jess as a baby. To drive home his deepest fear that had already come to fruition. That not spilling Jess's blood had cost Lorenzo his life.

The same blood that was pulling Lorenzo's soul to her now. And drawing Theo's with it...

anything else she wanted to sift through. But, as she debated on how to use Theo's presence here in Oblivion to her advantage, she played along.

"What did you do to him?"

"Some light bondage." He smirked. "We were just about to come find you when you reached out to me."

She dropped his arms. She didn't want his noxious touch, even if the waters *did* claim him. She glowered at him, and although she already knew the answer asked, "Why?"

Theo's bright eyes flicked over her. "I realized that Mara and the Fomors were losing. So, I thought to bargain with you. To trade Matteo's safety for my own."

A lie.

She saw through him. His soul had already hemorrhaged all of its secrets to her. He just didn't realize it. He'd seen the vision of her fears in the catacombs at Castle Nox. He knew what Mara had tried to do to her—to tether her soul. And, after Jess had severed hundreds of his sluagh from his soul, he'd fixed on tethering hers.

There were *no* lengths Theo wouldn't go to for more power. And there was nothing he wouldn't do to save his own skin. She realized that even now he hoped that his lies might grant him a way out of here. Anger and resentment drummed through her. And part of her responded to his words without conscious thought. Just as she'd furnished them with bodies, Jess drew from Theo's soul to craft their surroundings now.

Theo's gaze flew around them as he took in the shape of walls and furniture, etching itself on the air around them. "What the fuck?" He whipped around, examining the solidifying room encompassing them...

They still stood within the rush of water, but the semblance of a solid room now encased them. Jess analyzed the feel of the place. It emanated with Theo's energy.

Interesting.

Something the mage suddenly realized. Anger bristled over his wide face. "You're stealing my soul's energy for furnishings!"

"Similar to the way you would have used my sacred groves to furnish your study," Jess countered.

Fear clouded his bright eyes.

How does she know that? His soul asked.

She recognized the room she'd built: the suite at Castle Nox where the after-party was after the Enodians' induction.

Bitterness wound through Jess, and she knew precisely why she'd crafted this place. She remembered how in this room on the night of Theo's induction into Enodia, before she'd known how deep his darkness went, she'd felt so angry for the twisted upbringing Enodia had imposed on their young. She'd wished there was a way she could save him from the coven's destructive influence. She'd wished that when she got away from Castle Nox, her friend could leave with her. That was the final time she'd been with him and believed that beneath all the smarmy cunningness Theo possessed a heart.

"Welcome to your final after-party," she said as resentment bloomed through her.

His green eyes drank her in—what was that look? Something like awe. "Touché, Remi."

Jess's gaze traveled up as she caught movement above, on the gallery, and realized that Theo's fear had leaked into their surroundings. *She* hadn't formed the figure that flourished on the upper gallery. Theo's fear of the end now colored their environment.

His profile lifted to look at the figure. The woman swayed on the balcony. It wasn't Judith. This woman had raven hair and eyes and wore black, but the floaty tulle skirt and high-necked lace top gave her a quirky, old-fashioned look. Paired with the heavy Doc Martins, makeup, and wild hair, she had a grungy air to her. Her look and voice—she was singing—was far too expressive to be an Enodian's.

Jess *felt* Theo and this woman's history drift through her. She saw how he'd been dreaming of Von lately. That he'd nicknamed this singer Von Otherworld to mock the poor little thing who liked the *idea* of the supernatural but was so human. Theo had met her in Italy; she'd been the reason he'd been captured by the Triodia, staying in the Tuscan villa where he'd tethered Donna— the human soul with para abilities—for too long. He'd been waiting for Von when he'd been captured. And the shock of what Theo truly felt was laid bare: Von was the only person he'd ever *loved*. Some part of his soul that stared up at her thrummed with that truth, even as it called out with the heart-breaking question: *"Who could ever love someone like me?"*

With shock, Jess recognized that there was something vulnerable and human in Theo, that ached for love, and did love another being. Yet, she knew it was time to let go of the idea of what Theo might have been.

Because... the souls kept coming and the water level rose steadily. It was knee-level now. The urge to see what else she might be able to do with the energy of Theo's soul beat through Jess. If she could craft a way out, in the same way she'd crafted them bodies and the room around them, then she would damn well wring the last bit of energy out of him.

After all, there was *no* saving Theo. No more than there had been a way to save the thousands of Enodians and Unseelie that she'd cleansed from existence. Besides, if these were to be her final moments, she wouldn't spend them with this psychopath.

"I once thought you could be saved from yourself, but I don't believe that anymore," she said.

"I'll have you know, there are hundreds who would *kill* to save me from myself," he quipped.

The way he joked about death, about killing, here at the end shouldn't shock her, but it did. Jess wondered what would happen to Theo's soul. Did he have one left?

Jess felt the burst of acknowledgment from Theo though. He

knew she'd won, and hatred flickered through him. Hatred for her. For his defeat. But a flare of wilful, independent spirit refused to be completely conquered by her. If he was going to pass into the stream of Oblivion, then he was fucking well going to step into it, not be pushed.

"So long, Remi," he said, a smirk curling his lips. Anticipation flooded Theo and a flicker of the times he'd thrown himself through Heights portals, free-falling through the stinging cold and beneath the light of hundreds of stars flashed through him, just before he fell backward and beneath the water.

As Theo caught in the current, the structure around Jess began to fade. The walls were like mist until the lines of Nox blinked out.

Jess drew from his energy and from the other divisive magic around her. She tried to use it to create threads—a rope—one that could furnish her with a way out. Back to the world she'd fought to save. Yet, although she crafted the semblance of twine before her, when she tried to move forwards, it was impossible. When she pulled at it, its unattached line did nothing to aid her against the current.

Her failure to conjure a way out mingled with panic as the water continued to climb. And doubts about her own soul swam through her thoughts. What awaited *her* beyond Oblivion? In some ways, she was no purer than Theo. Thoughts of all the Enodians and Unseelie that she'd killed on the battlefield rippled through her. She had killed *thousands*. Any soul who had tethered another was being swept into Oblivion. All the death she was responsible for seemed to heap up within her.

Lorenzo's blood sluagh played on her mind again. She'd slain her own blood and so made the first para sluagh. That act had given Theo the knowledge to tether Lorenzo, to make more para sluagh, and to bathe the world in blood and destruction.

She tried to reassure herself. Hadn't lots of lives been saved by her? Astra would live the life she wanted in a united court. And

Eilea would live a life of freedom, too, untethered from the Unseelie who had enslaved her. And so many other countless Unseelie, Storm-born, and even Enodians—those young enough not to have tethered a soul yet—would lead a life absent of the divisive magic that had sullied the clans, covens, and courts.

As her concerns weighed her down, a ripple in the water caught her attention. Then, a musical voice caressed her soul. *Jess?*

Like sunshine on water, the voice danced through her.

With a gasp, Jess exclaimed, *Matteo.*

Relief battered her. She didn't know how Matteo had reached her. But he'd somehow found her.

The light shining down brightened.

You did it, he told her. *The Fomors, the Enodians, the Unseelie— they're dying.*

Her stomach twisted at Matteo's final word. She knew they were because their essences were roaring past her. And although their deaths had been necessary, wasn't their blood on her hands? Perhaps it was right that she seemed destined to follow them.

Her chest ached as she knew she only had so long to say good-bye. The water was at her waist. *I'm trapped here in Oblivion with them.*

Inevitability swarmed every ounce of her. *I'm... going to be swept away with them.*

But Matteo didn't seem to realize how trapped she was. His steady voice said, *Listen to me, dearest. You need to come home. You're a maker of worlds, Jess. You need to create. Create a way out. You've always made your own world. Remember, creation takes destruction—create from it now.*

His words conjured to mind how she'd shared with him the meaning behind her dreamcatcher. How she'd got it to remind her that she could build her own world. And here Matteo was, the last beautiful strand connecting her to the world she'd taken for granted most of her life.

But she also felt the crushing weight on her chest of this creating. This level of making was *too* big.

I tried, she gasped. *I tried to use the divisive energy around me to get out, but it's no good.*

But his stalwart voice came again. *Then keep trying. You're not giving up. Not on yourself. Not on us. I'm right here with you and I'm not letting you go.*

Her whole being thrummed with heartache, at the belief in his words. She seemed to feel the ghost of Matteo's touch on her hand as if he were running his thumb over hers.

Then, possibility flared through her. Hadn't she just thought that the problem with the rope she had tried to create was that it had no anchor to the other side? What if Matteo was the anchor she needed? Something fastened to the world she wanted to get back to.

A world she didn't want to lose. A world she *wouldn't* lose.

Her being vibrated and she felt as if she'd taken a huge steadying breath. Matteo's influence, the shafts of beautiful light glimmering on the water, were the strands she would weave to pull her back up to the surface. Back up to her world. Drawing from the destroyed energy around her, she spun the beams of light into threads, into a rope, one that was *taut.*

Talk to me, Matteo. It's you. Your voice is guiding me back.

I'm with you dearest.

As her determination grew, the shafts of light flashing through the water strengthened.

Keep going.

Each shimmering note of his voice tugged her back as she heaved herself against the torrent.

But even as she made progress, her awareness of the water rising gnawed at her. It was at her chest now. She had to hurry. Just then, something slick and slimy caused her to lose her footing. Jess slipped. She crashed into the deluge, and it wasn't just water that she thrashed around in. The slick had been the ooze of the disintegrating Fomors. Jess found herself wildly beating out at the wastewaters, trying to swim into the purer waters. As she found them, her hands grasped for the rope, and her legs kicked out, searching for the solid riverbed. But her fingers grasped at emptiness and all her feet felt was the pounding current ... dragging her away.

28

REMEMBER THE LIGHT

Matteo tackled Theo. With his hands tied behind him, he had no way of preparing for the crash. The mage made a good landing cushion though, and it wasn't without satisfaction that he watched Theo's head slam into the ground, his eyes scrunched up in pain.

Matteo used his weight to pin him down. "You're not going anywhere, you little weasel.".

He'd caught the look of fear as Theo had witnessed Mara's body falling from the sky. He'd watched the mage freeze in shock as he'd spied Rune's waters starting to wash the Fomors' filth from the plains. And Matteo had known exactly what Theo was about to do: retreat.

A smirk wound over Theo's face. Incensed, Matteo head-butted him, enjoying the sight of the asshole reeling from another blow.

He knew that when Jess accomplished what she'd gone to the Below to do—pull the divisive energy from the worlds the Fomors had invaded—even on Earth, Theo would, in theory, be destroyed. But the thought of the mage stealing away from the battlefield, holing himself up somewhere on Earth, and somehow escaping the death he deserved for all the countless crimes he had committed, enraged Matteo and kept him on the mage.

But then something hissed right beside Matteo. He flinched away as Lorenzo's blood sluagh suddenly manifested vividly on the air.

What the hell? Is this some kind of attempt at a distraction?

But Matteo was mystified as the mage underneath him stared at him dazedly as if he didn't understand why his own blood sluagh had appeared.

Maybe he's concussed. Is being concussed enough to make one's sluagh run amok?

The mage's features twisted.

Theo writhed beneath Matteo.

"Jess," the mage said.

Matteo's heart leaped in his chest. Was this Jess's doing? Had she managed to move the divisive energy in the Below onwards? Matteo had heard once from her. She'd reached out through the Between and told him that she'd made it to the Below. That she'd been about to penetrate to the deepest part of the Fomor kingdom.

Theo's body started to convulse, and Matteo pitched off of him. A strangled scream of pain fell from the mage's mouth. Then his face and body went slack. Similar shouts and groans erupted across the battlefield as if Theo's had ignited them. Matteo's gaze leaped across the plains, watching as too many of their foes fell in a strangely synchronized fashion: Enodians and Fomors alike fell like cut wheat across the plains, while Unseelie fell from the sky.

Matteo shook himself out of his frozen stupor—one that most of his allies were caught up in as they blinked in astonishment at their enemy felled all at once. His eyes flew to a dropped cloidem on the ground nearby. Sliding over to it, he sawed the leather around his wrist over the sharp blade.

Getting to his feet, tentative relief washed through him. Jess had done it. As he rubbed his wrists and stretched out his fingers, bringing the blood circulation back to them, he reassured himself that Jess would reach out again. She'd done it once. It had sounded effortless. She'd used the operation codenames that Astra had come up with. Her playful tone had brought a miraculous sense of joy as he'd battled through the hellish Fomor ranks. The *I-love-you* that she'd gifted him had given him a second wind, too, as he'd torn through the enemy ranks.

But with every second that ticked by, and as her scent and voice remained absent, his apprehension mounted. Already around him, voices were springing up: the sound of incredulity and hope. Matteo took in the carnage too though. Amidst the dying Enodians and Unseelie, there lay dead and injured Seelie, Triodians, shifters, and Storm-born. Some of his allies were already searching for the wounded, already trying to help those in need.

But he couldn't bring himself to move. He tried to clear his mind. Maybe it was his apprehension muddying the connection somehow. He closed his eyes, trying to quieten his thumping heart.

You did it. He told her as if she could hear him.

But nothing sounded amidst the blackness behind his eyes. And no scent engulfed his being.

As he tried not to give into the twisting terror, he let his mind form her name, reaching out again.

Jess?

A flash of Theo, just before he'd spasmed and screamed, then gone lifeless flickered through Matteo. Jess's name had been on the mage's lips. As if he'd known it was her who was pulling his life force to her. As if he'd sensed her.

Matteo's eyes snapped open. His gaze spun around the corpses on the ground. He drank in the sight of Theo's prone body, then darted towards it, throwing himself down beside it as if he were a dear friend.

He took hold of Theo's hand and Jess's ambery scent suffused his lungs instantly. *Jess?*

Matteo.

He felt as if his heart stopped at the sound of her voice. He heaved in a lungful of air as he spoke soundlessly to her.

You did it, he told her. *The Fomors, the Enodians, the Unseelie, they're dying.*

But unease tumbled through Matteo from Jess as she remained silent a beat too long. *I'm trapped here in Oblivion with them.*

Fear pummelled Matteo. *This* was the reason it was taking Theo's body to form a connection with Jess. She had been washed into Oblivion with the very divisive energy she'd moved on.

I'm... going to be swept away with them, she said.

Her comment crashed into him. He gritted his jaw, tightening his grip on Theo's hand as if it were hers.

Listen to me, dearest. You need to come home. He hated that he wasn't there with her, that he couldn't physically bring her back, but he reminded himself of the power in his voice, in his scent that she'd described to him. He needed to use those things to help her find a way out.

You're a maker of worlds, Jess. You need to create. Create a way out. You've always made your own world. Remember, creation takes destruction—create from it now.

I tried, she gasped. *I tried to use the divisive energy around me to get out, but it's no good.*

He felt her desperation. Everything within him ached to be able to hold her. If he was only there, he swore he would carry her back from the beyond to this world. But he wasn't. So, he had to make her believe in *her* strength.

Then keep trying, he said. *You're not giving up. Not on yourself. Not on us. I'm right here with you and I'm not letting you go.*

He felt his determination echoing through Jess. He sensed the hope firing through her. Her resolve grew, and he *knew* she was doing the impossible, crafting a way out of Oblivion. The seconds ticked by, each one feeling as if it grated against his lungs, waiting for her to speak.

Talk to me, Matteo. It's you. Your voice is *guiding me back.*

Elation seared through him. He knew it—Jess was finding a way.

I'm with you dearest.

He stroked Theo's hand in his as if it were Jess's once again, willing her, waiting for the moment that she'd tell him that she'd made it.

Keep going.

She was coming back to him.

Then, she screamed. Her fear smashed into him like icy water. It seeped into his bones, into his very marrow. It seemed to dissolve him from the inside out. Other scents marred Jess's: something rotten traveled through the inner-scape that linked them, making him want to recoil, but Jess was buried beneath that scent. Instead, Matteo breathed it in, letting the decay seep through him as he shouted, *Jess! Jess!*

Each breath felt jarring as if he couldn't get enough air, but all he could do was strain to keep track of Jess's muted energy. His hand squeezed Theo's until it hurt, holding on for dear life.

But Jess's scent *vanished*. Only decay and cold iron floated through him no matter how hard he squeezed Theo's hand.

"Erika!" Matteo's bellow flooded the battlefield. "Erika!"

Silence swathed the plains, but Matteo didn't hear any of it. His attention was still pinioned on the mingling scents of rot and iron that drifted through him as he mashed the mage's hand in his own.

I should have called the witch immediately. Why didn't I think of her earlier? Maybe the witch would have known how to help her.

His thoughts warred with one another. Torment pierced him as he kept searching the scent of iron and decay for warmth—for the amber and resin scent that was the trail to home. He felt the suffocating knowledge bear down on him: Jess had won the battle for them but... lost her own.

Matteo didn't notice the shouts, wingbeats, and footfalls around him as Jess's friends rallied towards his devastated roar. He existed in a world of metal and rot, unwilling to stop searching Oblivion for the treasure it had taken.

Then something brushed up against his soul, soft and almost Earthen in its energy. Like a forest full of firs. And between those trees, he got the distinct flash of wolves. *Running.* And something within that flash urged him not to let go of the mage's hand. It wasn't a voiced command, more of a feeling.

Matteo startled.

He felt the arrival of someone as they touched his shoulder, but he ignored them, squeezing the mage's hand. Matteo's eyes remained shut, desperately concentrating on that textured forest for other guidance.

He prayed that this wasn't his imagination. That the fir forest wasn't just his grief conjuring desperate desires from the dark. But the sickening sense that Jess *wasn't* here anymore crushed him, his chest felt as if it were breaking, and he was willing to hope against hope.

Please, he reached out, *she put whole worlds back together, freed thousands of souls from a tortured existence, help her. She deserves to be saved.* He begged for whatever it was that was reaching out to him through that forest fragrance. Begged that it really was a lifeline for Jess.

Once more, the soft whisper of the forest urged him. This time, faint words rippled through him: *Think of the future you have together.*

Faith flared through Matteo, and he clutched at *everything* that he'd thought of and not voiced in the cave when he and Jess had been together. His imaginings blazed across his mind's eye and... radiated through the depths, seeming to burn away the iron and decay. With closed eyes, Matteo watched the surface of a great body of water, torn between hope and heartbreak, as his deepest desires played out before him.

Jess sketched on the wall in a piazza, her face twisted in concentration. Bright sunshine cascaded over her skin, highlighting the smudges of graphite she'd absent-mindedly stained her cheek with, her face lighting up as she caught sight of Matteo...

The image changed. Soft morning light washed over him and Jess, sprawled in bed, stark-naked and deliciously spent from lovemaking. She drew lazy circles over his chest as she wondered aloud what they should do for breakfast.

Flickering once more, Jess and he played Scopa around the dining table in his parents' house. Firelight bathed Jess's laughing face as she won the round.

The electric light of the TV screen illuminated them—he and Jess slumped on a sofa at Villa Silva. Giovanni's laugh rang out as Piera chucked popcorn at Jess, sniffing at her sister's movie choice.

Then, the soft light of Eventide flooded a mountaintop, limning him and Jess. Astra clasped hands with Skiron in a handfasting ceremony. Rune and Eilea stood beside them, too, their faces alight with smiles as they watched the rite...

29

HYDROMANCY &...

HAPPILY EVER AFTER

Warmth was the first thing Jess grew aware of as consciousness returned. Her eyelids fluttered, her eyes slits as they adjusted to the bright sunshine. An echo of a lilting voice seemed to ripple through her head. Her memories scattered but something about the glimmer reminded her of Matteo.

His voice in Oblivion.

It's what had kept her from succumbing to the current threatening to steal her away. But another fractured piece of memory drove a shrill note of panic through her. She remembered, despite her best efforts to get out, the sickening sense of empty waters dragging her away. With hurried breaths, Jess's eyes snapped open. Dread pounded through her as she wondered what she'd see. Where had Oblivion taken her?

As she blinked at her surroundings, wooded panels awash with sunlight spilling through the window met her. She recognized the Sun Keep, but this room was smaller than hers. Her gaze skipped over the double bed she was in, the wardrobe, and froze on the armchair beside the bed. On the man sleeping in it.

His muscular form took up the whole chair, and his unruly

black hair was reminiscent of the last time she'd seen him, but the stubble on his jaw was thicker. Matteo. Her eyes glistened with moisture as she dared to hope.

Can this be real? Perhaps Oblivion washed me away to paradise.

Then dread gnawed at her. What if something had happened to him? He'd said that she'd succeeded—that the Fomors, Unseelie, and Enodians were dead. But what if he'd been wounded? Was that why Matteo was here beyond, too? A lump rose in her throat and she sat so still, too afraid to disturb him in case that fear turned out to be true. She couldn't face the prospect that he was dead.

But, as if sensing her movement, Matteo blinked his eyes open. He stared, drinking her in. She held her breath, still unsure whether he was a beautiful illusion. But Matteo had no such qualms, he launched himself at her, crushing her to him. The feel of him, his arms so wonderfully solid and his pine scent washing over her banished her fear.

Tears streamed down her cheeks as bone-deep relief and happiness struck her. The longing she'd felt in Oblivion to get to him shook through her.

"How?" she croaked.

"I don't know entirely," Matteo answered, knowing that she was asking about *how* she was here. *Alive.* He didn't let her go.

She shook her head. "Your voice was the only light down there. Somehow, you started to lead me back," she said. Yet, her voice quavered as she added, "but—"

He inched back, one hand falling to her waist, the other cradling her face, refusing to be separated from her. "Then Oblivion took you," he finished, his expression rigid.

The last memory she had was of the weight of Oblivion washing her on. "That's the last thing I remember." Her voice was thick, suffused with anxiety again that this beautiful reality didn't —*couldn't*—exist.

But Matteo's gentle voice continued, "When you slipped

under and your scent disappeared, I was desperate." His throat bobbed, and Jess reached out, stroking his cheek. Her hands wound down his chest, resting there, the feel of him anchoring her to the moment, reminding her of how his voice had been a tether of the best kind. "When I felt you slipping away, every-thing that I was losing flashed through my thoughts and that's when I sensed another kind of scent and a different kind of texture. It felt like a forest of firs. And there were flashes of wolves running, too."

Jess startled. "Wolves?"

Matteo nodded. "They wordlessly, somehow, urged me not to let go of Theo's hand-"

"Theo?" Jess exclaimed.

"Theo had bound me on the battlefield," he explained. "When you pulled the divisive energy out of Umbra, I was right beside him when he fell." His gaze prickled over her. "Just before he lost consciousness, he said your name as if he sensed you."

"He did. I saw him pass through Oblivion," she said. "I spoke to him, just before I heard your voice."

"The mage—like all the Enodians—*was* dying but his heart hadn't stopped yet. He was still, technically, alive. When you didn't reach out to me, I realized touching Theo might allow me to reach you."

Jess blinked in wonder. She hadn't been able to reach Matteo alone. Her energy had been too weak to reach through the Between. But Theo's body and his soul in Oblivion had acted as a bridge between Matteo and her.

"Theo was part of the reason I survived," Jess commented, staggered as she considered everything that had allowed her to be here: still breathing and blissfully alive. The sense of her surroundings—the soft bed, the air in her lungs, and Matteo's hands had never felt so good.

"Inadvertently, yes," Matteo said with a frown. "He was

looking for you on the battlefield to try to tether your soul like Mara tried."

She nodded. "I know, he told me—or his soul revealed his intentions in Oblivion."

Jess shook thoughts of Theo away and asked, "But I still don't understand what you meant about a forest and wolves."

Matteo continued, "When your scent disappeared and I entreated Oblivion to bring you back, that was when the scent of a forest drifted through me. And then the sense of wolves running between the trees rippled through my thoughts. I think they were souls. Maybe those you'd helped free from Yin."

"The Suang," Jess said in awe. "I sensed them in the Below, too, in a pack like us shifters."

"I think it was them who urged me then to picture our future," Matteo said. "And as I visualized what I'd imagined of our future, it flooded the waters of Oblivion." He stroked her cheek, a tender smile on his face. "The first thing I saw was you sketching in a piazza. You had pencil marks here and here." His thumb stroked her cheek and eyebrow.

She laughed, not just because of the mucky description, but because of the happiness of such a future. A future where she didn't create to try to escape being washed into Oblivion, but only for the pure joy of it. A future that wasn't just hers. But hers and Matteo's.

Our future.

Vision by vision, Matteo painted a picture of what he'd seen. Incredulously, Jess realized that it sounded like the Hydromancy that the Enodians practiced.

"You saw the future like an Enodian might in a large body of water," she said. "But in this case, the body of water was the waters of Oblivion."

"Exactly," Matteo said. "When I told Rune about what I'd seen he came to the same conclusion. He reckons the power of the Enodians flowing through Oblivion conjured the future in its waters. And that the pack of Suang pulling your energy back and anchoring you to me, as well as Theo's body still serving as a connection between us, brought you back."

Stunned, Jess absorbed all the minutiae of her rescue. The sheer force of love that burned through Matteo for her was, in part, responsible for bringing her back. Then the Suang, as well as the countless other souls in the waters of Oblivion that had projected that future and used it to save her. But no matter how it had happened, the thing that made her deliriously happy was that she was going to have the chance to watch that future play out in real-time.

Beside Matteo.

As Jess's astonishment allowed room for other thoughts, she exclaimed, "What about the battle? Is everyone else okay?" Her heart tore into a hurried beat as thoughts of her friends and family whipped through her.

"Everyone's fine, dearest," he assured her. "Your dad, Piera, and Dearbhla are currently on Earth. The shifters are holding a joint Rom and Rem ceremony for the shifters who fell in battle."

Jess swore that when she went back to Earth, she'd adorn the site of their burial with some of her groves in honor of all they'd given.

Worry tugged at her. Her dad hadn't been well enough for battle before. What was he doing portaling to Earth? "But my dad needs to rest—"

"He's fine, don't worry," Matteo assured her. "I think it was Theo's soul passing on. Giovanni almost seemed back to his normal self a day after."

"How long have I been out?" she asked.

"Three days," he said, the flicker of worry evident in the tension in his jaw. "When Astra and Eilea arrived back with you, Rune examined you and said he sensed your Earthen energy. Said that he was almost certain that you only needed rest after all the magic you'd expended."

Jess saw the ghost of concern in his expression and her heart squeezed.

"Speaking of which, I should go and let everyone know you're awake," he said.

But the memory of her own fear, of their disembodied conversation, that she thought had been their last, washed over her. "Don't let me go," she said, savoring the feel of his arms tightening around her.

For a while, their unfolding breaths, the feel of each other's inhalations and exhalations was the most beautiful thing imaginable. But as Jess looked up and caught the tender light in Matteo's eyes, she imagined his lips on her own. And the exploratory kiss they shared was an even better celebration of the most precious thing they had: time. With each slow and gentle movement that they basked in together, they exalted in the time that lay before them.

But, it wasn't long before Astra burst in, literally, in a flurry of feathers through the window. With a squeal, she launched herself at Jess, her wings and elbows bashing Matteo out of the way. Once she'd hugged it out, Astra rounded on Matteo. "Wing Woman should have been the first to be notified of the White Wolf's recovery," she scolded him.

Jess laughed at her friend's continued use of their codenames. The fae had been off to stretch her wings but had spent most of the last three days watching over Jess. She soon learned that Astra had been the only one who had managed to get Matteo to go eat and occasionally rest over the last few days. Matteo muttered something about the "small but mighty" under his breath.

It was only minutes after Astra had joined them, that a breeze drifted through the window and Rune suddenly manifested in a shiver of shadow.

The mixture of happiness and relief on his face told Jess that he'd sensed her Earthen energy when she'd woken, but that it was only when his eyes clapped onto her that he trusted she was back.

With barely any more restraint than Astra had possessed, he dashed over, gathering Jess to him. "You're a bloody Earthling, Jess. You're meant to keep your feet firmly on the ground."

"And let you take all the glory? Never."

Giving her an incorrigible smile, he settled back at the bottom of the bed.

"Ski said the battle up here was pretty epic," Astra said, throwing herself down on the foot of the bed, opposite Rune. "Umbra's shadows and waves tore apart the iron-tinged, Mara, and the Fomors."

Jess nodded. "In Oblivion, Theo's memories showed me your waves drowning the Fomors and Mara falling out of the sky," Jess said, looking at Rune.

Seriousness clothed Rune's features. "I'm not going to lie, it felt good to finally get vengeance for Umbra and for us both."

Jess's gaze strayed over the set lines of Rune's face. "I'm glad that Mara got what she deserved, too." Her bare arms tingled with the reminder of the queen's blade and what she'd tried to do to her. And the realization that the magic that Mara had tried to practice on her was truly gone swept through Jess.

"But the best move was Matteo's head-butting that little twerp and thereby keeping him in Umbra," Rune said, throwing a smile at Matteo.

"In this case, I totally agree, mine was the most heroic of all," Matteo answered, his thumb stroking circles over Jess's as he clasped her hand.

The shared camaraderie between Rune and Matteo took Jess aback for a moment. But then she realized that the two of them had spent a significant amount of time in each other's company the last few days, watching over her, waiting—*hoping*—she'd wake.

As Jess's thoughts went to the rest of her friends, she asked, "Are Sunny and Erika still here?"

Rune shook his head. "They left this morning. Erika was reluctant—she kept vigil over you almost as much as the rest of us. I think she blamed herself for what happened to you. But we thought it prudent that she checks that the Fomors' presence is gone from the other worlds. She and Sunny said they'd report back within a few weeks, a month at most."

"It's right that they went to check," Jess said.

Rune's lips twitched.

"What?" she asked.

"Well, you never used to be shy of laying blame on others, but you really have become quite magnanimous of spirit."

Jess laughed and flattered herself that she had.

Magnanimous Lord Alba and *Lady Silva*.

"Speaking of noble duties, I have to get to a meeting with Imber. There's a mirror call with the Triodians at headquarters. They're due to announce a new High Witch or Mage. Fern fell in battle," Rune added in explanation to Jess's frown.

A mixture of relief and guilt churned through Jess. "Oh, I see," was all she managed.

Because the death of the witch felt like a blessing. Perhaps with a more open-minded person at the Triodia's helm, the coven could be steered successfully into a period of peace and balance.

After all, Fern Trever had been a hypocritical leader who practiced death magic but prohibited its use to the wider coven. The welfare of her coven hadn't been her priority, but rather keeping control of it. And like most leaders, when she'd felt her control weakening over her people, she'd fought back with fear and violence. Jess hoped that the Triodia would choose a more *magnanimous* leader for the coven from here on in. And, maybe, with her influence as Lady Silva, the Great Goddess, Mother of Shifters, she would be able to lend a helping hand to whoever that duty fell to.

Maybe I should attend the meet–

Interpreting her restless look correctly, Rune shook his head. "You need to rest. I'll keep you updated." His gaze went to Matteo. "Make sure she stays put."

Jess laughed and couldn't resist hugging it out with her dad yet again, even if he was threatening imprisonment. It meant he cared, right?

A knock sounded on the door and Eilea wandered in, with Rune in tow.

"Storm Horse," Jess greeted her, her gaze roving over Eilea's cloudy wings and irises that churned like storm clouds. "You look amazing." Jess couldn't help admiring both features that had changed due to the freedom she'd gained.

"Thanks, White Wolf," she said with a smile.

With a leap of joy, she saw the way that Rune's gaze skimmed Eilea's vibrant form with something *more* than admiration, too. She bit back the cheesy grin and contented herself with the thought that things were definitely *developing* there. As Rune and Eilea joined them all, Jess felt full to bursting with the love she had in her chest for all of them.

But most of all, the gentleness and strength in Matteo's eyes were the greatest treasure, the light in them as beautiful as Eventide. The light that told her he saw all that they were together and all that they would be.

EPILOGUE
ONE YEAR LATER

Jess reached for that undertone of darker energy in the roots of the trees. She was in the library of the Triodia's headquarters in Rome. Drawing from the natural decay of vegetation in the ancient glade in the courtyard, she let the energy seep into the room around them—its timbers, its bookcases, its desks, and chairs. Every surface and crevice, she coated with the death dust. Like a sigh trailing away, she felt the room become veiled.

Even though the witches and mages around her had seen and felt this happen perhaps a dozen times now, there was a collective gasp, then whispers of excitement. To be fair, most of the witches and mages were between five and thirteen years old. But Jess found herself smiling at their rapt faces.

"This magic is in your blood," Jess said. "It's your heritage as a witch or mage to be able to harness the magic in the Earth, both its light and dark. This death dust is drawing from the past, from the natural decay within the dirt." She looked around at the varying expressions on their faces. A full range of emotions was apparent from apprehension to zeal. But Jess didn't temper her words. "Because creation *needs* destruction."

When she'd first mentioned *blood* in these sorts of speeches or *death dust*, there had been plenty of gasps and disapproving tsks from the older generation of Triodians. The topic of blood magic and any sort of death magic being deemed unsuitable for the new coven. But Jess had insisted on challenging their narrow-minded-ness. Necessity had helped. The fact that an alternative to glamour needed to be found to veil all the Triodias over Earth. King Imber's people hadn't been able to be forever at the Triodia's disposal. The fae had wanted to be back in their own world, rebuilding their community in the wake of the removal of the Fomors' magic. The new Triodian High Witch, Hannah Lang, another witch who had a natural affinity with spirits, was, help-fully, more broad-minded than Fern Trever had been. The next step had been to get Erika's permission for the Thokkal rings she'd left in Umbra to be used on Earth for maintaining the veil-ings. With the witch's permission granted, each of the Triodian institutes had been given a ring. With it on site, it had been enough to magnify the witches' and mages' power, allowing them to wield the death dust and veil the institutes.

Gradually, the Triodians had come to see that this death dust was how their institutes were to be kept safely secret from the human world. And they'd allowed the teaching of this magic within its different branches. There were enough mages and witches within each branch of the new Triodia Coven—now Earth's sole coven—to safely keep their branches veiled using death dust. But with this being such a newly learned skill, Jess was often asked into the various institutes around the globe to help foster this power in the coven's young.

Something she had actively wanted to be part of. It was evident that the instinct in many of the coven was to stamp out any magic that reminded them of the Enodians. But that wasn't fair. The coven's youth was a mixture of both Triodians *and* ex-Enodians. Hundreds of Enodian young, ranging from toddlers to the age of thirteen, had become part of the Triodian Coven.

Those who hadn't ever tethered, who hadn't possessed divisive magic in their soul, and had survived the destruction of the rest of their coven.

"Right, your turn," Jess said. "As you'll be able to tell, the books on your laps aren't veiled. I want you to draw from the decay in the ancient glade to veil them."

"Yes, Lady Silva," a few of the younger witches and mages returned. The older Triodians fell straight to their task. Some of the pupils closed their eyes with a solemn focus on their faces, others with wide-eyed apprehension as if they worried they'd summon fearsome tree walkers by trying to access such power.

All the ancient woods that had been taken to Umbra during the war had now been restored to the various Triodian branches. Some of them, too, graced Cemetery Romulus and Remus in honor of the fallen. In the first few months after the battle, Jess had healed the trees before seeing them safely portaled to their homes.

Now, with the veilings being maintained by the Triodia Coven, Jess had had enough time since the fall to enroll in art school. She'd wanted to be near family, near Matteo, her dad, and her sister, so had enrolled in Rome. After her afternoon's death dust class had finished, she left the institute and made her way from the para area and towards her school. Jess loved Rome's streets with their Greco-Roman architecture, and its deep-layered history was a heady blend full of inspiration.

It was Friday evening and ordinarily, she had a couple of beers with her friends in their studio, alongside working on whatever piece they were developing. At RUFA—Academy of Fine Arts— she keyed in the code to the building and wandered up to the second floor.

"Ciao, bella," Melody greeted her.

"Hey guys," Jess said, including Cici, who was tucked in at the back corner of the studio. Cici turned around, briefly, giving Jess a small wave before sinking back into the sketch she was working on at her easel. Melody returned equally swiftly to her sculpture.

Jess breathed in the scent of graphite, paint, and clay. Even the chemical scent of paint thinner on the air was one she somehow liked, associating it now with this space. Her creative space. It was a small-ish one: enough room for the four students to have an easel and a shared table space in the middle for bigger projects. The four of them at Christmas had also hefted up the salvaged couch from the street that now rested in their break area, with a mini-fridge and a tea and coffee station. Scattered throughout the room, they had various spare easels and lots of plastic folding tables. The simple surfaces throughout the room seemed truly magical for how much they created.

Jess stood in front of her easel, gazing at her work in progress. Her eye strayed over the half-finished painting of Theo in the waters of Oblivion, his face upturned to Von's grungy, regency figure in the background.

She'd be lying if she said Theo didn't play on her mind.

But not in the he's-haunting-me kinda way, thank the gods.

It was just that going to teach the young in the Triodia Coven always got her thinking about him. She couldn't help wondering how different things might have been if the emerald-eyed mage had had the chance to be one of them before he'd succumbed to tethering and let divisive magic take root in his soul. Her heart also ached for the ex-Enodians as they seemed to embody so much of the lack of belonging she'd felt in her life. They had been displaced from the only home they'd known. Albeit a despicable one, that had taught them to value themselves by the power they accumulated, rather than their own intrinsic worth.

"You working on the Haunted Mage tonight?" Melody asked.

Jess had sunk into her reflections, and at the sound of her friend's voice, answered, "Nah, I can't stay tonight."

Her friends in the studio saw Jess as their resident fantasy artist. And she'd gone with it. They didn't need to know that her subjects were far more every day fair than they thought. After all, as her friends said, there was a real market for fantasy art.

"Hot plans with that Adonis of yours?" Melody flashed her a grin. Matteo had been a hit with her and the other girls in Jess's class when they'd met him at a painting party that Jess had invited them to.

"Something like that," she answered. "We've got a friend's party to get to early tomorrow."

Once she'd found the painting she'd come for, she packed it away in her art folder and said goodbye to the girls.

Leaving RUFA, she felt positively giddy about the weekend. She and Matteo *did* have big plans in Umbra. She buzzed at the prospect of seeing her Umbran friends. It had been weeks since she'd visited. Rune was still being rightly cautious and hadn't left Umbra since his shadow self had been restored. He had plenty to keep him occupied there, too. The integration of the Unseelie young into the Seelie Court to make one fae court was something he was passionate about helping Imber with.

Outside of his duties to unite Umbra's people, Jess knew he took great enjoyment in passing his time with the Storm-born. Restoring their forgotten history and beliefs and teaching them to read and record it had been his favorite topic of conversation the last time Jess visited him. She, too, had been mesmerized by the theatrical skill and beauty of the Storm-borns' retellings. But smiling, Jess thought of how those fireside stories had been made even cozier for Rune by Storm Horse's company.

Overall, both Umbra and Earth's communities were slowly recovering and developing in the wake of the Fomors' magic. The humans that the fae had found in the Iron Keep had been relocated back to Earth; those with relatives had been put in touch with their families and those without had been given help to start over. The iron mines on Earth based in Scandinavia, which had been under Queen Mara's dominion and a source of division before, had become a supply of wealth for the humans who needed relocating.

The ex-vamps whose knowledge of the para world hadn't been able to be glamoured away had been aided by the wealth of the iron mines as well. Under the new Triodian High Witch, the ex-vamps were proving to be a wonderful bridge between the Triodians and humans. They were strong advocates for change in the human world concerning climate change and protecting the natural world.

Erika and Sunny would be in Umbra this weekend, too. They'd reported back to the Shadowlands that the other worlds that had been infected by the divisive magic were cleansed, too. When Jess had visited Umbra last time, Rune had passed on a message from Erika that she'd be happy to take her and Matteo world-walking. Jess had discussed the idea with Matteo, but both of them felt no inclination to go world-hopping at the moment. Maybe one day. But for now, they were both happy in their home world.

When Jess reached Triodia's headquarters again, she quietly nipped into The Silvan Reading Room to portal home; she had been allocated her own private room and collected the remnants of the Eventide prophecies onto its shelves. She'd told Hannah Lang that it was for nostalgia's sake that she had them around her. But in reality, they were far more practical than that. With the power in the pages—paper made from her most ancient glade— she was able to use them as her own private portal.

Ah, the graces of being a goddess.

In a moment, Jess portaled out into a garden in the Sabina countryside, complete with yew trees. That had been her and Matteo's only real stipulation when looking for a place. That they find one with yew trees, ridding themselves of a lengthy commute to get to Rome's city center, a fifty-minute drive—or a thirty-minute run in wolf terms—away.

For the first six months of being back on Earth, Jess had moved in with her dad and Piera. Neither the Roms or Rems, technically, needed an Alpha anymore, in that they weren't bound by blood oaths or the blood command to an Alpha. But the shifters of Earth had wanted representatives to express shifter interests to the Triodia and in dealings with the paras of Umbra. In time, the Rom and Rem Clans had chosen to elect Giovanni and Dearbhla. Giovanni had moved back into Villa Silva to serve the welfare of the Rom Clan. Meanwhile, Dearbhla had taken ownership of La Alba and the overseeing of the Rem Clan.

Jess and Matteo had naturally split their time between staying at Piera's in Rome and Matteo's apartment in Naples. The city was where his para squad, his parents, and his siblings were based, too. Now that the para squads didn't need to hunt down rule-breaking Rems, Enodians, and vamps, Matteo and the other paras within the Triodia spent their time largely checking that veilings were maintained, the Thokkal iron guarded, and most importantly of all, that the young within the very mingled coven were adhering to the rules of practicing no divisive magic. The onus these days was much more on education and the well-being of both the coven and clans' young.

Over time, Jess and Matteo had gradually grown to want their own space. Last winter, they'd bought this tumbledown villa in Sabinashire. Complete with a leaky roof, no central heating, and a fire that smoked. Winter had been hard. Giovanni had called it madness to move into such a dilapidated place in the height of winter. But Jess had even relished the push-back they'd gotten from her dad—his disapproval making her feel warm and fuzzy about how much he cared. But both she and Matteo had been firm and moved in after Christmas. It wasn't a holiday that the paras celebrated, but most of Matteo's family were human, and Jess had experienced her first proper Christmas where she truly felt like she belonged.

The tail end of the holiday had been spent in a dizzying slog of trying to get the house into some liveable state. They'd also spent a large proportion of nights in wolf form so as not to freeze to death. Yet, still, they held the villa as perfect because ... it was their home.

Jess let herself in the back door. Matteo's keys were on the kitchen surface. "Matteo?"

"Upstairs."

Jess wandered through the kitchen, her art folder still slung over her shoulder.

I think there's wrapping paper in our bedroom closet.

Wandering through the living room, her gaze went to the fresco—the creation from the painting party that she'd had her friends help paint this semester. It had trees and a white and black wolf slinking through the forest beneath a moon, commemorating Jess and Matteo's first proper "date."

Jess's hand wound along the smooth wood of the staircase, enjoying the scent of the sanded walnut. One of Matteo's brothers was a joiner and was helping them restore the beautiful wooden features within the villa. Gradually unearthing and restoring each one made the house feel ever more connected to the hum of the trees sweeping the countryside around them.

As Jess came up onto the landing, Matteo called out, "I think the shower's fixed."

The shower/hot water system in the house *had* been the bane of their lives lately. It was definitely another reason she was looking forward to the trip to Umbra: guaranteed hot springs at Skiron's house sounded like utter luxury.

Jess took out the painting from her folder and rested it against the banister then leaned in the doorframe, gawking at Matteo shamelessly.

Silva-lining about the constant DIY was that the sight of Matteo in nothing but jeans was a frequent one.

His lips quirked as he caught her. "Done looking at me like a piece of meat?"

"Never." She bit her bottom lip, an action calculated to bring about exactly what it did: Matteo climbed out the bathtub and greeted her with a kiss.

He caught sight of the painting. "The finished piece. May I?"

Jess grinned and retrieved it.

She'd painted the wedding scene except they weren't *allowed* to call it that. Astra had explicitly told them that it was a *party*. She and Ski might happen to be doing a hand-fasting rite, but it was still just a big party, where they'd all get totally bacae-berried.

Matteo stared down at the scene he'd glimpsed through the waters of Oblivion. Jess had had him describe it to her in detail. And Jess was secretly happy that all Astra had told them was that she wasn't wearing a dress. She couldn't wait to see her friend's face when she presented her the painting of her in the silver suit she *knew* Astra was wearing. Matteo had seen the studies she'd drawn for this but not the finished product.

"You've captured it perfectly," he said, his gaze roving over the six figures in the painting.

But then, a faint rustling sounded—like a bird ruffling its feathers.

Matteo rolled his eyes. Jess pushed the painting into his hands before wandering through to confront the disturbance. Her gaze drifted to the dresser opposite the window, where a potted yew sapling rested.

All six of their long-needled branches were wriggling, the ends of them like hands grabbing the air. Their roots had broken through the topmost soil, the biggest managing to shovel dirt over the pot's edge.

"Miles," Jess scolded, "we talked about this."

The sapling seemed to sigh as all their branches shuddered. Then, all bar one branch slumped. With the remaining limb, the sapling ... waved.

Jess smirked. "Fine." She let a wave of her Earthen energy ripple over the young tree. Another of its branches shot up and it looked as if it was showing off its biceps. She chuckled. "You're totally growing into a mighty warrior."

It had been six months since she'd dug up the tiny sapling from the Cathedral and nurtured them with a little Earthen energy daily. They could now move their branches and two biggest roots. She suspected it would be another year or two before Miles could properly use their roots like feet. Likewise, it would be years before their type of flowers told them whether Miles was male or female. Miles, which meant soldier in Umbran (although Jess and Matteo's pronunciation of it was definitively Earthen), was another wedding present for Astra and Ski.

"Are you sure about this?" Matteo came in behind her. He placed the painting on the bed before regarding the sapling. "The fae might not thank you, you know? Miles's pretty high maintenance."

Miles momentarily raised all five of their branches before flipping Matteo off.

Jess laughed. "Nah, Astra's gonna love them."

Miles proceeded to do a jiggly dance, as much as their bound roots allowed.

The sapling had always been intended as a present for Astra. The fae had never forgotten about missing out on witnessing fricking tree soldiers. Now, Astra would have her own she could grow and nurture over the years.

Matteo put his arms around Jess's waist, leaning his chin on her head, and she knew he was smiling at Miles's dance fondly, too.

"Besides, at Ski's, they'll have lots of company," she said.

With Ski, his brother, his dad, and now Astra living under one roof, there were a lot more people for the yew to be around. Whereas Matteo spent most days in Naples with his para unit, while Jess's time was divided between Art school and the Triodia institutes. The house was too quiet for the sapling to be properly stimulated. But as she stood against Matteo, watching Miles, a beautiful sense budded—and feeling sappy—imagined a time, perhaps not too far away, when it would be right for saplings.

"It really is beautiful by the way," Matteo said, turning them both to stare at the painting propped up on the cushions.

"I couldn't have done it without you," she said, a smile in her voice.

He huffed a laugh against her cheek. "No kidding."

Matteo had described the scene in the painting to her in detail: a flicker of the future that he'd seen in the waters of Oblivion. In the painting, the soft light of dusk lit up the Aedis Peak. Astra had told Jess where the ceremony was going to be, and the last time she and Matteo had visited Umbra, Jess had taken photos to help with her composition. In the center of the canvas stood Astra and Ski, their hands bound with ribbon. She and Matteo stood beside Astra, beaming. While Rune and Eilea were beside Skiron, their own hands clasped.

Occasionally, over the last year, Matteo had shared things like this scene with Jess. He'd tell her that he'd seen a particular moment they were in. But, most of the time, they enjoyed every moment for what it was: unknown. As of yet, unmade. And Jess found *that* to be the truest magic. Like the changing seasons or the light of Eventide, that's where magic was to be found. In the transitional. In the liminal. In the between of things.

Along her journey from human to shifter to goddess to half-goddess, she'd certainly learned that going through these transitions was nothing if not messy. But there were hidden joys lying in these between spaces that could only be found when you fully discovered yourself. Like the wonder that existed between her and Matteo, made even more special for their journey from friend to lover. He'd seen her fall apart, literally, but the falling apart was an essential bit of life. Just as destruction was essential for creation. And Jess knew, without a shadow of a doubt, that Matteo would always be there to help put her back together again. Just as she would him.

ALSO BY RAE ELSE

ABOUT THE AUTHOR

Rae Else is most at home in the spaces between reality and the imaginary. When in the real world, she lives with her husband on their sailboat in Cornwall. The Arete Trilogy is her Young Adult, Urban Fantasy debut. Her most recent series, The Dark Between, is a decadently dark YA Fantasy, featuring a whole cast of paras—shifters, vamps, witches, mages, fae ... and lots of soul magic.

Rae studied Classics at university and a lot of her stories draw on mythology and ancient worlds. In her twenties, Rae worked as a teacher and now writes full time. When not reading or writing, Rae loves to swim, kayak, and pootle from anchorage to anchorage. She finds the big blue to be like a good book—a portal to a different world.

You can connect with Rae on social media on Instagram @raeelse or Facebook @rae_else

Made in the USA
Columbia, SC
22 December 2022

74826398R00183